I0609491

DEEP SIX

*A Just Cause Universe **Novel***

IAN THOMAS HEALY

Local Hero Press

Deep Six: A Just Cause Universe Novel
Published by Local Hero Press, LLC
http://localheropress.ianthealy.com

1st Printing
Local Hero Press: trade paperback, November 1, 2013
2nd Printing
Local Hero Press, LLC: trade paperback, May 1, 2014

ISBN-13: 9781971445045

Cover art by Jeff Hebert
Book design by Ian Thomas Healy

This is a work of fiction. Names, characters, places, and incidents are either the product of the author's imagination or used fictitiously. Any resemblance to actual events, locales, or persons, living or dead, is entirely coincidental.

Books by Local Hero Press

The *Just Cause Universe*

Just Cause
The Archmage
Day of the Destroyer
Deep Six
Jackrabbit
Champion
Castles
The Lion and the Five Deadly Serpents
Tusks
The Neighborhood Watch
Jackrabbit: Big In Japan
Arena
Hero Academy
The Path
Cinco de Mayo
Search and Rescue
Rooftops
Plague
Soldiers of Fortune
Just Cause Universe Compendium
Destroyer of Earth
Flint and Steel
The Club
Jackrabbit: Rinse and Repeat
Posse
Extinction Event
Rain Must Fall

Pariah of Verigo

Pariah's Moon
Pariah's War

Three Flavors of Tacos

The Guitarist
Making the Cut
The Scene Stealers

Collections

Airship Lies
High Contrast
The Good Fight
The Good Fight 3: Sidekicks
The Good Fight 4: Homefront
The Good Fight 5: The Golden Age
Muddy Creek Tales
Caped

Other Novels

Assassin
Blood on the Ice
Funeral Games
Hope and Undead Elvis
Horde
The Murder Squad (2026)
Roast Wyvern (and Other Recipes)
*Starf*cker*
Strings
The Oilman's Daughter
Troubleshooters

Nonfiction

Action! Writing Better Action Using Cinematic Techniques

I am indebted to my own team of superheroes for helping to make this book possible. Jeff Hebert made a real bang-up cover that I think is his best yet. Tremendous thanks go to Sherri Cornelius and Allison M. Dickson for their feedback and editing help. I especially want to thank my wife for her insight into the inner workings of the prison system (she's not an inmate, she works for in one!) and my whole family for their everlasting love and support. Finally, thanks to you, my fans, for continuing to support my work! You're the biggest heroes of all.

For Amy.

We miss you.

PROLOGUE

(Excerpt from Deep Six: A Decade Under The Ground by William "The Neutralizer" Silbersack, 2004, reprinted with permission.)

It amuses me to see how people react when I tell them about my job.

I'm reminded specifically of a neighborhood barbecue I attended a couple of summers back with my wife. I was chatting with a nice young fellow who'd recently moved onto our block. I asked him about his work and he said he was a geologist for an oil company. "Have you found any yet?" I joked. "Here and there," he replied. "What do you do for work, Bill?"

His beer actually slipped right out of his fingers when I told him I was the Warden for Deep Six.

I get that kind of reaction a lot. When people discover you work in a parahuman prison, they make a bunch of assumptions. Some are fallacious, others are true. I'm neither a troglodyte nor a sadist. Actually, I've been told I'm a rather nice fellow, but thanks to Hollywood, people don't expect it of a prison guard. Would they be more comfortable around me if I were surly and cruel? I doubt it, but just the same I get more than my fair share of distant, carefully polite conversation, as if somehow I had the power to bring a world of trouble down upon someone from an imagined insult.

Once I've explained what I do, there are questions I am normally expected to answer. Everybody asks them in some form or another. I hope this book will serve to provide in-depth answers to those questions. In the ensuing chapters, I shall endeavor to go into these answers in far more detail, but in case you are the sort who likes to be teased, here are some of the most common questions (My editor informs me they're called FAQs) and my standard, pat answers.

Am I a parahuman?

Yes. I have the unique ability to prevent others from using their own powers, making me a logical choice to work for Deep Six.

What is a parahuman, anyway?

I'm no expert in the field by any stretch of imagination, but I can try to provide a short answer. A parahuman is anyone who has abilities or powers that would otherwise be considered impossible, such as flight, enhanced strength, or projecting fire. When most people think of parahumans, they think of Just Cause— the "Cause of Justice"—the iconic American superhero team that's been around since the Fifties. Names like *Lady Athena*, *Lionheart*, *Juice*, and *Doublecharge* have become household names as the team's various commanders.

What many people don't realize is that Just Cause is only one group of parahumans among many throughout the country and the world. Some, like the Lucky Seven or the New Guard, fight on the side of law and order. Others have banded together for less-benign purposes. Anyone who grew up in the Seventies and Eighties will remember the Weathermen and the Malice Group as they took parapowered crime from back alley muggings to blatant daylight attacks in Times Square and the Hollywood Bowl, or Destroyer's murderous sneak attack at a Just Cause member's funeral service in 1985, or the Cult of Destruction's reign of terror in the Nineties and the deadly cat-and-mouse game they played with parahuman heroes across the country.

Using parahuman powers in the commission of a crime automatically makes it a Federal felony. The problem with parahuman lawbreakers is how to keep them incarcerated. They retain their rights, just like anyone else. If bail is denied them after an arrest, they must be detained through court proceedings, and if they are convicted they must serve their prison sentences somewhere. Some parahumans can be safely held in a normal Federal correctional facility. Others require more specialized handling, and that means Deep Six.

Why is it called Deep Six?

The prison is six thousand feet underground.

Where is it? Are visitors allowed?

Deep Six is about seventy-five miles west of Billings, Montana. Visitors may come to the surface complex, but due to security requirements, only duly-appointed law enforcement and Bureau of Prisons personnel are permitted to descend into the hole.

Is it secure?

Deep Six maintains the highest possible level of security under the auspices of the Federal Bureau of Prisons. It is the next step above SuperMax. The entire premise behind Deep Six was to answer the question "how do you contain someone who can fly or walk through walls?"

Who's being held there?

Any parahuman whose powers would make incarceration in a standard prison facility impossible is held in Deep Six. The list of prisoners changes as sentences are served. I usually refer people to our website instead.

What's it like working there?

For the most part it's like any other job; repetitive and dull. But the nature of the prisoners does make for some interesting moments. I recall one incident where an inmate with enhanced strength—a power I cannot usually block—broke out of his cell and nearly made it to the elevator before guards were able to put him down. In the process, three guards were injured and he did so much damage that it forced a complete redesign of the wings.

Has anyone ever escaped?

No. I'm very proud of that fact.

"As of today, the Cult of Destruction and its leader, Misrule, are the top priority for Just Cause."
—James "Juice" Forsythe, Just Cause Commander

July, 2007
Denver, Colorado

The airport was a pandemonium of police, journalists, and strange, beautiful people in colorful costumes. Katie Malone stared at them in open wonder from the coolness of the concourse. The temperature was threatening to break the hundred-degree mark for the third day in a row, and the air conditioning strained to keep up. She watched the jet from Deep Six taxi across the tarmac. A woman with feathered wings circled over the plane as it came to a halt several hundred feet away from the airport proper.

Parahumans were uncommon in Ohio, where Katie had lived most of her life. She still had an outsider's fascination with the earthbound gods and their miraculous abilities. She'd recently discovered, to great surprise, she belonged to that elite group. Her power was nothing spectacular. She could only generate a small flame from her fingertip, as if she'd struck a match. It certainly didn't fall in the category of exceptional abilities—she wouldn't be climbing into a spandex costume and battling for the fate of the world anytime soon. On the other hand, it made her the first parahuman she'd ever known. Perhaps she should start smoking; it would give her an excuse to use the power. She raised her hand up, extended a finger, and watched as a tiny flame flickered to life at the tip.

"Wow, how did you do that?" asked the airport security guard who'd escorted her to the waiting area from her own plane. She'd forgotten he was even there.

She shrugged. "I don't know. I just can."

"I never met a real parahuman before."

"You still haven't." She nodded to the costumed figures on the tarmac below. "They're the real ones. I'm nobody compared to them."

The guard looked down at the heroes of Just Cause, the nation's premier super-team. Katie thought he looked a little bored, but she imagined that with the team headquartered there in Denver, the residents became a little jaded with the heroes' presence. "You ready to head down, Miss?"

"That's *Officer*," said Katie, used to making that particular correction.

"Sorry. *Officer*, then."

Katie flipped a compact open from her purse to check herself. She didn't make a habit of wearing makeup, but in order to make a good impression she'd applied some base, lipstick, and eyeliner, following some half-remembered advice from her mother. She fussed with her short auburn bob. The dry, high-altitude air was making it frizzy and no amount of combing or hair spray was going to fix it without more time than she had to spare. Satisfied that she looked good enough for the circumstances, she stood, smoothed her conservative business suit, and picked up the handle of her wheeled suitcase. The guard led her out the door and down the stairs to the tarmac.

The heat was a tangible thing, a shock to her system. She already felt a little lightheaded from the ridiculous altitude of what the locals called the Mile High City, and the addition of the sweltering temperature made her nauseous. At least the air was dry; Ohio humidity would have caused her to melt into a puddle in minutes.

Despite the massive police presence which cordoned off that entire section of the airport, far too many people roamed around unattended for her liking. As she crossed the tarmac, she scanned the groups and assigned each one a number and a threat potential, a habit she'd acquired in her former position at Ohio State Prison. Pairs of airport security guards like her escort roamed nearest to the concourse. Beyond them prowled the Feds, obvious in their off-the-rack suits and flesh-toned earpieces. Local police decked out in SWAT gear formed the outermost front. A forest of satellite booms from local, national, and international news outlets sprouted in the distance.

All other current events paled against the capture of the parahuman known as Misrule.

"Ms. Malone?"

She turned to see one of the Feds regarding her with cool detachment. His query was a formality; she'd have been shocked if they hadn't already identified her six times over already. She held up her badge for his perusal. "Yes, I'm *Officer* Malone." She emphasized her rank to the suit in case he'd forgotten that she not only belonged there, but had earned that right with her own blood and sweat.

He glanced at it without really looking, which confirmed her suspicion that he already knew everything there was to know about her from her middle name to her daughter's birthday to the incident details in her file from the Ohio State Penitentiary, where she had worked until two days ago. "I'm Ben Croft, U.S. Marshal. We're here to oversee the transfer of the prisoner. Have you checked in with your people yet?"

"No, I only arrived an hour ago and they wouldn't let me out of the concourse until the transport jet landed."

"Come with me."

Croft escorted her across the cement. He seemed immune to the sweltering heat despite his navy blue suit as he spoke into his radio. Shortly, an airport transport pulled alongside them, its quiet electrical motor drowned out by the sounds of jets landing and taking off along other runways. They boarded it and the driver steered toward the powering-down jet. The Fed's expression didn't change in the least, his eyes unreadable behind the mirror shades.

In a minute, they stopped next to the Deep Six jet. Three men dressed in navy blue tactical gear stood outside, smoking and sweating. Katie and the Fed stepped off the transport. The Deep Six men, deputies by their badges, regarded the newcomers with interest. One of them, a burly man with graying hair and mustache, extended his hand toward Katie, ignoring the Fed.

"You must be our transfer. They said you'd be meeting us here. I'm Lieutenant Frankes."

Katie gave him her best, firmest handshake. Prison guards understood strength, and it was imperative they saw her as strong first and a woman second. She'd spent years cultivating that reputation at OSP and hoped she could represent the same strength to the correctional officers at Deep Six. "CO Katharine Malone." She dug a folder out of the front zipper pouch in her bag. "Here's my paperwork."

Frankes made no move to reach for it. "I'm sure it's all in order. You come highly recommended, but we're not messing with petty offenders and minor felons at Deep Six."

Katie refused to be baited. "Good. I'm tired of playing with the kids sent up the river for stealing apples from the neighbors' orchard, *sir*."

Frankes burst into laughter. "Oh, that's rich. I'll have to remember that. Stealing apples." He snickered and turned to the other two men. "Officers Foster and Garcia," he said. Foster had short red hair, freckles, and sparkling blue eyes. He looked miserably hot in his gear with the sunlight blazing down upon him. Garcia's muscles bulged underneath his uniform and threatened to tear it at the seams. They both gave her polite nods.

"So when's the big event supposed to take place, sir?" Katie squinted across the hot cement, distorted by heat waves.

"We'll take possession of the prisoner as soon as Just Cause delivers him" Frankes glared at Katie's business suit. "Do you have any tactical gear stowed in your bag?"

"No, sir. I was told that Deep Six had its own special equipment."

"That we do. Foster, see if you can dig up something to outfit Malone here so she looks like she's playing in the same band as the rest of us."

Foster grinned. "I hope you can sing better than the Lieutenant. If I have to hear his rendition of *Feelings* one more time . . ."

He led her inside the jet. It was roomier inside than she would have expected; most of the seats had been removed, and blessedly cool. A hospital gurney was bolted down in the middle of the floor, surrounded by numerous monitoring devices and security features. She took a good look at it all as Foster rummaged through a supply cabinet. "I'm Tim, but everyone calls me Foster. Pleased to meet you, Katharine."

"Katie, please. Nice to meet you."

"So you were a CO at Ohio? How'd you like that?"

Katie shrugged. "It was a job. My dad and granddad both worked there."

"Why come to Deep Six?" Foster emerged from the cabinet with a handful of clothing and gear. "It's about as boring a place as you can imagine. We've got security that makes SuperMax look like a work release program."

She took the tactical ensemble from Foster. "I needed a change. I used to be married to another CO. He was very popular. We . . . separated. It became difficult to work there after that." She paused. "You going to watch me change, Foster?" Undaunted, she began to unbutton her blouse as she gave him a gimlet eye.

"Oh, uh . . ." He turned around, color rushing to his fair cheeks.

Katie stripped down to her underwear and bra, climbed into the one-piece blue jumpsuit and zipped it up to her throat. It turned out to be quite a bit larger than she'd thought at first and she felt like she was wearing a tent. "You can turn around now, Foster." She glanced out the small window and caught a glimpse of the winged woman as she cruised past in a slow glide. "She's beautiful. I don't remember her name, though. Eagle Woman?"

"Close," said Foster. "Desert Eagle."

"What's Just Cause really like?" Katie watched as Desert Eagle banked through a sharp turn; the white feathers on the underside of her wings sparkled in the sun. Just Cause was a venerable American institution—the team of heroes had been the cornerstone of parahuman law enforcement for more than fifty years. Like a sports franchise, the players changed over time but the name remained the same. The organization operated under the aegis of the government's recently-formed Parahuman Resources Agency.

"They're all right. I've only met one or two, and it was really brief. I doubt they remember me at all."

"Why should they?" Katie flapped her sleeves for emphasis, since she couldn't shrug clearly in the oversized jumpsuit. "They don't have time for ordinary assholes like us."

"I'm a para." His cheeks colored again. "Well, sort of."

"Oh?" Katie rolled up the cuffs of the jumpsuit legs and sleeves. Not for the first time in her life, she wished she'd inherited her father's or grandfather's height, instead of measuring only a few inches over five feet.

"Yeah. A lot of us at the Six are."

"What can you do?"

"I can almost turn invisible." He said the *almost* quickly, under his breath, as if he was ashamed of it.

"*Almost* invisible? What's that look like?"

Foster faded before her eyes. He grew darker, as if he stood in a shadow, and she realized she could see details of the plane cabin clearly through him. It only lasted a few seconds before he returned to normal.

"It's not much," he said. "It's better in low-light conditions. Then I'm almost impossible to see."

"Almost."

"It's useful for when I moonlight as a peeping Tom. Or a peeping Tim." Foster grinned.

"I bet." Katie took one look at the boots that went with the outfit and knew that she couldn't wear enough extra pairs of socks to make them fit her feet. She opened her bag; her own boots were inside. "I'm para too. Just found out." She held up a hand and sprouted a small flame from each fingertip. "Let me know if you need any candles lit or anything."

Foster laughed aloud at that. "Typical. We get the good genes, the same lucky turn of the cards as those Just Cause yahoos. They're out there fighting the big fights and we get to clean up the mess. It's like they're the circus performers doing gymnastics on the elephants and we get to walk behind them and shovel shit."

"And you have the soul of a poet." Katie laughed as she laced up her boots. "How in the world did you wind up at Deep Six?"

"They were hiring. I needed a job, and wanted to work with parahumans. Little did I know what I was getting into. Long hours underground, but at least the pay's pretty good and you can't beat the government benefits."

"How's the housing out there? I don't know a thing about Montana." Katie wrestled with the straps of the armored vest as she tried to arrange it comfortably on her chest. The damned things were not designed with breasts in mind.

"Not bad. We get subsidized housing, which means a small townhouse. But it's good enough for me and the boys."

"You have kids? A wife?"

"Two sons. Garth and Evan. Twelve and nine. No wife. She died seven years ago. Drunk driver."

"I'm sorry."

"It's all right. It happens. At least I've got the boys. You have any kids?"

"Just my daughter, Lindsay. She's five."

Frankes stuck his head into the plane door. "I hate to break up this love fest, but they're bringing him in now. Let's get a move on."

* * *

Maxim de Witte was born in Denmark in 1965 and became a naturalized American citizen in 1986. Sometime after that the parahuman known as Misrule debuted, and in the wake of his crime wave investigators found sufficient evidence to prove the two men were one and the same. Misrule specialized in large, spectacular crimes involving massive amounts of property damage and loss of life. He accumulated a group of parapowered followers who called themselves The Cult of Destruction. They moved around the country to battle various local superteams as they carved their way into the history books with such dramatic incidents as the Broward County Bloodbath, the Bank of Albuquerque Heist, and the Salt Lake City

Shootout. The Shootout had resulted in nineteen deaths —eleven police officers and eight civilians, half directly at the hands of Misrule—and the director of the FBI himself had asked Just Cause to focus their efforts on the Cult of Destruction.

The Cultists were wanted for crimes ranging from assaults to arson, burglary to battery, robbery to rape, and many, many murders. Misrule was at the top of that list, the Most Wanted parahuman criminal in the country. It seemed that not a law existed he hadn't broken, not a crime he hadn't committed. *Murder* was far too sanitary a term for the bloodbaths he often left in his wake. If convicted of even a tenth of the outstanding charges against him, his prison term would stretch into centuries, maybe even millennia.

Over the ensuing six years, Just Cause hunted down the Cult members one at a time. The cells of Deep Six became filled with captured Cultists, and by summer of 2007 only Misrule remained free, but had dropped completely out of sight. Just Cause's best investigators were unable to turn up the slightest bit of information on his whereabouts. Some of them theorized he was building up a new Cult and would turn up in some astonishing new crime of unbelievable scale. Others thought perhaps he had retired, having stolen close to half a billion dollars and uncounted valuables over the course of two decades. Still others believed he had left the country to work elsewhere in the world.

Nobody had expected him to show up at Just Cause headquarters to turn himself in.

* * *

"You dealt with paras before, Malone?" Frankes shouted over the roar of the Just Cause jet's engines as they idled.

"No, sir."

"Think of the worst offenders you've ever had to escort, and these guys are almost always harder than that."

"I've read the file on Misrule, sir."

"Maxim de Witte."

"What?"

"First rule of Deep Six is that you don't refer to the prisoners by anything but the name on their birth certificate. Calling them by the names they call themselves gives them legitimacy, and that's something we just don't want to do."

"I understand, sir."

"All right, lean in," bellowed Frankes to the others. The four correctional officers huddled together. "We've got most of Just Cause to cover our asses here, and that's a good thing, but we've also got a shitload of media types with zoom lenses and shotgun mikes, so let's not screw this one up. Foster, you administer the sleeper set. Garcia and Malone will cover. I'll drive the flatbed back to the jet once we get him situated. The file says he's bulletproof, super-strong, and generally one tough son of a bitch. But ultratasers should be effective if we need to motivate him to cooperate."

A normal taser like those issued to police officers was about the size of a flashlight. The ultrataser was developed specially for Deep Six and looked like an unholy union of shotgun and Super Soaker by way of Black and Decker. It could deliver anything from a standard taser charge up to a jolt equivalent to a lightning bolt. Katie felt the hairs on her arms stand on end as she took the ultrataser in hand and adjusted it to the setting Frankes recommended.

"All right, let's put on a good show for the press. Foster, watch your language around the press."

"I will shut the fuck up, sir."

"Nobody likes a wise-ass, Foster. Button it."

Katie thought she rather did like Foster's wise-assery, but kept that to herself and focused on the task at hand.

Foster unpacked the sleeper set from its carrying case. It used an electronic signal to induce a comatose state in the wearer. It was the safest way to transport prisoners who were strong enough to rip their way out of an airplane, or fly away if given the chance. At one time prisoners incarcerated in Deep Six had worn them twenty-four hours a day, but the ACLU filed a complaint about cruel and unusual punishment. The Supreme Court agreed and now the sets could only be used for transportation or extreme circumstances.

"Set's ready, Lieutenant," said Foster after he checked the settings on the device.

The aft door of the Just Cause jet opened, a ramp lowering down to the concrete. Frankes halted the motorized cart just at the base of the ramp. Garcia rolled off the cart to take a position at one side, his ultrataser at the ready. A moment later, Katie followed suit on the other side.

Misrule—*Maxim de Witte*, thought Katie as she remembered Frankes' words—stood at the top of the ramp. He was much larger than he looked on the archival video footage she'd seen. At nearly seven feet, he towered over the two Just Cause heroes who flanked him. His dark red, leathery skin contrasted sharply with the plain gray sweats he wore. Yellowed claws extended from his toes and fingertips. Pure white hair fell straight to his shoulders. His face was twisted into a demonic visage complete with ram's horns. Katie didn't realize she'd started to lower her ultrataser in awe until Garcia hissed at her and she focused again.

A length of sturdy chain bound Misrule's arms and a thick iron bar hobbled his legs, but he made no effort to battle his bonds. His head hung low and his shoulders slumped; he looked defeated. *He's sick or something*, she thought, recognizing the same stance her daughter had when she had a bad cold.

Doublecharge, the commander of Just Cause, stepped forward, resplendent in her black and white costume. She held out a tablet computer to Frankes. The screen was on standby mode, but Katie could see *Maxim de Witte "Misrule"* printed on a label across the top. Behind Doublecharge stood a handsome man with curly hair going gray at the temples and a sly grin that had graced hundreds of magazine covers for two decades. People called him the Face of Just Cause—Jack Raymond, known as Crackerjack, the Indestructible Man. He wore a jumpsuit similar to those worn by the Deep Six guards, weighed down with all manner of useful gadgetry and weapons. He'd been on Katie's list of celebrities she'd do since she'd been a teenager. She felt her pulse quicken at his presence, but he paid her no attention.

"He's been pretty docile and cooperative," said Doublecharge. "He claims he's got cancer."

Frankes tucked the tablet into a briefcase. "Nothing like free health care at the taxpayers' expense. Hard copy already sent?"

"It's on its way."

"Good. Let's go, de Witte. I'd like to be back home in time for dinner tonight. Know what we're having? Turkey. Know what we're having tomorrow? Turkey. And Friday? Turkey. Hope you like turkey, you asshole, because it's all you're going to get for the duration of your stay." A few of the Just Cause members looked uncomfortable at the taunts but nobody said anything. Katie could understand Frankes' lack of sympathy; the charges against Misrule could have filled a whole journal.

Misrule started down the ramp, but broke into a coughing jag halfway down. The man's bonds didn't allow him to hunch over as they wracked his body with heavy, wet sounds. Katie winced in unexpected sympathy as bloody sputum flew from his mouth to stain the concrete below.

"Maxim de Witte is being held on multiple outstanding warrants, and the detainee has been denied bond by the judge due to the high flight risk and lethal parahuman abilities," said Doublecharge. "All the information on his charges is contained within his file."

"Deep Six acknowledges the charges and accepts responsibility for the prisoner," said Frankes, following what sounded to Katie like official protocol. He turned to Misrule, who stood by the flatbed. Katie knew he was strong enough to break the chains and bars with ease if he made an effort. He could even fire destructive energy bolts from his hands, which didn't seem fair in the greater scheme of things; parahumans were supposed to be super-strong bricks *or* energy blasters, but Misrule was rare because he was *both*. Despite his tremendous level of power, he stood docile and awaited his fate.

Foster approached Misrule without hesitation. Katie wasn't sure she could have applied the same professional nonchalance herself. She gripped the ultrataser tightly, prepared to give the prisoner a powerful jolt if he so much as made an aggressive blink. Misrule remained placid as Foster ordered him to sit on the flatbed and installed the sleeper set on his head. It sat on Misrule's head like an aluminum skullcap. Katie thought it looked like a colander with electronic gizmos all over it. Foster had some difficulty fitting it over the prisoner's horns, but at last he twisted it just right and it settled into place. Foster activated the set and Misrule's eyes rolled back as he fell back onto the transport.

Foster caught him and lowered his torso onto the flatbed. "Christ, this guy's heavy."

"That's his muscular density," said Doublecharge. "His tissue is so dense that our MRI couldn't read his insides. He certainly seems sick, though."

Frankes nodded. "That he does. We've got special equipment back at the Six that ought to get us a look inside him."

"Good luck with that one. We've been after him for a long time."

"Warden has his cell all set to go. We've been expecting him." Frankes started the flatbed's engine, and then turned to Doublecharge. "Kind of funny that he gave himself up after all this time, don't you think?"

"Quite." She turned and walked back up the ramp into the plane.

* * *

Katie had expected someone else would pilot the jet back to Deep Six, but instead Frankes and Garcia went to the cockpit to perform a preflight checkup, leaving her and Foster to arrange their prisoner.

"You're not kidding about his weight. It feels like he's made of lead or something," she said as they struggled to move the comatose Misrule onto the gurney. She was no slouch about spending time in the gym—it was important for guards to be physically strong—but she and Foster barely managed to get Misrule into place. Her heart pounded and blood rushed in her ears as they strapped him down. "This altitude is a bitch. How do people live up here?"

"It's not so bad. Maybe we're just out of shape." Foster seemed just as winded and dropped into a seat at the aft of the cabin.

Katie joined him. "Are all prisoner pickups like this?"

"No. This one went smoothly. Thank God it's a short flight back to the Six from here. We won't have to do the icky part."

"Do I want to know?"

He smiled. "Ever install a catheter?"

"Oh. No."

The jet taxied to a runway and took off without delay. Katie caught a glimpse of the Rockies as the plane banked to the north. Snow still sat on the highest peaks, even in the middle of summer.

Foster got up, went to a cabinet at the plane's tail, and returned with two bottles of water. Katie accepted one and held the cool plastic against her hot forehead. "I had to manhandle a prisoner by myself back in Ohio once. He was about Misrule's—I mean, de Witte's—size, but not nearly as heavy."

"I wouldn't worry so much about calling him by his real name, Katie. Frankes is kind of a stickler for the rules, but we all know these assholes by their parahuman identities. If something happens and somebody tells you to go get de Witte, you don't want to waste time looking him up in the computer. I say *Misrule*, and you know exactly who I mean."

"I get it. Just don't say it around Frankes?"

"Not unless you want an ass-chewing. So what happened with your prisoner?"

She sipped her water. "I got him into a joint lock and introduced his face to a wall and held him there until someone backed me up."

"I'm surprised you had to deal with someone by yourself at all."

"Well, Ohio has always been kind of short-staffed, but . . ." She was unsure of how to explain the sexism, the constant tests of her ability to measure up to other guards, the general antipathy toward women, all of which had grown worse after she and Lindsay left Simon. Her ex-husband was very popular with the other officers and they'd all made it very clear whose side they were on, and it wasn't hers.

"You won't ever have to deal with anyone by yourself at the Six," Foster said. "These are the people who are too dangerous to hold even in a SuperMax. With the addition of him—" Foster nodded toward Misrule. "We've got the entire Cult of Destruction there now. We also hold the group that tried to rob the Denver Mint a couple of years back, and a slew of independents. Bad, scary people."

Katie nodded. She'd spent several nights paging through the Neutralizer's book and looking over Deep Six's and Just Cause's websites. "Are most of the staff members pretty easygoing, like you? Or . . . are they more like the Lieutenant?"

Foster chuckled. "That man has a real chip on his shoulder. He's jealous of paras, even if they're stupidly low-powered like you and me. He took the Musashi-Kitaro genetic test *twice*, and each time it came back negative."

Katie had never taken the MK test herself. It checked for the presence of the common genetic marker within most parahumans. She'd never had any reason to take the test, and now that she knew she had parahuman abilities, it was a moot point anyway. "So he hates parahumans. How many of us are on the staff?"

"Several. Garcia's one. He never sleeps. Ever. The man has been constantly awake for the last seventeen years."

Katie's mouth dropped open. It didn't sound like much of an ability, but then she thought about what she could do with another six-to-eight hours a day every day. "Wow."

"Yeah. He's got three degrees, his pilot's license, speaks four languages fluently, and three open-minded girlfriends."

"There are others?"

"Yes. You'll meet them soon enough. Nice folks for the most part."

"Good."

The jet's engines howled and they ate up the miles toward Montana and a very deep hole in the ground.

"How do you contain someone who can fly or walk through walls?"
—*Thomas Denton, Director of the Federal Bureau of Prisons*

July, 2007
Deep Six, Montana

"We're on final approach to Deep Six now. Our baby still sleeping?" Frankes' voice jarred Katie out of a sound sleep. Her early-morning flight from Ohio to Denver followed by the excitement of the prisoner transfer and finally another air journey to Montana had her jet lagged and exhausted. She sat up and checked on Misrule—*de Witte!* she corrected herself. He hadn't moved, which was a relief. In theory, with a sleeper set on he was incapable of any voluntary actions. She glanced over at Foster. He also dozed, his mouth hanging open, head tilted back against the seat. She smiled; her daughter slept the same way in the car.

"What the hell?" shouted Frankes. "Anybody awake back there? Some guards you are."

"Sorry, sir. We're awake. Misrule—I mean *de Witte*—is fine. He's still secured." Katie hoped there was an open microphone somewhere in the cabin and she wasn't just talking to the air.

Foster opened his bleary eyes and looked around. "We there already?"

The jet descended at a rapid clip and swung around toward an isolated runway. Katie couldn't resist pressing her nose against the window like a child, trying to get a better look as the runway rose up to meet them. "What happens next?"

"There's a secure hangar at the end of the runway," said Foster. "We taxi in there and once it's locked up, we can take the prisoner out. We're allowed to keep him asleep until we take the elevator down to Booking."

Katie shivered a little at the phrase *elevator down to Booking*. She wasn't claustrophobic, but had never been deeper underground than the basement levels of Ohio State. Deep Six was more than a mile beneath the surface. "What's it like, working so far underground?"

The landing gear touched down with a slight jolt and the engines' timbre changed as Frankes applied them to braking.

"Noisy. Between the air circulation, the plumbing, the generators, and all the electronic monitoring, there's a perpetual background hum that's occasionally loud enough you have to shout to be heard. It's also hot and humid. You ought to feel right at home, coming from Ohio."

Katie chuckled at that. The plane slowed and rolled into a hangar. She peered out the window at the reinforced walls as they bumped to a stop.

"We'd like to thank you for flying Deep Six airlines. Baggage claim is to your right, six thousand feet straight down," Garcia announced over the speakers.

The cockpit door opened and Frankes stepped through. "Everybody's a goddamn comedian." He stared at the comatose Misrule with professional intensity. "All right, let's get this asshole under the ground."

Foster opened the door. Several guards armed with ultratasers at the ready stood outside. One had a heavy-duty powered wheelchair. As they struggled to get Misrule's heavy body out of the plane, Katie glanced around the interior of the hangar. Tungsten- steel and concrete lined the heavily-armored walls, with numerous cameras mounted high above. Behind the plane, a massive shuttered door had sealed them inside. Ahead she saw a small building, which likely housed the elevator to the prison below.

They placed Misrule in the wheelchair and fastened his arms and legs into thick restraints. A brace kept his head upright while another clamped around his neck. For a moment Katie felt sympathetic for the man; the bonds seemed cruel. But then she reminded herself this man represented a far more dangerous and deadly felon than any she had dealt with in her previous position. Given his abilities, she wondered if the current restraints would even be sufficient to hold him when they removed the sleeper set.

The wheelchair operated via a remote control, and Frankes drove it into the elevator building under the watchful eyes of the surface guards. Katie noticed there were no operator controls inside the elevator, only a card reader and a plastic tube with a silicone tip. Frankes slid a card through the reader and blew into the tube.

"What's that tube?" Katie asked.

"Genetic reader. It's the same technology that Just Cause uses. The Command Center has sole control over this elevator, and they won't raise or lower it without a match to existing genetic codes, the card, and the verbal code," said Foster.

"Prisoners are a pretty resourceful bunch," agreed Katie. "But I can't imagine how someone could fool all three."

"I hope we never have to find that out."

Katie shivered. It was bad enough when normal prisoners escaped. "Same here. What happens if you lose your card or forget your verbal codes?"

"I suggest you don't do either," said Frankes, still facing the reader.

"Welcome back, Lieutenant." A voice sounded from several speakers mounted behind a heavy screen in the elevator roof. "Your authorization, please."

"Hopscotch. Green. Woodrow. Ablative."

"Thank you, Lieutenant. Beginning your descent."

The elevator jerked when it started and then dropped at a steady rate, sending Katie's heart into her throat as she thought about six thousand feet of dirt and rock over her head.

Frankes turned to her. "Welcome to Deep Six, Malone. You'll be issued an ID card and authorization codes once we've gotten this bastard locked down."

"What if I was a spy? Or an impostor?" she asked.

"Are you?"

She glanced at Foster, who shrugged. "No, of course not."

"Once you're under the ground, you can't get back without help from the Command Center, and they won't do anything without authorization codes and genetic verification. If you have parahuman abilities, the Warden can cancel those out. And if you don't, you're way out of your league if you're trying to sneak *into* Deep Six."

The rest of the elevator ride passed in interminable silence. Katie checked her watch and was surprised to discover the journey downward took over ten minutes. Garcia and Foster lounged against the walls. Only Frankes stood ramrod straight, his back to the others, facing the door. Eventually the car braked and came to a halt. The doors opened into a lobby. Two men waited there, one in a plain navy jumpsuit matching those worn by the guards, the other in medical scrubs.

"Welcome back," said the older of the two. He was in late middle age, with a paunch that years of calisthenics couldn't hide and hair the color of steel wool. His face was lined but pleasant and he carried about him a youthful energy which didn't match his appearance. It reminded Katie of her grandfather before he died. He only glanced at Misrule for a moment before approaching Katie and giving her a firm handshake. "You must be Officer Malone. Welcome to Deep Six. I'm William Silbersack, Warden of this facility. Pleased to meet you."

"Thank you, sir. I read your book."

He smiled. "Did you enjoy it?"

"Very much, sir."

"Always a pleasure to meet a fan. Now . . . we don't take much stock in the whole *sir* and *ma'am* thing down here in the Six. My friends call me Chief, and I hope you will too."

"I will, sir. I mean *Chief.*" Kate smiled. It was nice that he'd been so pleasant to her right off the bat without being condescending. He hadn't even let his eyes drop to check out her figure like most men did upon introduction. She'd grown so used to the male gaze upon her daily that she only noticed it when it didn't happen.

"This is Doctor Donald Mayfair. He's in charge of the prisoners' well-being."

Dr. Mayfair's mouth twitched as if he suppressed a grin before making his face once more a mask of professional neutrality. "This means I spend most of my days dealing with all manner of the imagined maladies to which prisoners are prone."

"All right, everyone . . ." Silbersack's manner turned officious. "Let's wake up Mr. de Witte and get him processed. Be on your guard. I can prevent him from using his destructive energy blasts, but he'll retain all of his strength. He shouldn't be able to break free of those bonds, but we've all been surprised before."

Katie wondered just what it took to surprise this bunch of jaded guards. The officers readied their ultratasers, standing alert as Frankes removed the sleeper set. Everyone tensed as it came off. Seconds ticked by; not in silence, for the prison was as noisy as Foster had said, but it seemed silent nevertheless as tensions increased.

"Usually they wake up by now," Foster muttered to Katie. Misrule hadn't moved a muscle since the set was removed.

"Check his vitals," said Silbersack.

Dr. Mayfair stepped forward, his stethoscope at the ready. "He's alive, but I don't like the sound of his respiration. It's very strained. He claimed to have cancer?"

"That's what the initial report from Just Cause says," Silbersack said. "Doublecharge has doubts about his claim."

"Just the same, I'd like to do a thorough examination as soon as you're done booking him."

Misrule's eyes snapped open. "Watch it!" called Foster. The huge red-skinned man flexed his arms and chest, straining mightily at his restraints. An inch-thick steel pin dropped to the floor in two pieces with a ringing sound like a quarter flipped through the air. Mayfair tripped over his own feet and fell in his hurry to get out of Misrule's reach.

Around the lobby, officers raised their ultratasers, each on a hair trigger. Silbersack took a step forward. "Hold it right there, Misrule."

"My apologies." Misrule's voice had all the smoothness of a well-oiled blade. "I forgot myself for a moment, and it can be rather a shock to awaken in restraints. I shall behave myself."

A booking technician stepped out of the back offices to face Misrule. She looked to be in her early thirties, but had the face of a teenager. Katie shivered a little; a cool draft followed the young woman around, like she had her own portable air conditioner.

"That's Cassie Haig," whispered Foster. "She can raise or lower the temperature around her by a few degrees. She hates being too hot."

"Mr. de Witte," said Cassie, "I'm going to ask you a series of questions and will need you to answer them honestly."

Misrule smiled. "Of course."

"State your full name."

"Maxim Aeschylus de Witte."

"Date of birth?"

"Six August, Nineteen Sixty-Five."

"Have you ever been known by any other names?"

Misrule chuckled at that before his laughter degraded into a coughing fit. Dr. Mayfair moved over to check on him, his sense of duty to the infirm overriding basic common sense.

"At times it has pleased me to call myself *Misrule*. As have others."

Katie stifled a yawn. She'd always found the booking-in routines to be boring. The questions continued, getting Misrule's basic personal information. His answers were quiet and complete, never hesitating, stammering, or any of the other obvious signs of dishonesty.

The list of charges against him spanned several pages. Cassie didn't dwell on reading them all. Instead, she informed Misrule a federal judge had denied him bond. Misrule didn't seem upset at that.

"I've spent twenty years running from this. I'm very tired now."

"Do you have any medical conditions that require treatment and if so, what medications are you taking, if any?"

Misrule's smile turned sad. "I have cancer. I have been told it is inoperable due to the nature of my body. I am not currently taking any medication for it."

"Who told you it was cancer? What kind is it?" Dr. Mayfair stared at Misrule, as if he could determine the nature of the illness by visual examination.

"My doctor told me. He believes it to be lung cancer of a somewhat advanced nature. His prognosis for my survival was . . . grim."

"Who is your doctor? Does he have records he can send us?"

Misrule met Mayfair's eyes with his own. "I will not disclose his identity to you. I do not know if he keeps records, but it is doubtful he would release them if he did."

"Bullshit," said Mayfair. "No legitimate doctor works that way."

"I never said he is a legitimate doctor. He practices on . . . the less-upstanding parahuman population."

Mayfair turned away. "So some unlicensed quack tells you you're sick and you believed him. I don't know who's the greater fool."

Misrule coughed, as if for emphasis. Bloody phlegm slid from the corner of his mouth.

"Check him out nevertheless, Doc," Silbersack said. "His lawyer will have a field day with us if you don't." He looked around as if he sought the origin of a rank odor. "Speaking of which, have we heard from his attorney yet?"

"Not yet, Chief," said Cassie.

"I have not yet contacted an attorney," said Misrule.

"I find that astonishing," said the Warden. "You're supposed to be fabulously wealthy and you don't have an ambulance chaser riding shotgun?"

Misrule shrugged shoulders like basketballs. "When you've been given only a few months to live, certain things no longer become a priority."

"Are we done here?" asked Mayfair.

"I believe so. Cassie?" Silbersack glanced over to where the booking technician typed notes into the computer.

"Yeah, we're done."

Mayfair stalked over to the secure door leading to the medical wing. "Well, bring him along and we'll see how sick he really is."

* * *

Katie stood in the Command Center with Foster and watched the video feed of Misrule being escorted to the prison level below. Even though he was surrounded by several armed guards, he remained cool and collected and didn't offer even token resistance as he went into his cell.

Like all cells in Deep Six, Misrule's had been customized to minimize the effectiveness of his powers. Silbersack's own ability to inhibit other parahuman powers required his concentration, and unlike Officer Garcia, he had to sleep sometimes. Therefore the cells had to be capable of holding an inmate indefinitely, or at least long enough that he or she could be subdued before breaking out. The technology used for the customization was an offshoot of that in the Just Cause training facility. Using the vast resources of the Earth itself, swarms of microscopic robots built appropriate layers into the walls and ceiling of each prison cell. Misrule's cell was reinforced with a titanium grid layer both within and without. Tiny zirconium crystals had been mixed into the grid which should diffuse his destructive energy blast into harmless visible light.

Katie relaxed as the door clanged shut and locked tight. Cassie switched the view to the feed of the interior of Misrule's cell. The great red-skinned man lay on his bunk, arms folded behind his head, and went to sleep.

Silbersack poked his head out of his office. "Malone, step in here, please."

Katie stepped in and stood at attention in front of his desk.

"Sit down, Malone, and for God's sake try and relax. You'll be under enough stress in this job without trying to follow protocols."

"I'm sorry, sir—I mean, Chief. I'm not used to this kind of setting. How can I help you?"

"I like to meet my new staffers and get to know them personally. Now that Misrule is safely locked away, it seemed like an opportune moment, since I have to give you your codes and genetic test anyway."

"Genetic test?" Katie wondered what that would entail.

"It doesn't hurt." Silbersack must have read her facial expression. He pulled a small device the size of a cigarette pack from within his desk. He touched a switch and several LEDs lit and it extended a small plastic nozzle. "Ever taken a breathalyzer test?"

Katie shook her head.

"Good. Take a deep breath and blow hard into that nozzle until it beeps three times."

Katie did as she was told. By the time the device beeped at her, spots danced in front of her eyes. She handed it back to Silbersack, who plugged it into a USB port on his computer.

Dr. Mayfair staggered into Silbersack's office and made straight for the coffee pot in the corner.

Silbersack raised an eyebrow. "Do come in, Doc. Have a cup of coffee. Make yourself at home."

Mayfair threw himself into an overstuffed chair, glancing at Katie. "It's a hell of a thing, diagnosing someone like him."

"Sir—I mean *Chief*—should I leave?" asked Katie.

"Not at all, Malone." Silbersack smiled at her and then turned his attention back to Dr. Mayfair. "Did he give you a hard time?"

"Hardly. He was more than willing to submit to every manner of test I could conceive of. Gentle as a lamb. I tell you . . ." He sipped at the hot coffee. "I don't know if he has cancer or not, but I've seen a lot of terminal patients in my time. When they finally accept their fate, they act a lot like he is now."

Silbersack straightened upright. "But you don't know if he has cancer or not?"

"It's a combination of his muscle density and the tensile strength of his skin," Mayfair grumbled. "I must have spent an hour trying to get a damn blood sample out of him. We don't have a needle sharp enough to penetrate his skin. I finally stuck a tube down his throat and tried vacuuming out some from his lungs, since he seems to be coughing it up now and again."

"Did that work?"

Mayfair took off his glasses and pinched the bridge of his nose. "I don't know. I wasn't very impressed with what I got. My nurse is running labs on the sample now."

"Did you put him in the scanner?"

"For all the good it did, yes. His body is so dense that I can't get a high enough resolution on the scanner to get any clear images. Look . . ." Mayfair tossed a thumbdrive to the warden, who caught it and slotted it. The doctor stepped around Silbersack's desk to point over his shoulder. Katie, interested despite an avowed squeamishness to all icky things, peered over the warden's other shoulder.

"What exactly am I supposed to be seeing here, Doc? Stuff like this is way beyond me." Silbersack looked askance at the blotchy black and white images on his screen.

"This is his chest cavity. Do you see this?" Mayfair pointed to a brighter area of the image."

"Yes?"

"It should be black. That should be a lung, but there's something a lot denser there, obstructing the scanner."

"What do you think it is?"

"I don't know." Mayfair finished his coffee. "But judging by all his other symptoms, I'd say there's a high probability that it's a tumor, and a big one at that. If I had to make a guess, I'd say de Witte only has at the most three months. He may not live to finish a trial."

Silbersack closed the file and handed the thumb drive back to the doctor. "But you're not sure."

"No, I'm not sure. Hell, we've both been in this business long enough to know that nothing is ever sure."

The Warden picked up a light pen and clicked it. A large wall-mounted monitor came to life. The technology casually available in Deep Six was far beyond anything Katie had encountered in Ohio. She resolved to become comfortable and competent with it as quickly as possible. Using the pen like a mouse, Silbersack opened the data file on Maxim de Witte.

"This is what's bothering me about the notion that he has cancer." He clicked open subsequent folders until he had the list of documented, estimated, and rumored powers showing on the screen. "Super strength, tissue density, hardened skin, energy blast . . . and *healing*." He highlighted this last, listed as a documented power. "The bastard can heal himself when he's hurt. So how can he have cancer?"

"I asked him about that, Chief, and it was the only thing that got him the least bit riled up. *Don't you think I've tried?* he shouted at me. Maybe the cancer is healing itself because it's part of his body, or maybe it's a side effect of his healing ability itself. I just don't know."

"Do you know of anyone who has a scanner with sufficient resolution to look through that hide of his?"

"The Parahuman Medical Institute in Paris."

"I can't authorize sending a prisoner halfway around the world."

"I'm well aware of that."

"Can you send them the raw scan data? Maybe they could somehow interpret it more clearly than we can."

Mayfair shook his head and finished his coffee. "It's not the data, it's the scanner itself. He'll need a new scan to get anything tangible."

"What would it take to get one of those scanners here? We'll probably need one eventually anyway."

"Oh . . . Probably Senate approval."

Silbersack didn't bat an eye at that. "I'll put in a request for one at the next budgetary meeting."

"I won't hold my breath for de Witte to still be alive by the time we have it." Mayfair stopped by the door. "Thanks for the coffee, Chief. Officer Malone, nice to meet you again."

"Anytime, Doc."

"Let's see, Malone. Where were we?" murmured Silbersack. "Ah, yes." He passed her a card with four random words on it. "Here's your pass code. Commit that to memory then destroy the card. It's only good once, so get used to memorizing. You'll get a new one each time you head to the surface. I've just uploaded your genetic code into our system. Our computers will now recognize you as a Deep Six employee." He placed the device into a box on the wall and sealed it. "Now I'm irradiating the sampler to eliminate any trace of your DNA for the next time I have to use it."

"I see, sir—I mean, *Chief*."

Silbersack sighed. "If it makes you more comfortable, Malone, you can call me *sir*. That is, you can until either I'm sick of hearing it or you're sick of saying it, and I won't pretend to suspect which will come first."

"Thank you, sir."

"I've read your personnel file from Ohio State, and I have to say it's quite impressive. Prisons aren't very friendly settings towards female COs. Commended seven times for outstanding work . . . exemplary behavior . . . bravery . . . Honestly, Malone, you have more credentials here than my assistant warden. You could have had your choice of assignments when you left OSP."

Katie said nothing.

"There are also quite a few reprimands here, I see. Almost all of them came during this past year. I assume this is why you wanted to leave?"

"Yes, sir."

"Want to talk about it?"

"There's not much to tell. I was married to another officer. It didn't work out. He had many friends among the guards. It became very difficult to work there."

"And dangerous?"

Katie wondered if Silbersack could read her mind.

* * *

Only a month ago she'd walked into a dangerous situation that might have been arranged by her venomous ex. An inmate was somewhere he wasn't supposed to be, a place he couldn't have gotten to without help. He jumped her and it looked as if his intent was to rape and murder her, and not necessarily in that order. Unarmed, trapped in a room without a camera, she fought him tooth and nail. He was much bigger than her, much stronger, and he got her down to the floor. Saliva dripped onto her cheek from his leering mouth, mixing with droplets from the bloody scratches she left across his face. She could feel his terrifying hardness against her thigh as he sought to tear away her uniform trousers. He only made animal noises as he slapped her until her head spun and she lost her edge. His hot breath smelled sour, like he never brushed his teeth.

Then flames sprouted from her fingers.

The sudden flickering light distracted him and one of his sleeves caught fire. As his hold weakened on her for a moment, she grabbed his head and thrust her thumbs, flames and all, into his eyes. It felt like she'd poked her thumbs into a couple of tomatoes. The flames from her fingertips set his hair on fire. He screamed, flung himself aside, beat at his own head, and tore at his ruined eyes.

As he rolled around on the floor with his head aflame, she kicked him. Hard. Over and over in places soft and hard with her steel-toed boots until he was more dead than alive.

The flames died out quickly, and weren't hot enough to do more than singe his scalp, but he kept blubbering that he was blinded. She left him locked in the empty room and called for backup. Then she marched straight into the Warden's office and requested an immediate transfer out of OSP. The Warden was very quiet as he filled out the paperwork while she stood in front of him, bleeding and squinting through eyes nearly swollen shut. When he asked where she wanted to go, she said *Deep Six*.

Then she went home and held her daughter for a very long time.

Her physical injuries had healed, although she still had a scar next to one eye and sometimes her ears would ring for hours. At night she would sometimes awaken with the memory of blood in her mouth and the smell of fear and burning hair filling her nostrils, moments away from screaming.

* * *

Katie looked Silbersack straight in the eye. She knew her file contained a sanitized version of the incident, replacing her raw terror with the dry, plain language of reporting. "Dangerous? Not any more so than any other prison, sir."

"I see." His tone suggested he knew the full story nevertheless. "You've been on duty for most of a full shift now and you haven't even been home yet. Why don't you knock off now and call it a day?"

She blushed. "Well, to be honest, sir, I'm not even sure where my house is. Or how I'll get there."

"We're not entirely without resources here, Malone, and we don't expect you to fend for yourself." Silbersack touched his intercom. "Officer Foster, please report to my office." He returned his attention to her. "I've received word that the movers will arrive tomorrow morning with the rest of your personal effects, furniture, and your car. Your house is furnished enough that you won't have to sleep on the floor. And the rest of your family?"

Katie didn't have to check her watch at all. She missed her daughter terribly, and it would even be good to see her mom again. "Their plane lands in four hours."

"Four hours," he said. "That should give you just enough time to check into your house, have dinner, then get to the airport."

Foster walked into the office. "Yeah?"

"Foster, you're on chauffeur duty for Malone tonight. See that she gets home, something to eat, and to the airport."

"You got it." He grinned at Katie. "Do you like Thai food?"

She smiled back. "I have no idea."

THREE

"The most important work you and I will ever do will be within the walls of our own homes."
—Harold B. Lee, president of the Latter-Day Saints Church

July, 2007
Deep Six, Montana

Katie's new residence sat amid a row of townhouses in a small neighborhood halfway between Deep Six and Billings. They looked like little cracker boxes with shared walls, each painted the same uniform brick red with cheerful white trim. Each had two stories and a small garage in the rear that most families just used for storage, said Foster. The basements were roomy, though, warm in the winter and cool in the summer.

"Does everyone who works at Deep Six live here?" asked Katie.

"Not everyone," said Foster. "Some of the folks don't mind the commute from Billings, and it's not bad if you've got a good stereo."

"Where do you live?"

"Right there on the end of the row. The house with the geraniums in the window box."

"You grow flowers?"

Foster drew himself up proud. "It's my hobby. Once you're settled in you'll have to come and look at my garden in the back."

"What, not to come see your etchings?" Katie felt she needed to nip any notions of her being date material in the bud. She'd promised herself after the divorce that she would never again get involved with another correctional officer. The emotional wounds were still pretty fresh and dating inside the industry would just exacerbate them.

"No, uh, nothing like that." Foster studied his shoes. "I was just going to say that since the rest of the neighborhood is undeveloped, we can spread out quite a bit. I've got a greenhouse back there, and some good landscaping. Nice place to spend a summer evening with a beer."

"Sounds like it. How did you get into gardening?"

Foster shrugged. "It was something my wife did and I helped. After she died I felt like it was something I should keep doing. Now I enjoy it. It's relaxing."

Katie unlocked the door and stepped inside, letting her eyes adjust from the bright sunshine. The front door opened onto a small landing at the bottom of a stairwell leading up. The living room was to the right. A realtor would have called it *cozy* but to Katie, it was just cramped. A couch that looked like a leftover from a doctor's office sat along one wall, facing a television that wouldn't have been out of place in a Super 8 motel. Beyond the living room was a tiny dining area, with a round wooden table and four chairs. Past that she could see the kitchen and a door leading to the garage.

"Ugh," she said. "Is it all as bad as this?"

"Dorm room chic," said Foster. "They were all like this when we moved in. Most everybody has since painted, changed the carpet, and sent the furniture back to storage."

Katie tried to imagine her own furnishings filling the rooms instead of the horrid pieces currently occupying them. Her couch was larger than the one in the living room, with several different covers that she changed with the seasons. Maybe some new drapes and her mirror paintings would brighten things up. Her kitchen set was in poorer shape than the one already in place. She though perhaps the addition of a dark mahogany stain would make the existing table look rather nice.

"It is kind of charming." She wandered into the kitchen to check the tiny quarter bath and the appliances. "In a shitty sort of way."

"Nicer than the cells in the Six, that's for sure."

"Silbersack said in his book nobody has ever escaped. Ditto for the website. But I know that stuff goes on that doesn't get outside the walls. What's the worst thing to happen while you've been there?"

"You ever hear of a parahuman named Egress?"

"No. Stupid name."

"Stupid criminal too. He was strictly farm-league. He could open holes in solid matter. He was a pretty careless burglar, though, and got pinched by regular police. Anyway, we brought him into the Six and one day his cell malfunctioned and he went through his door right as Napalm was passing through the hall for his daily exercise. Before we could get an ultrataser on anyone, Napalm lit up Egress right there in the hall. Burned him to charcoal before we knocked him out. Poor guy was only serving twenty-four months."

"Oh my God," whispered Katie. "I knew Napalm was a psychopath, but that's really messed up. How come nobody ever heard about this?"

Foster shuffled his feet. "The Chief decided to keep it quiet. Napalm's already serving consecutive life sentences. If the word had gotten out that Deep Six wasn't quite as secure as everyone thought, it would have been a huge fiasco. Parahumans are already walking a fine line right now, and there is more than one lawmaker who'd like to see a new Parahuman Registration Act."

"So you covered up the death of a prisoner to protect your jobs and all free parahumans everywhere?"

"Yeah." Foster's smile was wry. "Pretty noble of us, don't you think?"

Katie shrugged. "We covered up our own share of incidents at OSP. I guess it probably goes on in every prison out there."

"I won't tell if you won't."

Katie snorted in amusement.

"You really can make one of these places into a decent home. The boys and I have been here for four years now. They seem to like it. There are quite a few kids their age in the neighborhood, as well as some younger. Not too many older kids, though. I think there are only three in high school."

"How are the schools? And for that matter, where are they?"

"Well, the neighborhood is a little bigger than it seems. Most of it is on the other side of the highway. There's a K-8 school over there and a bus to take kids from here. The nearest high school is twenty miles to the east."

"Hmm." Katie opened the door to the basement and was rewarded with a refreshing cool breeze. She peeked down the stairs. The basement was finished as a single large room. The ceiling was low and the sound of the central air created a constant hum, but she could see how it could be an attractive place, even though it was empty at the moment.

Upstairs she found three bedrooms; two smaller plus a master. Each room sported a twin-sized mattress on the floor with nothing else. Besides the bedrooms there was a laundry and a full bathroom. She examined the walk-in closet in the master bedroom and pronounced it too small, which drew a laugh from Foster.

"It's truly hideous," she said. "But I see potential."

Foster chuckled, checking his watch. "Hey, it's a long ride out to the airport. If you still want to try Thai food, we'll phone ahead and eat on the way."

"I'm game," she said. "I'm hungry enough by now to eat almost anything."

* * *

Katie was pleasantly surprised at how good her Thai noodle bowl was. She opted to forgo the chopsticks in favor of a more conventional fork. Foster had urged her to eat while he drove since he didn't want her to be late meeting the incoming plane. She'd tried to be polite but after he laughed at her fastidiousness, she gave in to her appetite and shoveled in noodles, peanuts, and wonderfully spicy chicken. While he drove, Foster nibbled at his own dish, some kind of fried fish nuggets with a curry dipping sauce that made her nose twitch.

Her mother, a retired schoolteacher, and her daughter were flying in together. Her mom intended to stay and provide free daycare for Lindsay when Katie was working. Katie hoped her mother would opt for a house of her own in the neighborhood so Katie could have some privacy. Ever since the divorce, her mother had been so watchful over her that it bordered on psychotic overprotectiveness.

As they drove and ate, Foster told her more about his sons, Garth and Evan. The two were rascals of the same mind, only separated by their ages. They were away in the middle of a two-week summer camp where Foster expected both were already in some sort of trouble. Garth had started to discover girls, something Foster admitted he wasn't ready for yet. The older boy was a mediocre student but a superb artist who wanted to draw comic books someday. His younger brother Evan wasn't artistically-minded in the least, but brought home straight A's and several detentions every year, usually for some complicated practical joke he'd dreamed up and put into action.

"The kid's some kind of weird genius," said Foster with a laugh. "He's just so curious about the world and the way things work. He looks at stuff in a different light from everyone else."

Billings Logan International Airport was a bland terminal that looked like most other airports Katie had ever seen. Foster parked his Yukon in short-term parking and the two headed inside. They suffered the indignity of a half-hearted check by a bored TSA guard before being allowed onto the concourse.

A few other people waited at the gate. Foster dropped into one of the hard plastic bench seats, yawning. "It's been a long day."

"You're telling me? I was still in Ohio this morning."

"Oh yeah, I forgot about that. You must be jet lagged as shit. I mean, you're probably beat all to hell and gone. Sorry, I'm trying to tone my mouth down here."

"Foster, I've worked in a prison environment since I was twenty-one. You don't have to edit yourself around me. Trust me, I've probably heard worse than you. Just keep your mouth clean around Lindsay and my mom and we'll get along just fine."

Foster smiled at that. "Fucking-A right."

"Now you're just showing off."

The plane landed shortly and Katie stood right up against the glass to watch it taxi over from the runway. She bounced in place as the jet-way swung over to link up with the airplane's door and chewed on her knuckles. In a few minutes people started to trickle out and she watched anxiously for her family.

Then, with an earsplitting cry of *Mommy!* Lindsay ran down the jet-way, dodging around straggling travelers with her pink princess backpack bouncing from one hand. Her raven hair flew behind her like a midnight flag and then she was in Katie's arms, all kisses and tickles. Katie buried her face in her daughter's neck and breathed in her scent.

"Mommy, I flew on the airplane!"

"Yes you did, sweetheart. Did you have fun?"

"Yeah. Gramma let me have a Coke and some honey nuts."

"She did? Yum. I had some peanuts in my dinner too."

Her mother appeared with a bag barely small enough to be called a carry-on slung over her shoulder. "She was very good for the whole flight."

Katie stood to embrace her. "Hi, Mom. Thanks for coming." She remembered Foster, who stood off to one side and waited for the reunion to run its course. "Mom, Lindsay, this is my friend Tim Foster. He works with me at the Six. Foster, this is my mom, Gail Wilson. And this lovely young lady is Lindsay." Katie hefted her little girl up to her hip.

"Hi Mr. Foster," she said. "I'm five years old."

"Mr. Foster is my father," he said. "You can just call me Foster. I don't think I've ever seen three lovelier ladies in one place before."

"Oh, I like this one," said Gail.

Katie did look a lot like her mother; both had auburn hair cut to sensibly short length, the same brown eyes and a mouth that turned down at the corners when smiling. Lindsay had inherited most of her mother's facial characteristics, but her hair was the same glossy black as her father's.

Gail had no luggage besides her carry-on. In it she had three changes of clothes for her and Katie, as well as basic toiletries and necessities like Junior Mints, homemade peanut brittle, and coconut shampoo and conditioner. Katie still couldn't quite believe it; her mother normally couldn't take less than a full suitcase for a weekend trip, never mind moving across the country.

"The movers had better be here by tomorrow," Gail grumbled. "I don't know what I'll do if they're late."

"Gee, mom, you might have to run a really small load of laundry." Katie knew that her mother's frugality would never permit such a transgression as a washing machine at less than full capacity. "And they do have shops here, you know."

"Yes, with electricity and running water and everything," said Foster with a twinkle in his eye. "We're very modern here."

Katie laughed. Everything seemed so much better now that she was reunited with her daughter. The foursome left the terminal, Lindsay skipping alongside her mother.

Even though it was past the little girl's bedtime, Katie talked Foster into stopping for ice cream. They each got a cone to take on the drive back.

Foster ended up having to finish Lindsay's ice cream. They weren't back in the truck for ten minutes before the little girl nodded off, nearly dumping her cone in her lap.

"You going to be okay to make this drive?" Katie asked Foster with a yawn that nearly split her skull.

He cracked open a Red Bull. "I can drive all night on two of these, but one should do me just fine to get you ladies home."

"Good." Katie finished her ice cream cone and shut her eyes. It was just for a minute, she told herself . . .

* * *

An insistent beeping from her cell phone woke her from the quagmire of half-remembered dreams. She fumbled for it on a nightstand that didn't exist because it was packed in a moving van somewhere between Montana and Ohio. Finally she managed to locate the electronic menace. "H'lo?"

"Good morning, Merry Sunshine," said Foster. "Would you like a ride to work or were you planning to hitchhike, maybe?"

Katie sat up and looked around at the blurry, unfamiliar room. The sun peeked in through the window to her right. She recalled being dropped off late the night before, staggering inside with Lindsay in her arms after bidding Foster thanks and good night. He'd said he would pick her up in the morning.

Lindsay, snuggled next to her on the mattress, shifted and murmured something incomprehensible. Katie carefully rolled off the bed so as not to wake her daughter, and moved into the bathroom, still clutching the cell phone. "Shit. How late am I?"

"You're not yet. I thought you might be tired so I brought cop food."

Cop food meant doughnuts and coffee, both of which sounded wonderful and necessary. "How can anyone be so chipper in the morning?" she grumbled into the phone. She found her glasses and stuck them over her ears, finally catching a focused glimpse of herself in the mirror. "Jesus."

"What's the matter?"

Her hair was sticking straight up on the left side and straight out on the right. "My hair sucks." How was it even possible for it to get so messy in such a short time? It wasn't like she was doing underwater acrobatics in her sleep. "I need to take a quick shower."

"That's fine, I'll wait. I don't think the inmates will care particularly one way or the other, but the Prince always likes us to look professional."

"Who?" Katie squeezed a massive amount of toothpaste onto her brush, hoping to eliminate the taste of whatever had died in her mouth overnight.

"David Prince. Assistant Warden. He's running the show today. Technically it's Silbersack's weekend, but the man hasn't taken a full day off since I've been working there."

Katie twisted the shower knob and marveled at the water pressure, which had always been trivial at best back home. She spat out a mouthful of minty foam. "Okay, give me ten minutes."

"Take fifteen, but after that I can't promise any doughnuts will be left."

"There better be, or I'll pay an inmate a carton of cigarettes to shank you in the halls." Katie shut her phone and hit the shower.

Fifteen minutes later she stepped out of the house after whispering goodbye to Lindsay and letting her mom know she was off. She'd dressed in comfortable civilian clothing, managed to put her contacts in the correct eyes, and even found the motivation to squirt some gardenia-scented body spray in a couple strategic locations. She dug in her purse and found a hair tie, pulling her hair back into a short and sensible ponytail before opening the door to Foster's Yukon. Had she remembered deodorant? She gave herself a couple surreptitious sniffs as she arranged her hair. Yes, she had.

"Good morning," said Foster. "Here, leave this for Lindsay and your mom." He held out a drink carrier with a cup of coffee, a pint of milk, and a bag of doughnut holes.

"Are you this nice to everyone?"

"I have an ulterior motive." He sipped his own coffee.

She arched an eyebrow. "I don't date COs."

Foster chuckled. "Who said anything about a date? I was hoping your mom would be willing to do a little babysitting now and again."

Katie flipped down the visor and checked herself in the vanity mirror. "It's possible."

"They're good kids. Housebroken and everything. They've had all their shots."

"Are your boys as goddamned cheerful as you are in the mornings?"

"I can't help it. I'm a morning person."

"I may have to kill you."

"Let's talk more about this date you mentioned."

"To hell with the inmates. I'll shank you myself."

"Tease."

* * *

Always there was the pain.

Misrule gritted his teeth against it. Had someone been foolish enough to place a tungsten-steel bar in his jaws, he could have bitten it in two. Some days the pain encompassed the sum total of his existence, and it took every effort he could muster not to bring it to a premature ending. He'd earned the pain, the wages of sins past, present, and future. Like some infernal retirement plan, the cancer multiplied, compounding interest upon interest. Unchecked, it would eventually claim him as its own. The pain was his nemesis, but it was also his partner and his salvation, and he had learned to embrace it. One day, soon, the pain would disappear and he would be freed from its grasp.

He lay on the hard bunk in silence, arms wrapped around his chest, as if by cradling it he could protect it from the terrible war being fought within the confines of his own body. Cold sweat dotted his hard red skin. Like a surfer shooting a tube, he rode the waves of pain, letting them support him even as they threatened to submerge him, using the pain as a focus for his thoughts.

The light over his cell door came on, and a voice issued from the speaker. "Wakey wakey . . . eggs and bakey." The food dispenser thumped and slid through the wall. It was a sturdy invention, modeled after those devices used to make night deposits at banks. On its tray sat his unappetizing morning meal: a paper bowl of oatmeal with a cardboard spoon, an apple, and a pint of milk. Next to the food lay a toothbrush and a small packet of toothpaste. "You've got twenty minutes, and then we inventory the tray. Anything missing and you get the gas and we search everything from top to bottom, including you."

"I am well aware of your security procedures," Misrule said through clenched teeth. "However, I am not hungry."

"Your choice. Twenty minutes then I take it away."

Embedded just beyond the edge of the cell's air vent lurked a hair-trigger grenade filled with an anesthetic gas. Misrule had seen the Discovery channel special on Deep Six and knew that the gas was effective on anyone who breathed it. He knew he could rip the reinforced grate free from the ceiling, but that would release the gas into his cell. Doing so would improve neither his position nor his health, so he left it alone.

His palate, once used to the finest gourmet cuisine, found the breakfast uninspiring. He looked at it in disappointment, but knew that it was the best he would likely get during his stay. Sighing, he picked up the spoon and began to eat the tasteless porridge. Some days the cancer wouldn't let him eat at all; others it wouldn't let him keep his food. Today it seemed content to leave him to dine in peace. Halfway through his bowl, he found a small, hard object in a spoonful. He didn't find this at all unusual, and tucked it into his cheek, careful not to swallow it as he ate.

He finished the meal, left the trash on the tray, and returned to his bunk. The monster in his chest stirred, threatening to dislodge his food as it had so many times in the past. He coughed, hard, until blood spattered his hand. As he did, he spat out the small object that had been buried in his oatmeal. Hunched over to avoid being seen from overhead, he examined it. It was a polished piece of bone the size of a nickel. Scratched onto it was a single number: 2.

Misrule slipped the bone back into his mouth and ground it to pieces between his powerful jaws, swallowing the remains. Two days. Two days until he no longer needed his pain, no longer needed to suffer the indignities of the cancer raging through his cells; the constant cough, the perpetual taste of his own blood to nauseate him, the gasping to draw enough oxygen into his tortured lungs to allow him another few minutes of life. He brushed his teeth and left the toothbrush on the dispenser tray. Only moments after he did, the tray slid back into the wall and the sardonic voice came over the speaker.

"Good boy, you ate all your num nums. Mummy will be proud of you."

Misrule didn't dignify the man with a response. He had his number, and he had his pain to keep him company.

Always there was the pain.

* * *

Pleased to meet you, Officer Malone." Assistant Warden David Prince was a short, stout man of undistinguished features.

"Likewise, sir." Katie had changed into her duty uniform and met Foster in the Command Center.

"Have you been given a full tour of the facility yet?"

"No, sir, not yet."

"What do you think of our security? It's always refreshing to get an outsider's perspective. Not that you're an outsider anymore, of course."

Katie glanced over at Foster, who smiled in encouragement. "It's very good, sir. This is the best guard-to-prisoner ratio I've ever encountered. It's almost enough to make one feel safe."

"Indeed. One guard for every three prisoners, even given twenty-three hour lockdowns, would seem wasteful in most correctional facilities." Prince pulled up a list of names on his main screen. They were not the names by which the inmates were filed, but the names by which they had been known when they were fugitives from justice. Twenty-three names, a few of which Katie recognized. *The Etched Man. T-Rex. Napalm. Heretic. The White Dragon.* Their crimes had been spectacular, flamboyant, and of the worst sort. Prince looked back at her. "These are not typical prisoners. Fortunately we have our own parahuman resources to assist in their containment, although the truly high-powered paras have chosen the paths of fame and glory instead of the opportunity to do some real work down here in the Six."

Prince ordered Foster to give Katie a quick tour through the facility, show her who was in each of the five wings, and brief her on security procedures. Foster and Katie saluted him and marched out of the office.

"He does like to hear himself talk." Foster took Katie to the secure elevator which led down to the wings. "Security is pretty straightforward, just like it would be at any Maximum Security prison. Keep a locked door between you and the prisoners at all times. If you ever have to approach one, have someone on hand to back you up. There's a kill switch for every cell that dumps the gas. It knocks you out. You wake up a few hours later with a hell of a headache. We've all felt its effects so we know what to expect. I'm sure you'll get your chance too."

"I can't tell you how much I'm looking forward to that." Katie scanned her badge on the elevator door and repeated her authorization code. The personnel on duty in the Command Center verified her ID, checked her image against the profile in the computer, calculated a sufficiently high probability she was herself, and opened the door.

The wings were arranged in a **V**-shape, with the elevator lobby at the nadir. Each wing was divided into four blocks of five cells with a secure airlock between each block. Cells were only on the outer walls. Behind the inner walls were the environmental systems that provided water and removed waste, as well as the air conditioning that maintained the prison at a constant seventy-degree temperature. This deep underground, cooling was essential; the surrounding rock measured over a hundred degrees due to pressure from above and geothermal heat from below. Without the air conditioning and cool water circulating through the walls, floor, and ceiling, the heat would reach dangerous levels within hours.

The airlocks at either end of each block allowed the anesthetic gas to be dumped into an entire block without contaminating adjacent areas of the prison. They also had "escape hatches" for any guards unable to reach the elevator lobby due to a gas release or other environmental or security concern. "We've only had to use one once." Foster showed the discreet hatch cover to Katie. "Two years ago Sea Witch got angry about a tuna fish sandwich and blew out a water pipe. E-Block filled up to the ceiling. Scariest fucking thing I've ever seen. We thought we were going to wind up with a bunch of drowned prisoners, and Jaime Pasteur was on the wrong side of it all. He's a guard here."

"Wow, scary. What happened?"

"Pasteur went up the hatch. Silbersack got Sea Witch calmed down and convinced her to push the water back into the pipe."

"How did he do that?"

"I have no idea. He moved her to a different cell after that and she can't do much more than push her drinks around now."

Katie looked at the hatch. It would be very difficult to spot if you didn't know the exact place where to look, and opening it would present an altogether different problem. "The prisoners don't know these are here?"

"We hope not. Each block has its own exercise room, so prisoners only pass through a lock on the way to or from court or to begin their sentence."

They entered A-Block and Katie looked at the names stenciled over each cell door and cross-referenced them with their fanciful villainous names. Holcomb; *Kiloton*. Gordon; *Dissident*. Sanchez; *Pinpoint*. LeVaughn; *Napalm*. It gave her the shivers to know just how powerful those parahumans were. "Does it ever freak you out? Being so close to them? Like this guy here?" She pointed to the cell of Curtis LeVaughn, who chose to call himself *Napalm*. He had burned down an apartment building just to watch the inhabitants die. The only reason he hadn't been executed was the state in which he'd been convicted had no death penalty.

Foster shrugged. "It's really no big deal. Misrule's the first new resident we've had since Just Cause's big bust of the *Soldados* last year. They're filling up B-Block and part of C. That was exciting—nothing for two years then seven all at once. I thought Prince was going to have a heart attack."

"I guess I thought there would be more drama or something." They continued through the airlock into B-Block.

"Deep Six is pretty much like any other prison. Same shit, different day."

"That sounds like any job."

"Yeah, it does, doesn't it?"

"There was never anything by the wit of man so well devised, or so sure established, which in continuance of time hath not been corrupted."
—*The Book of Common Prayer*

July, 2007
Deep Six, Montana

William Silbersack began his long career as a costumed superhero in the time referred to by people of his generation as *back in the day*. Back in the day for him meant the end of the turbulent 1960s as a member of a group of young upstarts known as the Atomic Generation. They had seen themselves as the new generation of heroes, willing to do the things and fight the fights that the older, more conservative organization of Just Cause would not. They'd been cutting edge parahumans—hip, mod, hardcore, and spoke with the voice of the Baby Boomers. While Just Cause had hidden in their holes, pretending the problems of the world didn't exist, the Atomic Generation had faced those problems head-on.

Civil rights? The Generation had been right at the forefront of the marches, unafraid to link arms with their colored brothers and sisters. They'd burned their draft cards and worn masks so the government couldn't track them down. They'd been hippies, beatniks, bohemians. They'd listened to freedom rock, to soul, to poets spouting their masterpieces in smoke-filled clubs. They'd smoked dope, taken LSD, had free-wheeling free-love orgies, and once fought Just Cause to a standstill in New York's Central Park in '75.

In his heyday as an eager young superhero, Silbersack had worn his hair long and his sideburns longer. He'd called himself the Neutralizer because he could stop any parahuman's powers cold, demonstrated to great effect against Just Cause's finest. He'd kept Pony Girl from running, Kid Crash from setting off his explosions, Tornado from flying, and Sundancer from lighting things up. The only powers he couldn't stop were those that didn't actually *do* anything: the super strength of Lionheart, the rock body of John Stone, and of course, the robotic Steel Soldier was immune to his negation power. If not for those three, what the *NY Times* called the Battle of Central Park would have had a clear victor, and it wouldn't have been Just Cause.

He had to concentrate to maintain his block of others' powers, and the effect dissipated over range. Eventually other parahumans had figured that out and he became an early casualty of most engagements, usually knocked on his ass and bleeding. He retired from the superhero business in 1979 at the tender age of thirty. He'd spent twelve years running around in what he'd come to regard as uniformly ridiculous costumes and had little to offer the business world in the way of practical skills. He wound up going to work in a local prison and found out he enjoyed the job. As time passed, he'd risen through the ranks, eventually became an assistant warden, and then was promoted to the top job.

In 1990, three years after taking over leadership of Just Cause, James "Juice" Forsythe had asked him if he would be interested in taking charge of the development of a prison for parahuman offenders. Silbersack had laughed at him until he'd realized the man was serious.

The project had spanned monumental proportions, requiring the work of dozens of engineers, thousands of man-hours, and a Belgian parahuman called The Architect, who had the ability to reshape earth, stone, and metal. Without his efforts, the construction of Deep Six would have taken two to three times as long to complete. While crews dug a very deep hole in the middle of Montana, Silbersack got to spend months under intensive scrutiny at the Parahuman Medical Institute in Paris. The researchers there had learned everything they could about his powers, then worked with the most technologically-minded people in the world to duplicate those same powers using machines.

The key breakthrough was The Architect's development of the miniature robots that could reshape matter molecule by molecule. Once those had been perfected, it was only a matter of replicating a few billion of them to permeate the facility, customizing every cell to contain its occupant. When the prison was ready to open in 1994, Silbersack had been the logical choice for Warden, and he'd gladly accepted the appointment.

He was beginning to grow tired, though. Already on the far side of 65, he'd considered beginning what he jovially called his second retirement, but he couldn't conceive of spending his days rocking on the porch and drinking lemonade, which is what his own father had done with his post-employment life until it killed him. Silbersack didn't fear much, but the thought of being carefree and without responsibilities made him break out in cold sweat. More than anything in his life, he needed to be needed. For a great many years, he'd found a way to fulfill that requirement. But now, his highly-skilled subordinates had accomplished what he'd long thought impossible.

They'd made him feel superfluous.

* * *

Patience was a necessary personality trait for a man who could stop time.

He called himself Stopwatch. He could step into the space between seconds. And once he was there, he could do things. The things weren't especially impressive—he could only perform tasks that didn't exceed a single man's efforts in the allotted time. His time limit was three minutes twenty seconds, for reasons he had never been able to comprehend. He could bring time itself to a screeching halt, leaving the entire Universe poised to take its next breath, and he had two hundred seconds to do whatever he chose. One might expect objects frozen in time to be frozen in space as well, but Stopwatch could pick them up, manipulate them, and change them. He couldn't alter time with significant frequency—once a day was pushing it—but then, how often did he really have a need?

Nobody knew about his powers. Well, almost nobody. One man knew, and that man had paid him an obscene amount of money for a single usage of his power. He hadn't fulfilled that task yet, but the right time was nearly at hand. He reached into his pocket, fingering the heavy Rolex stopwatch. It had been an expensive purchase; he'd once spent a year mugging people without their knowledge to acquire the cash for it. But he wanted nothing but the best in his line of work.

The time was right. He closed his eyes in concentration. As he felt the power flow out from him, stopping the Universe cold, he clicked on the stopwatch and got up from his duty station. Time was of the essence; he had a lot of ground to cover in his two hundred seconds. He ran to the medical lab, grabbed a pair of latex gloves, and pulled them on as he hurried back to the Command Center.

He pulled a syringe from his pocket. It was filled with a mixture of saline and an infusion of 200 micrograms of batrachotoxin. The chemical was neither easy nor cheap to acquire, but fortunately Stopwatch hadn't been the one to foot the bill. Some Central or South American frog gave its life for the contents of the vial, and because of it, someone was going to die.

He moved into the office of Bill Silbersack and injected the solution into the Warden's neck.

He checked his stopwatch. He had less than a hundred seconds to dispose of the evidence. He hurried back to the medical lab and opened the drug storage cabinet. He selected a random syringe, injected it into the sink drain, and then dropped the empty needle into the Sharps container. He filled the syringe that had contained the poison with tap water, relabeled it, and then replaced in the spot where the real medicine had been. He dropped his gloves into the biohazard bag as the stopwatch beeped to warn him that he only had twenty seconds left.

Stopwatch ran back to his work station and assumed a neutral position once more. He concentrated on regulating his breathing. In four seconds, the Universe realized it had stopped and snapped back to full speed again.

Only Stopwatch heard the sound of Silbersack's head as it hit his desk.

* * *

Warden? I wanted to ask you about . . ." Katie stopped as she walked into Silbersack's office. Her first thought was that he was sleeping at his desk and hoped she hadn't awakened him. But even that small hope was dashed as the faint smell of feces and vomit overcame the air circulation to assail her nostrils. She ran around his desk and checked his throat for a pulse. Nothing. She grabbed her radio. "Medical emergency in the Warden's office! Repeat, medical emergency!"

She noticed a trickle of blood that had leaked from a puncture at the side of Silbersack's neck.

Officer Garcia, who'd been on duty in the Command Center, came into the office at a dead run and skidded to a halt as he saw Katie lifting the Warden up onto his desk.

"Garcia, help me start CPR," said Katie in the same tone she used with Lindsay when her daughter refused to get in the bathtub.

He rushed over and pushed his sleeves up. Katie overcame her disgust and wiped out the Warden's mouth the best she could. "You compress, I'll breathe."

Garcia nodded, wide-eyed, and began performing compressions on Silbersack's chest. After a five-count, Katie blew a lungful of air into the Warden's chest. The world seemed to shrink away around her as all her effort was put into inflating the man's lungs. She tried to ignore the sour-cheese taste of his vomit on her lips as she blew breath after breath into him. Then Mayfair was there, along with his assistant, wheeling in the crash cart.

"Step back," he said.

Exhausted, Katie stepped back. She'd been breathing so hard for the Warden that she couldn't catch her own breath. Her arms and legs felt like they'd fallen asleep. As she wavered, she felt a strong arm wrap around her and guide her into a chair. She looked and saw Foster. He spared her a concerned glance before turning his attention to the desperate lifesaving attempt as Mayfair tore Silbersack's shirt open and hammered a cardiac needle through the man's sternum.

"No response." The nurse clapped sensors onto the Warden as fast as she could move.

Mayfair squirted some conductive gel onto the crash cart paddles, shouted "Clear," and placed them onto Silbersack's chest. The Warden's body jerked as the current flowed into his heart.

"Nothing." The nurse injected a drug into the cardiac needle.

"Clear." Another jolt of electricity raced through Silbersack to no effect.

Katie felt faint. She bent forward to put her head between her knees.

"You all right? Do you need to throw up or something?" Foster asked.

She shook her head. "No, I'm all right. Just light-headed from the CPR."

"He's not going to make it, is he?" Foster's lips whitened as they pressed together.

"No, I don't think so," she said. "I've seen inmates die from drug overdoses before. They looked like that."

"What do you mean, a drug overdose?" asked Foster.

"There's a puncture wound in his neck."

Foster shook his head in disbelief. "Like a bee sting?"

"Like a needle."

Mayfair stepped back from Silbersack. "Goddammit," he whispered.

David Prince ran into the office. "Doc?"

Mayfair shook his head. "He was dead before we got to him. I need a stretcher from Medical. He's got an abnormal wound and I want to do an autopsy."

Prince's eyes narrowed. "Abnormal wound?"

"Needle mark on his neck here."

"You're saying he was murdered?" A look of creeping horror crossed Prince's face.

"I'm not saying anything." Mayfair's voice rose in tight fury. "Not until I perform an autopsy."

Prince looked like a lost little boy. "Oh shit. Lock this place down, right now!"

Nobody moved.

"Goddamn it, do I have to draw you all a picture? I'm ordering a full lockdown right now!"

Everyone jumped up to follow his command. Katie realized that if the Warden had in fact been murdered, as she suspected, the killer was most likely still in the facility.

* * *

In the elevator shaft leading to the surface, great blocks of steel-reinforced stone rotated into place, each one massing hundreds of tons, blocking access to or from the surface. The air pumps forcing surface air below ground halted and the ventilation shafts sealed themselves. All other connections except for the communications line to the hangar were severed or blocked. Deep Six would be completely cut off from the surface until the emergency was declared over.

The Command Center was a flurry of activity as the self-contained life-support systems activated. The great compressed air tanks above the main complex would provide them with sufficient air for a week. Likewise the prison contained sufficient water and food to keep everyone alive during the lockdown period.

"We're on canned air and water." Cassie's eyes were wide and staring as she read data on her display. Katie, who stood off to one side with Foster, shivered at the idea of being so isolated from the surface.

"Command Center, what's going on?" Lieutenant Frankes' voice came over the speakers. He was the ranking officer in the hangar above.

"Warden Silbersack is dead, possibly murdered," said Prince into the microphone.

"What?"

"Keep a close eye out for anything suspicious," said Prince. "We'll provide regular check-ins every half an hour or sooner if we have something to report. Until I'm satisfied that we don't have a murderer on the loose down here somewhere, the Six stays locked down."

"Understood. Frankes out."

Prince switched channels on the radio. "All officers report to the Command Center." He turned to Cassie. "Get me a complete duty roster. I need to know exactly who is down here right now, including any civilians."

"Yes, sir."

Six other officers were on duty besides Katie, Foster, and Garcia. The most notable of these was Lania, a Guatemalan expatriate whose body was made of antimatter. She clomped into the Center in her magnetic containment suit.

"Sir, I've got a list of staff on duty today. Nineteen people, including maintenance, booking, kitchen, and janitorial," said Cassie.

"Eaton, Coltrane, round up all civilian staffers and bring them into Booking. Lania, I want you standing guard on the Center. The rest of you, I need a physical verification of every inmate's location. Get sleeper sets on all of them. Travel in pairs. Nobody goes anywhere alone. Watch yourselves. We may have a rogue or an escapee in here somewhere."

Katie looked at Foster, still uncertain about procedures.

He motioned with a jerk of his head. "Let's go."

* * *

Misrule heard the increased activity in the corridors. The air itself seemed electrically charged, as if before a thunderstorm. Something had happened; something to worry the guards to the point of interrupting the prisoners' solitude. He knew they would soon come through his door, ultratasers at the ready, with one hand on the kill switch to fill the cell with gas. Doubtless they would bring with them the dreamless unconsciousness of the sleeper sets.

He'd planned for such an eventuality.

The pain had receded to a dull roar, like the ocean muffled behind walls of glass. Soon he would be able to leave it behind altogether. But first, he would have to add to it, take charge over it and direct it to work for him.

Hunched over on his bunk, he hid his hand with the bulk of his body. He brushed his fingers gently over his chest, feeling the irregularities of the malignant mass crouched in his torso, coiled like a sleeping serpent. He dug one of his claws into his flesh without hesitation. The pain was great, but after months of living with it, the acute sting of injury was almost refreshing. Eyes shut, he hissed with the discomfort as he explored the wound with the fingertips of one hand; ragged, moist edges, layered skin over fascia over muscle. Veins throbbed under his fingers like wires humming with power. Shortly he found what he sought, and pulled an object the size of a nickel from within the folds of twisted, sickened flesh. No natural object this; it shone dully in the fluorescent lighting of his cell. He regarded it for a moment, crouched in his oversized palm like a thin silvery spider. Within its flattened body was packed a complicated system of crystals, molecule-diameter wire, and a power supply. The only visible features were a band of hair-fine cilia around the object's edge and a switch so small that Misrule's sharpest claw could barely flick it. The tiny legs would also act as antennae, focusing the energies contained within.

Misrule paid a man in China fourteen million dollars for it. The man had guaranteed the device's functionality with his life and the lives of his family. Misrule had asked him matter-of-factly how he would collect if the device failed to work. The man hadn't been able to form a satisfactory answer, and Misrule had torn him in half. Then for good measure, he'd broken every bone in the man's elderly parents, disemboweled his wife, and thrown each child as hard as he could against a wall. In fresh, hot blood, he'd written *CAVEAT VENDITOR* on the wall. *Let the seller beware.* Perhaps some Chinese student of Latin had deciphered the phrase to try to understand why a family had been so brutally murdered.

He wiped his own congealing blood off the face of the object and coughed into his hand. Should anyone be watching him, they'd see the blood on his hand and think nothing of it. He steeled himself for the next pain; it would be far worse than anything he had yet suffered. He transferred the device into his other hand and he rolled over in his bunk, pillowing his head on it. He tripped the switch and brought the device to unholy life. The cilia began to twitch and the object disappeared into his ear.

It burrowed through his ear canal like a hungry insect with razors for teeth. Blood spurted from his ear as the machine chewed its way inward, a throbbing horror out of a Boschian nightmare. Grayness settled across his vision and he felt nauseated as it pushed deeper and deeper into his head until it felt like it had found its way deep into his brain. Had he been capable of such weakness, tears would have squeezed out of his eyes. Once it stopped moving, he concentrated his efforts on healing the damage it wrought along its journey.

Super-strength was a wonderful thing to have; dense flesh and hardened skin made him fearless in the face of an enemy. Blasting destructive energy from his hands felt better than the strongest eye-popping orgasm. But without his ability to heal himself, Misrule would have died many years previously. He hadn't been entirely honest with the doctor concerning his ability to heal the cancer ravaging his system. He hadn't tried to heal the tumors, because he needed them. They were crucial to his plan. He didn't know for certain if he even could heal his cancer, but it was a risk he'd been willing to take.

The reward would far outweigh the risk.

* * *

"Ready for this?" Foster asked Katie, his normal jovial grin absent.

"Yeah."

They stood outside Napalm's cell.

"All right, here's the drill. Keep your ultrataser on him at all times while the door is open. If he makes a move, or even looks like he's going to, blast him. Everything in the cell is fireproofed except me. There is a foam suppression system that will automatically engage if it detects him using his power. He's tested it once and it nearly suffocated him, so I don't think he'll try again."

"I understand." Katie's fingers ached from clenching so tight around the ultrataser stock.

"Once I'm inside, you shut that door and then you're on the kill switch. Watch on the cameras. Any screwing around on his part and you punch it. Worry about me after he's neutralized."

"Be careful, Foster."

He winked at her. "What, no kiss?" He drew a pistol-sized ultrataser. It didn't carry the excess of power that the rifles did, but was serviceable enough for close quarters.

"In your dreams."

Foster keyed the cell intercom. "LeVaughn, face the wall away from the cell door and assume the position."

They watched as the convict, who lounged in his bunk, stretched out one languid arm with his middle finger raised on high.

"We can do this as easy or as hard as you want it, LeVaughn. The hard way means you get zapped and maybe gassed. You want that hangover?"

The inmate slouched over to the wall and leaned up against it, arms above his head and legs spread wide. "Come and get me, faggot," he wiggled his ass. "You like that, you fucking screw?"

Foster ignored the jibe. "Open the door."

Katie threw the switch. In the Command Center, they confirmed that the request to open the door was legitimate and authorized it in a few seconds.

The locks clanked as they opened and the door dropped into the floor, giving Foster and Katie the most time possible to see into the cell prior to entering. LeVaughn turned his head slightly to watch them out of his peripheral vision. The two guards had their weapons out and trained on him.

"Remain where you are. If you move, you're zapped." Foster advanced into the cell.

"Like what you see? You're probably getting off on this, huh?"

Again taunted, again Foster kept his cool. He kept his ultrataser in a one-handed grip as he withdrew the sleeper set from his belt. Katie shut the door and moved over to the kill switch, her gaze locked on the cell monitor.

"We're putting you to sleep, LeVaughn."

"What's the occasion? You'd rather fuck someone who can't fight you off?"

Foster's grin turned acidic. "Much as you talk about it, LeVaughn, I think you must be pretty bi-curious. You sure you're not a little light in the loafers? Maybe thinking about sweet young boys and their tight asses gets you all hot and bothered?"

"I ain't no fuckin' queer!" LeVaughn forgot himself and spun around, fists balled up, ready to incinerate Foster.

Foster shot him between the eyes.

LeVaughn flew to one side of the cell as the ultrataser dumped thousands of volts into him. Foster was on him in a flash, wrestling him prone. LeVaughn groaned but his feeble struggles were no match for Foster's determination as he got the sleeper set mounted on the killer's head and switched it on. LeVaughn stopped moving altogether except for some unconscious twitching of electrified muscles.

Foster waved an *all clear* to the camera and motioned for Katie to open the door again. "Help me get this asshole back on the bunk," he said. "Why didn't you hit the gas?"

"You looked like you had everything well under control, tough guy," Katie said.

Foster burst out laughing. "I'm glad you didn't, especially given the circumstances." Then his laughter faded and he grew silent and introspective.

Katie remained quiet as well. She kept thinking about Warden Silbersack and how cheerful and pleasant he'd been to her.

They moved the comatose LeVaughn onto his bunk and wheeled in the monitor, which would keep track of his vital signs while unconscious. Foster stripped off LeVaughn's coveralls. He looked down at the comatose convict. "At least he didn't piss or shit himself. I hate it when they do that." Katie requested the Command Center detach the secured wall panel and it clicked open. From there they connected the sleeper set to building power; it would run as long as there was electricity present.

"Why would someone kill the Warden?" Katie couldn't imagine how anyone could hold animosity toward such a nice man.

"To avoid paying him his pension? I'm sorry, that was tasteless." Foster held up the catheter. "Do you want to do this?"

"Do I have a choice?"

"I'm sure he'd rather you handled it than me."

"I'm not so sure. He was trying awfully hard to convince you he was straight."

Foster grimaced in sympathy as he set the catheter in place. Katie watched the process with sick fascination. They put an adult diaper around his hips to catch any residual feces.

"The way I see it, it has to be an inside job. I think Prince is totally wrong. Nobody could have sneaked all the way down here past all our security and gotten to the Warden." Foster waited while Katie set an IV.

"They used to say people couldn't fly," she said. "But I think you're right. It has to have been someone already down here with us."

"Which means it was either an inmate who somehow got out or else . . ."

"Or else it was one of us. Someone on the staff."

The two were silent for a moment as they contemplated what it meant if the Warden had died by another officer's hand. They slowly looked at each other as it dawned on them that they were suspects.

"I don't think you did it," said Katie.

"Neither do I." Foster paused, and then added, "I mean, I don't think you did it either."

They both smiled at that.

In her time at Ohio State, Katie had met killers with the faces of angels, serial rapists that looked like librarians, and one child pornographer with the faith of a nun and the demeanor of a diplomat. And yet she could always sense that sliver of wrongness, the thing which had gone all black and rotten in their souls and made them perform monstrous acts. She couldn't find any broken place in Foster, and for that she was grateful.

Foster holstered his ultrataser. "Let's get the rest of these assholes on ice. I'll feel safer when everyone's making big Zs."

* * *

Misrule waited. Patient. The pain subsided to a dull roar, replaced by the distant conversation of the guards in his cell. The sleeper set crouched on his skull like a metallic daddy long legs. The guards thought he was comatose.

They were mistaken, so mistaken.

So he waited.

"What are you doing?"

Misrule could feel the man's warm breath on his cheek, smelling of coffee and menthol cigarettes. The man was bent over him. Misrule watched through slitted eyes.

"Just looking, all right?"

"Think he might be your daddy?"

"Blow me, Pasteur. No, I was looking at his skin. I always thought he was . . . tattooed or something, like that Etched Man guy down the hall. But he's really this color."

Pasteur looked disinterested as he catheterized Misrule. "Yeah, so what? You got something against folks who ain't white?" Pasteur's skin was the color of rich dark chocolate. His teeth sparkled in shockingly white contrast to it when he grinned.

"No, just against guys like this." He tapped Misrule's chest for emphasis with his ultrataser barrel.

The weapon made a muffled clinking sound as it bounced off the prisoner's dark red skin.

"What the hell?" asked Roggen. He prodded Misrule again. *Here* was a meaty thunk; *there* was another, but then . . .

Clink.

Interest crossed Pasteur's face at last. "What is that?"

Roggen set his weapon down and felt around the area of Misrule's torso. "Hey, there's something here." He tapped a spot under his finger.

"Well, he's got cancer, right? It's probably the tumor."

"A tumor wouldn't *clink.*"

"Then what is it?"

Roggen bent down again to feel the hard spot. "I don't know. You almost can't tell it's there. It's hard."

"Yeah, well, so is the rest of him. He's bulletproof, remember?"

"Pasteur, would you just feel this spot and tell me if I'm crazy?"

"All right, I'll grope the inmate while you watch. You going to need a minute or two alone when I'm done?"

"Funny."

Pasteur ran his hand across Misrule's chest. His eyes widened. "That feels like . . . like metal or something."

"What do you think it is?"

"I have no idea, but maybe we ought to tell Doc Mayfair about it."

Roggen started to reply, but Misrule's hand flashed up to close around Roggen's throat. The guard managed a surprised gurgle before the fist tightened and pinched his head off as neatly as one might pop a grape off its stem. Blood shot upward in a brief fountain to drench Misrule's face and chest. He laughed and licked it off his lips as he flung the grisly corpse at Pasteur.

Pasteur was a parahuman; he could turn insubstantial for all of two seconds. He flashed into his ghostly state but didn't make it clear through the wall before his power failed.

As Pasteur solidified, one of his legs was still within the wall structure. The sudden appearance of new matter within the molecular matrix of the wall was more than the laws of physics could handle.

A violent explosion shook the prison at the intersection of Misrule's cell wall and Pasteur's leg, tearing both asunder. The guard died before he could draw a breath to scream. His fluids flashed into vapor from the sudden heat of fusion and his body began to smolder.

Misrule rose from his bunk and freed himself from the tendrils of medical sensors that clung to him like cobwebs. The small spider robot had performed its task as promised; it had blocked the sleeper set's coma-inducing signal. He'd hoped to have more time before putting his plan into motion, but with the two officers about to discover his ace-in-the-hole, he'd been forced to act.

Alarms began to cry their warnings throughout the prison. Misrule wiped the stinking muddy paste of wall fragments mixed with the guards' blood from his face and as he stepped into the corridor, a leer of pleasure crossed his demonic visage.

The time for destruction had begun anew.

"None of you understand. I'm not locked up in here with you. You're locked up in here with me."
—Rorschach in Watchmen *by Alan Moore and Dave Gibbons*

July, 2007
Deep Six, Montana

"What is it? What's happening?" David Prince picked himself up off the floor. The explosion in the cell wings below had thrown everyone down. Most of the video displays in the Command Center showed either snow or blank screens. Of the four that still displayed live views, one pointed at a crazy angle and one showed a distorted view through a cracked lens. Bits of gravel had fallen through the ceiling and a long crack bisected the wall of the Warden's office. Multiple alarms screamed for attention while the radios remained silent.

Cassie brushed rock fragments from her workstation and tried to get the computer back online. "Some kind of explosion downstairs," she said. "Backup systems are functioning. I've got smoke and temperature gradients consistent with a small fire in C-Wing. Oh, no . . ."

Prince leaned over behind her to look at the display.

CONTAINMENT BREACH, CELL C-3, DE WITTE, MAXIM.

A heavy impact shook the floor, not as strong as the explosion had been but enough that everyone felt it. Another line appeared on the display.

CONTAINMENT BREACH, CELL C-4, BRAVA, MITCHELL.

"Who's down in C-Wing?" Prince asked.

"Pasteur and Roggen," said Cassie.

Prince grabbed a radio and held it close to his lips. "Officers Pasteur and Roggen, report."

There was only silence from the radio speaker.

"Pasteur? Roggen? Any officers in the wings sound off. That's a direct order."

Cassie fussed with her keyboard. "Radio systems are down. That explosion must have damaged the repeaters somehow."

CONTAINMENT BREACH, CELL C-2, FENCHURCH, KENDRA.

CONTAINMENT BREACH, CELL C-5, FELICIANO, GLORIANA.

"My God, it's a breakout," said another tech.

"Shut it down. Seal off C-Wing and blow all the gas you can. Blow everything!" said Prince.

Cassie's fingers flew over the keys. "I've got nothing, sir."

CONTAINMENT BREACH, CELL C-1, TELLEZ, JOSE.

"Who's down below besides Roggen and Pasteur?"

"Foster and Malone were in D-Wing. Judge and Garcia were in A-Wing."

A-Wing was directly beyond the elevator lobby, but D-Wing was at the far end of the east leg of the prison cells.

Officers Eaton and Coltrane returned to the Command Center, having rounded up all the civilian employees of the prison.

Prince turned to them. "We've got a breakout in C-Wing. I need you guys down there to help contain it. Foster and Malone are cut off." He looked over at Lania. "Lania, you go too. Your powers might be useful."

"Sir, you're leaving the Center undefended!" Cassie felt panic rising like a pot about to boil over.

Prince turned to face her, his eyes wide. "Haig, those parahumans down there aren't like the also-rans and losers on our payroll. If the guards can't stop them, nothing you or I can do will make a difference."

Cassie dropped her hands to her sides. "We're all going to die, aren't we?"

* * *

Katie coughed, keeping her head down near the floor where there was less smoke. "Foster, what the hell just happened?"

"No idea, but it sounded like the next wing blew up." Foster had small cuts on his face from a spray of gravel. "Command Center, this is Foster. What's going on?"

No reply.

A heavy impact from the next wing made more dust fall from the ceiling, followed by a shriek of overstressed metal being torn. Katie and Foster looked at each other wide-eyed. "Who's held in C-Wing?" she asked.

"Fenchurch . . . Feliciano," said Foster.

"No, goddammit, those don't mean anything to me. *Public* names."

He thought for a moment. "Brainstorm, Espada, Puño, the Etched Man, and . . . Misrule."

Katie didn't recognize the two Hispanic names, but Brainstorm and the Etched Man had both been part of Misrule's Cult of Destruction in the past. Brainstorm was a high level, single-power psi. She had the sole ability to scramble a victim's brain, but could do it so completely that even the best psionic healers and telepaths in the world couldn't repair the damage. The Etched Man powers were terrifying. He was covered with tattoos, images that moved of their own accords within his skin. He could *pull* a tattoo from his body, thus bestowing upon it form and a pseudo-life of its own, giving it the ability to act independently. Whatever he could envision, he could create with a tattoo.

And of course, then there was Misrule.

"We've got to do something," said Katie. "We're going to have a mass breakout on our hands in a minute. Why are there so few guards here?"

Foster sounded defensive. "The guard to prisoner ratio is one to three. That's better than any prison anywhere."

"Yes, but if two guards are taken out, that's twenty percent of the available forces. You and I, Foster, are twenty percent."

"Oh. Shit."

"Can we blow gas into C-Wing from down here?" Katie inventoried her gear. She had the ultrataser, good for two shots, one spare battery pack that would give her two more, a holdout knife clipped to the inside of her boot, and nothing else. Hardly enough to deal with a mundane prisoner, much less one with parapowers.

"Gassing an entire wing can only be done by the Command Center." Foster likewise checked his own gear. "If they could have, they would have already. The explosion must have damaged control circuits. I wonder what blew up."

"I'm sure we'll find out sooner or later. So do we stand and fight and hope for reinforcements from the front end, or do we run?"

The airlock door rang like a bell as a fist-sized bulge appeared in its smooth metal skin.

Katie and Foster looked at each other in horror. "We run," they said together, and headed for the escape hatch at the far end of D-Wing.

* * *

Misrule punched his way through the door into the wing beyond. From his research, he had a rough idea of the layout. His army was growing, but he wanted to clear one leg of the prison completely before starting on the other. The most important thing was to make sure nobody could come at him from behind.

A great weight had lifted from his heart when he saw the names over the cell doors in his wing. Two of his old Cult of Destruction compatriots were being held adjacent to him. Brainstorm was his psionic assassin, able to scramble anyone's brain. And of course, The Etched Man had his frightening tattoos which crawled across his skin like sub-dermal spiders. His emaciated appearance, shaved head, and general dislike for most clothing, made him more like a sideshow freak instead of a powerful parahuman. Of all the people Misrule had met, allied with, or fought against in his lifetime, only The Etched Man scared him.

They joined him without question once their sleeper sets were removed. The surprise of a sudden release by their old ally had been joyous for Brainstorm, who hugged Misrule tight. The two had been lovers many years ago and perhaps would be once more. The Etched Man, known for his emotional equanimity, had curled the corners of his lips upward in a vacant smile that reeked of inauthentic depravity. Anyone else would have turned back flips.

The other two prisoners released by Misrule hailed from the erstwhile gang of bank robbers, *Los Soldados*. Misrule gave them each a simple choice: join him or die. Espada—whose name meant *Sword*—didn't hesitate to sign up. Once freed from her cell, her arms flattened and hardened into organic sword blades. She looked dangerous and bloodthirsty. Puño—*Fist*—thought perhaps he'd argue the point with Misrule. Being both a bank robber and a muscleman meant thinking things through wasn't his strong point. Likewise, his sternum hadn't been a strong point when Misrule had spun around with a devastating spin kick that crushed the larger man's chest.

Part of C-Wing had collapsed as a result of the explosion. Rocks and debris lay everywhere. The wall opposite the cells had taken a lot of the explosive force, and the concrete had cracked and split in several places. What remained of Pasteur's body had burned and filled the air with greasy smoke that smelled of spoiled pork. Charred bone and ashes lay in and around a small crater blown into the floor.

"Etch, secure the far door. I would prefer not to be interrupted by the prison guards before I examine D-Wing." Misrule didn't bother to fuss with the door into the next wing. Instead he drove his fist hard into it. The shock of impact felt good to him. It had been months since he'd really used his strength for anything.

"Etch, secure the door," muttered the Etched Man, and tore what looked like a thick, ropy spider web from one of his arms. It grew in size and thickness as he flung it across the door. It stuck and spread out until it completed its seal around the door using its disturbing tendrils.

Misrule hit the opposite door again and this time punctured it. He flexed his arm, braced his feet against the frame, and yanked hard. Metal creaked and groaned, then snapped as the heavy door broke free from its tracks. Misrule laughed as he tossed it aside. The physical activity drove the monster in his chest back to cower in the darkness once more. "Knock knock," he called. "Anybody home?"

From the far end of C-Wing, he heard the door motors as they strained to overcome the Etched Man's seal. He knew the man's magic was proof enough against mere technology, and didn't even bother to see if the seal held. Instead, he bowed to Brainstorm and Espada. "Ladies, if you would be so kind to follow me."

* * *

"There's no easy way to say this so I'll just say it," said David Prince into the radiophone. For the moment they still had surface communications, but that could change at any time. Cassie continued to work her own variety of magic across the keyboard and rerouted connections as they failed. "We've had an accident down here resulting in a containment failure in one of the wings."

"A containment failure," repeated Doublecharge, the field commander of Just Cause. "Who's out, and what are you doing about it?" She never bothered with polite conversation. Under her leadership, the premiere American superhero team had made a gradual shift from the carefree reactive days under former commander Juice's tutelage to the proactive, paramilitary force it had become since its reorganization and subsequent separation from Homeland Security. Her lack of humor often made her a target for late-night television show hosts, but everyone agreed that Just Cause was the most professional it had ever been under her leadership.

"We have the situation under control. The inmates are cut off from the rest of the prison."

"I can't believe you're spinning this," Cassie hissed at him. Prince held up a warning finger toward her.

Doublecharge didn't buy the story either. "Exactly which inmates are out of their cells?"

Prince swallowed hard. "Roughly . . . all of C-Wing."

"And that would include?"

"Oh, just a couple of the *Soldados* . . . and a few of the Cult of Destruction alumni."

"Misrule?"

"Uh . . ."

"We're en route to your location now. I'll expect a complete report when we arrive in ninety minutes."

"Well, that's going to be a bit of a problem. We're under hard lockdown right now, plus we've sustained some damage to the facility. Until the situation is completely controlled and we've had a chance to assess that damage, we have to remain isolated from the surface at all costs."

"We'll see about that." Doublecharge broke the connection.

* * *

The hydraulics strained and groaned as they tried to open the airlock door into C-Wing. Officer Eaton finally stopped trying. His tactical gear rattled with his frustrated motion. He and Coltrane wore the helmets, kneepads, and vests of full riot gear, and were armed to the teeth with ultratasers, rubber bullets, gas grenades, sharp sticks, and harsh language. Lania had opened the vents in her suit to allow steam to flow gently out of them. In a heartbeat, she could drop her gloves and expose her antimatter flesh to the air. Without the weak force field her body generated, contact between anything matter and her skin would result in a massive release of destructive energy. She could control that power somewhat to eject single molecules like a particle accelerator. With such natural weapons at her disposal, she eschewed the arsenal the other officers preferred.

"It's no good. Something's jammed the door shut," Eaton said. "Command Center, can't you get this damned thing open?"

"Negative, Eaton. We have a temporary loss of function in that section."

"Wonderful."

Lania stepped forward. The two officers shrank back to put some distance between her and them. Their reactions didn't bother her; she'd grown used to the fact that people feared her. "I'll open it. Cover me."

Eaton and Coltrane looked at each other, then stepped back and raised their ultratasers.

Lania removed one of her gloves. Her skin, once brown from her native Guatemalan heritage, was now a luminescent periwinkle with traceries of energy crackling over it. Although at times she missed looking human, she'd never thought of herself as pretty until after the transformation. She touched the edge of the door and relaxed her force field a bit. Sparks shot out from around her fingertip to leave a ragged, blackened edge where she cut through the metal. Eaton and Coltrane squinted into the glare. The door shivered and settled slightly as she cut along its top. Then without warning, someone wrenched it away and pulled it inside C-Wing.

Misrule stood framed in the smoking, ragged doorway. "Please," he said, "lower your weapons."

Lania recoiled in shock from his unexpected, monstrous visage. Coltrane shouted, "Put your hands up, Misrule!"

Misrule smiled. "You don't really think you can stop me, do you?" He pushed through the remains of the door.

"S-stop, we're . . . we're warning you." Eaton stuttered. The barrel of his ultrataser started to waver.

"Surrender to me now and I will personally guarantee you won't be killed. Force us to battle you and I make no such promise."

"Eaton? What's wrong?" Lania looked on in surprise as sheer terror overtook the man. He looked at her with wide-eyed fear as his weapon dangled from nerveless fingers. Other prisoners filed through the door behind Misrule. Brainstorm. The Etched Man. Espada. Even the three inmates from D-Wing were there—Whisper, the psionic torturer; Kickback, who reflected energy; and the White Dragon, a white supremacist who could become the full-sized, fire-breathing, flying lizard of his namesake.

"You are hopelessly outnumbered and outgunned as well. And you are weak. See how easily Whisper toys with your emotions?"

"No," Eaton dropped his ultrataser. "Please . . . please . . . make it go away."

"Let him go!" cried Lania. "Coltrane, surrender to them. Please!"

Coltrane shook his head. "Lania, we can't let them get past us. We can't let them have the run of the prison."

The Etched Man spoke for the first time. His voice crackled like it came through blown speakers. "Silly man." He peeled a tattoo away and a shambling creature with too many legs and teeth crawled past Misrule toward the obstinate guard. "You can't stop us."

Coltrane backed away as the creature approached him. Eaton screamed as it brushed past him. He fell to the ground to grovel at Misrule's feet, begging to be saved.

Lania raised her hands, which glowed with barely restrained energy. "That's enough, Misrule. We surrender. Now stop this cruel game."

"I have yet to hear your companion surrender," said Misrule. "Perhaps I can't hear him over your prattling."

Coltrane blasted the ultrataser at the beast as it backed him into a corner. The electricity had no effect at all. He yelled in defiance as it sprang at him. Misrule watched as man and monster rolled across the floor, each fighting for the officer's life. Coltrane howled in agony as the creature ripped off his left hand. Blood spattered across the floor like a burst can of spray paint. The coppery smell mixed with the fecal reek as Coltrane's bowels let go.

"Surrender," whispered Misrule, an unholy gleam in his eyes as he watched the carnage unfold.

"For God's sake, call it off!" screamed Lania.

"Kill him!" shouted Espada in counterpoint, the expression on her face a mirror of Misrule's. Her sword-arms slowly crossed back and forth, as if to sharpen them in preparation to carve a holiday turkey.

Coltrane screamed again, a blubbering shriek of pain that Misrule interpreted as capitulation. He made a conciliatory gesture and the Etched Man nodded. The creature became smoke that drifted back to wrap itself back onto the man's tattooed skin.

"You've got to let me get him to the doctor." Lania rushed over to help Coltrane.

"Of course," said Misrule. "There is but the matter of getting up the elevator to the Command Center."

He smiled again. "But even if nobody upstairs will cooperate, I'm certain I can find someone down here to facilitate the journey."

Lania's eyes widened as she realized he intended to release all the prisoners in Deep Six.

* * *

Katie and Foster huddled in the small crawl space at the top of the ladder and wondered if they would be discovered. The narrow well was stifling and hot. It had been a frightening, exhausting climb in pitch black darkness, up twenty feet to the small alcove. They both barely fit, ignoring polite distance for a better chance of survival. A small emergency light provided just enough illumination for Katie to see Foster's face.

"Are we going to have enough air?" whispered Katie.

"I hope so. There's supposed to be ventilation."

"What do we do if they find the escape hatch?"

"Hope our insurance is paid up."

Katie elbowed him hard. "That's not funny."

"Sorry. There's a last-ditch system to block the tunnel the same way the main elevator shaft is blocked during lockdown. The idea is to make it more trouble than it's worth to dig us out."

Katie shivered at the idea of being buried completely underground. "That's not very comforting."

"Look here." Foster's shadowed hand pointed to a small red button at the end of the alcove. "That's our insurance. Push it if you'd rather be buried alive than dragged down by some inmate with a grudge."

"Not much of a choice, is it?"

They sat in silence and listened for any sounds of conflict or impending discovery below. A muffled *clang* echoed up the shaft. Then the sound of a man screaming in pain wafted up on the air currents.

Shivers ran down Katie's spine. "I feel horrible that we're hiding up here while people down there might be dying."

"It could be us dying down there," Foster said.

"We should do something."

"Like what? We've got an ultrataser and a half between us, your devastating ability to light candles from your fingertips, and my equally-impressive power to sort of disappear as long as nobody's really looking and it's not really bright out. We're fucking useless."

"Good point. Let's just sit here with our thumbs up our asses," retorted Katie.

It was quiet for a minute.

Foster sighed. "You're right. We should do something."

"Of course I'm right," said Katie. "I'm a woman."

"Yes indeed, and I must say that I can't think of more pleasant company to be hiding for my life with than you."

Katie felt her ears burn. "Knock it off. We have work to do. I think we can assume everyone in C and D-Wings are out. Do you agree?"

"And maybe B and A as well. If they can do that, I figure they'll clear out E, since that's the only occupied wing on the other side. We should probably expect twenty to twenty-three prisoners on the loose—all powerful, all dangerous, and probably looking for a little payback on us and each other."

"You figure some grudges might get settled?"

It was a matter of course that in prison riots, inmates often took the opportunity to eliminate rivals or those they hated.

Foster postulated Misrule was in charge, and with two of the more powerful members of his old Cult of Destruction group held in C-Wing, he would have the firepower to back up his claim to leadership. Anyone who didn't submit to his orders would be seen as a liability and eliminated. Katie agreed with his assessment.

"The next question is what do they want?"

"Simple. They want to escape." Foster snapped his fingers for emphasis.

"But that won't be quite as easy," said Katie. "It's almost impossible for a riot in a conventional prison to break outside the walls, never mind one that's over a mile underground. Even if they could get up the shaft to the surface, there's still the secure hangar above, and you know that Just Cause and maybe a couple of other teams as well will be waiting."

"So where does that leave them?"

Katie snapped her own fingers and released a small spark without meaning to. "Hostages. They'll use the prison staff as leverage."

"Which means they won't kill everyone. God, I hope you're right about that."

Visions of Lindsay danced before Katie's eyes. She forced herself not to dwell on her daughter, lest she lose whatever edge she had. She firmly swore she would return home alive and well, whether sooner or later.

She would see her daughter again.

"I'm right," she said. "I'm a woman. We already covered this."

Foster chuckled. "And I'm laughing in the face of imminent death. But seriously," he continued, more sober. "Negotiations will most certainly fail. The government isn't going to negotiate with terrorists, domestic or otherwise. They'll do what they can to get hostages released but ultimately aren't going to let anyone out of the hole."

A thought occurred to Katie, and she didn't like the direction it took her. "The Warden's death is awfully convenient, don't you think?"

"You mean how he was the one man who could single-handedly shut down a breakout here and said breakout began within a few hours of his death? Yeah, I was thinking that too."

"And what one thing has changed here in Deep Six in the last couple of days?"

"Besides your transfer?"

"I thought you didn't think I had anything to do with this." Katie's tone grew a little frosty.

"I don't, silly. But you're right. One new prisoner and suddenly everything is turned upside down."

"He gave himself up. Why would he do that after all this time?"

Foster's eyes widened. "He wants something. He needs someone who's here."

"Or several someones." Katie shivered. "Or all of them. Shit, if he organized the group that's down here, he could accomplish just about anything he wanted."

"Unless someone stops him."

Katie winked. "Or two someones."

" . . . it is the duty of a prisoner to escape if able to do so."
—General Orders No. 209, *Federal Secretary of War*

July, 2007
Deep Six, Montana

Cassie was getting very angry at her computer. It told her which cells had been opened and in what order. It told her security systems were offline. It told her internal communications systems were offline. It told her there were other unidentified malfunctions in environmental systems and it was unable to diagnose them. And that was all she could get it to tell her, no matter how many different subroutines she tried. She swore at it, at the hapless programmers who created it, and at everyone from Bill Gates on down.

David Prince leaned over her and looked at the display. Twenty-three inmates had been incarcerated in five of Deep Six's eight wings. Twenty-three names were listed with the words CONTAINMENT BREACH next to them. He looked like he'd aged twenty years in the last twenty minutes.

"Have you been able to raise any of the guards at all?"

"No, sir. Internal communications are still down." She sniffled a little, certain the guards were all dead. It was only a matter of time before the same fate would befall the staffers in the Command Center, as well as the service personnel milling around the Booking lobby.

"Get me a line to the surface."

Cassie flicked a switch and handed Prince the microphone. "You're on," she said.

He closed his eyes and sighed. "Lieutenant Frankes, this is the Command Center."

"Prince? This is Doublecharge. I have assumed command up here. What is your situation?"

Cassie looked up at her boss and wondered how he could possibly spin what had happened.

"I'm sorry to report that we have suffered a total loss of containment. All, repeat, all inmates have broken out of their cells. We have no communication with any guards and are assuming them to have been lost. I expect to lose the Command Center any minute now. I'm afraid I have to declare Deep Six a total loss. I recommend you activate the *Last Line*."

"That's not an option I'm prepared to accept yet. As long as you're alive down there, we're going to try to get you out and get those prisoners back into custody."

A light that had been dark lit up on Cassie's board. Her eyes widened and she stabbed a finger at it. It was a signal from a guard's radio. She held a set of headphones up to one ear so she could also listen in to Prince's conversation with the surface. The computer identified the radio as belonging to Officer Eaton.

"Eaton?" she whispered. "Command Center. What's going on?"

"Officer Eaton is currently indisposed. This is Misrule. Whom do I have the honor of addressing?" Misrule's rich, deep voice sounded satisfied.

Cassie waved at Prince to try to get his attention but he was engrossed in his conversation with Doublecharge. She gulped and spoke into her microphone with a squeaky, dry mouth. "This is . . . I'm just a technician."

"Is Mr. Prince available?"

She leaned over and smacked Prince on the arm. He glared at her. "What?"

She held out the headphones. "It's Misrule. He's on the radio."

Prince's protests died on his lips. "Stand by, Doublecharge." He touched the control to put the conversation on external speakers so they could all listen.

"Mr. de Witte, this is Acting Chief Warden David Prince. What do you want?"

"Why, I want what every prisoner desires, Acting Chief Warden David Prince. I wish to escape my confinement."

"You know we can't allow that, de Witte."

"I beg to differ. You are in no position to argue with me. I control this facility now, not you."

"You're not up here yet," said Prince.

Cassie's mouth dropped open.

"Really, that's hardly a valid point. The accommodations in the cell wings don't really suit me. I think I shall be far more comfortable in your office. You may either permit me access or refuse it. One way will be far more pleasant for you and your coworkers. The other will result in the deaths of . . . I'm told their names are Eaton, Coltrane, Lania, Judge, and Garcia."

"They're still alive?" said Cassie aloud.

"You wouldn't dare kill them," said Prince. "I've got Just Cause ready to come in."

"Wouldn't I?" Misrule's voice left no doubt in Cassie's mind that he would do exactly that. A crunching sound issued from the Command Center speakers followed by muffled shouts and sounds of retching. "I've just crushed Officer Judge's skull into paste. His death is now on your hands. Shall I kill someone else or are you ready to act in a manner more civilized?"

Cassie's own gorge rose and she pressed the back of her hand against her lips, trying to keep from vomiting. Prince's legs gave way and he sank into the seat next to her. "Oh, Jesus."

"Contrary to news reports, I don't particularly enjoy frivolous killing, Acting Chief Warden David Prince. I find it wasteful. You and your people are more useful to me alive than dead right now. Should that change, I will not hesitate to order your deaths. What is your preference?"

"All right, all right. We can make a deal. Just don't kill anyone else."

Misrule paused. "A deal," he said. "Very well, here are my terms. You do exactly what I say when I say and I won't tear you limb from limb. I'll give you thirty seconds to accept them and open the Command Center to my people. Otherwise we'll force our way in and kill you by inches."

Prince dug his fingers into his hair and stretched his face into a distorted mask of pain. "Do it," he told Cassie.

Misrule chuckled into the radio. The reverberations made every listener cringe. "I am pleased you are a man who can be reasoned with. I hope you will remain similarly sensible in our continuing relationship. Stand by, we're coming in. I expect no resistance from you."

* * *

Katie and Foster decided to try to force their way into the ventilation shaft. Foster chuckled about the cliché. Heroes traveling unseen through the air ducts were a staple of adventure movies. "But then, what else are we going to do? The corridors could be crawling with prisoners."

"Aren't the ventilation shafts secured to prevent just what we're doing?" Katie watched Foster's struggles to open the grille with his Leatherman multitool. She lit up her fingers, providing him enough light to see by as they crouched in the small alcove atop the escape ladder.

"I hope not," he grunted, then smiled as a bolt gave way. "Let's hope the designers planned better than that."

"Better?"

"Better for us." Another bolt dropped to the ground. "Prisoners here are supposed to be locked down twenty-three hours a day, under constant surveillance. The chances of them having the time or resources to do this were jack shit, especially given the security procedures and technology already in place."

"*Pride goeth before a fall.*" Katie watched as the third bolt came loose.

"Huh?"

"Everyone was so confident of the security here that nobody considered what would happen if there actually was a problem."

Foster paused in his work. "That's not entirely true. There is a final security option, one that's not known to the general public."

Katie didn't like the sound of the word *final*. "What's that?"

"It's not written down anywhere, but we all know about it. Warden Silbersack would have briefed you on it after your first month on the job. It's called the *Last Line*. It's a ten-kiloton nuclear device buried just below the prison."

"What?" Katie's eyes bulged out.

"They tell us it would be a clean explosion. You know, keep everything under the ground—all neat and tidy. It would vaporize the cell wings and a good portion of the elevator shaft to the surface, but in theory would be the one thing to keep the prisoners from escaping should all other means fail."

"A nuke. Goddamn it, I move my family out here and I'm sitting on top of a nuke." Katie felt like screaming and beating on Foster with her fists.

Foster resumed his attack on the last bolt. "They're not going to set it off. It requires a Presidential order. Nobody here has the codes. They don't trust us grunts with such delicate knowledge."

"So there's a nuke, but nobody can set it off. The President has to order it. Does he have the button too?"

"No. It's in the Command Center. But only he can give the launch codes. Just push it and nothing happens."

"I don't believe you." Katie thought about it again. "No, you're probably right. Since when did the government ever do something that made sense? Who'd set off a nuke knowing they were going to die in it?"

"Now you see why I'm not worried." The last bolt dropped and Foster lowered the grille to the ground. They both took a turn to peek up the long, dark shaft that seemed to rise into infinity. Foster grimaced at the narrow opening. "Suddenly I'm glad I skipped that extra doughnut this morning."

Katie thought perhaps she herself could have hit the gym a little harder in the years since Lindsay was born. "Have you ever done a chimney ascent?"

"No, but how hard could it be?"

"I'll go first. That way you can catch me if I slip."

"Yeah, well who'll catch me if *I* slip?"

"Nobody, so don't." Katie hung the ultrataser from her belt so it would be out of her way. She wormed her way into the mouth of the pipe. "Touch my ass and I'll kick yours."

"I wouldn't dream of it."

"Yes you would."

"You're the lady, you're right." Foster chuckled as Katie pulled herself up into the shaft.

She discovered that it widened just a little after the first few yards and there was a series of regular hand- and footholds to make the climb much easier. She told Foster.

"About time we had some good news for a change."

* * *

When the first elevator-load of escaped prisoners came into the Booking Lobby, Cassie felt like hiding beneath her desk. Misrule wasn't even among them. They strolled out of the elevator with all the attitude they could muster. Serial rapist T-Rex took the lead. His scaly skin gleamed with the natural oils he exuded. He flicked a boisterous forked tongue at Cassie and grabbed his crotch suggestively. She recoiled a little and clenched her teeth to keep from whimpering, even though she sat behind six inches of crystal-clear impact-resistant safety glass. He was the only ex-Cult of Destruction member in the first group. Four of *Los Soldados* accompanied him— Central American expatriates whose only claim to fame was a botched attempted robbery of a U.S. Mint. The water-controlling Sea Witch brought up the rear and left soggy footprints wherever she stepped from the constant condensation that ran off her skin.

Los Soldados rounded up the frightened staffers into one section of the Lobby while T-Rex and Sea Witch headed for the entrance to the Command Center itself.

Cassie looked at the leering video image of the reptilian killer outside the door. T-Rex had made the most of his odd birth defects by filing his teeth and tattooing colors into his scales to better resemble a poisonous snake or alligator. He claimed his ultimate goal was to scare his victims to death. According to his record, he'd succeeded on six separate occasions. She pleaded silently to Prince not to open the door, but the Acting Chief Warden triggered the lock and allowed the door to slide aside.

"Howdy," said the grinning lizard-countenanced man. "Misrule would be mighty obliged if y'all would join us down in the lobby."

Prince glanced back at the two technicians. "All right, we're coming quietly."

Cassie looked at her partner, Montell, and he back at her from where he floated in the air three inches above his chair. They stood and followed their boss out of the Center.

"Leave it open," said T-Rex. "Less'n we might wanna reach out and touch someone." He snickered at his own joke. Nobody else smiled.

The elevator doors opened and Misrule stepped out, followed by more escapees. As large as Misrule was, Black Hood dwarfed him. The giant man appeared odd and mundane without his trademark item of clothing obscuring his face. In converse, the Etched Man looked as frail as a blade of grass. The rest followed, all of whom Cassie knew by name, face, and deed since she'd booked them into Deep Six.

Misrule reached behind him and flung a bloodstained guard into the lobby, garnering muffled screams from some of the more sensitive staffers. Cassie's breath caught in her throat. It was Coltrane, and he looked like he'd been savaged by some wild beast. His left arm was tied off with his own belt in a rough tourniquet. Naught remained of his hand except a ragged, seeping stump.

"See to him," said Misrule.

Dr. Mayfair hurried over to examine the barely-conscious Coltrane. "I need to get him to Medical right away. He's lost a lot of blood and he's in shock."

Misrule nodded. "Hood, Heretic, Brainstorm . . . keep a watch on the good doctor. I doubt very much he will try anything suspect, but if he does you may kill him."

Mayfair glared at him but didn't say anything more except to detail his nurse to help him. Under guard, they got a stretcher and moved Coltrane into the infirmary.

Misrule watched the events unfold, his face devoid of expression. Finally he stepped forward, clearing his throat. "Ladies and gentlemen, I am Misrule, and this facility is now under my control. You are my hostages.

And as such, you are more valuable to me alive than dead. Thus I am keeping you alive." He walked across the lobby, shadowed by his companions who seemed like they would be far more willing to kill the staff without hesitation given the chance. "However, I do not require all of you. Any trouble and I will order the deaths of whatever number of you I deem adequate to quell it."

The elevator opened once more and disgorged four more guards escorted by more escapees. Cassie took a surreptitious mental inventory of who was there and who was missing. Foster, Pasteur, Roggen, and that new girl, whatever-her-name-was, were still absent. Counting the three prisoners who went to the infirmary with Dr. Mayfair, there were twenty escapees. It was hard for her to check on all of them without being blatant in her observation, but finally she worked out which prisoners had not arrived in the lobby along with the rest: Puño of *Los Soldados*, and two of the independents, Pinpoint and Squall. She wondered if they were still alive. Somehow, she doubted it. Misrule wasn't likely to leave any loose ends.

"Now," said Misrule. "I have a discussion to conduct with surface security. Am I correct in my assumption Just Cause is now waiting above, Acting Chief Warden David Prince?"

Prince swallowed hard and nodded.

"And you would have a scheduled time for contacting them?"

"Yes," said Prince.

"Excellent. When is your next check-in?"

Prince turned to Cassie, who felt all the color drain out of her cheeks. "How long, Cassie?"

She stammered out an answer, feeling T-Rex's lecherous gaze sliding up and down her.

"Fine. We shall give them something to worry about. You will miss your next scheduled communication deadline." Misrule looked around the lobby. "I require a room with some privacy, preferably one of some comfort. Where might I find the Warden's office?"

* * *

After detailing Whisper to see he would not be bothered, Misrule shut the door to the Warden's office and sank into the overstuffed chair behind the desk. The monster in his chest stirred. It yearned to be set free. He focused the sum total of his healing energies upon it. Now that he no longer required the tumors in his chest, he could concentrate on their elimination, removing one painful distraction in his plan.

He ripped away his prison garb and luxuriated in the feel of air against his skin once more. He had no need of clothing for protection; his skin was far superior to any cloth and, in his mind, far more attractive in appearance. His only concession to modesty was normally a simple pair of black briefs. Prisoners' underwear was white, but he wasn't too proud to wear it instead of his preferred color.

He returned to the distasteful task of poking and prodding his torso once more. The tumors there would dissolve to leave only the object which he had hidden there. He hissed at the pain as he dug his claws up and under his rib cage to peel away layers of skin and flesh. He ignored the droplets of blood that fell to the floor. Soon he had excavated far enough to uncover something black, hard, and metallic. He pulled and turned it carefully within his chest until an activation switch was visible and poking above the level of his chest. He concentrated on the healing again. The wound closed around the device, and he smiled as it stayed in place.

Misrule had always prided himself on his ability to foment destruction and chaos. He and his followers had staged numerous crimes using those aspects either as means to another end or the end itself.

Back when he had just been Maxim de Witte, before he'd transformed into Misrule, he had thrived on the power he could hold over others. Whether he'd tormented other children in the expensive boarding school he'd attended, tortured animals in the outlying farms, or abused the homeless men who lived under the bridge in his hometown, he'd lived for the simple act of controlling others. It made him feel whole, alive.

His first kill came at the tender age of fifteen. After spending most of a weekend torturing a homeless man he'd enticed to a secluded area with promises of food and booze, he'd taken a knife and slit the blubbering man's throat. As the man's life had poured out onto the rocky ground, de Witte had felt energized, like some kind of vampire who thrived on killing instead of feeding.

Not satisfied with mere physical domination, he'd studied psychology in school, and learned new ways to exert his power over people. He went to Amsterdam to sample the ways that people would allow themselves to be dominated. He learned that as satisfying as it was to kill, breaking people's spirits brought an even deeper thrill. He became a Dominant and a Master in the underground sexual subculture, where his crowning achievement was to convince his slaves to commit murder and suicide for him.

Bored with sex as a weapon, he'd drifted into organized crime. Where his studies had left off, his schooling on the street had begun, and he'd risen to prominence in the European underworld, learning money was yet another way to control others. Eventually he controlled a significant percentage of the drug and human slave trade which passed through northern Europe. He bought and sold human beings he'd never even met. Money was power, and at barely twenty, he had power undreamed of by most.

And still he hadn't been satisfied. He could dominate people physically, through violence; mentally, through psychology; he could buy and sell them with his ill-gotten gains. Yet something else remained, tantalizingly out of reach. He traveled to America, to test his skills in the land of opportunity. He built a gang of novice and hardened criminals around him, and took over Mob operations in the Great Lakes area in a bloodbath of shifting alliances, financed by his wealth earned in Europe. His natural avarice had fit well into the money-minded culture, and his hunger for further influence had carried him far, but even then not far enough for his satisfaction.

Perhaps it was through this desire for more that his parapowers had awakened. He'd fallen asleep one evening and didn't awaken for two weeks. In that time his body had changed into the form of Misrule. It had taken an assassination attempt by members of a rival gang to bring him from his slumber. He'd awakened to his new body, felt the power coursing through it, and knew *this* was what he'd sought for so long.

He'd slaughtered the rival gangsters with his bare hands and laughed as their bullets had bounced off his newly-hardened skin. He found so many new ways to break apart human bodies with his newfound strength, and the first time he blasted forth energy from a hand to incinerate an opponent, it gave him a more powerful rush than being brought to climax by one of his sex slaves.

So he'd cast aside the trappings of his former life, named himself Misrule and begun to build what he called the Cult of Destruction. His new abilities had made him formidable among even the elite parahumans, and eager troublemakers had flocked to him. He'd found ways to exert power over each of his newfound allies. Brainstorm had fallen in love with him. T. Rex had admired his physical prowess. The Etched Man had found a guiding hand for his madness. Others had followed, each with their own unique set of strings on which a gleeful Misrule had tugged.

He'd found a new object to control: groups. The others had seen the flashy crimes he'd planned as ways to garner wealth and attention, but Misrule had only seen them as means to an end. He could now control dozens of people with the fear he and his minions generated.

Then he'd seen the worldwide havoc wrought by a small group of non-parapowered terrorists in New York City one September morning, and realized that at best he was a rank amateur.

Once more, he'd cast aside his compatriots, all of whom were eventually captured by Just Cause. He'd gone into hiding, no longer content with controlling groups or organizations.

He wanted to control nations. Eventually, he wanted the whole world to operate at his whim. And he had been shown the way.

His healing of the self-inflicted wounds all completed, Misrule turned his attention to again curing his own cancer. That would be a longer process; it might take months to fully eliminate the rogue cells, but he would be able to spend those months as a free man. He called to Whisper, who stood watch outside the office door.

She stuck her head inside. "Yes, Maxim? Holy . . ." She trailed off as she saw the object which protruded from Misrule's chest. "What the hell is that?"

He smiled at her. "Our salvation. Will you send in the others please? Five at a time, if you will. I have an offer to make them which I hope they will all accept."

* * *

"Where the hell are we?" Katie looked around the nexus of ducts and vents.

"No idea. How far do you think we climbed?" Foster grimaced as he tried to work kinks out of his back. The ascent had been difficult, and they were both sore from the unusual exertion.

"In the movies, people just drop something and count the seconds until it hits."

"Yeah, and then they do some kind of math, right? Not really my strong suit." Foster looked at the various ducts leading from the nexus. "I think we climbed all the way past the Command Center level and we're above it, in the environmental systems. Feel how much colder the air is?"

Katie nodded and shivered. She could see her breath for a moment before it was carried away on the icy breeze.

"Somewhere up there are the primary air pumps. They'd normally draw fresh air down from the surface, compress and cool it, then blow it out into the prison. But they're off. We're running on canned air right now. Otherwise there might be ice all over these pipes."

"Can we get out onto the level itself? Maybe not have to crawl through ducts anymore?"

"You tell me, you've got the light source." Foster motioned to the flames dancing at Katie's fingertips. "How long can you keep those going?"

"I have no idea," she said. "This is the longest I've ever let them burn."

"Do you feel . . . *weird*, or anything?"

Katie considered carefully how she felt. "No. Scared shitless, half-frozen, but not weird, as you say. Why?"

"I get dizzy spells if I use my dimming power too often or for too long at a time."

"Well then I suppose it's good we're already in the dark. Wait here, I'll take a look down some of these other vents." She advanced into one, her hand held high so the candle flames wouldn't blind her. After a few meters it turned to drop straight down. She backed out into the nexus again. "Strike one," she reported.

Strike two also dropped straight down, but her third try continued level and ended in a sealed grate much like the one they had first opened at the bottom of the original shaft. Through the narrow grill openings she could see a rough-hewn stone passageway lined with conduits and strung lighting. She'd traveled further this time, and her arms quaked with exhaustion as she returned to the nexus.

Foster was asleep.

"Hey," she hissed at him.

He cracked open an eye. "I wasn't asleep. I was conserving energy."

"Liar. This vent leads to a passageway. Maybe we can open it from the inside."

"Okay. Do you want to do the honors?" Foster held out his Leatherman to her.

"So I can do all the work while you doze back here?" Katie snorted. "Get moving, Officer Foster. We've got a prison to reclaim . . . somehow."

He saluted her, weariness evident in his every move. "You're right, of course."

"Bright boy. You're learning."

Foster unscrewed the nuts on the inside of the grate and lowered it to the floor of the corridor beyond. He crawled out and then offered a hand to Katie. They both reveled in the ability to stand all the way upright, twisting their backs and necks to work out the kinks.

Katie looked down both directions of the hallway. They looked the same. "You want to make a guess?"

Foster gave it consideration. "I don't know that I've ever seen a blueprint of the environmental level, but it can't be that complex. Some of the environmental subsystems are up here—power, backup water and air. Then there's the maintenance section and the kitchen."

"Nothing else? Security systems? Computer cores? How about the armory?"

Foster's eyes widened. "No armory, but . . . Ohhh . . . I think the security monitoring server is up here."

Katie grinned. "That gives us some options if we're going to be fighting a war."

"A war?"

"How else would you describe it? We've got to stop thinking like we're prison guards now. We're combatants now, stranded behind enemy lines."

"I never thought of it like that, but you're right."

Katie winked at him and continued. "You and me, we're terrorists—or guerrillas if you prefer. We need to plan our attacks in that fashion. Be sneaky. Fight a war of attrition. Divide and conquer."

Foster grinned. "You sound like you've thought about this for awhile."

"Are you kidding? I'm making this up as I go along. But the longer we can keep them busy hunting us, the more likely we'll be to get some serious parahuman backup in to save our sorry butts."

"You mean Just Cause."

"I'm sure they've been called. They're not going to let Misrule or anyone else get out of here if they can avoid it, and they're going to be the only ones who can help us get this facility back under control again."

"What's first, Captain Malone?" Foster saluted.

"Let's turn out their lights and their cameras," Katie said. "Then let's go look at the cleaning and cooking supplies. I'll bet we can MacGyver up something to even the odds a little."

* * *

Misrule stepped out of his office and flung aside Sea Witch's body. Her face flapped like a torn sail where he'd ripped it off. She had balked at his offer. He hadn't given her the opportunity to reconsider. He didn't bother to wipe her blood off his hands. "I'm pleased the rest of you have decided to join me," he said. "There's nothing quite like the feeling of unity from a group like this."

More than a few of the other parahuman ex-prisoners looked uncomfortable and dismayed at how quickly the callous Misrule had dispatched a dissenter. They muttered amongst themselves. He ignored them.

"I shall now speak with those on the surface. Who can put me in touch with them?"

Cassie glanced at David Prince, who nodded at her. She raised a tentative hand.

"Excellent. You will accompany me back into your Command Center. Acting Chief Warden David Prince, I require your presence as well." Misrule was careful to pronounce every syllable of Prince's name and title, like he was mocking the man. "Rex, bring them."

Prince stood, his hands jammed into his pockets, and followed Cassie and Misrule back to the Command Center. T-Rex followed behind and stared at Cassie with furious, hungry intensity.

Prince tripped on the steps and went sprawling. Something flew from his hand to land at T-Rex's feet. The reptilian man picked it up and examined it, a lopsided, snaggle-toothed grin spread across his scales. "Give it back!" cried Prince as he staggered over toward T-Rex. He tried to wrestle the item away, but T-Rex shoved him in the face and knocked Prince to the ground once more.

Misrule looked back, annoyance on his face. "What is this delay?"

"Just let it go, David." Cassie helped her boss to his feet once more.

"What is it, Rex?"

"Aw, nuthin'," grumbled T-Rex. "Just a piece of shit watch. It ain't even got a band."

Misrule glared at him. "Petty theft, Rex? We're better than that. You're better than that. Give the man back his property."

"But . . . it's a Rolex."

"Rex . . ." There was no mistaking the warning in Misrule's tone.

"Aw hell." Rex tossed the watch back to Prince. "I always wanted me a Rolex."

"Why didn't you just steal one, dumbass?" called Kiloton from his vantage point at the far end of the lobby. "It isn't like you never had the chance."

"I just never thought of it when we was out doing jobs." T-Rex licked his lips. "Or when I was out trollin' for tail."

Cassie shivered in fear and disgust. She watched as Prince tucked the watch back into his pocket. Rolex or not, she thought, it wasn't worth him dying over, and she told him so.

"It's a family heirloom," he said.

Cassie slid into her seat and brought the computer out of standby. The *incoming communication* message flashed. She activated the radio and nodded at Misrule.

"This is Misrule," he said. "To whom am I speaking?"

"Doublecharge of Just Cause," said a brusque voice. "Misrule, you gave yourself up," she added with an accusatory tone in her voice.

"Let us say I have had a change of heart," he said. "I have decided I much prefer being free to being in prison. If our places were reversed, I'm sure you'd agree."

"I suppose it's pointless of me to order you to surrender, turn control back over to the Deep Six staff, and return to your cell."

"Indeed. Instead, I have some demands that I'm certain you will wish to carefully consider, given the number of hostages I am holding."

"How do I know you're holding anyone? For all I know everyone down there is already dead."

Misrule motioned to Prince, who stepped forward dutifully. "This is Assistant Warden David Prince. Misrule has released all prisoners and has killed one—"

"Four. Let us not play down the situation," said Misrule, his tone chilling.

"All right, *four* prisoners are dead, as are two guards . . ." he paused, as if waiting for Misrule to correct him. When the tyrant didn't speak, Prince's brow furrowed as he took his own mental inventory of the guards and found he had come up two short of the expected number. Cassie realized it at the same time and kicked him in the shin, making it look as accidental as she could. "Uh, yes . . . two guards, as I said. The rest of us are still alive, although Officer Coltrane is injured and being treated by Dr. Mayfair."

"How many, Prince?" asked Doublecharge.

Misrule took the microphone back from Prince before he could reply. "Twenty-four, Doublecharge, and all are alive so far. It's up to you to keep them that way."

"What are your demands?"

Misrule's voice took on a tone of satisfaction. "There is a parahuman in Holland—Amsterdam, I believe—known as Airlift. His given name is Ulrich Graf. I want him brought to this facility. I think twenty-four hours should be ample time for Just Cause to locate and have him brought here. Should you fail to bring him within the time limit I have just set, I will execute one hostage every fifteen minutes until you run out of stomach for the delay or I run out of hostages."

"Misrule, be reasonable. You expect us to find one man in all of Amsterdam, maybe all of Holland, and bring him here within one day?"

"He is a teleporter, Doublecharge. Once you locate him, which should not be difficult given the information I've passed to you, he can be here within seconds."

Doublecharge paused, and Cassie wondered what rapid-fire orders she relayed to her team in the interim. "You know how this works, Misrule. We scratch your back, you scratch ours. I want half the hostages released with his arrival."

Misrule laughed aloud, amused by such audacity. "You presume so much, Doublecharge. I'll hardly give up half my bargaining power for such a paltry sum."

"Then we have no deal."

His voice grew ugly. "You fail to understand. This is not a negotiation, these are my demands. Fail to comply and the deaths of twenty-four more men and women will be on your conscience and the lead story on every news report around the world. Do you want that kind of negative exposure?" He dropped to a low whisper. "I know how Just Cause is regarded by the current administration. How many high-profile mistakes will it take to see a reinstatement of the Parahuman Registration Acts of the '50s? The writing is already on the wall, Doublecharge. It's only a matter of time before you and your people will be fugitives like me and mine. Your best bet is for this matter to be resolved smoothly, quickly, and quietly."

Cassie was somewhat familiar with the political situation in Washington concerning parahumans. She knew Just Cause had been moved from the supervision of Homeland Security to the recently-formed Parahuman Resources Agency, which was in turn a part of the National Security Agency. The general scuttlebutt was the PRA was a clearinghouse for parahuman information—the government's way to keep tabs on the parapowered population. Registration with the PRA wasn't yet mandatory, but Congress kept trying to pass a bill to require exactly that, and it failed to pass by an ever slimming margin. She knew more and more public officials spoke out against parahumans. It was the same ignorance, fear, and intolerance that had hounded blacks in the '60s and AIDS victims in the '80s. Parahumans were the new pariahs, the untouchable caste in America.

Doublecharge sounded subdued when she replied. "All right, what happens after we bring Airlift here?"

"Pure simplicity. You send him down to us and he teleports us to a locale of my choosing. Once I determine we are free and clear, I permit him to send the hostages back. They will be unharmed."

"I . . . look, I can't make this kind of decision."

"Then find someone who can. Your meter is running, Doublecharge." His hand brushed against the object protruding from his chest. "If it will aid you in your decision-making ability, I have one other important piece of information to share. I have in my possession an explosive device containing just over half a kilogram of a V-series nerve toxin. I am told that as little as two hundred micrograms constitutes a lethal dose. If detonated, either manually or by means of a deadman switch connected to my heart, it guarantees the death of everyone within this facility, and by means of air circulation, everyone above it, with significant threats to everyone downwind as far as Billings. Have you ever seen someone die of asphyxiation, Doublecharge?" He paused for effect. "Imagine that multiplied by fifty thousand."

Cassie instinctively covered her mouth, even though she knew it was pointless to do so. He hadn't released any gas; if he had, they would already be dead. It frightened her to be so close to a weapon that could kill so many so easily. It was one thing to face a monster like Misrule who had slaughtered with his own hands even within the past half hour, and another to be within spitting distance of a fabled Weapon of Mass Destruction. Somehow Misrule knew that when Deep Six's air reserves dropped to critical levels, pipes would open automatically to access fresh air from the surface. The pumps would circulate out all the gas-laden air within minutes.

"You wouldn't dare," Doublecharge whispered.

"Of course I would. I have terminal cancer, remember? I have little for which to live and therefore I am a very desperate man. If you do not discover just how desperate, you may count yourself fortunate." Misrule broke the connection.

"You got cancer, boss?" T-Rex's jaw hung open.

"Not anymore, Rex. But they don't need to know that." He motioned toward the door, his polite demeanor at odds with his threatening reputation. "Now we wait while events above are set into motion. Perhaps Acting Chief Warden David Prince will count off the hours for us on his fancy Rolex."

Prince blushed and bowed his head, but said nothing.

"We must carry the war into every corner the enemy happens to carry it: to his home, to his centers of entertainment; a total war. It is necessary to prevent him from having a moment of peace, a quiet moment outside his barracks or even inside; we must attack him wherever he may be, make him feel like a cornered beast wherever he may move."

—*Ernesto Che Guevara*

July, 2007
Deep Six, Montana

Katie and Foster advanced down the hallway, their steps cautious and their weapons drawn and raised. The first door they had found led to a storage closet for sundries like toilet paper, rags, and paper towels. The next contained an inventory of personal hygiene supplies.

"It's like double coupon day at the warehouse store," said Foster. "We should come back later and stock up."

The next closet was labeled *Cleaning Supplies* and locked. They couldn't break down the heavy steel door without the aid of heavy tools or a willing parahuman with suitable strength.

"We'll come back to it. We may find something to get us in. I hate this, not knowing where we're going. I wish we had a map," Katie sighed.

Foster matched her sigh. "I wish we had a tank. No, screw that. I wish I'd been off today."

They found an intersection around the next bend in the corridor. The left-hand passage led toward the water purification and reclamation systems. A laminated card hung at the juncture. It showed a map of the entire level with emergency safe zones marked in red. In any other building, the map would show the way to fire exits and the like, but there was no such thing in the underground prison. Katie yanked it off the wall and held a flaming fingertip up to see it better.

"Quick, wish for something else," said Foster. "Winning lottery ticket. Free mac and cheese for a year. Man-portable rocket launcher."

Katie touched the map. "We're here. The kitchen is here, the maintenance shop is here, and the security systems are here, and there is the power room." She looked up at Foster. "X marks the spot. Everything we need."

"I bet everything is locked."

"Look at this . . ." Katie moved her finger across the map. "Support staff locker rooms. I wonder if anyone leaves his keys in his locker on his days off."

They continued around the corridor with greater urgency now they had an idea of where they needed to go. As they passed the kitchen, Katie stopped. "Wait, let's go look around in here first." She glanced past Foster to look at the kitchen with interest.

"Why?"

"You don't cook much, do you?"

"I make a pretty mean meatloaf." Foster looked wounded at the accusation.

Katie snorted. "That's not cooking. Anyone can make meatloaf. I mean *cooking*. Like making things up completely from scratch."

"What's your point? I doubt anything that leaves this kitchen was ever made completely from scratch. You've tasted what passes for food here."

"Any chef, even one who works primarily with prepackaged junk, will have a drawer or bin full of tools and implements that he thinks he might need sometime. A lot of them won't necessarily be things you'd expect to find in a kitchen."

Foster shrugged and followed Katie into the institutional kitchen, full of stainless steel tables, a huge freezer and cooler, all stocked full of government-selected foodstuffs suitable for prisoner requirements. Foster opened a large door and regarded the rolling steel racks within, mystified. "What are you looking for?"

Katie crowed with success as she found a plastic tub on a rack beneath a table. She lifted it out and Foster came over to see what treasures were contained within.

"You're kidding," he said as she withdrew a screwdriver large enough to be a chisel, a ball-peen hammer, and even a set of bolt cutters. "Do you have this shit in your kitchen too?"

"No, but I do have a junk drawer. Anyone who cooks acquires miscellaneous crap like this. Now we don't have to force our way into every locker." She held up the bolt cutters for evidence. "I'll bet the maintenance guys never knew this was even here. They probably lost it years ago and just requisitioned a new one."

As they left the kitchen, Katie looked around at the commonplace items with a new perspective, wondering which ones might make good improvised weapons. One item, a can of cooking spray, caught her fancy and she shook it to test how full it was. Foster raised an eyebrow at that and opened his mouth as if to make some joke about it.

She raised a finger, lit it, and sprayed a brief blast of butter-flavored aerosol across it. The atomized cooking oil and propellant formed a highly volatile mixture and a burst of flame illuminated the kitchen for an instant. Foster jumped back in surprise. Katie smiled in satisfaction and slipped the can into a pocket of her jumpsuit. "Might come in handy, don't you think?"

"My partner, the human blowtorch." Foster struggled to regain his composure after being startled.

They headed for the locker rooms. The chambers weren't much larger than the storage closets they'd examined earlier, but the restroom facilities were most welcome. After they had attended to personal needs, Foster and Katie began to clip locks in the men's lockers. They found a lot of clothing, some wallets, two cartons of cigarettes, and other useless personal items, but nothing else.

"Not even any contraband," said Foster with a sigh. "What a bunch of boring upright stiffs we have working here."

"Come on, let's check the ladies' room," said Katie.

She found the women's locker contents much more interesting. She found some shades of eye and lip color she thought might suit her, marveled at the pictures of nude male models taped inside one locker while Foster looked at the ceiling, and clucked in disgust at one woman's taste in sweaters. The third from last locker they opened turned out to be the most valuable of all. A set of keys and a duty schedule for the cleaning staff hung inside the door.

Katie grinned and swiped the keys. "Let's go do some damage."

* * *

They found a working computer terminal in the maintenance supervisor's office. Foster slid into the battered office chair while Katie looked over his shoulder. He tried to access the camera system first, but the terminal had no direct connection to any security systems. "Just when some intelligence would have been really useful," he grumbled.

"Can we get to the Command Center? Maybe somebody there can tell us exactly what's going on."

"We could do it through DSIM, but I'm sure the Center has been overrun already." Foster moved the mouse pointer over the Deep Six Instant Message icon on the screen. "I don't want to risk us being discovered."

"I have an idea. If the initial message reads like a standard computer check or something, it wouldn't be an immediate giveaway to anyone except one of our people."

Foster looked up at Katie. "That's a good idea."

He began to type.

* * *

Cassie inhaled sharply as the unexpected messenger window popped onto the corner of her screen with its characteristic doorbell sound. T-Rex looked up from where he lounged in the doorway of the Command Center. Misrule had returned to the Warden's office, but he'd ordered Cassie to stay in the Center under T-Rex's watchful eye. He wanted someone available who knew how to operate the complicated system. She huddled in front of her terminal, wishing she had any kind of useful power, instead of the fantastic ability to alter room temperatures by seven degrees. She tried to make herself as much of an unlovely, shapeless mass as possible in the hope that T-Rex wouldn't be interested enough to approach her with the intent to do her harm.

Impossible words appeared in the messenger window; they shouldn't have been there at all, and they made no sense. *ENVIRONMENTAL SYSTEMS DIAGNOSTIC COMPLETE: PLEASE INPUT NUMBER OF PERSONNEL AND INMATES PRESENT TO CONTINUE.*

T-Rex ambled over. His fetid breath washed across her like the odor from a slaughterhouse. He looked down at the screen while Cassie cowered. "Whuzzat?" He pointed at the messenger window.

"En-environmental systems check." She hoped she sounded convincing enough to him.

He seemed satisfied at that, but didn't immediately move away either. He leaned closer, and a little bit of drool leaked out between his sharpened teeth. "So how you doin', sweetcheeks?"

She felt tears at the corners of her eyes. "Please," she whispered. "Please just go away."

"Now that just ain't polite," he said in a low voice, and flicked his long tongue out to caress her cheek. It tickled as if a fly had brushed across her face. "Mmmm . . ." He grinned around a mouthful of sharpened teeth. "You taste real good, sweet thang."

"Please," she whispered again as tears started rolling down her cheeks in earnest. "You have to leave me alone."

"Aw, honey, I ain't gonna hurt ya. Leastaways, I never mean to. Y'all can't help if y'all are so fragile." He leaned even closer and made his tongue flick around her neck. Shivers of terror coursed up and down her spine, but she didn't dare move. "But mebbe when Misrule gets us all out of here, you and I can have a little fun. Fella can only pull his pud so many times afore he's looking for someplace wet to stick it. Five years has been one helluva dry spell." He laughed at his own joke.

"Hey, Rex, quit bothering the hostages," called a voice from the door of the Command Center. Cassie looked past the reptile man's scaly shoulder to see Dissident. The fair-haired man could turn himself into a two-dimensional being, a unique if not exceptionally useful power.

T-Rex's eyes narrowed to slits. "I weren't doin' nuthin'." He picked at something underneath a thick, yellow fingernail.

"Then you can do it over here. Misrule trusts you not to fuck this up like you usually do. You should be glad for the opportunity."

"Kiss-ass." T-Rex slunk back to the door, sending a venomous glare at Dissident's back.

Cassie gulped, tasting bile at the back of her throat from the close call, and turned her attention back to the mysterious message. She hesitated and glanced back toward T-Rex to see if he was watching, but he seemed to have lost interest in her for the moment. Then she typed *19 INMATES, 24 PERSONNEL*.

The reply only took a moment: *+2*. Then it was followed with *CLOSE WINDOW*.

She closed the window before anyone else could wander in and see that tell-tale *+2*. It could only mean one thing . . . Katie Malone and Tim Foster were still free within the confines of Deep Six.

Cassie's heart beat a little faster. She would do what she could to help them from her post in the Command Center. Whatever they were planning, they would need information. She started watching the inmates once more, but out of hope instead of hopelessness.

* * *

Fearful shrieks and surprised curses emanated from the hostages and the escapees when the lights went out. The oppressive darkness pressed in on everyone and made chests constrict with fear and panic. The intercom system beeped twice and a recorded voice announced "Emergency power activated." The dim emergency lights powered up, which sank the prison into perpetual twilight.

"What the hell?" T-Rex looked around in confusion before he focused his attention on Cassie. "You. You did something, you sly little bitch." He stalked toward her, lustful vengeance on his ugly face.

Cassie screamed and dove underneath the control board for what little protection it offered.

"Rex, I swear I can't leave you alone for five minutes. What's going on?" Misrule made only a shadow in the doorway, backlit by the rotating warning lights outside the door.

T-Rex hooked his claws in the back of Cassie's blouse, and he dragged her from under the console as if she was nothing more than a paper doll. "This gash made the lights go out. I saw her messin' with the computer just afore it happened."

"Let her go, Rex."

Cassie, too frightened to scream, managed a high-pitched hyperventilation. T-Rex ignored Misrule's order and pressed Cassie up against the console with one hand. He used the other to pop her buttons open in one swift motion.

Suddenly Misrule moved right behind the convicted rapist, wrapped one powerful arm around his throat, and squeezed. "Manners," whispered Misrule. T-Rex's eyes bulged as he tried to dislodge Misrule's choke hold. The reptilian, though much stronger than a normal human, couldn't match Misrule's power. His struggles weakened, then ceased altogether and he slumped into unconsciousness. Misrule lifted his minion by the neck and one leg and hurled him through the thick bulletproof glass. Hostages and escapees scattered as shards of glass flew in all directions. T-Rex hit the floor hard and bounced several times.

Misrule sighed with irritation before extending a hand to Cassie. "What's your name?"

Cassie didn't accept his helping hand. Instead she tried to hold her ragged shirt together.

"Come now . . . at the very least I've just saved your dignity. You can't reciprocate by giving me something to call you besides *hey you*?" Misrule lowered his head and gazed at her from under his thick brow ridge with a grim smile. "Or perhaps you'd prefer *bitch* or *gash* like my unfortunate colleague does?"

"C-Cassie."

"There, you see? No harm done. Now . . ." He stepped closer to her, suddenly deep inside her personal space, and had her trapped against the wall with his face only inches from hers. He moved so fast she had no time to react, to dodge. Whereas T-Rex enjoyed making his victims afraid with the anticipation of his approach, Misrule utilized economy of motion. He didn't waste an iota of energy with idle threats or posturing. He turned her face back toward his. "Did you, Cassie, shut down the lights?"

"N-no," she said.

"And what was your *messing with the computer*?"

"I was . . . I was responding to an alert by the environmental monitoring system."

"Do go on."

"It said it d-detected abnormal air usage in the Booking Lobby. There have n-never been this many people in Booking. The system flags anything odd like that, runs a diagnostic, and—"

"Please." Misrule released her face and Cassie shut her mouth with a snap. "Don't bore me with your technical details. Stay right there and touch nothing."

Cassie froze except for her quaking knees.

Misrule leaned over the console and called out the window, "Brainstorm, see to Rex. If he's still alive and conscious, inform him that I have given Espada permission to castrate him if he slips up again." Espada, her arms still formed into razor-sharp blades, gave him a predatory smile. "Acting Chief Warden David Prince, I require your presence here in the Center."

Prince appeared at the doorway a moment later. "What's going on?" He looked suspiciously at Cassie, as if it had all been her fault.

"I would like you to check your memory very carefully and tell me if in fact you have accounted for all your personnel. If I perceive you are lying to me, I will kill this young woman in front of you."

Prince turned his eyes toward Cassie and for a moment she saw he was prepared to let her die before his face softened and he looked away from her. "We have two guards that we haven't located."

Misrule's face was impassive. "I see. Never lie to me again and you may yet live to spend your retirement. Assuming your missing guards are responsible for turning out our lights, where would they most likely have accomplished such a task?"

"Maintenance level." Prince wouldn't meet either Misrule's or Cassie's gaze.

Misrule looked out the window at the gathered escapees in the lobby. "Kickback, Napalm, I have a mission for you."

* * *

Neither Katie nor Foster knew anything about engineering, power systems, or things mechanical, but they had found where the main local power grid connected to Deep Six, thanks to convenient warning labels. They improvised an explosive by taping together a case of spray lubricant cans and placing them right at the connection. Cotton twine soaked in the kitchen fryer made a serviceable fuse, and Katie lit it. For a moment, they stared at the tiny flame at the end of the cord, wondering if they had watched too many adventure TV shows as kids. Then the grease caught in earnest, and the flame raced up the line to where they had painted the cans with sludge scooped from the grease pit. The cans began burning bright, and Foster and Katie gaped at each other with dawning realization that they had built a bomb.

A moment later, they flung themselves to the floor behind the backup generator as the makeshift explosive detonated, sending flames and aluminum shrapnel everywhere. The room plunged into darkness as the backup generator wound itself up to speed. Backup lighting came online. Katie and Foster peeked out from behind their cover to see the power conduit a shredded, smoldering mess. They looked at their smudged faces and smiled. The sprinklers flashed on, dousing the room if not their spirits.

"Did we do that?" Foster snickered with glee. "Maintenance department's going to absolutely have a shit hemorrhage."

Katie coughed from the smoke in her lungs. "Let's get out of here. Misrule's going to send someone to check on this."

They retreated back to the maintenance office. "Now what?" Foster asked.

"We'd better prepare for a fight."

They rooted through the cleaning and industrial supplies for anything they could use. Katie examined the map. "They'll come up this way," she said, pointing at a route. "We should make our stand here, so we can retreat through the kitchen if needed."

"Why the kitchen?"

"There's enough clutter in there to make it difficult for a straight-up fight," explained Katie. "And we don't know who's coming up. If there are five or six of them we're going to be in trouble. At least you might be able to get dim and hide in the freezer or something."

"What about you?"

"I'll think of something. Let's be optimists."

Katie looked at her tiny arsenal of impromptu weapons: two baggies filled with pepper and one with flour, the can of cooking spray, a butcher knife, and a bottle of hot sauce. Foster regarded them with wry amusement. "I have a very good feeling about this plan."

"That's the spirit." Then Katie drew in a sharp breath, for she heard footsteps in the corridor beyond. "Shit, they got up here faster than I thought."

Foster checked the charge on his ultrataser for the umpteenth time. Katie motioned to him to head to the other end of the kitchen. As he stepped away, he faded to a mere ghost of himself.

Flickering firelight lit the hallway outside the kitchen. Curtis LeVaughn stood by the doorway and looked in. *Napalm.* "I smell smoke," he said. Of all the inmates who Misrule could have sent, why did it have to be the scariest one of the bunch? Another man joined him. Katie didn't recognize the newcomer. She shrank back a little further into her hiding place.

"There's a fire in the power room, shithead," grunted the other man.

"No," retorted Napalm. "Fresh smoke. In here." His fists became balls of flame. "Come out, little chickenshits. I promise I won't hurt you . . . much."

Katie shivered. The ultrataser she held felt small and pathetic compared to the fire burning in Napalm's hands. Her finger tightened on the trigger, ready to unleash the stored electricity in the weapon.

Napalm stepped into the kitchen. His hands lit the room like two torches. "Come out, come out, wherever you are."

"Yeah, come downstairs and join the party," said the other guy. "We're gonna play Twister."

Katie didn't move, barely even dared to breathe. *One more step*, she thought to herself. Napalm took that step, and she shot him.

The tiny darts melted before they struck his skin and the ultrataser expended its charge into the floor instead of Napalm. Next to him, Foster's darts glanced off the other man to stick into the wall. "What the fuck?" the unnamed escapee cried.

"Watch out, Kickback," shouted Napalm. "I knew I was right. You're gonna burn, bitch." A gout of flame sprayed from his hands toward Katie. She dove across the floor and rolled behind an oven. She wondered how the hell they were going to overcome the two powerful parahumans. She knew that Kickback reflected energy and physical attacks directed at him, making him difficult to take down. And Napalm was, well, Napalm.

Heat washed across Katie's back and she realized the stovetop above her was aflame. Fire crawled up the grease-stained wall and across the hood over the burners. She yelped and jumped across the open space between the oven and the stainless steel counter tops. Napalm saw her and loosed another blast of flame. Katie crouched under the counter. Fear sweat poured off her.

"Surrender, Dorothy. We've got you bitches outgunned," called Kickback.

Foster appeared out of the smoke and faded into full view from dimness, a fire extinguisher clutched in his hands. But instead of turning it on Napalm, he loosed the contents at Kickback.

"Hey!" Kickback reflected a portion of the sticky foam back at Foster, but he couldn't deal with the entire cloud, and was soon coated from head to toe in white residue. He choked and coughed from the thick powdery goop.

Napalm ignored Foster and Kickback to stalk into the kitchen after Katie. "I'm going to cook you slow, whore."

All her improvised weapons seemed pathetic and useless against the man's massive firepower, and Katie was trapped under the counter. She tried desperately to scrunch a little further back and something behind her moved. She looked and saw a five-gallon plastic bucket. The faded label read *Lard*, and the bucket was nearly full. Suddenly she recalled something she'd read in Napalm's file, and she closed her fingers around the wire handle. She had no time to wonder about flammability or combustion temperatures or anything like that. It was animal fat, and it would burn. She heaved herself out from under the counter, spun around like a hammer thrower in the Olympics, and let the bucket fly right toward Napalm. His predictable response was to blast it with flame.

The bucket didn't so much ignite as explode.

Burning fat flew everywhere. Several bits hit Katie, which burned and sizzled where they struck. The white-hot bucket handle whistled past her face and took a painful notch out of her right ear as it passed. Blood flowed warm and wet down the side of her neck. She would have cried out had she not been so desperate to avoid being burned to death.

Napalm caught the full brunt of the flaming mass of lard. It splattered against his chest and abdomen and coated him in raging fire. As he drew in breath to scream, the flames raced down into his lungs to sear him from the inside. He jumped backwards in reflex and fell into the corridor. He may have been able to shoot fire from his hands, but he didn't have any immunity to flame or ability to control it. He flailed about on the floor as the hungry flames ate into his flesh.

As Napalm exploded in flames, Foster went straight for Kickback, who flailed about helpless because the foam had blinded him. Kickback wasn't much of a wrestler, and it only took two moves for Foster to get him into a headlock. Kickback struggled for a few moments until consciousness fled him.

Katie found another fire extinguisher and sprayed down Napalm, afraid she'd been all too effective in her attack upon him. He lay curiously still as the foam enveloped him and added its thick chemical smell to the odor of barbecued flesh in the hallway. He remained unmoving as she emptied the extinguisher completely and tossed it aside.

"Katie, you all right?" Foster called over his shoulder as he pulled the unconscious Kickback into the hallway.

The pain from her damaged ear hit her. She yelped and clapped her hand to her head.

He was there in an instant, gentle hands pulling carefully at hers. "Katie, you have to let me see it." She couldn't see through the tears of pain, but she let Foster pull her hand away from her ear. "This?" he asked. "This scratch?"

"How bad is it?" she whimpered.

"It's not too bad," he said. "I'm sure you'll still be able to play the piano, and it will make for some interesting stories at the bar."

The post-combat shakes and the shock of her injury weakened her resolve and she giggled. "Oh God . . . that's wonderful. I never could play the piano . . ."

Foster checked on his captive to ensure Kickback was still unconscious. "The trick with him is to get in close. You'd think a guy like that would learn how to grapple, but he always assumes nobody will get that close to him. Looks like you did a number on Napalm too."

"Oh, yeah," said Katie. "He was easy too. I just b-burned him . . ." She collapsed into nervous laughter, unable to stop herself until she dug both fists into her mouth. "Oh shit, Foster . . . I think I killed him." A shriek of lunacy escaped between her hands.

Foster grabbed her by the shoulders and shook her. "Katie, get a hold of yourself. Come on, I need the serious Katie now. We can make all the jokes we want when this is over, but you've got a better head for details than I do and if you lose it, we might as well march right downstairs and let Misrule turn us into steaks."

She gasped for breath. "I'm sorry, Foster. It's just . . . I've never killed anyone before."

"Me neither," he said. "Let's hope it doesn't become a habit."

* * *

The indicator on Cassie's monitoring board lit up and she took a step toward her station before she froze as she remembered Misrule's strict warning for her not to touch anything. She couldn't quite see the nature of the alert from her seat by the entrance to the Command Center. Misrule had ordered her to remain nearby should anything require her attention, but he made it clear that if it didn't require his attention, it didn't require hers either.

Dissident had replaced T-Rex as the Command Center guard. The soft-spoken man barely moved a muscle, content to remain seated and still. His posture made Cassie wonder if he was meditating. He was serving the shortest sentence of all the Cult of Destruction members: ten years for felony burglary. His ability to become completely flat helped with breaking and entering, and Just Cause had been lucky to capture him at all. His cell had been constructed without seams in the walls, floor, or ceiling, and had an intricate multi-tiered arrangement of joints around the door making it impossible for him to slip through. Cassie remembered the day she'd booked him. He had been polite and even smiled at her, and since then had been a model prisoner and would have been up for parole in eighteen more months.

"Um, excuse me? Something on my board just lit up and I should go check it out," she said.

"Of course." He motioned her inside and followed her into the Command Center. He stood where he could observe her every action from over her shoulder.

The board indicated a fire with sprinkler deployment on the maintenance level. She reported this to Dissident, who in turn sent for Misrule.

Misrule didn't seem concerned. "Doubtless our friend Napalm has seen fit to use his power. We shall learn of the results of his actions soon enough. Has there been any communication from the surface?"

"Nothing," said Cassie.

"Interesting." Misrule spun on his heel and returned to the Warden's office.

A minor commotion erupted outside the Command Center, and Cassie recognized Dr. Mayfair's voice. "Oh for God's sake, I'm a doctor," he said.

"Let him in, Kiloton," said Dissident. Mayfair stomped into the Center, bloodstains on his coat. He looked tired and angry. "What's the problem, Doctor?"

Mayfair pushed his glasses up his nose. "I understand that this young lady was attacked. I'm going to need to examine her."

"No, really, I'm fine," she said.

Mayfair's eyes bored into hers. "You'll let me be the judge of that, Cassandra."

In all the years that Cassie had been in Deep Six, not once had he or anyone else ever called her Cassandra. Something was on his mind; something important enough for him to come to her despite the risk.

"Well, all right, if you think so. He did scratch me a bit," she said.

Mayfair glared at Dissident. "Well? Do I have permission to perform my sworn duties or not?"

"Who else can perform her duties while you have her in Medical?"

She was about to open her mouth to reply but Montell drifted up to the doorway where he hovered at his usual altitude of three inches above the floor. He couldn't fly any higher than that if he'd wanted to. "I can," he said.

"Very well. You may go." Dissident waved them away. Cassie wanted to say something to Montell, to let him know about the message she'd received from Foster and Malone earlier, but didn't know how she could without alerting Dissident. She squeezed his arm as she passed by. He smiled down at her with forced cheer.

Mayfair led her across the lobby. As they crossed, Mayfair paused and called back toward Dissident. "If we're going to be down here for awhile, you might want to start thinking about feeding everyone."

Dissident nodded his head once but said nothing.

The doctor harrumphed and headed towards Medical fast enough that Cassie almost had to jog to keep up. "There are three of them in Medical," he said quietly enough that she had to strain to hear him. "They're bored stupid." He raised his voice. "All right, Cassandra, let's check you over."

As they walked into Medical, Cassie saw Officer Coltrane lying on a bed, his wounds dressed and his wrist wrapped in a thick bandage. Numerous wires and sensors hung off him and the nurse stopped by every few minutes to check his status. "How is he?" Cassie asked, nodding her head toward the guard.

"He's fine, resting comfortably," said Mayfair, his voice unnaturally loud. He got Cassie seated on an adjacent bed and drew a privacy curtain to partially block them from view by the three escapees who were supposed to be on guard duty. Instead of fulfilling their required roles, Brainstorm idly toyed with an otoscope, sticking it into her own ear. Heretic was barely awake, and Black Hood's stentorian snores rattled the test tubes on the counter. "He's dead," Mayfair whispered, his expression neutral as he strapped a blood pressure cuff over her arm.

Cassie bit her tongue to keep from exclaiming in surprise. Mayfair was up to something, and had a reason for keeping their watchers in the dark about Coltrane's true status. Whatever it was, she knew the best thing would be for her to play along. "Oh, that's good," she said. Heretic laid his head on his hands and his eyelids drooped shut.

The doctor proceeded to apply antibiotic ointment to the scratches on her chest while he kept a surreptitious watch on Brainstorm. She yawned, stretched, and got up from her post. She headed back to the lobby, probably to use the bathroom. Mayfair nodded at his assistant and she moved to a different location where she could watch for Brainstorm's return.

Mayfair spoke quickly. "I've autopsied Warden Silbersack, and I know how he was killed. Whoever did it injected him with a biological toxin. It shut down his respiratory system almost immediately."

"That's horrible."

"Yes it is, but there's more. The killer was careful, but not thorough enough. I went through the sharps container and found a needle that shouldn't have been in there. That led me to find the one which originally contained the poison. I've examined it and I believe I may have found a fingerprint on it. I'm sure the killer wore gloves to carry out the act, but may have handled it without them at some point in the past."

"Why are you telling me this?"

"Because I need you to access employee records and see if you can cross-reference it with anyone here."

"I can't do that." Cassie almost raised her voice too loud. "The Command Center is being watched constantly."

"So am I, but by incompetents. I've connected the laptop monitoring Coltrane to a computer simulation instead so it shows him still alive. You can use it to access the network." Mayfair showed her the computer.

"How will they let me work on it?"

Mayfair tapped a couple of keys and the simulation froze. "I'm having computer trouble. You're the best tech here. You can fix it."

Cassie gulped and nodded.

She started to work with her various passwords to access different parts of the database. Montell would certainly notice her actions in the system activity log. She had to trust him to keep quiet about it—what other choice did she have?

"Even if we can find out who killed the Warden, how does that help us now?" she murmured.

"I'm convinced it was an inside job," said Mayfair. "And I think whoever did it is working for Misrule."

"Why?"

"What better way to kick off a mass breakout than by eliminating the one man who could cut it off right from the start?"

"That makes sense." Cassie smiled as a back door in the system allowed her into the employee records. She didn't have authority to access them, but over the years she'd handled so many varied tasks that she had acquired far more knowledge about the ins and outs of Deep Six's computer system than just about anyone else. She pulled up the scan of the fingerprint that Mayfair had lifted from the syringe and loaded the comparison application. A thought occurred to her and she turned to the doctor. "How do I know it wasn't you? Or how do you know it wasn't me who did it?"

"You don't, and I don't, but sooner or later we have to trust somebody or we can't ever trust anyone. I don't believe you're capable of committing murder, Cassie, and I choose to trust you." Mayfair looked over his glasses at her.

He was either dead serious or a great actor, she thought. But he had a point about trust, and she decided she'd trust the doctor who had been in Deep Six longer than she had. "I'm running the match now," she said.

"Hey, what's she doing?" Brainstorm walked back into Medical and kicked at Hood and Heretic's chairs to wake them.

"The damage throughout the prison seems to have affected my monitoring system. Cassandra is trying to repair it so I can continue to care for Officer Coltrane." Mayfair took his glasses off to polish them and glared at Brainstorm. "Perhaps you'd like to read my mind and confirm that?"

"I can't read minds," she hissed. "But I can destroy them. I could destroy yours right now."

Mayfair shrugged and turned his back on her. "Whatever. But if you do, you'd better hope nobody else requires medical attention."

"Huh? What's he talking about?" grunted Heretic.

"He's full of shit," said Black Hood. "He ain't gonna lift a finger to help one of us inmates. Do him, Brainstorm. Do him slow, so I can watch."

Cassie shrank back in her seat. The fear of being caught in a crossfire made her feel like she was being strangled.

Mayfair rounded on the three escapees. "I swore an oath once to provide assistance to those who need it, no matter what their crimes may have been. And by God I am going to practice my medicine here with or without your blessing." He folded his arms across his chest, as if daring them to do anything.

Heretic and Brainstorm backed down, and a moment later Black Hood stepped back and folded his arms. "You just watch yourself, old man, or you're going down. I don't care if you're a doctor or not," growled the hulking brute.

"Christ, I need a cup of coffee," grumbled Mayfair.

"A prisoner of war is a man who tries to kill you and fails, and then asks you not to kill him."

—Winston Churchill

July, 2007
Deep Six, Montana

Napalm was dead; Kickback was alive. Dealing with Napalm was easy. Katie and Foster dragged his charred corpse into the walk-in freezer in the kitchen. Kickback presented a more complex problem altogether. Katie found some duct tape in the maintenance supplies and they bound him hand and foot and placed a strip across his mouth. He awoke while they finished moving Napalm and when they returned, he glared at them in baleful silence.

"Think we ought to kill him?" asked Katie. "He'd have done us without a second thought."

Kickback shook his head and yelled behind his taped mouth.

Foster looked at their prisoner. "Yes, but do you want a second death on your conscience? Napalm was self-defense. This is different. This would be murder."

Katie sighed. "It's true. I don't really want more blood on my hands. It's too bad we can't keep him unconscious. Oh!" She stopped as an idea struck her.

"What?"

"Sleeper sets. We can still use them, right? They'll operate without a direct connection to the computer system." She gestured with her hands, trying to illustrate her idea in bad pantomime.

"Good idea. Only problem is that all the sets are in Medical, and there are a couple dozen bad guys in between us and them."

"There's got to be a way to even the odds."

"If you think of one, let me know."

"What about the knockout gas?"

"That's another great idea. If we could only get into the Command Center we could trigger every grenade in the entire facility, assuming the relays are all still functioning. I suspect that if they could have blown all the gas, Command would have once the first few escapees got out. I bet the system's down. And that doesn't help us deal with this asshole here." Foster prodded at Kickback with his toe. "Want to just throw him in a locker until we figure out something better?"

Katie nodded, still trying to imagine a scenario where they could acquire some of the potent knockout gas. Kickback shouted against his tape again as Foster used a combination of plastic wrap from the kitchen and duct tape to wrap up Kickback like a gothic mummy.

They lugged the trussed-up convict to the men's locker room. Foster thought it might be more of a kindness to use the women's, because it would smell a little better. Katie vetoed that on the grounds of it being just too weird. Besides, she explained, any locker he spent more than a few hours in would develop its own peculiar funk and she wouldn't wish that upon any of her sisters.

Cramming Kickback into a locker proved to be more difficult in practice than in theory. The lockers weren't quite tall, wide, or deep enough to contain him, especially when he struggled against them as much as he could in his shrink-wrapped state. Finally Katie decided she'd had enough of his shenanigans and held up the roll of duct tape in front of his bulging eyes. "Listen, either you cooperate or I'll tape your nostrils shut and wait for you to die on the floor."

He gave up his struggles, resigned to his fate. "Look, I know this is pretty junior high school of us," said Foster, "but the whole point of this is to avoid killing you. I'm sure you understand. What's that? I can't hear you. Oh, must be because you've got tape over your mouth." He winked at Katie, who snickered into her sleeve.

"Huck hoo," said Kickback from behind the duct tape.

"That's the spirit." Foster pressed the man into the locker. Katie shut the door carefully so the escapee's reflection power wouldn't throw it open again. Once it was shut, Foster took one of the padlocks they'd cut earlier and stuck it through the latch. "Look good to you?" he asked Katie.

"Definitely."

"Now we need some kind of big diversion that'll let us get down to Medical. There are canisters of the knockout gas down there as well as a supply of sleeper sets."

An idea occurred to Katie. "How big a diversion do you want?"

"Really big."

"Then come on. I saw a cutting torch in the maintenance section."

"That sounds promising." Foster turned and tapped twice on the locker. "S'all right?"

"Huck hoo," Kickback answered.

"Okay. We'll be back to get you once we've got the prison back under control," said Katie.

"Don't go anywhere," added Foster.

* * *

Cassie looked at the data on the screen and tried to keep her voice calm and collected. "Dr. Mayfair, I think I might have fixed the problem. Will you come take a look?"

He stepped around the bed to look over her shoulder. Cassie had run the fingerprint matching application twice and each time it came up with the same match. According to the software, the fingerprint which Mayfair found on the hidden syringe was a 98% match for David Prince.

Mayfair set a heavy hand on Cassie's shoulder. A slight tremor shook his voice. "Yes, Cassandra, I think that'll do nicely. Thank you for your help." He leaned down and touched a couple keys to close the application and bring the monitor simulation back up once more.

"I'm . . . I'm glad I could help, Doctor." Cassie stood up and the room began to swirl around her.

"I'll let you know if . . . Cassie, are you all right?"

She grabbed onto the back of her chair for support. Her sanity wanted to take a little mental vacation, but she knew she now had to be strong. Cassie clenched her teeth and willed herself to be well enough. She had a new mission: to watch Prince. He couldn't be trusted any longer. He'd already given Foster and Malone up to Misrule, and they were probably dead or captured because of it.

One way or another, she'd see to it nobody else died because of Prince's traitorous actions.

She waved off Mayfair's ministrations and staggered back into Booking. She didn't see Prince through the shattered glass of the Command Center, so he was either in the bathroom or in the Warden's office.

"Jesus, Cassie, you look like you've seen a ghost," said Officer Garcia. He, Lania, and Eaton huddled together under the watchful eyes of Nightmare and several of the *Soldados*. "Come, sit with us. We'll make

sure nobody else bothers you like that asshole did."
Garcia waved in the direction of T-Rex, who swayed in
a chair by himself. He muttered to himself and
occasionally squeezed his head as if doing so would
lessen the pain.

Lania growled through the speaker of her
containment suit. "I'd blow this entire facility to hell if
there weren't so many civilians down here. These
animals don't deserve to live."

"Easy, Lania. There's no need to go all mad bomber
on us yet. They may have overrun the prison, but they
haven't reached the surface yet." Garcia placed a
comforting hand on her arm. "We've got a lot of allies
up there on the surface. You can bet they're not going
to let these jerks out of here."

"You didn't see them. You didn't see how they made
Eaton grovel and beg, or how they mutilated Coltrane,"
grumbled Lania.

Cassie looked at Eaton, who had finally succumbed
to unconsciousness. He lay with his head in Lania's lap.
Sweat dampened his brow and his lips pulled back into
a defensive snarl.

"How is Coltrane, anyway?" Lania sounded worried
even through the speaker in her suit.

Cassie glanced at the escapees that surrounded
them. Like those who guarded Dr. Mayfair, boredom
had taken its toll on them as well. Only Nightmare
appeared alert, but she was the furthest away from
them. The other guards deserved to know Coltrane's
fate, and Cassie lowered her voice to a bare whisper.
"Don't react, but he's dead. Mayfair is pretending he's
still alive so he can keep a computer running."

Misrule stepped out of the Warden's office, followed by
a meek David Prince. They went to the Command Center.
From her vantage point, Cassie could see them speak into
the microphone, once more in communication with the
surface. She wanted to tell the other guards about Prince,

but didn't want to condemn him on the basis of a single partial fingerprint. It might have been valuable evidence for a court case, but on its own was hardly enough to prove him guilty beyond a reasonable doubt. She decided for the moment to keep silent about hers and Mayfair's suspicions.

Misrule strode back into the lobby, his face darkened and thunderous. Everyone shrank back a bit from him; even the other escapees took involuntary steps away, or looked at the ceiling or floor—anything to avoid giving him further offense.

"Please, I'm sure they're doing the best they can," said Prince from behind Misrule. "You've got to give them enough time to find him."

Misrule swept his arm backward and caught Prince across the face. The Assistant Warden tumbled away with a bloodied nose. Misrule didn't bother to look back at him. Instead, he swept the room with his imperious gaze as if to search for someone to execute. His eyes came to rest on a couple of the kitchen staffers and he started toward them, but then halted.

"Where are Napalm and Kickback?" he asked of no-one in particular.

The other escapees looked at each other in surprise. None of them had noticed the two men Misrule dispatched earlier had not returned.

Misrule looked up at the ceiling in thought.

* * *

"This is going to get us killed," said Foster. He and Katie had scrounged through the maintenance shop and retrieved the oxy-acetylene cutting torch and a roll of heavy-duty wire.

"I hope not," Katie said. "I change my own oil, but besides that I'm not much of a backyard engineer."

"You change your own oil? Shit, for a minute there I thought I was only dealing with an amateur."

Katie smirked, and then winced as the motion caused a sharp twinge from the cut on her ear. "Okay, here's the plan. Once we blow the elevator, things should get pretty chaotic for a few minutes. We sneak down to Medical and grab the gas canister and a couple of breathers."

"We can only blow all the gas simultaneously from the Command Center," pointed out Foster. "It's sure to be watched, and we don't know that the system is even working."

"We've got to assume it is. We're running out of options. How hard is it to activate?"

"It isn't. There's a panic button." He showed her its location on the map.

"Look here . . ." Katie pointed along the map. "We can drop right down into the Command Center from this ventilation shaft. The gas only takes a few seconds to take effect, right? One of us should be able to get to the switch. All we have to do is stay alive for those few seconds and everything's golden. As long as we have uncontaminated air."

"Sure," said Foster. "Stay alive for a few seconds with Misrule and everybody else trying to kill us. Not a problem."

Katie elbowed him. "Stay optimistic. It's our best chance for success. Once we pop the gas, we can get sleeper sets on everyone."

"What about Misrule?" Foster asked. "He had a sleeper set on—we put it on him ourselves. Somehow he woke up from an induced coma. That's not supposed to be possible."

"Don't you figure he's planned this whole breakout? I'll bet he's even behind the Warden's death somehow. I wouldn't at all be surprised if he's figured out a way to beat the sleeper set. Can we alter them somehow? Change the frequency or something?"

"We can't," said Foster. "But Doc Mayfair could."

"All right, we'll keep that in mind. Let's get these tanks to the shaft."

They had decided the best, most useful diversion would be to destroy the elevator that led to the surface. That way, even when the security blocks were removed from the shaft, there would be no easy way to reach the surface. It should put a crimp in any plans to evacuate the facility that way, and would create the panic that they needed to put their own plan into effect.

Katie's ex-husband had been a car guy, and among his tools he'd had an oxy-acetylene torch. One winter night while she was seven months pregnant with Lindsay, she'd sat in the garage watching him work on his truck. That particular night he'd been cutting some sheet metal with the torch and he'd explained to her how it worked. She didn't think she'd paid much attention at the time, but enough of it seemed to have stuck that she had a bare-bones idea of how to get the improvised bomb to work.

They unwound and cut off a section of the wire, and Foster used his pocket multitool to strip away the plastic coating, and then untwisted the braided end into two narrower strips. Katie attached the other end of the wire to the darts of her ultrataser. "I hope this works," she said, "or we're wasting a shot for nothing."

She'd expended one shot against Napalm. The test-firing they were about to perform would use up one more. She had her spare battery pack that would be good for two more. If the test was successful, they would need to utilize yet another charge to detonate their bomb, leaving them each a single shot remaining.

Foster fashioned a crude frame out of duct tape and paper clips to hold the wire forks near each other without touching, then set his creation down on the floor and backed away. "Ready," he reported.

"Here goes nothing," said Katie, pointed the ultrataser into a corner, and pulled the trigger. The darts shot out and bounced to the floor. Foster, watching the other end, whooped with excitement. "Did it spark?" asked Katie.

Foster seized her hands and grinned. "Like a tiny bolt of lightning. You're a genius."

Katie blushed. "No, I'm just practical. I don't like the idea of standing next to the tanks, trying to set them off with my fingers." She locked gazes with Foster without meaning to, and a long moment passed before she shook herself. She was surprised and a little embarrassed at the flush of heat in her center, something she hadn't felt since well before she left her ex-husband. She reminded herself that this was neither the time nor the place to entertain such foolish notions.

And besides, she didn't date COs.

"Yeah," said Foster, who likewise seemed a bit out of sorts. "Let's, uh, get this thing going before I change my mind about it being a good idea."

"Did I give the impression this was a good idea?" Katie slapped the replacement battery into her ultrataser. "It's the only one I've got. If you can provide a better alternative, I'm ready to listen."

"I got nothing," said Foster after a pause.

They wheeled the cutting torch to the elevator that led back down to Booking. Foster coiled the wire around the base of the torch so it couldn't be dislodged, and then affixed his framework just underneath the tanks. Katie muscled open the elevator doors with a crowbar she'd taken from the maintenance shop. Unlike the convenient lighting that always seemed to be present in movie elevator shafts, this one was pitch black and had an odd echo within it. She peeked in, shining her flashlight up, then down. Only a few feet above the top of the door was the first of the giant steel-reinforced stone blocks which had slid into place to block the elevator shaft during lockdown. Each block was fifteen feet high, and six of them were spaced at thousand-foot intervals to seal the shaft with countless tons of stone and steel. Twenty feet below she saw the top of the elevator. There was no cable. Instead, it ran along a chain track set into the side of the shaft.

"This might be a problem," she said.

Foster leaned out to take a better look. "Oh, shit." They hadn't counted on the long drop to the elevator's roof.

They would have to lower the heavy torch setup down and do it quietly enough not to alert the escapees in Booking. Then one of them would have to open the valves on the tanks and climb out again before succumbing to the gas.

"This idea is getting worse all the time." Katie knew it would have to be her unleashing the gas because she was smaller and lighter than Foster. She unrolled enough wire from the coil to stretch down to the elevator, and then ran the rest of the length down the hallway, around a corner, and into the kitchen where she hooked it to the ultrataser.

They used a heavy strap from Maintenance to lower the torch, grunting and straining with the effort. Once the unit rested on the elevator roof, they skittered down the handholds in the side of the shaft to make sure their trigger was still set.

Katie untied the strap from around the tank and fastened it around her waist while Foster made a few last minute adjustments. When she finished, she handed the end of the strap to him.

"Once I open these valves, this shaft is going to fill very quickly. I'll only have a few seconds to get out. You just keep pulling on that strap and I'll keep climbing and hopefully I'll clear the shaft before it's too late."

"Katie . . ." A variety of emotions vied for control of Foster's face.

She held up a hand to his lips to forestall any platitudes, because she could tell he was about to go all dumb and chivalrous on her. "Foster, listen. We both know it has to be me. I'm a tough little chick, but I don't know if I could pull you out of here. I'm trusting you to lift me out. Deal?"

He nodded.

She swallowed a lump that suddenly appeared in her throat. "If I fall, there won't be time to come get me. You can't let the gas get into the hallway up here or you'll blow yourself up too. You'll have to shut the doors whether I'm out or not."

"No way," said Foster. "I'm not leaving you behind."

Katie smiled. "That's sweet of you. Stupid, but sweet." She surprised herself by stretching up on her tip-toes to kiss his cheek. "See you soon, cowboy."

Foster climbed the twenty feet back to the maintenance level and cursed under his breath the entire way. Once at the top, he wrapped the slack around his own waist. Katie's eyes met his. She placed her hands on the valves for the two tanks. When Foster nodded, she spun the valves open as fast as she could. Acetylene and oxygen started to hiss into the shaft.

Katie felt lightheaded almost immediately as the gas sprayed out. It made her feel drunk and filled her eyes with flashes, making it hard to see. She staggered over to the ladder and began to climb.

Halfway up, she missed a handhold and slipped.

The shaft spun around her as Katie swung at the end of the strap. Somewhere above her, Foster struggled to pull her out of the deadly fog. She couldn't see anymore and was too dizzy to think. She caught the ladder with one of her flailing hands and retained enough presence of mind to start to climb again toward the light above her. After what seemed like an eternity, she stuck a hand above the plane of the maintenance floor and then Foster was there, her arm clutched in his sturdy grip. He pulled her free from the deadly miasma, got her clear of the doors, and shut them.

Katie sank to the floor and put her head in between her knees to clear it of the fuzziness. Foster bent down next to her. "Are you all right?"

She managed a weak thumbs-up. He helped her to her feet and they hurried down the hallway to outrun the sweet garlic smell of the acetylene that made her hungry for spaghetti.

They crouched down in the kitchen. Katie still felt terrible and woozy. "You'd better do it."

"When?"

"No time like the present."

He nodded and pulled the ultrataser's trigger.

The darts bounced off the wall, but nothing else happened.

"Where's the *kaboom*? There was supposed to be an earth-shattering *kaboom*!" Foster's jaw hung open in surprise. "Should I go back and check it?"

Katie shook her head. "The shaft's full of gas now. It could go at any moment." She looked at the ultrataser with its single remaining charge. "Try it once more."

Foster hurried to reattach the wire. "Cross your fingers," he said, and pulled the trigger.

* * *

Misrule pointed at Espada. "Take your team upstairs and find the missing two guards. I want them brought to me . . . alive."

Pistola leaped to her feet. "What do you mean, *her* team? Last I checked, *I* was leader of *Los Soldados*!" Several small, misshapen chunks of metal spun in tight orbits around her head.

"Not anymore, *pendeja*." Espada grinned like a hungry shark. "*Señor* Misrule put me in charge."

"Over my dead body." The metal lumps that swirled around Pistola accelerated into blurs and whistled through the air.

Espada reshaped her arms once more into straight, razor-sharp swords. "If you insist."

Misrule folded his arms. "Resolve this. Now."

Espada charged at Pistola and screamed obscenities in Spanish. Her blades flashed in the dim lighting.

"Dirty gutter wench!" Pistola flung the metal bits at her teammate like bullets.

The chunks struck Espada's shoulders; one blew through completely to skitter across the floor, leaving a trail of blood in its wake. The wounds didn't stop or slow Espada's advance. Pistola's eyes widened in surprise as she realized her attack had been ineffective. Espada lopped off her head with a heavy backhanded swing.

Several of the hostages screamed as Pistola's body tipped sideways. Blood sprayed from her severed neck. Her head rolled to a stop at Misrule's feet, an expression halfway between fury and surprise frozen on her upturned face. He smiled and stepped over it to where Espada stood. Her own blood ran down from her shoulder wounds to mix with Pistola's on her arm blade.

"Nicely done. I knew I made a good choice in you. Etch, do something about these wounds."

"Etch, do something about the wounds," muttered the Etched Man. "Do this. Do that. Always the same. Always glad to help. Glad to be the bitch."

Misrule raised an eyebrow at the man's tirade but said nothing more and turned away.

Nevertheless, the Etched Man withdrew a tattoo that looked like a tangled spider web. It floated onto Espada and coated her wounds. She smiled her approval and turned to face her horrified teammates. "The rest of you *putas* have any problem with that?"

Azote, Escudo, Cañón, and Cuchillo looked at each other before shrugging it off.

"I never liked that bitch," said Azote.

"Find me those guards. I want to talk to them," ordered Misrule.

They headed for the elevator.

Azote looked sharply at Cañón and sniffed. "Hey, fucker, did you rip ass?"

Cañón shrugged his massive, oversized arms and wrinkled his sizable nose. "No. I was just going to ask you that."

* * *

Kaboom!

* * *

An explosion tore the elevator asunder. The heavy steel doors ripped away from their tracks and whirled outward in precession of a blast of searing flame. Escudo somehow managed to get his force field activated in time and encapsulated himself and Espada in the impenetrable dome. The others weren't so lucky. Azote and Cuchillo were flung backwards like fiery missiles against the impact-resistant glass of the Command Center office and hit with sickening meaty thuds. One of the elevator doors struck Cañón so hard that he didn't hit the floor before he crashed against the far wall of Booking and crumpled into a heap of shattered bones and smoldering flesh.

The heat flashed out to knock people off their feet and blister the skin of those closest to the elevator. The sound struck a moment later, louder than thunder in the enclosed space of Booking. With nowhere for the sound to exit, it reverberated off the walls and beat on the inhabitants with almost tangible force. Fortunately, all the hostages had been held at the far end of Booking and suffered the least.

Cassie drew in a shaky breath and nearly fainted. The fiery explosion had used up a sizable portion of the oxygen in the room. She pressed her face toward the floor and found it a bit easier to breathe. The temperature sensors registered the change and triggered the sprinklers, which doused everyone with tepid water and put out the lingering fires from the explosion.

Misrule sprang back onto his feet, his red skin sooty and his expression thunderous. Doctor Mayfair and his assistant ran in from Medical with crash kits, followed by the escapees assigned to watch them. The two began to treat burns and shrapnel wounds. Escudo turned off his force field, a look of abject horror on his face as he saw the remains of his erstwhile teammates. Espada shrugged at the carnage and turned to Misrule for further direction.

Misrule stalked across the floor to the elevator. His feet kicked up splashes of dirty water. The walls had buckled from the tremendous heat of the explosion, and smoke still escaped from the charred metal. Undaunted, he stepped into the elevator. It creaked with his weight but stayed in place, possibly fused to the walls of the shaft. The force of the explosion had split the elevator's ceiling. He stiffened his fingers and punched upward to penetrate it first with one hand, then the other. He flexed his mighty arms and pulled downward. Then, with a shriek of overstressed metal, he wrenched the ceiling free from the elevator and flung it into the Booking lobby.

He pointed Espada. "Take as many as you need. Find them and bring them to me alive."

She nodded and began to recruit escapees to follow her into the shaft.

Misrule turned to Doctor Mayfair. "See to your people."

Mayfair paused from his application of a bandage to glare at Misrule. "I don't need your permission to treat the injured. None of this would have happened if you'd stayed in your goddamn cell."

Misrule nodded, as if to acknowledge that the doctor had scored a point. Then he looked to Cassie. "Cassandra, I require your assistance in the Command Center. And I also need Acting Chief Warden David Prince."

Prince started at the sound of his name. He had a scratch across his forehead from a piece of shrapnel, dotted with beads of blood.

Cassie glared at him before she followed Misrule across the floor. Water from the emergency sprinklers mixed with ash and soot to make a gooey black mud that clung to whatever it touched with remarkable tenacity, including her feet and legs. An incongruous thought about her ruined shoes crossed her mind.

"Out," Misrule ordered to Montell, who protested that he could do whatever Misrule needed and to leave Cassie alone. "I prefer her presence to yours. See that I don't prefer you dead to alive."

Montell went pale, making his dark skin appear gray.

"Good Lord, Misrule, how long is this going to go on?" asked Prince.

"That is what I intend to discover. But first, tell me if there is a method by which I may address whoever is causing these difficulties." He directed this last toward Cassie.

She nodded. "There is a prison-wide speaker system."

"Activate it, and pull up the missing guards' personnel files. I want to see who I'm dealing with."

She touched the appropriate button and then handed the microphone to Misrule.

* * *

Katie and Foster stood in the hallway, mouths agape, and stared at the blackened burns which emanated from the mouth of the elevator. The smell of burnt paint fought for space alongside the stink of hot metal and ash. Katie coughed.

"Wow, look what you did. I bet you get written up." Foster chuckled as he cleared his throat.

Katie elbowed him. "You helped."

"You're the perp. I'm only the accomplice. I'll get probation and community service, since I just did the heavy lifting."

"You better not be calling me *heavy*," Katie cocked her ear toward the elevator and listened for the sounds of anyone approaching.

They hurried back to the ventilation shaft and found the first flaw in their plan. The tube leading down to Medical was much smaller than the one they'd ascended earlier.

Foster shook his head. "There is no way I'm fitting into that."

"I think I could squeeze into it," said Katie, "but I think I'd have to go down head-first."

"So what do we do? Plan B?"

"Give me your multitool." Katie held out her hand. Foster dropped the Leatherman into it. "I don't have a Plan B. You have anything?"

"No."

"Then we're going to have to split up."

Foster looked down the hall in the direction and frowned. "I don't like that plan at all. Two people working together are five times more effective than when working separately."

"You made that up."

"Yeah."

"I'll be fine. Somebody's got to get down there."

"Just be careful. I've kind of gotten used to having you around."

"Hush. If they catch me, I'll tell them you're dead."

"How sweet of you. They're certainly going to catch me, you know."

"With your power, you've got a better chance of hiding in plain sight than I do. But if they do find you, Misrule will want to know what happened. He'll insist on us being taken alive, at least initially." Katie tried to sound confident.

"Then I guess I have no choice but to tell him the truth," said Foster. "Napalm got you. I'm so damn upset that I can't even think straight." He grinned.

Katie punched him gently on the arm. "Get out of here, cowboy."

Foster tipped his imaginary hat. "Ma'am." He turned and hustled down the hall. Katie watched him go and thought maybe she should have kissed him.

"The general who is skilled in defense hides in the most secret recesses of the earth; he who is skilled in attack flashes forth from the topmost heights of heaven. Thus on the one hand we have ability to protect ourselves; on the other, a victory that is complete."
                                        —*Sun Tzu, The Art Of War*

July, 2007
Deep Six, Montana

Katie grunted as she wriggled her way downward through the ventilation tube toward Medical. Her head ached and her vision blurred from the blood pooling in her head. Her labored breath made her sound like a petite feminine Darth Vader in the tight space. The descent was terrifying since she had nothing against which to hold herself from falling except friction.

Fortunately, she thought, her extra pounds provided enough of that needed friction to keep her from dropping like a pinball. She kept a tight hold of the Leatherman, deathly afraid she'd drop it, it would slip out of the grille at the bottom of the shaft, and she'd be stranded.

Only the small circle of light which grew slowly beneath her kept her from blind panic. She reached the bottom of the shaft sooner than she expected. It seemed like one moment it was still yards away and the next her hands bumped against the grille at the bottom. She wished she had a dental mirror or a SWAT fiber-optic camera so she could check out Medical. But then she laughed to herself. She'd probably made enough noise during her descent that anyone in the room would have had to investigate.

She began to consider ways to get out, and quickly, because her arms quaked with the effort of supporting her body. Even though the friction of the shaft walls took some of the burden, she knew she couldn't hold herself up much longer. The grille was only held on by four short screws, but the heads were on the wrong side. Katie thought perhaps she could use the multitool's saw attachment to cut through the protruding shafts of the screws and then let herself drop. Her weight should break the grille free.

But what would she land on? She'd have no way to slow her fall from the ceiling and keep from plummeting head-first onto whatever lay beneath. She blinked away tears of pain, as red tinged the edges of her vision, and tried to focus on what she could see through the small grille openings. She nearly burst out laughing in relief when she realized a hospital bed lay almost directly beneath her.

She began to saw away at the first screw. The hardened steel of the multitool made short work of the protruding shaft. One of her arms began to cramp and she slipped further down the tube. She sawed furiously at the second screw, then the third. Her arm felt like it would tear itself to shreds any moment.

Before she could attack the last screw, her arm gave out and she crashed down onto the grille with a muffled yelp. The weakened screws gave way and the grille bent downward to spill her out onto the bed below. She bounced off the edge, and crashed to the floor below in a heap. She lay there for a few seconds and tried to catch her breath. After a quick inventory of her body, she discovered numerous spots of pain, but nothing which indicated worse than bumps and bruises. She didn't dare wait to see if anyone would come investigate the noise of her fall, and hurried to cover her tracks.

She glanced up toward the ventilation tube and realized the grille still hung from a single screw, bent at the corner. She found the multitool underneath the bed and unfolded the screwdriver tip, then climbed onto the bed and quickly removed the last screw and took the grille completely down. It left a gaping square hole in the ceiling, but it would certainly be less noticeable than the bent grille hanging by a thread.

She took stock of potential assets in the Medical wing. She knew she and Foster would need breather masks for when they blew the gas. They'd also require a supply of the reagent to negate the gas's effects so they could awaken other prison staffers.

And then Misrule began to speak over the prison intercom, and all her thoughts of strategy melted away.

Misrule said, "Officers Foster and Malone. I order you to surrender to my people. If you do not within five minutes, I will begin slaughtering one hostage every five minutes until you comply. When I run out of hostages, I will go claim your family members, one by one. If you wish all that blood on your hands then by all means, continue eluding those I have sent to collect you. I promise that if you cease your pitiful acts of resistance that you will not be killed. I give you my word: surrender, and live. Resist, and you will bear witness to the deaths of these innocents. You have four and a half minutes remaining."

It took every ounce of willpower Katie had not to run out of Medical and fling herself at Misrule's feet to beg for the lives of her mother and daughter. Nevertheless, she moved to the edge of Medical where she could peek down the short hall to the main Booking lobby. She needed to get a sense of what she fought for

—not just the lives of her family, but for Foster's boys, the other guards, Doctor Mayfair, and the mostly-unseen civilian workers who kept Deep Six running on a daily basis. She saw them, huddled together in groups, surrounded by palpable fear. But yet . . . she sensed glimpses of hope from them as well. She couldn't let those people down.

Then a voice echoed across Booking from the ruined elevator shaft, and it made her blood run cold.

"We got one of 'em!"

* * *

"Officer Timothy Foster," said Misrule as the frightened man stood before him. Misrule had appropriated the Warden's oversized chair and dark-grained desk, luxuriating in one and resting his clawed feet on the other. "I am pleased to see you have the good sense to quit when you've lost the battle. In all fairness, I must give you your due. The elevator stunt was unexpected, and it has forced me to alter my own plans."

"I aim to please." Foster tried to put on a show of bravado. "You know what they say about the best-laid plans. Mice and men, right?"

"Indeed." Misrule paged through the hard copy of Foster's personnel file, content to let the man stand nervously while he waited. Kiloton, one of Misrule's fervent supporters within the Cult, stood behind the guard. The contact blaster's hands emitted a slight glow, indicating his ability to make things he touched explode. "I see you are a parahuman, Officer Foster," said Misrule. "I am curious what being dim looks like. Please . . . indulge me."

Foster shrugged and became transparent enough that Misrule could see Kiloton behind him. "It's nothing, really. A stupid power."

"So it seems. How disappointing that you cannot turn fully invisible."

"It's a cross I have to bear."

"Your partner, Officer Malone. Where is she?"

Foster gulped and took a deep breath. "She's dead."

Misrule raised an eyebrow. He'd studied enough psychology to recognize when someone was lying to him. Foster was an excellent actor, but Misrule had caught a brief flicker of guilt on the man's face before he spoke. It might have been the guilt over a dead comrade, but Misrule doubted it. "And how did she die?"

"Napalm got her while I was wrestling Kickback," said Foster. "She used a bucket of lard or something against him. It exploded all over both of them."

"I see. And Kickback?"

Foster raised his head. "I killed him myself."

Misrule snorted. "Unlikely."

"The man was a bad fighter," said Foster. "His powers made him lazy about it. I got him in a choke hold. And I held it. He's dead."

"I see. And the bodies?"

"In the deep freeze at the back of the kitchen."

"You want me to go check that, Boss?" asked Kiloton.

Misrule didn't answer right away, instead searching Foster's face for any giveaways. "No," he said at last. "It is better we remain together as a group. Officer Foster, you may rejoin your people. I trust I shall have no further trouble from you."

Foster nodded and stepped out of the office.

"You're not going to kill him?" Kiloton's mouth dropped open. "At least let me do it, Boss. He took two of our people!"

"Perhaps," said Misrule. "But Officer Foster may yet prove useful to us. He stays alive. See to it everyone knows, lest they incur my wrath."

"Okay, Boss." Kiloton fell all over himself in his hurry to exit the office.

Misrule smiled. Kiloton was a simple man, full of simple thoughts—easily dominated and therefore the perfect soldier. He had been one of Misrule's earliest successes in recruiting and was by far the most loyal of the Cultists.

Before the office door shut once more, Misrule caught a glimpse of Brainstorm, glancing back toward him over her shoulder. Her loyalty had been purchased through seduction, and she still loved him even now, despite the things he had required her to do in his service. He knew he could rely on her to do anything he asked, no matter how despicable it might seem, so long as he continued to make her believe he loved her in return.

The loyalty of the other Cultists troubled him. T. Rex's inability to control himself was fast becoming a liability. He had been useful to Misrule in the past, but even then he'd had to keep a tight rein on the scaled man. T. Rex had joined the Cult because he liked being near power. His lusts ran deep, and what didn't express itself sexually transformed into voyeurism.

Dissident was an enigma, and Misrule had spent years trying to discover why the man had chosen to side with him. His ability to flatten to two dimensions not withstanding, Dissident was intelligent enough to see through many of Misrule's psychological ploys. And yet, for whatever reason, he chose to follow. Misrule suspected that should he find a sufficient reason, Dissident would reject the Cult out of hand to find his own path. Misrule compensated by keeping Dissident on the fringes, away from the centers of action. That way, should the man choose betrayal instead of compliance, it would cause less harm to the Cult.

The Etched Man had come out of his cell with a troubling defiant streak. He seemed as if he no longer wished to follow Misrule, and did so solely because of the breakout. The man's powers frightened Misrule, because he didn't understand them. He was one of the most powerful parahumans Misrule had encountered, with his ability to create *anything* from the magical tattoos embedded in his flesh. The Etched Man was psychologically unstable, prone to aberrant behavior, as if the disturbing images on his skin had become imprinted on his very soul. Or perhaps the opposite was the case: the man's twisted, diseased psyche expressed itself directly onto his skin, like a fruit rotting from the inside out. Whatever the case, thought Misrule, he would have to watch Etch very closely. He might have to die before the escape came to its successful conclusion.

Misrule set down Foster's personnel folder. "Your move," he whispered to the empty air of the office. Then he picked up Malone's folder and began to read it.

* * *

Doctor Mayfair stalked up the hall, followed by Black Hood, the massively-strong murderer. Katie shrank back into the shadows, afraid to move toward a better hiding place lest she be spotted.

"Where do you think you're going, Doctor?" asked the escapee.

"I'm going to check on my other patient, if you don't mind."

"I'm coming with you," said Black Hood. "No funny business."

"Suit yourself. Perhaps you'll be interested enough to take up a career in medicine whenever you finally serve your entire sentence," said Mayfair. "Geriatrics is a growing industry."

Katie bit her tongue to keep from snorting. The joke went over Black Hood's head. He followed the doctor down the hall toward Medical. As he walked past, Mayfair glanced in Katie's direction. His eyes widened as they met hers but he didn't miss a stride. He proceeded to put on a magnificent show of checking out a man lying on a gurney. Katie chewed on her knuckles as she realized the man had been in the room the entire time and could have seen everything she'd done.

"Don't touch that," growled the doctor as Black Hood picked up a piece of equipment and looked at it with curiosity. The large man set it down with a guilty look on his face.

Mayfair disconnected the monitoring computer from the man on the gurney and drew the sheet over his head.

"Why'd you do that?" asked the escapee.

Mayfair rounded on him. "Because Officer Coltrane is dead, thanks to you and your people." He stalked over and poured a cup of coffee but didn't ever raise it to his lips. He rounded on Black Hood. "None of this had to happen. None of it. Come on, let's go report yet another death to which you're an accessory."

"Huh? Me? I didn't kill him," grunted Black Hood.

"Accessory," repeated Mayfair. He marched back out of Medical and didn't glance in Katie's direction at all. Black Hood followed right after him. Katie was once more alone in Medical.

She knew Mayfair had seen her. She'd watched him like a hawk to see if he might accidentally give her away. He had pulled off the secrecy with great skill, but something didn't sit right with her nevertheless.

The coffee, she realized. Nobody in the Corrections industry ever left coffee untouched. Why would he pour it and then leave it on a table?

She poured the cup carefully out into a corner of the sink. With a quiet jingle, a set of small keys spilled out. She smiled as she realized Mayfair was a sneaky old bird. He must have had some idea of what Katie could use in Medical. She pocketed the keys and poured herself another cup. She slugged it down as quickly as she could stand it. Her stomach nearly rebelled from the sudden influx of hot, bitter liquid, but Katie needed the caffeine fix to keep going. She had been running on pure adrenaline for the past several hours and knew she was close to exhaustion.

Her stomach churned to remind her she hadn't eaten since breakfast. She then realized that probably nobody else had either. Misrule would have to allow them to eat sooner or later. Even the inmates would be getting hungry, and that would make them short-tempered and more likely to kill. She wondered if anything could be salvaged from the ruins of the kitchen. Between herself and Napalm, they had done a lot of damage to it. Katie put thoughts of food out of her mind, trying to focus on the task of finding the knockout gas.

She kept an ear out for anyone approaching from the direction of Booking as she searched through Medical. It would have been nice to find a large canister labeled *Knockout Gas* conveniently on a table but she wasn't surprised when she didn't. Using the keys Mayfair had left for her, she searched through locked cabinets, and soon found the stash of sleeper sets, each loaded with a battery and ready for use. Katie smiled, but knew they would be of no use if the escapees remained conscious.

A large bottle plastered with warning labels and a valve showed promise. She read the content label but could make no heads or tails from the complicated chemical names. She cracked the valve for a moment to make sure it had pressure. The bottle released a puff of whitish vapor. Surely a whiff couldn't knock her out. It would probably just make her a little dizzy.

As the floor rushed up at her, she knew she'd made a terrible mistake.

* * *

Misrule stepped into the Command Center. Cassie hunched down in her seat, wishing she could become invisible. The damage done by Foster to the prison's power grid had reduced the effectiveness of the air conditioning, and the ambient temperature had climbed above eighty degrees now. Cassie used her power to keep the Command Center a few degrees cooler.

"Acting Chief Warden David Prince," called Misrule. "Come here."

A stab of hatred stuck Cassie right through her heart at the mention of Prince's name. She could barely stand to look at the man as he sidled into the Center. The stress of the day's events had taken its toll on him. His hair stuck out as if he'd been grabbing handfuls of it and squeezing. A papery gray tone had come over his skin. His eyes had become hollowed and his lips webbed with dried saliva. Great circles of sweat stained his underarms and Cassie could smell the stink of it from across the Center.

"Hmmm," Misrule said at length. "You're a mess, Prince, a real disgrace to your position. Tell me, Acting Chief Warden David Prince, aren't you the least bit ashamed of yourself?"

Prince looked away and didn't answer. Cassie glanced at him sidelong. It was a strange question Misrule had asked him. And where he stood, at Misrule's side, he seemed almost like a lackey instead of a prisoner.

"Acting Chief Warden David Prince, I think it is an opportune time to request a status update from your friends on the surface."

Misrule nodded to Cassie and she opened a channel to the secure hangar six thousand feet above them. "This is Deep Six requesting Doublecharge. Please respond, over."

"I'm here," said Just Cause's leader. "What do you need?"

Misrule took the microphone away from Cassie with a polite nod. "This is Misrule. How does your search for Airlift progress?"

"It's slow," said Doublecharge. "We have people all over Amsterdam, and broadcasts are going out on all local networks, but he hasn't turned up yet. Are you sure he's even in Holland?"

"The only thing of which I am certain, Doublecharge, is that if you do not find him a great many people are going to die." Misrule's eyes narrowed.

"A show of faith on your end would go a long way toward convincing my people you're willing to work with us. I'm getting a lot of pressure from the Feds to halt the search. They say this is just a delaying tactic of yours."

"Do they?" Misrule dug his claws into the console next to him and left bright furrows in the dull finish. "I imagine that even the indentured media would have difficulty putting a positive spin on actions that allowed the deaths of twenty-four innocent hostages."

"Think of Ruby Ridge," said Doublecharge. "Or Waco. The government will risk a black eye to solve the problem you've created. Give yourselves up, Misrule. We can still end this before it gets out of hand."

"Out of hand?" roared Misrule. "I'll show you *out of hand.*" He rushed out of the Command Center. A commotion and chorale of screaming ensued from the hostages. Misrule reappeared, half-carrying and half-dragging a young Hispanic man who gibbered with fear.

"Misrule?"

Misrule shoved the microphone in the man's face. "What's your name?" he shouted.

"*No . . . no hablo ingles . . .*" Tears streamed down the frightened man's cheeks.

"*Su nombre! Cómo te llamas, hombre?*"

"Fe-Federico!"

"Doublecharge, meet Federico. Now say goodbye." With one swift motion, Misrule tore the man's throat out and splattered blood from one end of the Command Center to the other.

David Prince leaned over and vomited on his shoes. Cassie was too stunned to move, even as she felt droplets of hot blood running slow and thick down her face. Federico made a horrible gobbling noise as he died. Cassie would never forget the sound of it. Misrule dropped his grisly debris onto the floor.

"Misrule? What did you do?" asked Doublecharge, sounding panicked.

Misrule shoved the blood-streaked microphone in Cassie's face. "Tell her. Tell her what I just did."

Cassie opened her mouth but no sound came forth.

"Speak, bitch, or you're next." The look on Misrule's face said his patience had run out.

"He . . ." Cassie swallowed as her bile rose. "Federico is dead, Doublecharge. Misrule killed him."

Misrule looked satisfied at her words. "Now tell me again about things getting out of hand, Doublecharge. You're acting like you're running the show but you've got exactly shit. I'm in charge here, whether you like it or not. Who's in charge?"

"Listen, I can't—" began Doublecharge.

"Kiloton, bring me someone else. I don't care who."

"Misrule, please!"

Kiloton appeared at the doorway to the Command Center with a middle-aged woman from the kitchen staff.

"What's your name?" Misrule screamed.

"Brenda," said the woman through clenched teeth. In spite of the knowledge of certain death, she held her head high and refused to cower before the bloody killer in front of her.

"Misrule, for God's sake!" cried Doublecharge.

"Who's in charge?" he asked.

She paused before whispering, "You are."

"I didn't quite hear that."

"You are."

"That's right," he growled. "And don't you forget that." He motioned for Kiloton to take the woman away. "Now, find Airlift, and we'll see about keeping things from getting *out of hand* again. You have six hours."

"Now wait a minute," said Doublecharge. "We still have twelve from your original deadline."

Misrule smirked. "Deadline . . . such an appropriately humorous word, given the circumstances. I wonder if Federico would find it funny. Twelve hours is now too long for me to wait. You have six. It's now your move, Doublecharge. See that you don't waste it."

"All right," she said. "We'll find him."

"A wise plan." Misrule flung the microphone down and stalked out of the Command Center.

Cassie waited a few moments until she couldn't bear the sound of Federico's blood dripping onto the floor and she, too, fled the Center. None of the escapees made a move to stop her as she staggered across the floor, until her legs gave out and she fell to the floor by the surviving guards. Her hands and shoulders shook like she had palsy. Officer Foster put a comforting arm around her and she clutched at him like a drowning man to a piece of driftwood.

"You all right?" he whispered.

"No." Tears began to spill down her face.

"Hang in there. As long as we're still alive, there's hope."

"Foster, what's the current score?" asked Garcia. He was doing something with tiny, torn pieces of paper on the floor. Some were blackened with soot; others remained white.

"I don't follow you," said Foster, still holding Cassie.

Garcia pointed to the two clusters of tokens. "These are the escapees, and these are the staff. Black pieces are dead people." He paused. "These two were for you and Malone. I had you both down as alive. Is she still at large?"

Foster looked away. "She's dead," he said.

Cassie squeezed his arm. "I'm sorry," she whispered.

Suddenly one of his eyelids dropped in a very fast wink. "It's all right," he said. "I'm sure she's in a better place than the rest of us."

Cassie's eyes widened at the emphasis in his voice. If she understood his hints right, Katie Malone might still be alive. Maybe there was some hope after all. She hid her joy in case it would give something away. She wiped away her tears and looked at Garcia's chart. "So who's down among the escapees?"

Garcia ticked each one off by moving the black pieces. "Azote, Cuchillo, and Cañón died in whatever Foster did to the elevator shaft. Espada killed Pistola, and Misrule killed Sea Witch. We haven't seen Puño or Squall, so we're assuming they're dead. Misrule wouldn't have left them behind."

"You can add Napalm to that list, and Kickback," said Foster. "Although Kickback isn't dead. Unless they find him and release him, he's a non-factor."

"Fine." Garcia flipped two more pieces from the group that represented the escapees.

Cassie counted the remaining white tokens. "Twelve left, out of twenty-three. Not bad. How are we doing?"

"Coltrane and Judge are dead. We haven't seen Roggen or Pasteur, but they were in C-Wing when everything started. We think they're gone too, and you said Malone's dead. Then there's the civilian that Misrule just did."

"How can you be so cold about it?" asked Lania. "He was an innocent victim."

Garcia gave her a cold glare. "There will be time enough to mourn the dead. Right now we need to worry about staying alive. We may yet get a chance to do something." He pointed to the scraps of paper. "Twenty-three alive, six dead. We're doing better than the escapees so far."

"What about the *Last Line*?" asked Foster in a low voice.

Garcia shrugged. "It's out of our hands. We can't trigger it without the President's codes, and we couldn't reach the detonation controls even if he ordered us to."

Eaton broke into ragged giggles, and then subsided into mumbles. As Lania stroked his head, tender in spite of her containment suit, he closed his eyes to sleep.

"What's the matter with him?" asked Cassie.

"That *puta*, Whisper. She messed with his mind. I think she destroyed it. He's coming apart inside his head."

Cassie shivered at the thought of an intellect fragmented beyond repair. "I'm wiped out."

"Go ahead and sleep," said Garcia. Cassie knew he didn't sleep at all. "I'll wake you if there's a problem." He shot an evil look toward the Command Center. "I'm hoping to see some more dissension in the ranks there. It would save us a lot of trouble if they'd kill a few more of their own."

Cassie shook her head. She feared the dreams that would come to her if she did pass out. "I can't. I've got to stay in the Command Center. I can't . . . I can't let Misrule find a reason to kill someone else."

Foster put a hand on her leg. "Just a minute," he said, and called to Dissident. "Hey, if she's got to go back in there, can we at least clean the place up first?"

Dissident shrugged. "Do what you want. No funny business."

"Lania, stay with Eaton. Come on, Garcia, you and I are on mop detail. Hey, Doc? Can you give us a hand?" Foster whistled toward Doctor Mayfair, who nodded.

"Thank you," whispered Cassie, squeezing his arm.

"Just another day at the office," said Foster.

* * *

Katie lifted her head and wondered why in the world she lay on the floor. The room spun around her for a few seconds and she had to press her cheek against the cold tile floor until it stopped. An unpleasant metallic taste filled her mouth as if she'd been sucking on a dirty steel washer. She closed her eyes for a moment, and then remembered everything that had happened.

She sat bolt upright and clamped her teeth together as if doing so would help control her nausea. She couldn't believe nobody had walked in to find her there passed out on the floor. She wondered how long she'd been out. It couldn't have been more than a few minutes, considering the tiny amount of the gas she'd inhaled. She stood and her stomach flip-flopped, but being empty, she had nothing to regurgitate.

She regarded the large canister of gas and wondered how she'd manage to distribute it into Booking and the Command Center from Medical. It was powerful stuff, to be sure. She considered the notion of opening the valve and rolling it down the hallway, but dismissed that as being too obvious and easy to stop. She needed some method more subtle.

The ventilation system was the obvious answer, but going back up the shaft to the environmental systems level was out of the question, and Medical had no other exits. Whatever she did, she'd have to do it from her current location. What she really needed was a change in airflow direction, but she didn't have the slightest idea how to accomplish such a task.

Her eyes fell on Doctor Mayfair's laptop where it sat by Coltrane's covered form on the gurney. She grabbed it with the hope she wouldn't need a password to log on after awakening it from its standby state.

A standard desktop appeared, with full access to the Deep Six software package. Katie grinned. Her good luck was holding. She opened the instant messaging program and thought very carefully about how to word her request.

"We feel free when we escape—even if it be but from the frying pan to the fire."

—Eric Hoffer, American author

July, 2007
Deep Six, Montana

The Instant Messenger icon flashed on Cassie's screen. She looked around to see if anyone else noticed it. Foster, Garcia, and Doctor Mayfair had done a good job of bagging Federico's remains and cleaning up the worst of the mess. She tried not to look around lest she discover a spray of blood they might have missed. Misrule had left the Command Center for the time being and conversed with the other ex-Cultists. David Prince stood in the doorway, not quite a part of their conversation but listened in nonetheless. Cassie noticed they made no special efforts to hide anything from him, which served to further cement her suspicions of him. For the moment, though, she was not being watched. She opened the window.

ENVIRONMENTAL SYSTEMS ALERT, it said. MANUAL REROUTING OF PRISON AIRFLOW REQUIRED.

Cassie read the words twice. Foster had said Malone was dead, but it couldn't be anyone else. Everyone else was being held in Booking. The new guard must have somehow bypassed the escapees.

CONFIRMED, she typed in reply. FROM WHERE TO WHERE?

MEDICAL TO BOOKING. NOTIFY WHEN COMPLETE. The window closed.

Cassie realized what Malone intended to do. The anesthetic gas used in the cells below was stored in Medical. She must have found it and intended to distribute it through the ventilation system. She looked out at the escapees. The gas worked best in higher concentrations, which is why it was so effective in the prison cells. Booking was the single largest open space in the entire prison. She wondered if they could get the gas into Booking fast enough to have any effect before currents carried it away.

"What's up, Cassie?" David Prince's voice made Cassie jump. She never heard him come up behind her.

"N-nothing." She knew she must sound as guilty as a kid caught smoking her father's cigarettes.

"Really?" She could tell he didn't believe her.

Her mind raced, frantic to changed the subject. "Hey, I've been meaning to ask you something."

"Yes?"

"How come you're all buddy-buddy with Misrule? You've practically been in his hip pocket the entire time he's been here."

Prince opened his mouth as if to reply but no words came forth. For some reason, he jammed his hand into his pocket as if he sought solace. The watch, she thought. Something about his watch. He cleared his throat. "I'm trying to learn his plans. He doesn't seem to mind me hanging around him."

"No, I guess he doesn't, does he?" Cassie's heart felt as if it would hammer its way out of her rib cage.

"I guess not."

Prince stared at her for a long time. She returned his gaze, unwilling to back down first. "Was there something else, Acting Chief Warden?"

He spun and walked back to the Command Center door. He paused there and turned his head slightly to speak over his shoulder. "Whatever you're thinking, you should keep it to yourself, Ms. Haig. We need to remain united at a time like this." He left.

"My ass," she muttered, and typed in the commands to access the environmental control systems.

* * *

"More coffee?" Doublecharge and Crackerjack turned to see Mustang Sally holding up a thermos. The young speedster was having a harder time with the interminable wait than some of the other Just Cause heroes. Being able to run five hundred miles an hour wasn't conducive to patience.

"Not the yucky stuff from here, I hope." Doublecharge pushed her mask back and massaged her temples. Costume masks were a relic of days-gone-by, back when heroes had to hide their identities from the law as well as those they battled. Then Congress had passed the Parahuman Anti-Discrimination law and gave heroes the ability to be licensed, and some of the masks had come off. Many of the newly-legal heroes had kept their faces hidden, even when their identities had become public, as a testament to those who'd had to fight from the shadows. Even today, fifty years after a senator from Wisconsin had led the charge against the heroes of American Justice, some still wore their masks. Doublecharge remained one of those proud to cover her face.

"No, I went to a place in Billings. It's still hot." Sally cracked the thermos open and allowed the scent of mocha cappuccino to waft forth.

"You are an angel." Jack gave her his best million-dollar smile.

Doublecharge shook out her long blonde locks and nodded at Sally's bright red and yellow outfit. "I'll bet you gave them a start."

"Yeah, well." Sally shrugged. The trip to Billings and back—approaching a hundred and fifty miles—had taken her just twenty minutes. She liked Montana with its straight, flat roads where she could really get up to top speed.

"Juice called from Washington." Doublecharge sipped at the piping hot beverage. She'd succeeded him as commander of Just Cause while he'd gone to head the government's new Parahuman Resources Agency. "He says he's proud of the way we're handing things so far."

"But we haven't done anything," said Sally. "We're just sitting around here drinking coffee, waiting to see if Holland authorities can find one parahuman who may not want to be found."

Jack sipped at his own coffee, wishing he had a scone. "What else can we do? Go in?"

"Well . . . I mean . . . we're *Just Cause*. We're not supposed to just do nothing."

"Even we have limitations, Sally," said Doublecharge. "Who here could get through the reinforced blocks in the shaft?"

Sally kicked at the ground; she knew Doublecharge was right. "Did Juice say anything else?"

Doublecharge's cell phone rang. She flipped it open before the first ring stopped. "Go."

Sally watched as Doublecharge listened to whomever spoke on the other end. "Well?" she asked when the call was finished.

"They've found Airlift."

Sally's eyes widened. "Really?"

"Yes. He just teleported into a passenger lounge in O'Hare Airport in Chicago."

Jack spoke quickly into his radio. Outside, the Just Cause jet fired its VTOL engines and lifted into the air.

"He can't just 'port here?"

"No, he can only teleport to someplace he's been and knows well. Apparently he's been to Chicago several times and that's the closest he could get. We can have him here in three hours. That's faster than anybody else can."

Sally sighed as she thought of the joys of speed. "So what happens now?"

"We call Misrule, and then we wait. Things are going to happen very quickly."

"About time." Sally smiled.

* * *

"Three hours. Very good, Doublecharge. I may have underestimated your leadership abilities." Misrule picked dried blood from under his claws.

"We've done as you asked," said Doublecharge. "Now I want to see a show of good faith on your side. Release some hostages."

"Now how would I go about doing such a thing?"

"You're going to have to open the shaft eventually. Airlift can't teleport down to you."

"No, I don't suppose he can. Very well. Contact me again when he arrives and in the meantime I'll consider my next move."

Cassie could hear in his voice that he already knew precisely what he would do next. She touched the control that broke the connection.

"I won't need your professional services for the next couple hours, Cassandra. Perhaps you'd like to take a break? Have a bite to eat?" Misrule had ordered two of the escapees to escort a few of the kitchen staff upstairs to prepare some food in what remained of the kitchen. They had returned with a mass of turkey sandwiches, canned fruit cocktails, and the report of Napalm's body in the freezer. They hadn't said anything about Kickback, and Misrule didn't ask.

"No, that's all right. I'd better just stay here in case something goes wrong."

"Indeed. Acting Chief Warden David Prince seems to think you're a troublemaker."

"You trust his opinion?"

"Why should I not?"

Cassie shrugged and turned away. "He's your inside man, isn't he?"

"Perhaps."

"Well, if he is, you should think about this. He's broken one trust. What makes you think he won't break another?" She cringed and wondered if she'd just signed her own death warrant, but Misrule smiled and turned away.

"You imply I trust him at all, Cassandra. A fallacy, I assure you."

Cassie typed as fast as she could. She had managed to work out a method to alter the airflow in the prison, and she set her plan into motion.

Elsewhere in the ventilation ducts, some fans stopped blowing altogether while others increased their speed. Two reversed direction, their vanes shifting to accommodate the change in rotation.

On her screen, arrows indicating flow direction shifted. Cassie smiled and closed the environmental systems monitor window and prepared to send a new message update to Malone.

"I knew it! You traitorous bitch!"

Cassie spun around to see David Prince behind her. She screamed and scrambled up and over the console. She flopped through the broken window and dropped to the Booking floor in a heap. Heads turned to look in her direction as Prince leaned out the window and pointed at her.

"She's trying to kill us all!" he cried, his face red with growing fury.

Cassie retreated toward the surviving guards. Lania, Garcia, and Foster leaped to their feet, fists clenched, ready to defend her. The Etched Man cast a tattoo forth and suddenly her legs were entwined with a thick, gummy substance. She fell forward and shrieked as it started to ooze up her torso. Prince caught up with her and rolled her over with his foot. "Thought you'd take it into your own hands, did you? Thought maybe you'd rather die a hero?"

The stuff the Etched Man had thrown upon her constricted. She could barely breathe. "Better than living as a coward and murderer," she gasped.

Prince cocked his leg and Cassie clenched her teeth in anticipation of a hard kick, but it never landed. Garcia leaped forward, catching Prince across the face with his forearm. Foster swept Prince's legs out from under him. The Acting Warden fell next to Cassie and like her, gasped for breath.

"Woohoo, a tussle!" called T-Rex from where he rested on some chairs. "Kill that bitch and save me the best parts."

"Let her go!" Montell coasted over and tried without success to pull the twisting, constricting form away from Cassie.

The Etched Man only cackled, waved his fingers, and watched the tattoo respond to his direction.

The blood pounded in Cassie's ears as she struggled to draw in one more breath, but her chest had no more room to expand.

"Hold! Nobody move. Release her, Etch," Misrule ordered as he stepped in with Espada at one elbow and Brainstorm at the other.

"Release her, Etch," repeated the tattooed man under his breath and glared at Misrule from under his lowered lids. The restricting tattoo flowed away from her like fog from a river and wrapped itself back around one of the Etched Man's legs.

"Now, Acting Chief Warden David Prince, what is the meaning of this outburst?"

Prince got to his feet. Blood streamed from his nose and he spat out a tooth. "She . . . she had a schematic open. On her computer."

"A schematic," said Misrule in an ugly tone.

"Of the prison," said Prince. "She was doing something. I'll bet she was trying to set off the *Last Line*, but she can't without the President's code."

Garcia's eyes widened. "Oh goddamn, will you shut the fuck up already?"

Misrule was very still, and a cold fire burned in his dark eyes. "*Last Line* . . . A last line of defense, perhaps? What would that be, Prince?"

Cassie coughed as she tried to draw a breath. She caught the subtle change in Misrule's attitude toward Prince.

Prince shot a triumphant glance at Garcia. "It's a nuke. Under the prison. If she sets it off, we all die."

"There is a nuclear device here? And you didn't think to tell me that? You didn't think that constituted *need-to-know information*?"

"Why would he tell you?" shouted Garcia.

Cassie wheezed, "He's the insider. He killed the Warden."

Garcia lunged forward for Prince's throat. Prince jammed his hand into his pocket, withdrew his watch, and disappeared.

* * *

David Prince—Stopwatch—panicked. He stepped into the space between seconds, but knew he had already used two hundred seconds within the past day and probably only had a minute or maybe two before his power failed. And where could he go? Misrule had promised him a spot in the new Cult of Destruction, but the chances of that seemed remote now. He wondered if he had enough time to get sleeper sets on all the escapees but dismissed it as impossible. Whatever he was going to do, standing in Booking wasn't going to help him.

He ran toward Medical. Maybe he could start injecting random stuff into the escapees. It had worked on Silbersack. He doubted the hostages would accept him, now that they knew his secret. Although . . . if he could bring an end to the jailbreak, he might be able to sway sympathy in a court of law. He could say he'd been under psionic compulsion. The defense was rare because of the difficulty in proving it, but given his close contact with numerous parahumans, it might be his only chance.

He skidded to a stop. Someone was already in Medical. Stopwatch's eyes widened as he recognized Officer Malone. The woman had fastened a length of rubber tubing to the nozzle of a large gas cylinder and was frozen in the process of feeding it up into a ventilation shaft. Stopwatch changed his mind; Malone was half responsible for the destruction of the elevator and the deaths of several of the escapees. Misrule was known to be generous to those who assisted him, and enjoyed his vengeance on those who interfered with his devious plans. If Stopwatch could take down Malone, Misrule might forgive him for failing to disclose the existence of the *Last Line*.

Time snapped back, two minutes early by Stopwatch's count, and Malone began to feed the line upward once more, oblivious to the man who stood behind her. Stopwatch knew he had perhaps only seconds before Misrule's people found him here. Barely daring to breathe, he wrapped his fingers around a wheeled IV stand nearby. He raised it and wound up for a home run swing at Malone's head.

* * *

Katie froze as she saw a distorted reflection in the cylinder of someone behind her. She spun around and raised an arm in defense just in time to deflect a heavy blow that would have knocked her brains out of her skull. She tumbled across a table through a bank of beakers. The pain made her see double—an astonishing vision of two David Princes attacking her. The Acting Warden's face had

171

transformed into something ugly and hateful, and he rushed at Katie, bloodlust in his eyes.

Katie scrambled backward and rolled to one side just as Prince brought the IV stand down in an overhead swing that cracked the tile. She lashed out with a foot and caught Prince just under the kneecap. The man grunted and leaped back out of range. Katie clambered to her feet and dodged as Prince lunged again and again at her with the hooked end of the stand. She saw an opening and caught the stand under her good arm and shoved herself backward. Her body weight yanked it right out of Prince's hands.

Prince's eyes widened as Katie jabbed the stand into his belly like a spear, then popped it upward to catch him under the chin. He staggered and she smashed the end into his face. Blood poured from his forehead and he started to fall before he caught himself on the gas canister.

Heavy footsteps approached from Booking. Katie glanced around for someplace to hide. She dove underneath the gurney which held Coltrane's body.

The door to Medical crashed open and Misrule rushed in, followed by Kiloton and Brainstorm. Misrule's eyes narrowed as he saw Prince by the gas bottle. "What do we have here?" he said, his voice oily like a diplomat's.

"It was Malone!" cried Prince as he wiped blood from his eyes. "She's alive! She's here. She was going to gas us all. I stopped her."

"Was she." Misrule glanced to either side. "I do not see her. Neither did I pass her in the hall. Perhaps there is another exit from Medical?"

"No, but—"

"Perhaps she turned invisible, or slipped through a crack in the floor."

"Look at my face! You think I did this to myself?"

"You could have."

"The gurney! She's underneath it! She's got to be!" screamed Prince.

"Indeed?" Misrule bent down to look beneath the bed.

Katie held her breath and prayed her muscles wouldn't give out. Instead of staying underneath the gurney, she had wedged an arm and leg underneath Coltrane's sheet-covered body and hung off the edge. She braced herself up with her other leg and hand and hid alongside the mattress. It was an obvious hiding place, she thought. Nobody in their right mind would try such a stunt.

"I see nobody," said Misrule, and stood. He stalked toward Prince. Kiloton flanked the Assistant Warden while Brainstorm stood ready by the hallway.

"She's got to be here. I swear to God she was just here." Prince blubbered.

"I'll tell you what I think," whispered Misrule. "I think Cassandra was right to remind me that a traitor cannot be trusted. I think it was you all along who intended to use the gas."

"No, it's not like that at all."

Misrule leaned down, his face only inches away from Prince's. "Would you have killed us all in our sleep? Claimed sole credit for containing the escape?"

"Please, oh God, I don't want to die." Prince groveled.

"How could I ever turn my back on you after this?"

"I wouldn't . . . I won't ever do anything to you."

A wet, popping sound echoed through Medical.

Katie nearly cried out in terror at the noise.

"No, you won't."

Misrule straightened, his hand buried deep in Prince's chest. Prince made a peculiar grunt and a trickle of blood leaked from the corner of his mouth. With a twist of his wrist, Misrule pulled his fist clear, clutched in it a piece of muscular tissue which dripped with gore. He flung it aside and it splattered against the wall.

"Leave me," said Misrule. Brainstorm and Kiloton hurried from the room. Prince's body fell to the floor, a look of horror frozen on his face. Blood gurgled out of the gaping hole in his chest where his heart had been, and spread across the tiled floor.

Katie held her breath for fear Misrule might hear her.

"Officer Katherine Malone," rumbled Misrule, and Katie nearly squeaked in surprise. He couldn't possibly see her . . . could he? "I presume you are still here. I do not believe that Prince had the brain capacity to formulate a plan such as this. He was a tool, and like so many others, outlived his usefulness to me. You, on the other hand . . . I've read your file. Throughout your career, you have displayed initiative, creativity, and a propensity to solve problems. Admirable traits."

He didn't move while he spoke, as if he didn't care whether he found Katie or not. It was like he trusted his voice and words to bring about the results he desired.

"Because I too admire those traits, and you have impressed me with your efforts to stop me thus far, I am going to offer you a proposal. My minions and I will be leaving this facility shortly. You will remain behind. I believe you will cause me further difficulties should you manage to accompany us on the next leg of our journey. I will not tolerate that. I promise you that if you do, I will seek out your mother and your daughter and exact my revenge against them. And then I will proceed to slaughter everyone I can in their proximity until I feel sated. You I will leave alive as a witness. If you wish to surrender to me now, I give you my word I will not harm you."

He waited by the doorway. Tears leaked out of Katie's eyes. She knew he calculated his words to cause such an effect, but she couldn't bring herself to surrender. Her sense of duty outweighed her fear. She remained hidden, muscles aching.

"Very well," said Misrule at last. "Perhaps I misjudged you. Or perhaps Officer Foster spoke the truth that you are in fact dead, and I am truly speaking to an empty room.

Nevertheless . . . No further problems. I will kill your loved ones, and I will kill many innocents, and their blood will be on your hands, Officer Malone."

He left Medical.

Katie swore to herself in that moment that one way or another, Misrule would not survive the breakout. Not after he'd threatened her mother, and her daughter.

Even if she had to kill him herself.

* * *

Cassie's eyes fell on Misrule's blood-soaked hand, and she couldn't look away. The congealing gore on his skin didn't seem to bother him in the least. She tried to scoot away as he approached, and squeaked in fear when she backed into Black Hood.

"Congratulations, Cassandra. I've just arranged for your promotion." Misrule extended his clean hand down to her in an offer to help her stand.

She struggled to her feet without his assistance. "Promotion?" she asked, afraid she already knew the answer from the fresh blood upon his hand.

Misrule's teeth were shocking white amid the dark red of his face. "As this facility is under my control, it falls to me to hire and fire as I see fit. David Prince has been fired. I have selected you as the best candidate to replace him from the current pool of applicants. You are now Acting Chief Warden."

"Oh." Cassie felt very small. "What . . . what do you want me to do?"

"At the moment, if you would simply contact our friend Doublecharge, it would suffice admirably."

Cassie walked with heavy feet toward the Command Center. She had mixed feelings about David Prince's death. Certainly he had committed an unspeakable act with his willful assassination of Warden Silbersack. And yet, he had been corrupted by this monster that stood behind her as he waited for her to establish the connection. She doubted

Prince ever could have become a killer without Misrule's sly goading.

"Misrule," said Doublecharge. "Airlift is here."

"Ahead of schedule again," said Misrule. "Very good. I would like to speak to him."

There was a pause, and then a new voice with a thick accent came over the speaker. "This is Airlift. What do you want?"

"You will teleport a group away from here."

"What if I do not?"

"Then I will kill everyone down here. And then I'll come find you and let you watch while I slaughter everyone you know, everyone you love."

"You would not dare!"

"Don't try me," said Misrule. "I have no compunctions about demonstrating my willingness to slay."

"I cannot teleport down to you. I have not been there."

"I would be surprised if you had. We will come to you."

"Okay."

Doublecharge took up the conversation once more. "Misrule, we've gone out of our way to provide what you asked. Now you need to give some consideration to us. Release some hostages."

"Perhaps in time, Doublecharge. For the moment I am quite content for them to remain here with me. I do believe in giving fair trade value, though, so I will offer up this choice bit of information. The party responsible for the death of Warden Silbersack was none other than the Assistant Warden, David Prince."

Doublecharge snorted. "I doubt that."

"Last year, Mr. Prince received a payment of one million U.S. dollars into an account with a private bank in the Cayman Islands." Misrule rattled off a fifteen-digit number from memory. "I advanced those funds to him as payment for his services."

"You could have set that account up in his name yourself," said Doublecharge.

"True, but in fact he gave the number to me. I'm certain you can verify information with the bank in your own time."

"It's not enough, Misrule. You've got to give up some people."

Misrule sighed. "Very well. Tell Airlift to prepare for us to receive him. I will release four hostages. The number is not negotiable."

"Would you consider a trade?"

Misrule raised an eyebrow. "A trade of what and for what?"

"For hostages," said Doublecharge. "I will give up any and all members of Just Cause, including myself, as your prisoners in exchange for the remaining hostages."

"You're rather free with the lives of your team, aren't you?" Misrule threw his head back and laughed. "I wonder if they'd feel differently if you discussed it with them first. What kind of fool do you take me for, Doublecharge? I don't believe for a minute that we could hold you and your team, any more than you could hold me."

"Think it over, Misrule. You'd have us, the group who took apart your vaunted Cult of Destruction. Isn't that tempting?"

"You'll forgive my lack of enthusiasm at the prospect. I believe there are only three of you remaining from the pre-September Eleventh team. It wouldn't be nearly as satisfying."

Cassie recalled that Just Cause used to be headquartered in one of the World Trade Center towers, and more than half of the team perished in the attacks.

"Think it over," said Doublecharge.

"Oh, I have. And I'm not interested. I have another agenda entirely, and dealing with parapowered prisoners of my own is not part of it." Misrule looked down at Cassie. "Clear the shaft."

"I'll do my best," she said. "But I don't know what kind of damage it has sustained."

"What was that?" said Doublecharge. "I didn't hear."

"The elevator has been damaged," said Misrule. "We will ascend by other means."

"Such as?"

"It will be a surprise." Misrule broke the connection.

* * *

In the main shaft, motors spun to life and transmissions whined as they struggled to move the massive blocks of stone clear. Cassie monitored the process from her board. Her heart thudded as the lowest block grated to a halt for several seconds before lurching the remaining yards back into the side wall of the shaft. The two minutes it took the blocks to shift were the longest of her life. In the end, each block lay nestled back in its niche.

"Should I try the elevator?" she asked Misrule.

"No, Cassandra," he said. "I believe The Etched Man will once again provide a solution. Come." He held out a hand to her. She refused to take it, but stood and followed him from the Command Center. The way he had risen to meet every challenge and obstacle without losing sight of his eventual goal was impressive. She could see how he attracted such a following. He was a natural leader, and it was too bad he'd chosen to waste those talents as a criminal.

She wondered what he really wanted from her.

Then she wondered how much longer he would keep her alive.

"Breaks balance out. The sun don't shine on the same ol' dog's rear end every day."
   —Darrell Royal, University of Texas Longhorns football coach

July, 2007
Deep Six, Montana

Escudo wrapped himself, Kiloton, and the Etched Man in his force field. Misrule pointed to the surviving guards. "You four. Your services as hostages will no longer be required. You will accompany my people to the surface. Count yourselves fortunate that, for now, you get to live."

Foster looked at Garcia, and Lania, who still held the catatonic Eaton. "You'd better go," he told the Guatemalan woman. "And take him."

"Why me?" Tiny sparks shot from Lania's eyes.

"Your suit will need recharging soon," said Garcia. "If it runs out of juice, it doesn't really matter what happens to the rest of us."

Foster turned to face Misrule. "Send one of the civilians instead of me, Misrule." Cassie's heart caught in her throat.

"Yeah, me too," said Garcia.

Misrule snorted. "Your chivalry is antiquated. I'm giving you the opportunity to return to your families."

Foster shook his head. "Take a civilian. This isn't part of their jobs."

"Neither is it yours. However . . ." Misrule's eyes narrowed and Cassie realized he'd had an idea. "Very well, I accede to your request. Officer Garcia, though, does not intrigue me in the least." Misrule directed his attention toward the Hispanic man. "Stay if you wish, but I will not replace your vacancy with someone else."

"Go," said Foster. "We'll be all right."

Garcia clasped the other guard's hand. "Good luck, Foster. We'll send out the cavalry just as soon as we can."

"I know."

Garcia walked over to stand beside Lania, who carried Eaton like a baby against the bulky shoulder of her suit. Black tendrils drifted from within Escudo's force field and the Etched Man directed a tattoo as a platform. It lifted them into the air and walked on tentacles that belonged on ghostly jellyfish.

Misrule and Black Hood wrenched the remains of the elevator out of the way. The inky tattoo crawled and slithered across the floor and began to flow up the shaft on a fibrous black web.

* * *

While everyone's attention was focused on the departing group of escapees and guards, Katie lunged out of a shadow, grabbed one of the civilian hostages, and dragged her back into the shadowed corridor leading to Medical.

"You'll thank me for this later," whispered Katie in her ear as she sprayed a puff of anesthetic gas into the woman's face from a small aerosol can she'd found in Medical. The woman succumbed to unconsciousness immediately. Katie stripped off the woman's coveralls and shrugged into the sky-blue one-piece that was the standard garment for civilian employees. She spread soot across her cheeks, nose, and forehead, which darkened her skin. Then she pulled a mixture of sooty water through her hair, wincing at the thought of what it might take to remove it later. When she finished, her hair looked kinkier and much darker. She dragged the woman down the hall into Medical, heaved the woman up onto a bed and tossed a sheet over her.

Nobody noticed when Katie slipped back into Booking. She opened the door to the bathroom then shut it. Anyone who glanced in her direction would have assumed she was exiting the bathroom. She walked across the room with the trudging lope of one who felt hopeless. She took care to walk across Foster's field of vision and checked to see if he noticed her, but his attention stayed fixed upon the elevator shaft. Katie sat down by herself on a chair, resting her elbows on her knees and her chin on her palms.

She needed a plan.

* * *

"I've got movement in the shaft," said Jack, looking up from his motion sensors and cameras. "Something's coming up, and it's not the elevator." He pulled his light intensification goggles over his face and peeked over the lip of the shaft. "Can't see what it is. It's dark. Coming up fast, though." He pulled his pistol from its holster.

"All right, everyone, look sharp," said Doublecharge. "Nobody moves without my direct order. That means you, Jack. Keep your safety on."

Jack muttered something under his breath. Once they'd confirmed the stone blocks had been removed, he'd suggested he could go down the shaft himself with a canister of the anesthetic gas, trusting to his total invulnerability to keep him alive. The idea of a six-thousand foot BASE jump without a chute into darkness exhilarated him, but Doublecharge had nixed the idea, saying they couldn't risk accidentally setting off the device Misrule purported to have on him.

Mustang Sally waited as patiently as possible for a speedster and hugged herself as her fingers tapped in a blur on her arms. Her huge fiancé, Mastiff, stood beside her. He cracked his knuckles, his muscles barely contained by his gray-and-brown bodysuit. Far above them, Desert Eagle perched on a support beam of the hangar. The winged Amerindian woman had the eyesight of her namesake and could see the platform as it rose up the shaft far more clearly than even Jack with his cutting-edge technology. "Twenty seconds," she reported into her throat microphone. "I count seven . . . Kiloton, Etched Man, and Escudo plus four hostages. One looks like that antimatter guard in her containment suit." Desert Eagle undid the flaps on her holsters, ready to pull her customized .50-caliber pistols at a moment's notice.

"Roger that," said Doublecharge. "Stand by, everyone." She looked over the youngest members of her team, rookies by any stretch of the imagination, wishing she could imbue them with the kind of courage that only came with experience. Ment, slender and wrapped in a long black trenchcoat, needed no weapons besides his psionic abilities. Condensation swirled around the feet of Snowball, the genetic dwarf with frost powers; she seemed especially nervous. Her friend Minerva placed a comradely hand on her shoulder, keeping the other on the sword she'd inherited from her grandmother Lady Athena, who had co-founded Just Cause. Carver, resplendent in red and purple, cut parallel stripes in the floor with the high-speed vibrations of his fingers, and Octane paced back and forth as his shiny black flesh flowed like liquid vinyl.

They were the greatest heroes in the world, and they quaked in their boots with fear.

Beyond the heroes, the topside security forces of Deep Six stood their ground, with ultratasers and assault rifles, riot shields and helmets.

The group from below rose out of the shaft, borne on a swirling, smoky platform that caused headaches in anyone who stared at it for too long. The Etched Man grinned at them from behind Escudo's force field. "Airlift, come," he called in his high-pitched voice.

"Release the hostages first." Doublecharge hovered several feet in the air to get a better vantage point.

"I want to see him," said the Etched Man.

Airlift stepped out from behind a couple of security men. He was a small, unassuming man dressed in an expensive Italian suit with wraparound sunglasses and black leather gloves. "I am here," he said in his thick Dutch accent.

"You two, get off." Kiloton pointed to Lania, who still carried the hapless Eaton. He turned to Doublecharge. "You get the others once Airlift is here."

Lania moved beyond the first cordon of guards with her burden and was whisked away to safety by Ment's telekinetic abilities.

Airlift stepped across the open space between the guards and the shaft entrance. Kiloton kept moving, trying to look in all directions at once. "Keep your distance," he warned. "Or I start blowing people up in groups."

Tension levels rose quickly throughout both groups. Jack stood up, his hands well away from his weapons. "Kiloton? Man, you look like shit. Prison's not been good to you."

Doublecharge almost jumped down Jack's throat, but suddenly Kiloton focused solely on him, and she realized the canniness of Jack's strategy. The escapee was on a hair-trigger, and could kill a lot of people if he chose. Jack could prevent that occurrence by keeping Kiloton's attention on him.

"Crackerjack?" said Kiloton. "I can't believe you're still hanging around this group of losers."

Jack smiled. "The hours are good, and you can't beat the benefits. And I love the attention."

"I should have killed you when I had the chance." Kiloton licked his lips.

"Buddy, you never had the chance. Maybe you hadn't heard. I'm immune to explosions like yours."

"You haven't experienced mine," said Kiloton, his eyes narrow.

"Remind me to tell you about the time I dropped out of a plane without a chute. You wouldn't believe the mess I made when I hit."

Airlift made it to the floating tattoo platform and Escudo expanded his force field to encompass the Dutch teleport. The Etched Man gestured and the shifting base of the platform dumped Garcia and the civilian to the floor of the hangar.

"Another time, Crackerjack," said Kiloton.

"Count on it."

The platform descended into the shaft, nearly as fast as if it had fallen.

Doublecharge breathed out a sigh of relief that the situation hadn't gotten out of hand. "Get those people to debriefing right away," she said. "I want to know everything that's going on down there."

* * *

The escapees descended on the cloud of the Etched Man's mobile tattoo like actors riding a giant floating moon in a Broadway musical production. Katie watched them file out of the elevator shaft, their feet surrounded by tendrils of ink that flowed back onto the Etched Man's skin. Lania, Eaton, Garcia, and the civilian were gone, replaced by a small man with light blond hair pulled back into a short, severe ponytail. He looked around with distaste at the damage done to the Booking lobby. He seemed loath to touch anything and kept his arms and gloved hands close to his sides.

Katie moved behind Foster. "Don't worry, *señor* . . . I'm sure everything will be *muy bueno*." She spoke with a bad movie-villain Spanish accent.

Foster turned and saw her. His eyes widened but he bit down on his tongue to keep from saying anything that could get them both killed. "It's all right, Miss. We won't let anything happen to you."

"*Muchos gracias,*" she said.

"For Christ's sake, don't overdo it," grumbled Doctor Mayfair as he stalked past her toward Airlift.

Katie's mouth dropped open for a moment. Then she shut it with an audible snap and sat down, her pride deflated.

"And here you are at last, *Mijnheer de Lift van de Lucht,*" Misrule said with a wry smile. "I am pleased you chose to join our little party."

"I am only here because I wish nobody to be hurt," said the man in his nearly-impenetrable accent.

"And if you do as you are told, nobody will be. If you deviate from following my orders . . ." Misrule didn't finish his sentence, but the implication that Airlift's life was at stake was clear.

Airlift nodded in understanding. "You wish to leave here. To where?"

"I am given to understand you can only teleport to someplace with which you are familiar. Is that correct?"

"*Ja.*"

"And am I correct in assuming Just Cause has a special location where they wish you to bring us?"

Airlift didn't reply, but bowed his head slightly, his cheeks flushed.

"Come now, you didn't really expect me to fall for such a simple plan, did you?" Misrule shook his head. "Espada, search him."

The bloodthirsty woman grinned as she turned one of her arms into a sword. "With pleasure. You want to do this the easy way or the hard way?"

"No! Don't touch me!" Airlift backed away.

Misrule dropped a heavy hand onto Airlift's shoulder and held him so that the smaller man couldn't twist away. "She won't hurt you. Do you hear me, Espada? Do not hurt this man."

Espada licked her lips and ran the flat of her sword-arm along Airlift's neck. He stiffened like he might scream.

"Oh, for God's sake, Misrule. Stop teasing him and tell him where you want to go!" cried Cassie.

Misrule spun around. She stood her ground, her arms folded, and glared up at him in righteous fury. "You're right, Acting Chief Warden Cassandra Haig. How callous of me to simply use people for my own amusement. I am properly chastised."

Several of the escapees broke into rude laughter as Misrule bowed his head in mock shame. "I will be exceedingly disappointed in Doublecharge if she has not given you a global tracking device, Airlift. Surrender it to me now."

Airlift reached into a pocket and withdrew a small object the size of a cell phone. He dropped it into Espada's outstretched hand. She looked at it, shrugged, and passed it to Misrule, who squeezed it into tiny pieces.

"Now, you are no doubt familiar with my fellow prisoner, Whisper." Misrule held out his hand to the psionic assassin.

"Devil spawn!" spat Airlift. Whisper had been convicted for the killing of a German diplomat and her family in Washington DC. Germany had permitted the trial to take place in the United States. The trial had been a sensational media event, and Whisper was vilified throughout Europe.

"No need to be impolite," said Misrule. "However, she will ensure that you do not take it upon yourself to be disobedient. Do I make myself clear?"

Airlift nodded, not taking his eyes off the dark-haired woman who could kill with a thought.

"Fine. I'm glad we've reached this understanding. You are, of course, familiar with Berlin. You will transport everyone within this room to Tegel International Airport."

Katie and Foster glanced at each other.

Airlift looked horrified. "No!"

"I'm going to give you the option to reconsider your answer, and if it hasn't changed, I will tear off your arm," said Misrule. "And if you still haven't changed your mind after that, I'll take the other."

Katie clenched her fists and wished she could do something—anything—to stop Misrule.

Tears streamed down Airlift's cheeks. His eyes turned away from Whisper to the shiny black object which protruded from Misrule's chest.

"You needn't concern yourself with this." Misrule tapped his chest for emphasis. "As long as things go as planned, it will remain where it is. If things go awry, well . . ." He smiled. "You won't need to worry about it then either."

* * *

"He's got an army, a weapon of mass destruction, and a plan to get them out," said Lania. Her suit was plugged into a high-voltage power line that a Montana Power serviceman had run over from the main branch. It was a miracle of post-modern engineering: a containment suit that could safely hold her antimatter body. Even so, Jack felt uneasy around the woman who could accidentally blow a hole in the U.S. the size of Iowa. He wondered if even his invulnerability would be proof against such a blast.

"And what is he planning to do?" Doublecharge had pulled down her mask at last, irritated by the dusty Montana climate, and revealed the face of a woman in her mid-30s who'd seen far more combat and destruction than anybody should. Her eyes were dark blue and had a fine network of lines from stress and age around them. She didn't smile often and laughed even less.

"I don't know." Garcia sat hollow-eyed next to Lania. "But he killed anyone who didn't accept his plan." He swallowed and grimaced. "There are a lot of dead people down there." Only he and Lania remained in debriefing. The civilian had been cleared to leave and was being taken home to his family. Eaton was on a helicopter heading for St. Vincent's Hospital in Billings. Because of the damage Whisper had done to his brain, he'd had to be sedated and restrained.

Jack finished listing the escapees on a large pad of paper. "Can you tell me who among the escapees is dead?" he asked, pen poised to scratch out names.

Lania and Garcia together managed to come up with a complete list of the ten escapees they knew or believed to be dead: five by Misrule's or Espada's hands, and five by Officers Malone and Foster.

"Malone and Foster?" asked Jack in surprise. "Wait a second. We've looked at their personnel files. Yes, they're both parahumans, but at almost nonexistent levels. How could they take down five high-powered baddies on their own?"

"I don't know about Kickback and Napalm, but they set off some kind of bomb that took out the other three, as well as the elevator," said Lania.

"Amazing." Doublecharge shook her head. "And they're still below?"

"Foster is," said Garcia. "But Malone is dead."

"Is she? I'm not so sure." Lania looked thoughtful behind the faceplate of her helmet. "We only have Foster's word on that, and he may be protecting her. She could still be sneaking around."

"All right. You two have had a busy day, and I'm sure you'd like to rest and recuperate," said Doublecharge.

Garcia shrugged. "I don't sleep. Some coffee and sandwiches and I'm good to go. I'd like to stick around. Maybe I can help out somehow. I'm not an A-list para, but I am a guard at Deep Six, and that ought to count for something."

Lania nodded. "I'm stuck in this suit until full power is back on downstairs anyway. There's a room-sized magnetic bottle around my quarters. I might as well stay here."

"Do you need to eat or anything?" asked Jack.

"No. The only nourishment I need is electrical energy." Lania's voice turned wistful. "Although I long for the day someone invents an antimatter pizza."

A unit on Jack's vest beeped. He read the information on the display. "Airlift's GPS beacon is no longer transmitting."

Doublecharge nodded. "We expected that," she said to Lania and Garcia. "But we're hoping he hasn't got the ability to detect or eliminate the other beacon."

Garcia raised an eyebrow. "Another beacon?"

Doublecharge and Jack led them from the break room that she was using as a temporary office back out onto the hangar floor. The youngster Ment sat upright at the edge of the elevator shaft. His shiny black trench coat spread out behind him like a puddle of oil. His dark glasses were pushed up on top of his head, hair sticking out wildly around the edges of the lenses. His eyes were closed and his brow furrowed in concentration.

Minerva sat patiently by his side and stroked one of his arms in a slow, intimate manner. She carried the sense about her of being at peace with the world and completely in control of herself.

"They haven't found my brainhack," murmured Ment without opening his eyes. "I don't think they can, and they don't have anyone to break it if they do. Psionic halo is building, though. I think he's getting ready to teleport."

"Stay on him, Ment," said Doublecharge. "I want to know the exact location when they arrive."

"Here we go." Ment's voice rose in pitch with excitement. "The window's opening in five . . . four . . . three . . . two . . . one!"

Everyone around Ment and Minerva tensed as if they expected something grandiose. Instead, the only noticeable effect was that Ment's sunglasses cracked and their lenses tinkled to the cement around him.

"Did they teleport out? Have you got a fix on him?" asked Doublecharge.

"Yes. Not yet. I'm tracing the line." Ment leaned back to lie face-up on the cement floor, his arms straight out from his sides as if he were being crucified.

Minerva lay next to him, resting on one elbow and looking down at him. "It might be awhile," she said, knowing that Ment's speech centers no longer functioned as he devoted every spare neuron to finding the psionic tracer he'd laid on Airlift's brain.

TWELVE

"I tried to go as long as I can and as hard as I can. But I put my team in a deep hole early and that was it."

—*Jason Marquis, MLB pitcher*

July, 2007
Deep Six, Montana

The hostages and escapees watched as Airlift cleared a space in the middle of the Booking floor. The escapees seemed nervous and on edge now that they were on the verge of getting out of Deep Six, some for the first time in twelve years.

"Everyone stand in this area here," said Airlift at last, placing himself in the center of the open space.

"Do we need to touch you or hold hands or anything weird like that?" asked Dissident.

"No."

The hostages, resigned now to their fates for better or worse, moved to the center area, watched closely by the escapees. Katie stayed next to Foster amid the huddled group. She took his hand in hers, and he squeezed back, full of strength and reassurance.

In the center of the group, Airlift took a deep breath and held it in concentration. The air around them seemed to thicken as time slowed down to a crawl. Airlift's body became limned in pure white light. The light flowed out from him like a thick liquid. It enveloped those closest to him and blocked them from sight. Katie tried to shrink away from it as it touched her, but she had frozen in place. The bright whiteness covered her and it dulled all of her senses. She couldn't see anything but white. She heard nothing—not even her own blood as it pounded in her ears. She couldn't feel Foster's hand in hers, but she knew it was there, and that comforted her.

The bright light around her transformed into a light pink then deepened further into red. The light passed through the colors of the rainbow until moving beyond a purple too dark to distinguish from black. The absolute darkness engulfed her and she was totally alone—a single star in a silent universe. Then the blackness pulled away from her and the others, and her senses returned. The darkness shrank back into Airlift and then time snapped back to full speed again.

Nausea clawed at Katie's throat. Several of the hostages as well as Dissident and Black Hood fell to the tiled floor and retched. Katie blinked in surprise as she realized they had left the Deep Six Booking Lobby.

They had arrived in a large concourse lined with glass windows, beyond which Katie could see the lights of a major airport and past that, those of a large city at night. It had been late afternoon when they left, so she guessed it was early morning in Berlin, if that was in fact where they were. Only a few people moved through the concourse—late-night travelers, crew members, and several janitors who cleaned windows and vacuumed the carpeting. Everyone stopped what they were doing to stare at the ragtag group that had appeared out of nowhere.

Misrule looked at the gate number, frowned, and turned to the nearest person, a mustachioed man who wore coveralls and held a squeegee and bucket. "You. Where are we? *Wo sind wir?*"

"B-Berlin," stuttered the man, wide-eyed as he looked up at the red-skinned giant.

"*Wo in Berlin? Tegel Flughafen?*"

"*Ja.*"

Misrule looked around. People milled about, uncertain what to do. One man spat out rapid-fire German into his cell phone. Misrule filled his lungs and bellowed, "Run away if you want to live! *Laufen Sie weg, wenn Sie leben möchten! Laufen Sie!*"

The man with the mustache didn't hesitate. He dropped his squeegee and bucket and ran like his coveralls were on fire. Others didn't move immediately. Misrule frowned at their hesitation. "Etch, encourage them."

"Etch, encourage them," muttered the sullen Etched Man. Then he cackled with glee and tore monstrous animation after monstrous animation from his skin and hurled them at the civilians. As the horrible and vile creatures pursued them, the airport denizens screamed and ran. A few couldn't outrun the apparitions and fell. The shadow creatures savaged them with tendrils like flexible knife blades, cutting wherever they contracted.

Misrule ignored the sounds of torment behind him to face Airlift. "And now, as I promised, you will have nothing to worry about." He bowed his head in a slight nod and a sly smile spread across his face.

"What?" asked Airlift.

A moment later, one of Espada's sword-arms popped out through the teleport's chest, streaked with gore and tissue. He looked shocked and affronted for a moment and then vanished with a soft inrush of air. Espada stood behind where he'd been with a predatory grin on her face, Airlift's blood and entrails dripping from her arm-blade.

"Hey, where'd he go?" asked Dissident.

"Somewhere to finish dying. It does not matter," said Misrule. "Collect the hostages. We move out now. Prepare for a running fight. Our destination is a cargo hangar where I have secured transport."

"About time," grunted White Dragon in his Southern twang. His body twisted, reshaped, lengthened, as he transformed into his namesake: a fifteen-foot-long white-scaled dragon. He unfurled his segmented wings and blew a small puff of flame from his gaping jaws like a pilot clearing the guns. His platinum-colored claws raked furrows in the carpeting and his tail flipped a row of chairs across the open concourse.

Nightmare shrugged and discarded her human aspect in favor of her natural state of a demonic horse. Hostages shied away from her and she snorted in disgust at them. Dissident flattened onto a paper-thin two-dimensional representation of himself. Heretic became a roughly-human-shaped shadow who could envelop a victim and drain them of life like a proverbial vampire. And Espada, of course, already had her arms transformed and was looking around, eager for a new victim.

T-Rex threw off Black Hood's support and grunted with discomfort at his injuries. "'Bout time we had us a real fight. I got me some mighty bad frusterashuns to work out."

None of the other escapees needed to alter themselves to use their powers. They bullied the twenty remaining hostages into a tight block. Escudo extended his force field around them, not to safeguard them but to keep them close. Misrule hurled a ticket counter through the double-paned glass of the concourse. "Etch, a stairway, if you please."

"Etch, make a stairway. Etch, make an elevator," whined the tattooed man. "Do this, do that." A twisted, spiral staircase formed from smoky inkblots and the escapees moved down it to the tarmac.

"Dragon, give us air cover as we move. Hood, you and Rex secure that baggage train and we'll use it."

Misrule pointed at a parked tractor with several empty trailers behind it.

Katie noticed flashing lights in the distance and nudged Foster. Several vehicles approached across the field, police or security forces by the look of them.

"*Halt!*" cried a voice from above. Everyone turned to see three airport security guards who stared down through the shattered window at them, pistols leveled.

Misrule sighed and glanced toward the Etched Man for a moment. The skeletally-thin man glared back at him almost in open defiance as if he dared Misrule to order him about once more. Katie held her breath as she wondered if things would finally come to a head between them, but then Misrule backed down, much to her surprise. She saw something in his eyes that could only have been fear. He turned to Black Hood. "Hood, deal with this."

"About damn time." Black Hood wrenched the last cart loose from the baggage train.

"*H-halt! Bewegen Sie nicht!*" shouted one of the guards.

Black Hood twisted around once like an Olympic hammer-thrower and hurled the empty cart at the side of the concourse. The guards dove aside as the heavy cart whistled through the air like a pinwheel. It crashed against the side of the concourse and shattered several more panes of glass.

"Rex, go," said Misrule.

"All aboard," cried Rex. "I alluz wanted to say that." The Diesel engine coughed to life and the tractor kicked up a cloud of fragrant black smoke. The escapees bullied the hostages onto the cart right behind the tractor as it lurched forward.

Sirens yowled their discordance as police cars sped across the tarmac toward them. With a sound like thunder, White Dragon hurtled past overhead. Dust devils spun in his wake as he dropped to low altitude. His sides expanded as he drew in a massive breath and then expelled a jet of flame that stuck to whatever it hit like jelly. Two police cars ignited and skidded to a halt on bare rims as their tires melted away. The officers within tumbled out and pelted away from the burning cars before their fuel tanks exploded. As the cars blew, one officer moved too slowly and a whirling trunk lid cut him down.

Rex spun the wheel on the tractor and whooped like a rodeo cowboy. The rearmost baggage car whipped around and tipped, snapping off the steel tow ball like it was made of cheap plastic. A police car caught the corner of the heavy baggage cart and spun to a stop, its left front wheel dangling from a thread of shattered axle.

Misrule smiled at the carnage as it developed. This was destruction, his bailiwick. He resisted the desire to leap into the fray as was his wont. He had to protect the device in his chest. The time to release it would come, but not yet.

"There," he shouted over the din and pointed. "Head for that hangar, Rex."

The remaining police cars screeched to a standstill and the officers leaped clear. They took what cover they could and fired their weapons at the dragon as he wheeled around for another charge. Bullets ricocheted off the flying lizard's armored hide. Policemen scattered as another jet of flame carved across the parked cars. One of the officers screamed as flames engulfed him.

Rex bashed the tractor between two burning cars and flung them aside with a shriek of stressed metal while Nightmare herded away the remaining panicked police.

The baggage train continued on, unimpeded, on course for the hangar and apparent salvation.

* * *

"I lost him," choked Ment, his face drained of all color.

"Are you sure?" asked Doublecharge.

Ment leaned over and retched. Minerva stroked the back of his head and whispered soothing words in a language that was old when the world was young. "I think . . . I think he's dead." The boy spat into the open shaft beside him. "Airlift. I had a good lock on him and then nothing but pain. He moved again and I lost him."

"Ment, are you all right?" Doublecharge crouched down beside him.

The boy nodded and sniffled. "It . . . his death . . . caught me by surprise. I'll be all right. In time."

"Did you find out where he'd gone?"

"Back to Germany. That's all I got before he—he died." Ment rubbed one of his eyes. Minerva touched him between his shoulder blades. The tender concern in her demeanor belonged to someone far older than her nineteen years.

Doublecharge turned to Jack. "This is a mess for sure. What do you think we should do?"

Jack shrugged. "You're the boss."

"Don't give me that. You're the oldest, most experienced person on this team. I trust you, Jack."

Jack nodded toward the elevator shaft. "We'd better head down there. They may have left something or someone behind who can tell us where Misrule and company went."

Doublecharge nodded. "Gear up."

* * *

Oddly enough, none of the current members of Just Cause had ever been *down the hole* in Deep Six. Therefore it fell to Lieutenant Frankes to act as guide for the heroes as they searched the complex for any survivors. Only Doublecharge, Desert Eagle, and Minerva counted flight among their parapowers, and until a new elevator could be constructed, it was the only way to descend into the prison. Frankes had nearly balked at the idea of being carried down like a damsel in distress by Minerva, but when Doublecharge had shrugged and said they'd simply go without him, he relented. Jack smiled at him and snuggled a little deeper into Desert Eagle's muscular arms. They had been lovers for the past ten years and speculation ran high through the parahuman community about when they would finally relent and tie the knot.

Jack considered proposing to Desert Eagle—Sondra to her friends and teammates—fairly often, because he wasn't getting any younger. He'd planned to several years ago, but then 9/11 had happened and half the Just Cause team had been destroyed when their headquarters in the World Trade Center suffered the first impact. Then the team had relocated to their new headquarters in Denver. Then something else came up.

Something else *always* came up.

Damn it, he couldn't let things keep standing in the way. He looked up into Sondra's dark eyes as she flexed her wings. "Hey, honey, do you want to get married?"

"Oh my, you sure know how to sweep a girl off her feet." She chuckled.

He gave her his best magazine-cover grin. "Nothing's too good for my girl. So how about it, huh?"

"When?"

Jack paused. He hadn't expected to have to start working through details. "Soon."

"Sure, why not? The ring is forthcoming, I presume?"

"I left it in my other gun belt."

"Ah."

He looked over at Doublecharge. "Hey, boss, we're getting married!"

She raised an eyebrow at him from behind her mask. "Congratulations. I'm thrilled for the two of you. Now let's get under the ground."

The descent was harrowing. Doublecharge and Minerva flew by means unknown and drifted downward like leaves, but Desert Eagle had wings, and she could only safely descend by cupping those feathered extremities and spiraling downward. Jack smiled a little at Frankes' twitchiness. Minerva didn't precisely carry him; she laid a hand on his arm and conferred upon him flight ability of his own. Unskilled with such a new power, the Lieutenant jerked as his body tried to prevent him from falling despite the gentle descent.

Emergency power was still functioning, but Doublecharge held her hand high and caused electricity to arc between her fingers like the spines of a Jacob's ladder. Minerva carried a naked sword that seemed far too large for her small hands. It glowed with an innate luminescence as if it was a living creature. Desert Eagle had the eyesight of her namesake, and she could pick out minute details that the others might miss. Jack and Frankes relied on standard-issue flashlights strapped to their ultratasers. Frankes wanted to forgo the stunning weapon for something with more reasonable stopping power. Again, though, Doublecharge ordered him to carry something less lethal or else remain behind. Frankes relented, but not before looking pointedly at Desert Eagle's custom handguns.

Jack picked up a twisted piece of metal with something that might once have been a wheel attached to it. "What do you suppose happened here, Minerva?"

Minerva turned around slowly, hovering a few inches above the surface. Frankes twitched as he realized her eyes had either gone completely white or else rolled back into her head. "First he lets her go, then he goes back up there." Minerva inclined her head toward the entrance to the maintenance level. "They have a tank . . . a cutting torch . . . and they have made it into a bomb. She sets it to explode, then he pulls her to safety before it detonates."

"Who are they?" asked Desert Eagle. "Escapees? Maintenance workers? Guards?"

"Correctional Officers Tim Foster and Katie Malone."

Doublecharge turned to Frankes. "Does that sound right to you?"

Frankes nodded. "Foster's been here several years. Malone is new. She transferred in at the same time we brought in Misrule."

"Short, auburn hair?" asked Jack. Frankes grunted his agreement. "I remember her. Anything else, Minerva?"

Minerva's eyes returned to normal. "They're not down here now. Nobody lives beneath us in the cells." She pointed toward the medical wing. "But there is someone unconscious in there. It sounds like a woman."

They went to investigate, mindful of potential traps, and found a Hispanic woman stripped down to her underwear. She was unconscious but otherwise unbound. "She's been dosed with sleep gas." Minerva sniffed the air. "She's not a guard or an inmate. She smells like cleaning solution. She's probably a janitor."

Jack looked at Frankes and asked if he recognized the woman, but the Lieutenant only shrugged. "I never paid much attention to the civvies. It's more important to keep an eye on the prisoners."

"That worked out well for you." Minerva looked around at the destruction in the main lobby.

Doublecharge gathered the unconscious woman in her arms and flew back up the elevator shaft with her. While her commander was gone, Minerva drifted through the administration level, her eyes glassy and white. Doublecharge returned several minutes later, tired from the exertion of carrying the woman over a vertical mile.

"Have you found anything else?"

"One other heartbeat. Above us, on the environmental systems level. I sense nobody else, here or below in the cell blocks. Only death." She pointed to where several bodies had been draped with sheets.

"All right, then. Let's go." Doublecharge rose straight up until she was even with the entrance to the corridor leading to the kitchens and repair shop. Jack scampered up the debris after her, followed by Frankes and the others.

"Wait a second, you're going to bypass the entire prison level on the word of a kid?" Frankes' mouth hung open in surprise.

Minerva raised an eyebrow at him but said nothing.

"Minerva is extraordinarily observant," said Desert Eagle. "She's never been wrong about her interpretations of events."

"How does she do it?"

Minerva shrugged. "I just do. It's only a matter of paying attention to details and using your senses."

"For you, maybe," said Desert Eagle. "I met your grandmother once when I was younger. She was only good at it, but you're scary."

Someone else might have blushed at the compliment but Minerva merely nodded. They entered the maintenance level, following Minerva's lead. She guided them to a locker room and pointed to a narrow locker. "He's in there," she said.

They became aware of a muffled sound, a quiet tapping of flesh against metal.

"How do you know it's a guy?" whispered Frankes as he lifted the ultrataser to his shoulder, sighting at the locker door.

"Men smell different than women." Minerva made no move to raise or lower her own weapon, carrying her sword in a neutral fashion more like a tool than a blade.

Desert Eagle rested her hand on the locker latch and looked first to Doublecharge, who nodded, then to Jack, who likewise indicated his readiness. She yanked it open to reveal a man, shrink-wrapped, duct-taped, and gagged. His bloodshot eyes squinted from the flashlight.

Frankes gasped. "Kickback!"

"That's him," said Minerva. "He's the only one still here." She almost smiled. "He has to pee."

Doublecharge removed the gag from his mouth.

"Oh, God, you gotta get me out of this," he cried. "I got muscle cramps everywhere and I gotta piss so bad I can taste it."

Doublecharge didn't move. "Do you understand that you are still a convicted felon and a prisoner and this in no way constitutes any form of release from your lawful incarceration?"

"Hell, yes, whatever. Please!"

Doublecharge nodded to Desert Eagle, who slid a wicked-looking knife from an innocuous sheath strapped around one shapely leg. She sliced through the tape and shrink wrap around Kickback with care. Frankes lowered his ultrataser and slung it across his back in favor of an aerosol sprayer loaded with Deep Six's favored anesthetic gas. Kickback flexed his arms, neck, back and legs in turn as they were released and groaned as his muscles returned to their normal resting places. His eyes dropped with interest toward the large caliber pistols holstered on Desert Eagle's thighs.

"Don't even think about it," she said without the slightest glance upward from where she'd bent over to cut away the last of the binding from around his legs. "I'll introduce you to a world of pain you didn't even know existed."

"Don't be making eyes at my fiancée." Amusement sparkled in Jack's voice.

"I wasn't going to." Kickback hobbled over to a stall on legs that were still numb and urinated long and loud, his bodily needs taking precedence over any modesty.

"Why are you here and not with Misrule, Kickback?" asked Doublecharge.

"That bastard never did come looking for me," said the prisoner over his shoulder. "Two guards overpowered me and Napalm. Killed him. Then they locked me up in here."

"Where is Misrule going?"

Kickback flushed the toilet and turned around. "Don't I get to have a lawyer present during an interrogation?"

Frankes swore under his breath.

Doublecharge's tone turned ugly. "No. This is a matter of life and death and I'm not going to play stupid games with you. You can answer the question or you can join the others . . . how many, Minerva?"

"Nine."

"Nine dead prisoners," said Doublecharge. "And it's all the same to me if you'd rather join them, because who's to say what happened down here?"

"You can't do that!" Kickback yelled. "There are witnesses here! You can't kill me like a dog!"

"Did you hear something in the hallway just now?" Desert Eagle directed the question toward Frankes.

"Why yes, I did. Let's go check it out," he said, catching on.

"I'm not an unreasonable woman," said Doublecharge. "If you cooperate, I'll make a favorable recommendation on your behalf at your first parole hearing. That's my final offer. Now, I'm going to ask you once more and what happens to you next will relate directly to the honesty of your answer. Where is Misrule going?"

He told her.

* * *

"I think somebody should go after them," said Jack. "And it ought to be us."

"It isn't just that simple." Doublecharge looked troubled. "We can't just go flying out of the country. I don't think the government is going to look fondly on us getting involved in an international incident."

"Then I guess it's a good thing we've got a contact at Parahumans 'R' Us." Jack spat the organization's title like it was a curse. Most of the heroes within Just Cause felt similarly about the government watchdog.

Doublecharge pulled her phone from her belt and dialed a number she had long ago committed to memory.

"Hello, Stacey," said the familiar voice of Juice, erstwhile leader of Just Cause. Very few people had his personal cell phone number. Even his superiors in the National Security Agency contacted him via other lines.

"James," said Doublecharge. The two were very old friends, having worked together for fifteen years. Her electrical powers complimented his ability to convert electricity into muscular strength and density. "We're in a hell of a situation here." She relayed the latest information on the escape to him. "I need two things, and I mean expedited."

"Go ahead," he said.

"I need authorization for Just Cause to pursue the fugitives out of the 'States, and I need you to coordinate us with local parahuman assets." She started to chew on her nails, realized she still wore her long black gloves, and forced herself to lower her hand.

"I'll do what I can as far as contacting local paras," he said, "but I'm not optimistic about you being let out of the country. The administration is very paranoid about parahuman terrorism these days, and with Deep Six opened, who knows where Misrule and the Cult could turn up."

"That's not you talking, that's the Agency," said Doublecharge. "Where's my friend James?"

"Things are different now," said Juice. "This isn't the old days when we could buck the system and do whatever we wanted. Congress could yank funding from Just Cause in a heartbeat."

"You wouldn't do that."

"No, I wouldn't, but I'm not really in any kind of power here, Stacey. They put me here because I'm a troublemaker, and a popular one at that."

"Keep your friends close and your enemies closer?" asked Doublecharge.

"Something like that. But they know how much swing I have in the parahuman community. With my law background, I was the best candidate for the job at the PRA. But I'm not really much more than an errand boy for the NSA."

"Is it as bad as that?"

"It's worse. There is a lot of talk up on the Hill about a new Parahuman Registration Act. It's been rewritten. They think this one will pass for sure. More than a few senators and congressmen would like to see you all quietly just go away."

A surprising idea popped into Doublecharge's head. "Hang on, James. Better yet, let me call you back. It would be better for your career if you don't hear this."

"I'll see if I can get hold of Feuerwerke." He referred to a German hero group and broke the connection.

"Jack, I think you've got some vacation coming," said Doublecharge.

"I do?"

"You do," she said. "In fact, you should take it right now. I hear Germany is nice this time of year."

"Is it? I mean, yeah . . . I was thinking about going there. They've got salad that's made of meat."

"I'll have Reed take you. That way you don't have to deal with commercial airliners. I'll make a small oversight in fuel expenditures. Inform Reed that I'll get very stern with him if he logs the hours of this flight."

Jack hesitated. "You realize that Berlin's a good seven or eight hours away at top speed?"

Doublecharge nodded. "I do, but we haven't got anything or anyone faster, and we can't just sit here and do nothing. They're our escapees. They should be our responsibility to recapture."

"Got it. Let me collect my gear and I'll be off. You think I'll be missed?"

"Not if I have anything to do with it. Be careful, Jack."

He winked at her. "I'm indestructible."

"You Americans often forget that there are far more parahumans outside of the United States than inside it. Make no mistake, they are every bit as powerful and competent as you are . . . in many cases even more so."

—Big Bear, commander of Russia's Peacekeepers

July, 2007
Berlin, Germany

As she hustled into the hangar along with the other hostages, Katie noted only one jet was parked in front of the great doors, white with a sky blue tail and the disturbing word *SYRIANAIR* printed in block letters and Arabic over the strip of windows.

Foster noticed it at the same time. "Holy crap, are we going to Syria?"

"I hope not," said Katie.

"Me neither. My passport isn't current."

"Malone?" Cassie looked shocked as she recognized Katie underneath her hasty disguise. "Thank God, I thought you were dead."

"The rumors of my death were greatly exaggerated," said Katie with a small grin.

"Why didn't you get away when you could?"

"What, and miss all this fun?"

"Do you have a plan?"

"Of course I have a plan." Katie snorted as if the very thought was ridiculous.

"Oh, good," whispered Foster. "And I thought we were still in improvisation mode."

"What do you think is going to happen next?"

"I overheard two of them talking," said Cassie. "Misrule is forming a new Cult of Destruction, and it'll be funded by Middle Eastern terrorist organizations."

"Parahuman terrorists." Foster shook his head. "That's fucked up."

"We've got to stop that plane from taking off," said Katie. "Or we're going to all wind up as ticker items on CNN."

"No talking," said Heretic from several feet away.

Misrule detailed T-Rex and Black Hood to tear into some innocuous crates stacked against one wall of the hangar. The lizard man whooped in triumph as he withdrew a long tube from one. From the olive green coloration and the way he lifted it up to his shoulder, it could only be a rocket tube of some kind. Black Hood found a stash of automatic weapons, packed in oilcloth.

"The police will be regrouping and preparing to move in on us," said Misrule. "We will be most vulnerable as we taxi clear of the hangar. I expect you to clear a path . . . by whatever means you deem appropriate."

"Appropriate? Hell, I'm gonna blow me up some lawmen with my bazooky, and I don't care if they's German." T-Rex waved his rocket launcher for emphasis. Black Hood began passing out weapons to whoever wanted one.

While Heretic and Nightmare watched the hostages, Misrule moved a stairway truck up next to the cabin door and ascended into the plane. A few moments later the cockpit lighting came on and Katie could see him behind the windows as he began preflight procedures.

"*Kommen Sie aus den Hangar heraus! Sie widen umgeben! Ausliferung jetzt!*" shouted an amplified voice from outside the hangar.

Misrule appeared in the doorway of the jet. "Take firing positions and open the doors. Escudo, show off the hostages."

Escapees scrambled to find cover, preparing to fight. Escudo placed another force field around the group of hostages and marched them to the front of the jet.

"This is getting old fast," grumbled Dr. Mayfair. "I wish they'd either shit or get off the pot. Being paraded around like a damn fool is pissing me off."

The hangar doors slid open. Katie had an excellent view of a large number of guns pointed in her direction as they did. The police had arrived in larger numbers, and had blocked the hangar exit with several cars and vans, and behind them sat two hulking behemoths that must have been airport fire trucks. Half the policemen seemed to be normal cops with service pistols, but the rest were of the kneepads-and-riot-helmets variety, leveling wicked- looking submachine guns at them.

"*Zeichnen Sie Ihre Waffen auf! Es gibt kein Entweichen!*" called a man cowering behind a squad car with a megaphone.

"Speak Ainglish, ya mow-ron," cried T-Rex. He hadn't taken cover with the others; instead he stood to one side of Escudo, his rocket launcher pointed straight at the police beyond the hangar door.

The man with the megaphone passed it to someone else, who then spoke. "Throw down your guns. You are surrounded. There is no escape."

"Y'all throw down your own damn guns! We got hostages here and we ain't afraid to kill 'em if you don't git while the gittin's good."

There was silence as the German police tried to translate T-Rex's slang. Katie heard a new noise underneath everything: a growing whine of high-performance engines. Four vehicles raced across the tarmac in a tight formation at unbelievably high speed. As they streaked under the lights, they resolved into a group of heavily-customized Porsche Carreras, which Katie recognized only because she dreamed of owning one someday. They were painted in brilliant yellow, red, and black—the colors of the German flag—and each braked to a smooth stop off to one side of the police cars.

A single occupant emerged from each car. The first was wrapped in a high-tech suit of powered armor of gunmetal gray and brown. From clawed boots and gauntlets to wings that unfolded as he moved to a helmet full of sensors with points that rose like ears, he looked like a cybernetic bat. A huge man squeezed out of the second small coupe. He was sealed in heavy iron armor complete with a horned helmet, and carried a massive axe. The third man, not quite as large as the armored behemoth, seemed to be made entirely of stone and was nude save for tight-fitting biker shorts and metallic bracers around his wrists and ankles. The final member of the quartet was a diminutive woman, dressed in a revealing red costume. Her pale skin glowed with purplish light and sparks crackled between her limbs and torso as she moved.

Feuerwerke!

The word raced throughout the police, who seemed to relax at the arrival of what could only be a German superhero team. Katie's hopes rose; perhaps they could bring a halt to this untenable situation. Every minute away from her daughter felt like a splinter burrowed deeper and deeper toward her heart.

* * *

Misrule watched the *Feuerwerke* team arrive and fumed a little. He'd hoped they would be too far away to make a difference in his plans—the German heroes were famous for their skill in combat and infamous for their willingness to engage in it. He finished his preflight and started the engines. His Syrian contacts had done well, first by stocking the warehouse with arms for his people, and second for providing a fully-fueled airplane.

As the engines warmed up, he went to the door behind the cockpit and ordered his people to bring the hostages inside. "As soon as we clear that barricade, we leave."

The four heroes of *Feuerwerke*—it took him a moment to recall their names: The Bat, Visigoth, Wall, and Glamour—approached the hangar door, oozing confidence with every step. The Bat, his suit loaded with sensor technology, probably already had all the escapees marked, identified, and tagged by potential threat level. Visigoth slapped the haft of his axe with a gauntleted hand. Wall slowly grew larger and broadened as he absorbed the stone in the cement tarmac to add to his own body. Glamour's glow brightened and gave off static sparks of lavender and white as she hovered overhead.

"Surrender, Americans," said The Bat in a grating, processed voice.

T-Rex sniffed in disdain. "Hell, I ain't impressed much. I seen scarier shit in Texas. Although . . ." His tongue lashed out between his sharp teeth. "I wouldn't mind getting' to know the purdy little slit ya brought with ya."

Misrule sighed. T-Rex had become a liability. His time spent in prison had done nothing to mellow his demeanor. If anything, he was even edgier than he had been at the time of his conviction. Perhaps the time had come to cut him loose. T-Rex glanced up over his shoulder to see Misrule gazing down upon him. Misrule pointed at the police cars and made a parting motion with his hands, then nudged the airliner forward a few inches.

T-Rex saw Misrule's signal, yelled "Git outta the way, assholes," and fired his rocket tube. The rocket sailed past all the police cars to impact somewhere out on the tarmac. T-Rex whooped, threw aside the spent weapon, and charged at *Feuerwerke*. Black Hood and Espada followed only a few steps behind, ready to inflict grievous harm on anyone and anything which stood in their way. Kiloton brought up the rear with parcels of explosive energy circulating around his hands.

With a shriek borne of Hell, White Dragon dropped out of the sky onto a police cruiser. He dug his prodigious claws into the roof, shattering the glass in the doors, and beat his wings mightily. He couldn't have accomplished this with a heavy American car, but he was able to drag the smaller German car several yards.

The *Feuerwerke* heroes startled at the dragon's appearance. The hesitation nearly cost them their lives as T-Rex and the others bowled into them. The Bat leaped back to use his arms and legs defensively as T-Rex went after him. Misrule found the differences in their fighting styles interesting to observe. The Bat was a finesse fighter, and used a combination of martial arts styles with a firm grounding in the long kicks and punches of French Savate. T-Rex brawled mostly with joy, a devastating roundhouse, and a penchant for using his head as a weapon. The two fell into a flurry of exchanged blows. T-Rex's tough hide absorbed a lot of punishment, but the Bat's claws left bloody furrows in his green scales. The German hero didn't pass unscathed either, losing one of his cybernetic wings to T. Rex's exuberance.

Black Hood waded into Visigoth. He ducked underneath a swing of the massive axe that would have cleft a girder in half and drove both his fists into the giant's midsection. Visigoth staggered backward and Black Hood grabbed for the axe. The two wrestled over the haft as each tried to get the proper leverage to wrench it away from the other. Hood twisted his shoulders suddenly and ripped the axe clear away. Visigoth, overbalanced, stumbled and fell to his hands and knees.

Hood whooped and raised the axe, gleefully victorious, with intent to smash the titan beneath him. Visigoth kicked out hard and bent one of Hood's knees sideways in a direction that made even Misrule wince in spite of being long inured to acts of interpersonal violence. The escapee dropped the axe, howling in pain, and fell to the cement floor of the hangar with his leg a mangled mess.

Glamour rose out of Espada's reach. The swordswoman swore at her in a mixture of English and Spanish. Glamour doused her with lavender sparks which made Espada twitch and jerk about, her arms shifting back and forth between joints and blades.

Kiloton didn't mess around with Wall. He plunged both hands to the ground, discharging his energy. He couldn't affect living things with his power, but anything inanimate was vulnerable. The tarmac all around Wall exploded energetically, tossing chunks of cement shrapnel fifty feet in the air. The German parahuman crumpled and leaked very real, human blood from cracks in his stony exterior.

"Inside the jet or you all die here." Dissident pointed at the stairs. The hostages didn't argue; it was always better to be under cover when parahumans fought. Close bystanders often paid the price for their interest. Misrule nudged the jet forward again even before all the hostages had boarded.

White Dragon blasted more flame down upon the police cars. Cops ran for cover and fired their weapons at the great white monster, but with little effect. The dragon roared again and bulled full-speed into the side of a van to send it tumbling out of the way of the taxiing jet.

The Bat gained the upper hand against T-Rex. He had extended his fighting claws to full length, swinging them viciously at the reptilian man. T-Rex no longer tried to fight back, trapped on full defense as the whistling blades sliced new gashes in his skin. Blood ran freely down his limbs, and he left gore-streaked footprints on the cement. Suddenly Espada, recovering from a blast from Glamour, whirled and whipped her sword-arm across the back of the Bat's left leg to sever it. Instead of tissue and blood, sparks and wires trailed from the cut. Then Espada crumpled and convulsed as a stream of Glamour's sparks felled her once more.

Visigoth picked up his axe and spun it through his fingers like a drum majorette twirling a baton. The keen edge whistled through the air as Black Hood tried to crawl away. Like an executioner of old, Visigoth swung the axe up and over his head to bring it down across Hood's neck. The razor-sharp blade didn't slow in the least until it hit the concrete below with a shower of sparks. Hood's head flew aside and rolled underneath a baggage cart. His body twitched a few times as blood emptied from the stump of his neck.

Kiloton grabbed a fist-sized chunk of debris off the ground, charged it, and threw it toward Glamour. It exploded only a few feet away from her and peppered her flawless skin with razor-sharp bits of rock. She screamed and retreated out the door of the hangar. White Dragon spotted her and tail-whipped her as he flew past. She slammed hard against the side of the building with a sickening crunch and fell in a jumble of impossibly-twisted limbs.

* * *

The hostages scattered throughout the main cabin. Katie glanced at Foster and dropped into a seat near the tail. He sat down next to her and squeezed her hand. "Hi," he whispered.

"Hi yourself."

"I'm glad to see you, but why are you here? You could have stayed behind."

"Call it a swollen sense of duty," she said. "I couldn't leave you to have all the fun, could I?" She shrugged. "Besides, you're good company."

"Misrule killed Prince, didn't he?"

"Yeah." Katie shuddered. "He was an asshole for sure, but nobody ought to die that way."

"Bad?"

"I don't want to talk about it."

"Okay."

Katie looked down and realized she and Foster still held hands. She smiled and left her hand where it was. She felt comforted with his hand clasping hers, to feel his pulse. It reminded her they both still lived and with luck, they could still come out of the craziness in one piece.

"So what do we do now?" asked Foster.

"Me? Why is it up to me?"

"Because you're always right." He winked at her.

"Well, there's that."

Katie peeked around the edge of the seats to look up the aisle. Several escapees, heavily-armed with the weapons they'd found in the hangar, paced back and forth. They looked occasionally at the hostages but mostly watched the battle outside the jet. It gave her an idea.

"Do you think we could stop the jet from taking off somehow? There's got to be a way."

Foster shook his head. "Not from here. The cockpit's out. Maybe if we got to the avionics somehow, but I wouldn't have the slightest idea what to do with them if we did." He slouched down a little more as Dissident marched past and headed for the bathrooms at the tail of the plane. "Not to mention we're a little outnumbered and outgunned."

"The hangar was pretty well-stocked with arms," murmured Katie. "And they're military-grade. I think this operation is bigger than just Misrule."

"How so?"

"That bomb thing in his chest," Katie said. "Cassie told me it's filled with nerve gas. You can't just pop down to the Walgreen's and buy that. The weapons. This jet. He's got a powerful organization behind him for all this, and I bet they're terrorists."

"Why terrorists?"

"Rich. Influential. Access to WMDs."

"Okay, I'll buy that."

"Good, because you're going to stop them, Mr. Invisibility," said Katie.

Foster's jaw dropped. "I can't do that. What am I supposed to do, take over the whole plane?"

"I'm sure you'll think of something."

Suddenly Dissident stood beside them. "You two, move up front with the others."

Foster looked back at Katie and stood up.

An idea struck her and she began to act sick, moaning and holding her stomach. "*P-por favor, señor . . . Los baños*," she groaned.

Dissident glared at her. "All right. Go." He motioned toward the bathrooms.

Katie hurried back, hunched over, and locked herself into the bathroom.

Once inside the cramped room, she took a deep, shuddering breath. It had fallen to her again to be the instrument of change.

She hoped she was up to the task.

* * *

Brainstorm stalked up to where Cassie sat, huddled in miserable fear with her coworker Montell. "You," growled the woman with a feral hatred. "He wants you up front. With him."

"Why me?" asked Cassie.

"It doesn't matter why!" screamed Brainstorm. Her face was so red it nearly matched Misrule's natural skin tone. "Get up before I turn your brain to dogshit."

In that moment, Cassie understood Brainstorm loved Misrule. Misrule's interest in Cassie, whether professional or something she wasn't even remotely prepared to consider, threatened Brainstorm's attraction to him. Cassie understood all this and gained a dangerous sense of feminine sympathy for her captor. It was dangerous because as a hostage and the ranking survivor of the Deep Six staff according to Misrule, she couldn't afford the luxury of feeling anything but distrust and anger towards the escapees. She resisted the impulse to say something to Brainstorm and instead headed forward to the cockpit.

Montell patted her hand. "It'll be okay," he whispered. She smiled at him as she stood up.

"Dogshit," whispered Brainstorm as she led Cassie through the First Class cabin to the open cockpit door.

"Ah, Cassandra. Sit down. No, up here next to me," said Misrule as Cassie started to drop into the nearest seat. She changed to the copilot's chair and found it far more comfortable than she would have expected. It never occurred to her that pilots had better seats than passengers on airliners.

"Oh my God," said Cassie aloud as she saw the end result of the battles in front of the hangar. As she watched, a burning police car exploded and flipped up and over its hood to land on its roof. Visigoth supported the Bat, who was missing his lower leg, and swung his axe to keep the bloodthirsty T-Rex at bay. Black Hood lay dead and headless, his body forgotten by the others. Kiloton had Espada in a fireman's carry and was bringing her back toward the rolling plane; she was either unconscious or dead, her skin blistered, blackened, and smoking all over.

Visigoth reached Wall, who lay unmoving in the center of a crater. He shouted something in German and four of the police officers rushed in to help carry the stone-skinned man clear. Others fired at White Dragon, who wheeled about in the sky for yet another charge at them. Bodies were strewn everywhere—cops, airport workers, firemen. Many bore the marks of White Dragon's fire.

Others had been cut down by Kiloton's explosions. Police cars burned, surrounded by smoldering debris.

"This is my world." Misrule opened his arms as if to encompass the scene unfolding below.

"It's horrible," said Cassie.

"And yet had they not interfered, none of this would have happened." Misrule smiled as if he were privy to a great secret.

"Why did you want me here?"

"I enjoy your company, Cassandra."

Cassie shook her head. "I'd rather take my chances with T-Rex."

Misrule's tone grew acidic. "That could be arranged. However . . . I have decided he has outlived his usefulness to my cause." He turned. "Brainstorm, are Kiloton and Espada aboard?"

Brainstorm spoke from her post at the door to the cockpit. Cassie realized the woman had never left. "Yes. Only Rex and White Dragon are still out there."

Misrule turned his attention to the controls of the jet. "Dragon can catch us once we're out on the tarmac. As for Rex . . . It would be best for all if he does not accompany us on this journey. He would find the lifestyle . . . constraining."

"I—I don't understand."

"I do not wish Rex to set foot on board this plane. See to it he does not."

"You want me to . . ."

"Perhaps I have not made myself clear. Perhaps Cassandra would prefer to do the honors instead. I'm sure she could find it within her to take revenge upon the man who would have raped her without my intervention." Misrule ignored Cassie's scandalized outcry.

"No," said Brainstorm through clenched teeth. "I'll do it without her goddamn dogshit help."

Misrule touched a button on the console. "Tower, this is SAA001."

"SAA001, we are currently experiencing a ground-level emergency—"

"I'm taking off on Runway 35 in five minutes. I suggest you clear any traffic out of my way, because I don't intend to stop."

"What?"

Misrule negotiated the jet past the burning wreckage of the police cruisers. "Runway 35. I won't repeat it again. Clear the pattern."

Cassie's eyes widened. "What if they don't?"

"Then this should be very interesting."

* * *

Most of Jack's gear was already stowed on board the *Rita*. He only had to accumulate what he'd offloaded when Just Cause arrived at Deep Six. A few minutes later and he jogged across the pavement to where the jump jet waited. He ran up the ramp and was about to order the pilot, Reed, to get airborne when he realized he wasn't alone in the cabin.

Correctional Officers Lania and Garcia sat in the cabin. They looked eager and nervous at the same time.

"Out," said Jack. "I'm not going to risk anyone else on this mission."

"With all due respect, go to hell," said Garcia. "Those are our people, and we're going to do whatever we can to help get them out safe."

"I don't have time for this shit," said Jack.

"None of us have time for this shit," said Lania. "You might need us."

"Look, no offense meant, but you guys are prison guards. This goes way beyond your training."

"Nobody knows those prisoners better than we do," said Garcia. "We know their capabilities and powers. We've spent years preventing them from using those powers."

"But . . ." Jack felt his resolve weakening in the face of their strong logic.

"We brought sleeper sets, anesthetic sprayers, and ultratasers," said Lania. "We're prepared to deal with these escapees. Are you?"

Jack felt a spark of pride at the devotion the two guards held for their jobs. "All right. When it comes time to handle the prisoners, you're in. Until then, you follow orders. Understand?"

Garcia smiled and showed Jack his middle finger. "Perfectly, Crackerjack."

Jack nodded, more amused than offended. "Reed, get us out of here."

Almost before Jack finished speaking, the *Rita*'s engines revved up to a high-pitched scream. The jet flung itself into the air as if it were a bird escaping a cage. Like a Harrier, the *Rita* had thrust nozzles that could rotate down, which allowed it to launch vertically. The acceleration forces made the passengers' blood pool in their feet and their vision dimmed for a few moments until the *Rita* transitioned into horizontal flight.

"Destination, sir?" asked Reed over the cabin speaker.

"For now, Berlin, and don't worry about saving on fuel economy."

"Roger." The *Rita* heeled over and leaped forward as Reed kicked on the afterburners. The jet vibrated as it outraced sound.

"Doing all right?" Jack asked as he noticed Garcia looked a little green.

The muscular guard burped. "Sorry . . . this is a little different than our prisoner transport jet."

"Yeah, *Rita* is a capricious girl, given to sudden bursts of speed and unexplained quivering at times." Jack placed one hand on his chest and extended the other out to the side as if lampooning a professional orator. "And yet, she's pulled our bacon from the fire more times than I can count." He paused, reconsidering. "Well, our last jet was like that. The *Bettie*. She was a lovely lady."

"What happened to her, er, it?" asked Lania.

"Shot down by dragons and crashed in a field."

"That doesn't make me feel any safer, you know," grumbled Garcia.

"Well, we're going to have a few hours before we get there," said Jack. "And our destination could change pretty quickly. I think the best way to pass the time would be for the two of you to brief me on everything you can about the escapees."

"You've got the files already," said Lania.

"Yes I do. But as you said, you know these escapees better than anyone. I suspect your information will be a lot more useful when the chips are down than anything I read in the files. Not that I'm going to ignore them. Doublecharge would have my ass in a sling if I missed something for being a slacker." Jack opened a cabinet and withdrew weapon after weapon until he had laid out enough arms in the center of the cabin to outfit a full SEAL team. He followed up the arsenal with an amazing array of tools that ranged from simple screwdrivers and wrenches to handheld cutting torches and electronic lockpicks.

"You think it's going to be enough?" Lania cracked a smile behind the window of her containment suit.

"I like to have choices. Usually I just have to grab whatever and run. Extensive planning is a rare luxury in this business." Jack looked up. "Think I should bring some grenades? You never know."

"Shit, go for broke." Garcia picked up a handgun that seemed to be made entirely of plastic and ceramics.

"Good idea." Jack chose a selection of five different grenades. "Better to have them and not need them than otherwise. Oh, you like that one? You can have it. I've got six more back in my stash at headquarters. It won't set off airport security devices."

Garcia's eyes bugged out. "You're serious?"

Jack averted his eyes. "Well, uh, it hasn't yet at any rate. Don't ask. We'd better start going over your soon-to-be-recaptured prisoners."

Lania and Garcia began to talk.

* * *

The jet's engine noise increased. T-Rex looked behind him just in time to see the plane leave the hangar. His reptile brain was in charge, and he stared at the jet without comprehension.

"Surrender, American." Visigoth stood guard over his injured comrade, the Bat. "Your friends are leaving you behind."

"Huh?" T-Rex struggled to regain some of his higher brain functions. It took several seconds of alternately keeping an eye on Visigoth and checking on the plane's progress before something clicked and he realized that Misrule was leaving without him.

A look of confusion crossed his scaly face. "They . . . he . . ." T-Rex was unable to put together a coherent sentence and looked helplessly at Visigoth for a moment before he turned and sprinted after the departing jet. "Wait up!" he cried. "Hey, Boss, don't leave me here! Don't forget about yer pal Rexie!"

T-Rex pelted for all he was worth, and because of his greater-than-human strength and endurance, he closed in on the wing and squinted into the hot exhaust from the engine that hung underneath it. A shadow passed over his head: White Dragon. He'd have called out to Dragon if he'd had any breath to spare for it. T-Rex pumped his arms and legs to stay close to the jet, but had no strength to spare for a leap onto the wing. He felt a sudden sting in his side, then another in his cheek, and he realized someone had shot at him. The bullets hurt, but didn't penetrate his scaly skin. One caught him on his ankle and he went down with a howl. White Dragon didn't turn or even slow in his pace. As the great beast drew alongside the body of the jet, his form shrank back to human and he settled in the open cabin door.

Rex leaped to his feet and sprinted after the jet once more, angry tears in his eyes. "Goddammit, wait for me!" He ignored the sound of more guns firing at him and the twinges as bullets bounced off his flesh. The adrenaline that surged through his system gave him the speed and strength to hurl himself into the air over the wing. He managed to catch the ridge of a flap and haul himself up onto the metal surface.

The wing bounced up and down, nearly dislodging him from his precarious perch. He dug his finger and toe claws into whatever seams and ridges he could find and crawled along the wing toward the body. The air blowing over the wing's surface threatened to blast him off onto the tarmac below. It made his eyes water. He wasn't crying. Not T-Rex. Someone opened the door over the wing and he grinned through his tears as he recognized Brainstorm. He reached out a hand toward her.

"I'm sorry, Rex." Her words barely carried to him over the noise of the engines and wind.

He opened his mouth to question her, but before he could speak Brainstorm unleashed her power and destroyed his mind in a rape as violent as any he had perpetrated on his own victims. Everything that was, had been, or ever would be T-Rex spun away into nothingness like a leaf blowing away in the onslaught of a hurricane. He wavered for a moment on the wing, his face devoid of emotion. Spittle flew away from the corner of his toothy mouth. Then he fell without a sound and bounced on the tarmac like a discarded rag doll.

Chewing on her lip, Brainstorm dogged the hatch shut as the jet swung around onto a runway and began to accelerate in earnest.

* * *

"Incoming transmission," said Reed from the cockpit of the *Rita*. "It's Doublecharge."

"Pipe it in here, please," said Jack.

"Go ahead, ma'am."

"Jack?" Doublecharge's voice was so clear she might have been sitting in the same cabin with them instead of half a continent away. The *Rita* blasted along at her maximum supersonic speed, ramjets engaged and white hot, only minutes from the Atlantic Ocean.

"I'm here, boss."

"We have a situation update from Berlin. Misrule has managed to take off in a jet from the airport after a firefight with local authorities and a German hero team."

Jack and the two guards looked at each other and winced. "How bad was it?"

"Initial reports are two fatalities and one additional casualty on the German team . . . one fatality—Black Hood —and two casualties among the escapees, including T-Rex, who was recaptured. There is . . . some confusion as to the nature of his injuries. Three civilians were killed, six injured, all police or airport security."

Garcia shook his head. "Black Hood and T-Rex. That's two fewer psychopaths and the world is better off for it."

"What's his heading?"

"East southeast," said Doublecharge.

Jack immediately pulled up a map of Eastern Europe and traced a line along it. "That's not very helpful. He could be heading just about anywhere except home to Denmark," he muttered.

"Jack . . . it's a Syrian Arab Air jet."

Jack examined the map. Syria was well within the course Misrule had chosen, and the jet would certainly have the range to reach it. "Shit. Reed, are you listening in?"

"Yes, sir."

"Can we intercept the jet before it reaches Syria?"

There was a brief pause as Reed did some course and speed calculations on his navigation computer. "Not at our current speed, sir."

"Well, shit."

"Hang on a minute," said Garcia. "He said *not at our current speed*. How fast would we need to intercept him . . . say . . ." he hunted on the map. "Here," he pointed to the eastern edge of the Mediterranean. "Near Cyprus?"

"Average speed of Mach three-point-five," said Reed. "The *Rita* tops out at about Mach one-point-eight."

"Where are you going with this, Officer Garcia?" asked Doublecharge.

"We just have to go faster." Garcia looked excited and animated for the first time since he came on board.

Jack raised an eyebrow. "And how the hell do you propose to do that? Get out and push?"

"No." Garcia pointed at Lania. "Not me."

Lania looked stunned. "Huh? What do you mean?"

"It's simple. We'll make you into a pulse drive."

Silence filled the cabin.

"Oh, for the love of God . . . doesn't anybody read but me?" Garcia rolled his eyes. "Just because the rest of you have to sleep every day. A pulse drive." He waved his hands as he explained. "We use a series of antimatter explosions to push the *Rita* faster. Lania's powers let her release antimatter particles. They'll explode when their containment breaks down. Boom!"

Jack raised a finger. "Excuse me, but isn't it bad when antimatter explodes? No offense meant, Lania."

"None taken," said the woman. "But he's right. I can fire off tiny bits and they'll make energetic explosions."

"How do we keep them from destroying us?" Reed sounded interested.

"We have to reconfigure the magnetic field in Lania's suit to make a cone—a bell housing like a rocket nozzle," said Garcia. "That's the hard part."

"Okay, then what?" Jack raised an eyebrow.

"I'm still working on the rest of it."

The word *Syria* seemed to pulse on the map as Jack looked at it. "Work faster."

FOURTEEN

"To invent, you need a good imagination and a pile of junk."
—*Thomas A. Edison*

July, 2007
Berlin, Germany

Cassie dug her fingers into the edge of her seat as Misrule brought the jet's engines up to full thrust and sent the plane careening down the runway. She had never liked to fly, but watching it from the copilot's seat was like having a ringside seat at a WWF match. If anything went wrong at takeoff, she'd see it before anyone else and be the first one to hit the ground in a crash. It made her nerves sing like over-tightened violin strings. The end of the runway approached way too fast, and she winced in anticipation of the jet's inevitable tumble off into the grassy field beyond, fuel tanks exploding and metal crumpling. Then Misrule pulled back the stick and the jet's nose rose into the sky to leave the end of the runway far behind.

Frantic voices came from the cockpit speaker as air traffic controllers tried to warn them out of the traffic pattern. Misrule banked the jet and angled it onto a new course with no regard for any other planes in the sky. As the angry controller's voice rose in pitch and volume from the tower, Misrule grew irritated and took up the microphone. "Enough, or I turn this plane around and crash it into your terminal."

The voice stopped almost instantly, bathing the cockpit in silence except for the hiss of the engines and the quiet beeping of electronics. Cassie glanced at Misrule and saw he smiled at her, devoid of humor. "It would appear they have taken me seriously."

Cassie remained quiet and wondered what would come next.

"Brainstorm," called Misrule into the intercom. A moment later she appeared at the cockpit door. "Report."

Brainstorm sniffled a little, and Cassie noticed her eyes were puffy as if she'd been crying. The escapee ran a hand through her short blond hair. She looked disheveled and shrunken inside her prison garb. "Dragon, Kiloton, and Espada are back on board. Espada is hurt pretty bad. The Doc is looking her over."

"And Rex?"

"He . . ." she swallowed hard. "He's gone."

Something in her tone made Misrule's eyes narrow. "You did it yourself?"

She nodded and wiped at a single, angry tear that escaped her left eye.

"Well done. Go rest yourself," he said. "And, Brainstorm? Think very carefully should you get any ideas about taking down anyone else."

Brainstorm gasped in restrained fury, turned on her heel and was gone.

"You really inspire loyalty." Cassie's words escaped her before she could choke them back.

Misrule was unfazed. "I prefer to think of my leadership quality as that of an iron fist wrapped in a chamois glove. Sometimes one must set an example."

"You had her kill one of your teammates!"

"His body is not dead, but his mind has been destroyed. Rex will never again commit acts of wanton lust. Surely you find that agreeable after nearly becoming a victim yourself?"

"I—" Cassie realized with sick understanding that Misrule was right. Destroying T. Rex was a beneficial act to the rest of the world. "It's still wrong."

Misrule was unperturbed. "I have my reasons. I sense a growing division within the ranks of my people. I hope by setting this example it will cause others to think twice before raising their voices in dissent."

"You're just afraid to let them go."

"Not afraid. Disappointed, perhaps." He turned his head to look at her. "But I am considering the possibility of replacements."

Cassie couldn't meet his gaze. She feared what she saw behind those sulfurous eyes. She turned away and looked out the cockpit windows. "You're in charge here. I'm just along for the ride."

"Indeed. And what will you do when we arrive?"

"Are you going to release us?"

"It is my intention to do so, assuming things do not change between now and then. Perhaps some of you will select to remain behind of your own volition." He adjusted some controls on the huge, complicated panel, and released his hands from the wheel and stick.

"Aren't you supposed to hold onto those?"

"You need not fear. I am an accomplished pilot. With a reasonable fortune and plenty of time, one can acquire a professional-grade simulator. And fortunately, I have wealthy, patient benefactors."

"Let me guess . . . Syrian terrorists, right? I figure they're pretty good at flying planes, but I hear their landings need work."

Misrule chuckled at that. "Well-spoken, Cassandra. Go speak to Doctor Mayfair now. I want a status report on anyone who is injured, whether of your people or mine."

He lowered his head and offered a dark, toothy smile from under heavy brows. "I'm likely to order the death of anyone he feels requires more medical attention than he can provide. You might convey that to him."

Chills ran down Cassie's spine from the venom in his tone. In spite of his cultured demeanor he was still an evil, soulless killer. Something about the way he spoke to her, the way he looked at her, gave her what her mother had always called the *screaming meemies*. He wanted something from her, but she couldn't tell what it might be. The way he spoke to her . . . not like an equal, perhaps, but like a professor who lectured a student. She shivered at the thought. Did he want to recruit her somehow? Or was his interest more carnal in nature, she wondered as she glanced at Brainstorm, who huddled on one of the oversized seats in First Class and whispered to herself.

She didn't look up as Cassie passed.

* * *

Katie sat on the closed toilet seat in the cramped bathroom and tried not to panic as the plane lifted clear of the runway. She didn't know where Misrule would take them, but she suspected someplace unfriendly to Americans. There had to be a reason they were aboard a Syrian airliner. She had seen plenty of news reports about Americans being kidnapped, humiliated, and killed because they happened to be in the wrong place at the wrong time. She swore to herself she would not end up on the wrong end of an executioner's knife or worse. By God, she would go down fighting hard if it came to that, right down to her last tooth and nail. And as long as she fought, she told herself she would live to see her daughter again. That thought kept her going, so she looked for weaknesses and opportunities she could exploit, and especially for ways she could turn the escapees against one another.

Back in Ohio, she'd been through one prison riot, and until she was assaulted and nearly raped, it had been the most terrifying experience of her life. It took seventeen hours for the guards to regain control of the prisoner population, and when the last inmate was locked back down in his cell, nine of them were cooling in the morgue, victims of their own hate and anger, killed by fellow prisoners over slights real or imagined. If she could recreate some of that visceral emotion among the high-strung escapees, the schism might bring a premature end to Misrule's plans.

Of the escapees remaining, Katie felt Brainstorm, Escudo, and Dissident were the most likely to sour on Misrule's current plan of action, and the Etched Man seemed to have a sizable chip on his shoulder about being told what to do. She wondered if dissent would cost them their lives. Brainstorm had begun to question Misrule's authority, to herself if not openly. The nature of Escudo's powers made him a defensive thinker; he shielded those weaker than himself with his abilities, and he seemed fearful of Espada's bloodthirstiness and had no taste for it himself. Dissident was very much a mercenary, following the money, but he was no fighter and rejected authority out of hand wherever he encountered it.

Exhaustion had taken its toll on her. Katie started as she realized she'd drifted off to sleep, only awakening when her head hit the bulkhead. She felt like she could sleep for twelve or fourteen hours herself, but didn't dare let down her guard. She'd sat for too long. It was time to move, to act. She looked around the tiny bathroom in the hope there might be some kind of floor or ceiling hatch through which she could escape undetected. Unfortunately, the plane's designers had neglected to consider the possibility someone might need to leave via other means besides the door.

She knew there had to be some way down into the cargo area under the passenger deck. It would probably be in the stewardess station, which was only a few feet from her current spot in the bathroom, but unless she could get there without being seen, it might as well have been in another country. She wished she had Foster's dimming power. Even that would be preferable to her flame-tipped fingers at the moment. What she really needed was a diversion of some sort, something to keep the hostages and escapees looking away from the tail of the plane while she made her quick exit below.

And at that moment, over the rushing howl of the engines, she heard shouting.

* * *

Cassie came back from the cockpit. She looked disheveled and frightened. Her roving eyes found Foster's and she dropped into the seat next to him.

"How are you doing?" she asked him.

Foster made a noncommittal noise. "Not bad for a hostage. How are you and Misrule getting on?"

"Famously," Cassie said. "I'm supposed to be back here checking on Kiloton and Espada. Then I have to go report to Misrule and hope the news isn't so bad he opts to kill the messenger. How are they, anyway?"

"Kiloton is fine," said Foster. "His injuries were superficial. Doctor Mayfair just ordered him to rest. Espada's not doing so good. I think she's dying."

The Hispanic swordfighter was in shock from her burns, her skin blackened and blistered from her fight with Glamour. Mayfair and his nurse struggled to keep her alive, but neither looked optimistic. They raided the jet's small first aid kit for supplies. Espada shivered despite the blanket covering her. The nurse emptied salt and sugar packets into water bottles to make an improvised electrolyte solution. Mayfair monitored the escapee's vitals and checked her pulse and respiration constantly.

"Is there anything we can do to help?" asked Cassie. Convicted felon or not, it was hard to watch someone suffer so much pain.

"Yes. Tell Misrule that if he wants to keep her alive, he needs to land this plane now. The medical kit here is a joke. Worthless. She needs a hospital."

Cassie stood, as did Foster. "I'll tell him, but I doubt he'll consider that as an option."

Mayfair wiped sweat from his forehead with his sleeve. "If he doesn't, she'll be dead within an hour. There's nothing more I can do. She's losing this fight."

Foster put his hand on Cassie's arm. "Want me to go with you?"

Cassie swallowed hard. "No. It's better if you stay here. Besides, the natives are getting restless." She nodded her head toward Whisper and Nightmare, who glared at Foster with open hatred. "They don't like you much. You killed too many of their companions."

"The feeling is mutual, believe me," muttered Foster.

"What was that?" grunted Heretic from where he stood in the aisle, his gun held across his chest.

"I said you're a cocksucking prick."

"You want to eat a bullet, you fucking screw?" Heretic raised his voice and his gun together.

"You're an idiot if you keep listening to Misrule." Foster likewise raised his voice.

"What are you doing?" hissed Cassie, but Foster ignored her.

"This is a Syrian jet," shouted Foster. "You think we're going on a little pleasure jaunt across the Mediterranean?"

"What do you care? You're just meat. Just a walking insurance policy." Nightmare sidled up beside Heretic, sparks dancing behind her eyes.

"He's turned his hand," said Foster. "He's trying to escape to a country friendly to terrorists. Do you think for one second the U.S. is going to allow him to get there?"

Cassie looked around helplessly. She was afraid that Foster was about to get himself killed. Suddenly she noticed some motion towards the rear of the plane. A bathroom door opened and a figure hurried out and disappeared behind the aft bulkhead. She steeled herself, afraid that her face might give away some indication of what she'd seen.

"What are they going to do, shoot us down?" Heretic's laugh wasn't amused in the least. "Not with you on board. Now sit down and shut the fuck up before I decide you're not worth the effort."

Foster opened his mouth to continue the argument, but Cassie yanked hard on his arm and he sat down. "That's enough," she whispered. "It's out of your hands now."

His eyes widened and he turned to face straight forward in his seat, not daring to look anywhere toward the rear of the plane.

Cassie stood. Heretic, still looking for a fight, growled at her. "Where do you think you're going?"

"Back to the cockpit. Misrule's request," she said. "Perhaps you'd like to argue the point with him?"

A flash of something that might have been fear crossed Heretic's face before being replaced by a more stolid expression. In spite of her dislike for Misrule, she felt a small thrill at the power even his name carried.

"I thought not," she said. "Now piss off." She turned her back on Heretic and stalked back through First Class.

* * *

"Try it now," said Garcia.

Lania shrugged inside her suit and closed her eyes and focused on the magnetic fields around her. She detected a definite bulge in the field in front of her that extended out a couple of feet.

"I think that's got it," she said. Garcia grinned. The two of them, with Jack's inexpert assistance, had managed to rewire her suit and alter the software in the monitoring computer to create the bulge. "Now what?"

"By detonating particles just beyond the edge of this bubble, it should compress into an inverted bell. That makes a rocket engine." Garcia set down his tools.

"You know that for a fact?" asked Jack.

"No," said Garcia. "But it sounds good in theory."

"People thought Betamax sounded good in theory," grumbled Jack.

"What's Betamax?" asked Lania.

"Something from before your time." Jack stood up and began to fuss with a heavy harness.

The *Rita* had a tail-mounted airlock so the flying members of Just Cause could enter and leave the jet while in flight. Jack described how they would strap Lania inside the airlock and tie her down every way possible to keep her from falling. Then Reed would open the lock wide to give her an unrestricted field of view to the rear. At that point they would try the pusher-plate drive Garcia had imagined. It would either work, or it was back to the drawing board. Jack even went so far as to track down a propulsion engineer he knew in Phoenix to see if such a half-assed idea would work. She told him he was nuts, but agreed the theory was sound. It didn't make him feel any more confident. His indestructibility often led him to take risks that would be foolish for others. If the *Rita* blew up in midair, or crashed headlong into the ocean, he'd survive it. But he could still drown, he could still suffocate, and he could still have to live with approving a plan that might kill everyone else on board.

They buckled Lania down as tightly as they could and braced her against the solid bulkhead. Garcia had no idea what kind of pressure would be exerted on her or the airframe of the jet when she started to fire off antimatter particles behind them. He'd asked her time and time again if she was sure she wanted to assume the risk of being crushed into paste. She was sure. She'd do whatever it took to rescue the hostages.

Jack and Garcia retreated back into the cabin and strapped themselves back into their seats. Jack attuned the monitor to show the airlock camera view. "Lania, are you ready?"

She gave a thumbs-up.

"All right, Reed, open the lock."

The plane shuddered with the change in its aerodynamics as part of the tail section retracted, leaving Lania alone on a platform open above, behind, and to the sides. She didn't move, which relieved Jack; they'd tied her down tight enough.

"All right, let's do a test firing. Reed, stand by. Lania, on my count. Five . . . four . . . three . . . two . . . one . . . fire!"

A bright point of light emerged from within Lania's suit and burned out the camera in the lock.

WHAM!

They felt a brief lurch of acceleration, then nothing.

"Lania? Report in . . . are you all right?"

"*Si* . . . Yes. That was intense. Did it work?" She sounded shaken but still had a lot of strength in her voice.

"Reed?"

"My airspeed indicator jumped about a tenth of a Mach unit. But the Rita handled the shock, so I'm going to say it was successful. One thing though . . . the engines won't handle the strain of traveling faster than Mach 2.5, so if we manage to top that, I'll have to shut them down and dead-stick it."

"I understand," said Jack. "Well, everyone . . . if anyone wants to offer a different idea, I'm ready to entertain it." He paused. "No? Anyone? Anyone? Bueller?"

Garcia grinned at the movie reference.

"Okay then, Lania. Light us up."

WHAM!
WHAM!
WHAM!

* * *

"Espada is dying." Cassie flopped into the seat beside Misrule. "Unless you land now, Doctor Mayfair says she won't survive this trip."

Misrule didn't turn his head toward her, keeping his gaze on the clouds. "That is disappointing."

Cassie's mouth dropped open. "That's it? That's all you have to say about her? She's dying because she fought for you."

"I could recite a long list of others who have died on my behalf," said Misrule. "I am not concerned with anything but the results of their actions."

"That's horrible."

At that, Misrule looked at her, and Cassie felt her bones turn to water and her blood to ice. "I am a horrible person, Cassandra. You would do well to remember that."

"You're going to kill all of us, aren't you?"

He returned his attention to the controls once more. "Perhaps. Are you considering some pointless act of martyrdom? Grab the controls and dash the plane into the ground?"

The idea had occurred to Cassie, but she didn't see how she could accomplish such a task with Misrule in the cockpit with her. All he had to do was reach over and crush her skull like an overripe fruit. "No," she muttered. "I won't kill everyone. You'll have to do it."

"As I said, perhaps. The difference is that if I do choose that course of action, I will still be able to face myself tomorrow. I have come to terms with my heinous acts. I have no illusions that I am anything besides a monster, but I am not bothered by that nomenclature."

"You don't care about anyone?"

"No. I only care about results."

"And what is your ideal result from this escape you have orchestrated?"

Misrule didn't answer immediately. Cassie wondered if he even knew what he wanted. But he was only organizing his thoughts. "Arriving at my destination without incident will be satisfactory. It is my desire to see the majority of those I released to remain with me. My sponsors have agreed to provide exceptional succor and compensation in return for their efforts."

"What efforts are those? Or is it the kind of thing where you could tell me but then you'd have to kill me?" Cassie decided that if Misrule felt like talking, she'd try and get as much information from him as possible.

"Don't insult me by suggesting I need a reason to kill you." Misrule spared her a sulfurous glance. "I will be performing actions against American interests, at the behest and sponsorship of a group that is at odds with those interests."

"You'll be a terrorist."

"Semantics, Cassandra. I have always been a terrorist. It just happens that now I have found a group that will pay my way, instead of having to support myself." He glanced down at the device protruding from his chest. "I think, however, I shall keep this toy. People seem to be more inclined to behave themselves around me if they know I have the capability to destroy their entire city if they attack me."

"They'll never let you get away with it."

"Who is that?"

"Just Cause. The other teams. They'll find you, and bring you down."

"Just Cause. The other teams," mocked Misrule. "They never did locate me even after all those years of looking. I turned myself in. I have no fear of them. I see them truly for what they are."

Cassie didn't like the direction of the conversation, but felt powerless to stop it. "What is that?"

"Targets. Nothing more. Your government has already declared them as such. Surely you can see that."

"What do you mean?"

"Your president has decided parahumans are a threat to his national security, to the fascist state he has created in all but name. He will see to their elimination, first by enacting new versions of old laws, then by quietly arresting, incarcerating, or executing anyone exhibiting a parahuman gene. Even those with trivial powers."

"No, that won't happen. That could never happen," said Cassie.

"It has happened countless times throughout history," said Misrule. "Those in power fear those who have the capability to usurp that power. Why do you think the Parahuman Resources Agency was created? It's a registry of active parahumans." Misrule looked straight at her. "A hit list. Soon, being a parahuman in America will be like being a Jew in Germany circa 1938."

Cassie couldn't find the words to reply. Things couldn't be that bad. But Misrule had raised some questions in the back of her mind that could not easily be set aside. She was a parahuman too. Even such a trivial ability as hers was enough to set her apart by the tags in her genes. Would that make her a target in Misrule's dark future? She decided he was wrong. It was better to think that way than the alternative.

But just the same, she knew she would evermore be more aware of political undercurrents should she survive this ordeal.

* * *

Juice called Doublecharge, and he was angry—a rarity for a man who normally possessed great reserves of patience. "Stacey, who's in the *Rita*?"

"The *Rita*?" asked Doublecharge, as if she hadn't heard him correctly.

"Yes. NORAD monitored it leaving Deep Six within minutes after you and I last spoke, and you said it might be better if I didn't know what was going on."

"Well . . . maybe you should consider that I was right about that."

Juice sighed. "Cut the crap, Stacey. We've been friends too long to do this to each other. Off the record . . . who did you send? I'm guessing Jack."

"Good guess. But I didn't send him anywhere. He requested to take some vacation time and I granted it."

"Vacation? We both know Jack hasn't taken a vacation in twenty years."

"Then I guess he's overdue."

"And you just happened to authorize him to take the *Rita*, leaving you and the rest of the team stranded in the middle of Montana."

"We're not actually stranded," said Doublecharge. "Deep Six flight personnel have kindly offered to take us back to Denver once we've completely secured the facility and made sure it's safe to reopen."

"Stacey, for the last time, you've got to tell me what's going on. I may be the only one who can keep you out of trouble. I've had two calls from the President today . . . the first one he wanted my advice. The second time he was demanding an explanation, and what you tell me will determine what I tell him. He's expecting my call in ten minutes, so you've got to tell me the whole truth. I'll protect you the best I can."

"I know, James," said Doublecharge. "Nobody ever worked the attorney angle better than you did. All right, here's the story. Jack and two guards from Deep Six are flying to intercept Misrule's jet before it reaches Syrian airspace, assuming that's his destination. His course is questionable right now."

"Indeed. Heading straight south. He could be making for Libya, or he may be intending to skirt the Adriatic, then cross Greece and follow the Turkish coast into Syria. We've contacted Syrian Arab Air and they have confirmed this jet was supposed to be under repairs and out of circulation."

"And of course, everybody is denying culpability or responsibility?" Doublecharge's voice was bitter.

"Of course. The President has placed the Sixth Fleet on high alert, and every satellite that can see it is tracking that jet. We'll know where it lands, and be ready for it."

Doublecharge detected the cynicism in Juice's phrasing. "You don't think so?"

"Off the record, no I don't. The President is inclined to blow it out of the sky and claim the escapees detonated a bomb themselves."

"He's willing to slaughter those hostages?" Doublecharge couldn't believe it.

"They play by different rules here in Washington," said Juice. "A jetliner loaded with explosives and carrying hostages is blown up by the hijackers. That'd make a nice thirty-second sound bite in between lottery numbers and a look at the weather. Americans don't care what happens halfway around the world, and the media will report whatever the government tells them is the truth."

"My, you've gotten cynical in your retirement."

"I've opened my eyes, and it doesn't look so good."

"What are you going to tell the President?"

"The truth. That Jack took the *Rita* himself to try to rescue the hostages, against your advice and authority."

Doublecharge felt a new headache threaten. "He's the sacrificial lamb."

Juice's voice became conspiratorial. "Stacey, he's a celebrity, a media darling—the face of Just Cause for the past two decades. Everybody knows who he is. The man has hosted Saturday Night Live three times, for God's sake. If he fails in his attempt, he'll survive it because the public loves an underdog, even when he loses. If he somehow succeeds, it makes Just Cause look even better, and right now you need any positive press you can get. And if anyone can pull off an improbable rescue mission, it's him."

"I hope you're right, James."

"So do I, Stacey, so do I. Now, I have something else to ask from my science people. What in the hell is exploding off the back of the *Rita* that's making it go over Mach 3?"

* * *

"How long can you keep—" *WHAM!* "—this up?" Jack had to shout into the radio to be heard over the constant explosions of the antimatter pulses.

"I have—" *WHAM!* "—no idea." Lania had success-fully boosted the *Rita* to the target speed. After some trial and error with Reed's calculations, she was maintaining a constant flight speed with one detonation every two seconds.

Jack was invulnerable to every kind of damage imaginable. He had been shot at, burned, stabbed, blown-up, electrocuted, sprayed with acid, irradiated, magicked, and buried underneath the World Trade Center towers when they collapsed. He began to wonder if sound was his Achilles' Heel. Every explosion seemed like it went right through his skull.

"Reed, are we holding together?" *WHAM!*

"So far," said the pilot.

"What are you going to do—" *WHAM!* "—when we catch Misrule's jet?" asked Garcia.

"I've got a plan in the works." Jack had dredged idea after idea from the dark recesses of his brain and tried to draw upon years of the covert and commando missions that had been his specialty as a member of Just Cause. He tried to shut out the noise of the detonations aft of the *Rita* and focus on the problem at hand. The goal, of course, was to rescue the hostages and recapture the felons, in that order. While they were on the plane, neither goal seemed to be within reach. And if the plane was allowed to land at whatever destination Misrule had decided upon, it was likely he had reinforcements at that location.

Whatever plan Jack put into effect would have to take place before the jet reached its destination, which meant they had to somehow deal with it while still airborne. The *Rita* was heavily-armed, and could shoot the jetliner out of the sky with a minimum of fuss and bother, but that was akin to police shooting a suicidal jumper to keep him from killing himself. Perhaps they could force it down and make Misrule land prematurely. Again, Jack argued against the idea with himself. The escaped prisoners could slaughter all their hostages before the plane touched down, and Misrule could still detonate his nerve gas bomb. To minimize or eliminate potential civilian deaths, the only safe place to force the plane down would be over the Mediterranean, and a water landing was likely a death sentence for all aboard.

The puzzle of the jet wasn't helping his headache. It was like a doctor having to perform surgery wearing boxing gloves. Jack was used to dealing with his problems up close and personal, and trusting his personal invulnerability to protect him. Trying to rescue hostages he couldn't see, to dispatch opponents he couldn't touch, made him feel almost impotent.

WHAM!

WHAM!

WHAM!

He wished he could just leave the *Rita* entirely so he could think. The noise was intolerable.

And then it hit him.

He could board Misrule's jet and take it over from the inside. He had a tank of the fast-acting anesthetic gas used by Deep Six. He had a bag full of sleeper sets. And he had an ex-Air Force pilot in Reed who could talk him through an emergency landing.

WHAM!

"Reed, I'm coming up front. I need to talk to you. Come on, Garcia."

Jack led Garcia through the cabin to the cockpit. When he shut the door, he was astonished to discover that the antimatter explosions only registered as dull thumps.

Reed Ferguson was in his mid-40s, his military regulation haircut starting to gray around the edges. Ten years retired, he still carried himself with the professionalism and competency of a combat veteran. In the first Gulf War, he'd flown over fifty missions in a tank-busting A-10 Thunderbolt. Once he'd had half a plane shot out from under him and still managed to limp it back to an airbase.

"Good insulation in here." Garcia voiced Jack's unspoken thought.

"Sound canceling technology," said Reed.

"How come we don't have it back in the cabin?" asked Jack, mouth agape.

"Lack of funding. I cobbled this together myself last year. You wouldn't believe how loud it can get up here with all the background noise. I was losing my hearing."

"Fine then. We'll just keep you company for a spell," said Jack. "Now, here's my idea, and I want you to tell me how we can make it happen."

"Shoot."

"I want you to get me on board that jet without anyone noticing." Jack grinned, tucked his hands behind his head, and waited.

Reed actually turned around in his seat to stare at Jack. The look of incredulity on his face matched Garcia's. "Run that by me again? I'm not sure I heard you right."

Jack said, "I want you to get me on board Misrule's jet so I can take down the escapees."

Reed shook his head. "That's what I thought you said. No way, it's impossible."

"This is Just Cause, buddy. We make the impossible ordinary."

"I don't care about ordinary. I'm telling you that you can't get onto a jet in midair. This isn't some Hollywood movie where the laws of physics can be set aside if necessary."

"I'm not trying to change the laws of physics," said Jack. "Just bend them a little. Come on, what are parahumans if not violations of the Law of Conservation of Energy?"

"Huh?"

"Hang on a second," said Garcia. "Reed, what are the factors against this succeeding? List them for me."

"Altitude and airspeed, primarily," said Reed. "The only way you could get into a jet in flight without the crew noticing would be for you to come in underneath, into the cargo section. That would mean cutting a hole in the hull, which would immediately depressurize the plane and alert them to your presence. Not to mention the inherent difficulties in performing such a task while you can't breathe and are freezing to death."

"Go on," said Jack.

"The jet is probably cruising at about five hundred miles per hour. Sticking your head up in that would be like hitting a cement wall. You couldn't hold onto anything. It would be ripped from your hands. That means you'd lose your tools to cut into the plane's skin, assuming you could even manage to get a grip on it at all."

"Sounds impossible," said Jack. "Fortunately we've got some time to work around those problems."

"How good of a pilot are you?" asked Garcia.

"Damn good," retorted Reed. "I'm flying the *Rita* at three times her rated top speed, aren't I?"

"You could get us close underneath Misrule's plane? Like to within touching distance?"

Reed considered. "Yes. It would be hard as hell, but I could do it."

"But could you do it inverted?" asked Garcia.

"What?" asked Jack and Reed simultaneously.

"Could you fly the *Rita* inverted underneath the target jet? At touching distance?"

"What the hell are you getting at here, Garcia?" asked Jack.

"Well," said Reed slowly. "Now you're talking really difficult. Yeah, sure. Why not? It'd give me some good stories to tell at the Old Pilots' Home. And I intend to retire there, by the way—not get shot down or crash over the damn Mediterranean Sea in a stupid rescue mission."

"What if you opened the bomb bay doors and extended the nose landing gear?" continued Garcia. "That would give easy access to the other plane as well as create some air eddies that might reduce the wind speed to a more manageable level."

The *Rita*, being first and foremost designed to facilitate rapid deployment of Just Cause members, had multiple ways to offload passengers. The fastest was by means of the bomb bay doors, which opened at the front of the cabin. The doors were designed to open in such a way as to shield the heroes from the jet wash of the engines. As the *Rita* was also optimized for combat, and often dropped her passengers into the middle of combat situations, her landing gear was armored and covered by a plate to deflect incoming attacks.

Reed's eyes widened. "You're crazy. I don't even know how to simulate that here. You'd have to be a top-level aeronautical engineer to even try and figure out whether it would work."

"Do you have any better ideas?" asked Jack.

"No," said the pilot.

"Then we'll run with this until somebody tells us it can't be done or we come up with a better idea."

"That only solves part of the problem," grumbled Garcia. "We still don't know how to do the rest of it."

"I've got a rare-earth magnet that can hold me onto the skin of the jet," said Jack. "It's attached to a heavy line and fires from a compressed-air charge. Then I've got a microtorch that Orb made for me. That'll make short work of the hull."

"That's great. Now all we need to do is figure out how to keep from depressurizing the plane." Garcia rested his chin on his hands, deep in thought.

"A vacuum jar," said Reed suddenly. "Or something like it. If you can fasten some kind of airtight sleeve around yourself before you cut into the hull, it will trap the escaping air and not noticeably affect the interior pressure. It should work."

"Sure, I've got a vacuum jar back there in one of the cabinets," said Jack.

"Really?"

"No, of course not. But you can bet I'll start carrying a man-sized one in the future. That doesn't help us right now."

"What about the life raft?" asked Garcia.

Reed jumped on that. "Yeah, that might work. It's flexible so it could fit tightly around you and it's meant to be airtight already. It would also be easier to affix to the hull with a good seal."

"I have some fast-acting adhesive gel that would do the trick for sticking it to the hull," said Jack. "But what do I do when I get aboard? Surely the sleeve wouldn't last the duration of the flight."

"Once you're aboard, you just need to cover the hole. The plane's interior pressure will hold it in place."

"Brilliant," said Garcia.

"Or just incredibly foolish," said Jack. "But it's as good a plan as anything. Let's get to work on it."

"Let us be thankful for the fools. But for them the rest of us could not succeed."

—*Mark Twain*

July, 2007
Over the Mediterranean

Katie awoke with a start.

She'd dozed off in the empty cargo bay, lulled by the constant roar of the engines and the whisper of air underneath the hull. In spite of her care, she realized she was in plain sight, leaning against the curve of the interior wall.

She cursed at herself and got to her feet to look around in the dimmed light and get her bearings. Towards the aft of the jet was the ladder that led to a hatch in the galley. The cargo bay doors were designed to be opened from the outside as far as she could tell. Since she had no desire to suddenly depressurize the entire plane, she didn't explore them further as an option. She continued forward through the empty hold and sought anything that would give her an idea of what to do next.

At the front of the cargo hold, she found a wall with both a ladder that led up it to another deck at eye level and a narrow door into it. She checked the door and found a cramped passage that was lined with computer modules, labeled *Avionics*. She decided she would come back to explore it more, as it might present her the best solution to somehow disable the plane. The modules were mounted on shelves surrounding a large, sealed column that she thought was probably the nose landing gear.

The ladder ended in a small square panel and she shivered as she realized she was right underneath the cockpit. Misrule was probably only a few inches above her. She hoped the demonic man couldn't hear her over the noise of the flight. She resisted the impulse to listen at the panel. No help there, so she went back down the ladder again to look at the computers in greater detail.

A monitor sat amid all the modules with its own keyboard and mouse that rested snug in a socket to one side. The monitor was in standby mode but it awakened when she picked up the mouse. Information covered the screen, many filled with numbers, others with information relayed in Arabic.

She groaned.

To demolish or disable the computers would probably be the most efficacious way to take down the jet, but that smacked of the kind of permanence she wished to avoid.

Suddenly the plane took a sharp dip and the motion hurled her into a rack. She clipped a shelf with her head and pitched forward into blackness.

* * *

Cassie once more found herself seated next to Misrule in the jet's cockpit. Normally she couldn't stand to travel in silence, but even the thought of working information out of Misrule felt like far more of a chore than she could handle. Exhaustion had taken its toll and dulled her mind. Her eyes heavy, her head began to loll forward as she drifted in and out of fitful sleep, waking herself with a start before beginning the cycle anew. After the fifth or sixth time she'd jerked awake she shook her head and looked out the window to her right.

Someone looked back in at her from outside the plane.

She yelped in surprise. Misrule glanced at her, noticed the man pacing the plane, and his brow wrinkled. "Interesting." He switched off the automatic pilot.

The man seemed unaffected by the cold or low air pressure, and flew without any apparent means of locomotion. He wore an intricate exoskeleton which extended up into a fanciful falcon's-head mask that obscured his face in favor of the birdlike visage. His arms were bare except for the mechanics of the exoskeleton that ended in heavy bracers around his forearms. Cassie could see long capes stretched back from each arm and shoulder that loosely resembled wings.

The man stared in through the window of the plane. His unblinking falcon's gaze made Cassie feel guilty in spite of herself. She turned away and gasped as she saw someone else outside the opposite window.

Misrule growled deep in the back of his throat as he too saw the other figure—a woman who glowed painfully bright like a comet. Her face was turned toward them as well, with dark red eyes and mouth visible through the brightness of her flesh. Her legs seemed to be fused into a single beam that darkened into a smoky contrail. Cassie thought she looked more like a beam of light with humanoid tendencies than a human imitating a beam of light.

"Who are they?" she asked.

"Italian heroes," said Misrule. "Falco and Lumina. Fascinating. I would have expected them to shy away rather than risk me raining death upon their nation. Perhaps they are not aware of the cargo I carry."

The radio crackled. "*Resa ora!*" said a masculine voice.

"Surrender?" asked Misrule. "Have you recently acquired a sense of humor, Falco?"

"I order you to change course, land in Sicily, and surrender to the authorities," said the man in a heavy Italian accent.

"Now I am certain you are joking," said Misrule. "Did you hear about me on CNN and decide to play hero? It is a pity you did not wait for the full story or you would be aware of the nerve toxin I am carrying aboard."

"Nerve toxin?" said a static-laden female voice, undoubtedly from the glowing woman outside Misrule's window.

"Indeed." Misrule made no move to alter his course in the least.

"Then we shall destroy you here." Lumina's voice was a deadly hiss.

"You would slaughter the innocent hostages aboard this jet? I suspect the American government will look most unfavorably on such an act."

"You are a terrorist. Americans will tolerate heinous acts if they are perpetrated against terrorists."

Misrule turned on the intercom. "Etch, come to the cockpit." He returned his attention to the Italian parahumans outside the plane. "The two of you cannot be comfortable at such altitude. Perhaps you would be happier closer to the surface."

The plane's engines changed pitch and Cassie gasped as the nose dipped, and the jet dropped into the cloud cover below. The two parahumans followed suit and flanked the cockpit but took no other action. Cassie realized Misrule's observation was most likely correct. The Italian heroes had intercepted them rashly, without a plan or regard for the safety of anyone aboard the plane.

The Etched Man slunk into the cockpit. His inked skin radiated heat as if his tattoos themselves were infected. "Oh, look, new playmates."

"Yes." Misrule glared out the windscreen at the Italians. They had moved to fly next to each other, just outside Misrule's side of the cockpit, and were having an animated discussion. They cleared the clouds and the great blue expanse of the Mediterranean sprawled beneath them as the plane continued to descend. "Can you deal with them from in here?"

"Of course I can. I'm not useless," snapped the tattooed man as he selected an image from the small of his back. The creature had a mouth like a lamprey and a belt of four triangular wings around its middle. Its tail was a barbed lash that flicked back and forth and nearly creased Cassie's cheek. It flung itself forward and through the windscreen like a shadow to latch onto Falco's back. He screamed and fell helplessly as the monster attacked him. Lumina blasted energy at it and it dissolved into ash, carried away by the wind.

The Etched Man sniffed in a disappointed way.

Misrule was more verbal in his displeasure. "That is the best you can do?"

"No, of course not," snapped the thin man, and he rummaged around his flesh for more monsters to cast at the Italians.

Since the escapees had struck the first blow, the Italians must have felt it their duty to respond in kind. Falco, bleeding from a circular wound on his back and trailing bits of shredded exoskeleton, flew up and aft, out of view of the cockpit windows.

"Etch, go see what he's doing," said Misrule.

"No," muttered the Etched Man.

Misrule let go of the controls and drew himself up to his full height until his white hair brushed the cockpit ceiling. "Reconsider," rumbled the red-skinned man.

"No. I'm tired of you telling me what to do. I'm not your bitch. I was playing this game long before you ever crawled away from whatever whore spawned you." Blackness swirled around the Etched Man's hands as ink played across his skin.

"I made you into what you are today." The ire in Misrule's voice made Cassie want to crawl underneath the flight controls. "Without me you are nothing. You can go back to your pathetic, laughable super-villain antics of terrorizing rural farmsteads and catching teenagers necking on darkened roads."

"Stop it! Shut up!"

"You're a joke, Etch. A punchline. You always have been. At least when you're beside me you gain a semblance of respectability."

The Etched Man screamed in fury. Black tendrils shot forth from him to wrap around Misrule. Cassie gasped as the ink poured off of him, leaving his papery skin withered and unmarked in its wake. Then Misrule punched his arms clear of the darkness which swirled around him and closed his hands around the Etched Man's head to squeeze the life out of him.

Tattoos flowed like smoke and pulled desperately against Misrule's iron muscles. The Etched Man's eyes bulged out as he struggled to free himself. Ink thrust itself into Misrule's very body, through his nostrils and between his clenched teeth to smother and choke him. The two stayed locked together for several seconds, each trying to overcome the other's will. Then Misrule roared and tore out the Etched Man's throat with his teeth.

Ink sprayed across the cockpit. Horrible images briefly appeared on the walls before they ran together, turned to smoke, and disappeared. Cassie gasped as Misrule dropped the body to the floor. The Etched Man had no blood. As she watched, the man's body deflated like a punctured balloon and crumbled into dust.

Misrule coughed once and spat up something black against the wall. He turned to Cassie. She feared he'd become kill-crazy, desperate to slay and slay again in a berserk rage until nobody around him lived. The musky scent of his sweat filled the air of the cockpit and made her head spin. She saw the bulge in his shorts and realized he'd been overcome by a different sort of lust. He reached for her and she screamed and tried to flee.

Lumina moved right in front of the windscreen, flying backwards with her exhaust whipping all around the nose of the jet. She flashed like a flare going off. Cassie yelped and dug her fists into her eyes. Whether her eyes were open or shut, she only saw a floating green and red blob except in her peripheral vision.

The plane quivered suddenly. Almost immediately thereafter, an insistent, repetitive buzzer sounded through the cockpit. Misrule spun around, his lust forgotten, and examined the flight data readout.

"I apologize, Cassandra. That was very rude of me. Sit down and I will not harm you."

Cassie, blinded, fell into a seat. She wished she could have fled, but somehow she understood that her presence in the cockpit was keeping the other hostages alive. She concentrated on her pathetic parapower. Maybe if she cooled the air in the cockpit, Misrule would likewise cool down.

Misrule clicked on the intercom. "Falco has holed a fuel tank. Anyone who eliminates the man currently punching holes in our portside wing will earn my gratitude."

A thundering roar blasted through the jet as a pair of fighter jets overtook them, passing overhead and underneath, rocking the plane in their wake before they split up, arcing back around behind them once more. "Syrian Air Tango Three Niner Three, this is Lieutenant Will Holmes of the United States Navy. Come about to zero-eight-five degrees and prepare to be escorted to an EU airbase."

"Motherfucker," said Misrule under his breath.

* * *

WHAM! WHAM!

"Jack, call from Doublecharge," said Reed from the cockpit. "Do you want to take it up here?"

Jack set aside his project and nodded at Garcia, who continued to work. They had broken into the emergency stores on the *Rita* and started to cannibalize what they could. The life raft was spread across the cabin with a large piece cut from one side. That piece had been carefully reformed into an inflatable suit into which Jack would cram himself when the time came. Garcia was attaching an emergency breather to the wetsuit Jack carried in his regular gear. The breather contained about ten minutes of concentrated air but had nothing to secure it to the wearer. Jack would be exposing himself to winds in excess of two hundred miles per hour, which was Reed's best guess as to what the air would be like in the space between the two planes. Anything not securely fastened to his body would be torn away like leaves in a gale.

Jack stepped into the cockpit. Lania reported she was growing tired and her suit's power reserves were getting low. She'd promised them another ten minutes but that time was approaching rapidly. Reed prepared the *Rita* for self-powered flight once more and seemed to be everywhere at once in the cockpit.

"This is Jack, go ahead."

"Jack, we have a problem." Doublecharge sounded thoroughly exhausted.

"Just one? Oh, good. I can deal with them singly. What's up?"

"Can you confirm how far you are from intercept? We're estimating another twenty-five minutes."

Reed shook his head. "We'll be decelerating to normal cruising speed in a few minutes. Lania's exhausted herself. Call it forty minutes."

"Did you get all that?" asked Jack.

"Yes. Dammit. I hope you're not too late. We've got a three-way battle developing that looks like it could get very ugly."

"Three sides?"

"The escapees, two Italian heroes, and United States Navy jets."

"Is that all? Shoot, I thought you were going to tell me about a problem," said Jack. "Which Italians?"

"Falco and Lumina."

Jack's face fell. "Oh, I see."

The thumps from the rear of the jet stopped. A moment later the status screen showed the airlock closing. "Beginning deceleration," announced Reed. "Who are Falco and Lumina?"

"They're hotheads."

"Who's a hothead?" Garcia opened the cockpit door.

"Couple of Italian heroes," said Jack. "They're the kind of people who rush into a situation they know nothing about and exacerbate it with their presence, when the better choice of action would be to sit back and gain intel."

"Sounds like what we're doing," said Garcia.

Jack opened his mouth to speak, but then snapped it shut as he realized Garcia's assessment was accurate.

"Your suit is ready," said Garcia. "I think I used about a whole roll of duct tape holding it together."

"I hope it's enough. I've fallen from planes before, but never from thirty-five thousand feet. I'm not anxious to experience that today."

"Juice is messaging me as he gets information," said Doublecharge. "I don't think he has time to even call. I've got the team scrambled and we're on a Deep Six transport heading east. We'll rendezvous with the *Marilyn* in Chicago and then make for your part of the world."

The *Marilyn* was an older version of the *Rita*, used by Just Cause's Second Team from their headquarters in Richmond, Virginia.

"You may not make it in time to do anything but pick up the pieces," said Jack.

"It's a chance we'll have to take," said Doublecharge. "Parahuman relations with the U.S. Government are strained to the breaking point. If this thing blows up and we end up with a bunch of dead hostages at the hands of escaped prisoners, or dead Navy pilots at the hands of foreign paras . . . I don't even want to think what might happen."

"You realize you're breaking a direct order," Jack said. "As is everyone else on the team."

"Jack . . ." said Doublecharge, and stopped. For a moment he wondered if they'd lost the connection. "We found a survivor, an escapee, in Deep Six. He told us Misrule's plan. He's going into the wholesale terrorism business. He's got wealthy sponsors in the Middle East fronting everything for this escape operation. In return for their investment, he's going to hit whatever targets they select, with a new Cult of Destruction."

"Holy shit," whispered Garcia.

"Think about it, Jack. Parahuman terrorism. How's the President going to react to that? It's going to be 1953 all over again, except this time they won't just be registering parahumans, they'll be rounding us all up as potential threats and we'll either be held in camps or just quietly disappear. I have to do whatever it takes to stop that from happening. If that means Just Cause has to take the fall for all the others . . . what other option is there?"

A muscle twitched in Jack's jaw. "I won't let you down, Stacey."

"I know you won't. Good luck and God bless."

* * *

"I'll say it once more, Lieutenant Holmes," said Misrule. "I have American citizens aboard this plane. We are under attack by foreign parahumans. You are obligated to defend us." He banked the jet to swat at Falco and Lumina as they fussed around the wings. Lumina's powers were mostly non-offensive except for her bright flash, but she used it effectively to keep the Navy jets at bay while Falco worked at opening another section of the wing fuel tanks.

"We can't just attack without direct orders, Mr. uh, Misrule," said the pilot. "They are not replying to our communications."

Misrule snapped his head around to face Cassie. "Cassandra, go back and make a list of the names of all hostages and bring it back here. Quickly or I'll dash this plane into the sea."

Cassie jumped up and hurried back to the cabin to do his bidding, even though she could barely see after Lumina's bright flash.

"Lieutenant, do you see that stream leaving my port wing? That is fuel and the more I lose, the less likely I am to be able to comply with your orders. You have a duty."

"I can't."

"Lieutenant, we are going to die," said Misrule, his patience at an end. "You have a higher calling to defend Americans. Are you prepared to deal with the public outcry for failing to act?"

The plane shuddered as Falco ripped a flap free.

"Shit," muttered the pilot aloud. "*Eagle One* to *Eagle Two*, clear your guns. Give them some warning shots. Do not—repeat—do not fire directly on them or on the target."

"Roger that," said the pilot of the other jet.

Tracer rounds illuminated the sky in pale imitations of Lumina's bright energy.

Cassie returned to the cockpit, a scrap of paper clutched in her hand, and gasped as she saw one of the Navy jets flash past them. Misrule flung the microphone at her. "Read your list aloud, slowly and clearly, Cassandra, and repeat it until I tell you to stop."

She wished she had a drink of water to moisten her lips, but Cassie cleared her throat and began to read. She knew someone in the Navy had to be monitoring their communications would order the pilots to protect the jet. "Roberto Gonzalvo, Renata Washington, Dr. Donald Mayfair, Laura Danforth, Jose Lopez, Bibiano Lopez, Timothy Foster, Montell Plummer, Ahmad Gordon . . ." She continued to read the names until she thought she would lose her voice.

Falco left the wing alone and took a position above one of the Navy jets as Lumina flanked the other. Cassie thought they might be communicating with the American pilots.

Misrule examined the data on the monitor above the control stick and frowned. Cassie paused in her litany as two words on the screen jumped out at her.

Low fuel.

Her eyes started to throb from Lumina's previous flash at the cockpit. She blinked several times to clear her vision but it stayed persistently blotchy. It felt like someone had poured sand into her eyes. Tears coursed down her cheeks as she realized she couldn't even read the list she held any longer.

"I . . . I'm sorry . . . I can't . . ." she said in a quavering voice. "I can't see."

Misrule turned to look at her, but she only saw a dark red blotch against the painfully bright sky beyond. "My apologies, Cassandra. I sometimes forget not everyone can heal injury as easily as I. You may leave." He turned back to the radio. "Lieutenant, I no longer have sufficient fuel on board to turn around. Therefore, I will continue on my present course. If you do not back off, I will begin killing hostages."

The Navy jets peeled off and dropped from view.

"Are th-they gone?" asked Cassie.

"For now. I suspect they will keep pace and await their orders to shoot us down."

"They're going to kill us?"

"They will try."

* * *

"All right, I've used up every favor I had," said Juice when Doublecharge answered her phone. "The Navy has pulled its jets back and the Italians are returning home. I hope you know what you're doing."

"So do I, James." Doublecharge popped a couple of Tylenols for her growing tension headache.

"Can you tell me what Jack's planning? Something foolish, I'd bet."

"I think he's going to try to board the plane and take it over from the inside."

"Yes, that sounds like something he would do. I wonder if his invulnerability is going to his head."

Doublecharge smiled. "It's Jack. Everything goes to his head. The man has an ego the size of Cleveland."

"Of course. How could I forget?"

"I'm worried. I'm afraid his luck may finally run out. I don't have a good feeling about things this time."

"Neither do I, but don't let that show. Those kids you've got on the team now, they need you to be strong. They look up to you and Sondra and the others. You're more than just their boss, you represent everything that is Just Cause."

"Thanks for the pep talk. I feel so much better now." Doublecharge rubbed her temples, feeling a tension headache throbbing with every pump of her heart.

"Rah rah rah, you're doing a great job." Juice chuckled.

"How did you deal with the pressure when you were team leader?"

"I had someone I could talk to . . . someone I trusted, who understood the kinds of problems that only parahumans have."

"Who was that? Oh." Doublecharge blushed as she realized he referred to her.

"Stacey, you need to build relationships like you and I have with your team members. You can be their friend and still be their leader. They want to be close to you. Let them."

"Are you moonlighting as a psychologist now?"

"All lawyers are psychologists," said Juice. "I've got to go now and brief the President. I hope to have good news the next time we speak."

"Thanks, James, for everything."

"Anytime, Stacey."

"Destruction, hence, like creation, is one of Nature's mandates."
—Marquis De Sade

July, 2007
Over the Mediterranean

"Ten minutes. Get ready," said Reed. "Check all your gear once more. You forget anything, you can't come back for it."

"Thanks for that comforting thought, Reed," said Jack.

Jack's gear bag, loaded with sleeper sets, knockout gas, and other odds and ends he thought would be useful, was strapped to his back and reinforced with layers of duct tape. He'd decided against bringing any firearms with him. A bullet hole in the fuselage would do more harm to the hostages. Instead, he carried an ultrataser pistol holstered at his waist and likewise secured with additional tape. A sheathed knife went inside his wetsuit, which he'd need to cut himself free of all the layers of tape. He also carried several doses of the injectable antidote for the knockout gas. They assumed Tim Foster still lived and possibly Katie Malone, and if so Jack could revive them and make use of their experience.

Lania put her gloved hand on Jack's shoulder. "So you knock out everyone on the plane. Very good. What then, hotshot?"

Jack grinned. "Then Reed talks me through an emergency landing in Greece and we'll all have spanakopita and baklava for dinner."

"You can fly a plane?" Garcia raised an eyebrow.

"Sure. I've flown dozens of them." Jack coughed. "In simulation."

"Are you kidding me?"

"I've logged hundreds of hours on the best flight simulation software out there. Can you say the same?"

Garcia shrugged. "I've played *Ratchet and Clank* for an entire week nonstop. That's over a hundred and sixty hours of continuous gaming. Does that mean I'm qualified to take on an entire galaxy with an arsenal of odd munitions? I've *got* a pilot's license."

"To fly the Deep Six transport, not a jumbo jet," said Lania. "You know that's not the same thing."

"It's still practical experience."

"If you've got any better ideas, it's a little late to start spouting them now," said Lania.

Garcia paused. "Okay, I guess I don't. I just wanted to know where we stood with things."

Jack held out his arms. "Hook me up."

Garcia taped the adhesive gel tube underneath one arm and the microtorch on the other. Around Jack's chest went the spinneret with its rare-earth magnetic anchor. Then he climbed into the body bag they'd made from the life raft. He reached up and pulled the wetsuit mask up and over his head, leaving the breather off. He wouldn't use it until the last possible moment.

"Five minutes. Garcia and Lania, you'd better come up here and strap in. I can keep the cockpit pressurized." Reed's voice was intense.

Garcia shook Jack's hand. "Good luck, buddy. You're absolutely shit-crazy for doing this. I hope you pull it off."

"God bless you, Jack," said Lania. "And good luck."

Jack looked at the two of them from inside his yellow cocoon. "Neither of you are going to talk me out of it or volunteer to take my place?"

Garcia laughed. "If you fall into the ocean, we'll swing around, pick you up and you can try it again."

They exited the cabin, leaving Jack alone.

"Inverting in ten seconds," said Reed.

Jack reached out and grabbed onto the handles atop the seat backs. A moment later, the *Rita* flipped over onto her back. Jack stood on what had been the cabin roof, wondering if he was going to be sucked out into open air like in the movies. There was a thumping sound from somewhere over his head.

"Landing gear deployed. Bomb bay doors opening in ten seconds. Prepare for depressurization."

Jack slipped the breather into his mouth and clenched his teeth around it.

Normally the bomb bay doors could be opened in a flash, but Reed opened them slowly so as to avoid any unusual turbulence around the *Rita* or the target jet. Air whistled around the crack in the doors, and then hit Jack like a steamroller across the chest. He held tight onto the seatback handles over his head, buffeted by the strong air currents. Frost formed around the edges of his goggles almost immediately and his ears popped several times in quick succession.

The doors finished opening and he could see an expanse of aluminum aircraft skin only a few feet away from the hole above him. The wind lessened somewhat with the doors fully open and he released his hold on the seatbacks, testing his strength. He only had a few minutes of air from the breather, so he had to hurry.

He fired the spinneret. The compressed air charge fired the heavy magnet straight up. The high wind in the space between the planes deflected it but it still bit and stuck on the metal skin of the passenger jet above him. He wasted no time and squirted thick gobs of adhesive gel around the top of his cocoon. It would remain sticky enough for the few seconds it would take to traverse the intervening feet of open air. Or so he hoped. He crouched down, held the bag up and over his head, and tapped the button on his wrist to retract the spinneret.

He flew out of the *Rita* at dizzying speed, catching an impossible glimpse of the bottoms of two jets nearly atop one another before he slammed into the belly of the escapees' jet. The air currents beat upon him with the enthusiasm of drunken European football hooligans with sticks, but the adhesive held and with some judicious pressing around the edges, Jack found himself in a wind-free bag. He lit the microtorch and started to slice into the aluminum. A single puff of air inflated the bag around him, but it held true and didn't pop off the jet's surface.

He carved an oval hole he estimated just large enough to admit him to the cargo hold over his head, and then he reached up and hauled himself upward into the belly of the plane.

* * *

Katie groaned and rolled over. Her poor head had taken the kind of pounding normally reserved for heavyweight prizefighters. She felt at the lump on her temple and her fingers came away marred with drying blood. She sat up and winced as throbs of pain ran through her entire body. Her ears popped, and then popped again hard enough to make her grimace. She became aware of a change in the sound within the cargo bay. It hissed and whistled like wind around power lines. A painfully-bright light illuminated the swirling dust in the air.

A small section of deck plating popped upward and Katie saw daylight underneath. She wondered if they had landed while she was unconscious. But no, the engines still ran strong, and their noise increased a dozen decibels with the hole in the floor. She took a hesitant step forward, but then ducked into a shadow as someone climbed up through the opening.

The man was dressed all in black, with goggles and a duct-taped mask to cover any facial features. She watched as he opened his outfit and withdrew a knife, then cut through the strips of tape holding down various pieces of equipment.

Katie was at a loss how to proceed. Was he another escapee or a rescuer? And how had he boarded a flying jetliner? Answers to her questions would have to wait, but all the same she wished she had a better weapon than a sneak attack from the shadows.

The figure uncovered his face and Katie recognized Crackerjack from Just Cause. Relief flooded through her and she stepped out of the shadows. "Crackerjack!"

Jack moved with unbelievable speed, He ducked and rolled across the floor and came up with an ultrataser pointed at her. "Freeze!" he hissed.

"Don't shoot. I'm a friend. Officer Katie Malone, of Deep Six."

"Prove it."

"Shit. Okay, um . . ." Frantic thoughts raced through her head. "All right, when we picked up Misrule from you all in Denver, Lieutenant Frankes teased him about turkey."

Jack considered for a moment. "All right, that works for me." He holstered his weapon.

"How did you get here?"

"Blind, stupid luck, mostly." Jack grinned. "We need to seal this hole before we depressurize completely. I need a piece of something big, flat, and sturdy."

Katie pointed. "How about that cargo container?" The container was designed to be filled with baggage and fit snug inside the cargo bay's confines. It had an aluminum skin.

Jack rapped his knuckles on it. "Should be good enough," he muttered. "Watch your eyes." Using his knife, he cut free a small cutting torch taped to his right arm. With a few deft strokes, he sliced a large section of plating from the cargo container. Unmindful of the hot, sharp edges, he dragged it across the floor and stood it up right next to the hole he'd cut. Katie remembered that Jack was invulnerable to harm. He tossed a tube to her. "Squirt this around the edge. Make sure you don't touch it unless you want to spend the rest of the trip stuck there."

Katie nodded and squeezed the adhesive out of the tube around the edge of the hole. She had only just finished when the yellow fabric flapping under the hole tore. Her ears popped painfully and the air rushed from her lungs as Jack forced the plate over the gap. The whistling in her ears lessened and she found she could breathe once more.

"Okay," said Jack. "What's the situation upstairs in thirty seconds or less?"

"Misrule's flying the plane," Katie said. "There are ten escapees left, armed with automatic weapons . . ."

Jack held up his hand. "That's good enough for now. Here's the plan. I've got two pressurized canisters of your knockout gas from the Six, and two breather masks good for ten minutes apiece. We'll gas the interior, and then you start installing sleeper sets while I take the jet down to about eight thousand feet. Then we purge the cabin. The higher pressure in the plane should blow out enough gas for us to operate without the breathers. I've got four injectors to cancel out the effects of the gas. I suggest you wake up the Doctor and one other person to help. Are there any other guards left?"

Katie nodded. "One. No offense, but this sounds as half-assed as the plan he and I came up with to try to stop the breakout and look how well that worked."

Jack handed her a gas canister and the ultrataser.

"What about you?" Katie took the weapon.

"I'm invulnerable to harm," said Jack. "I don't have to shoot people to keep them away from me, and I know enough infighting to do well up close and personal."

Katie shrugged and checked the charge on the ultrataser. Full up. She approved.

They headed for the air conditioner units in the center of the bay. Jack examined each unit before he selected a candidate tube. He withdrew a flat pouch from his bag and unrolled it to reveal a small but complete tool kit. In a few deft moves, he clamped the line shut, and then spliced in a connection in for the gas canister. "How quickly does this stuff work?"

"Seconds. I can attest to that personally."

Jack did some mental arithmetic. "Air circulates through a plane this size in about two minutes. That's too much time for someone to do something stupid and dangerous. I'll go back to the ladder up in the tail. Thirty seconds after you start the gas here, I'll head through the cabin with this canister open." He patted the second bottle for emphasis. "The higher concentration of gas should be very effective and with luck, Misrule won't have any warning anything is wrong until it's too late."

Katie shrugged. "Sounds as good as any other idea I've heard today."

Jack handed her a breather mask which looked like a SCUBA mouthpiece attached to a pair of golf ball-sized tanks. She took a nose clip and pinched her nostrils shut so she wouldn't accidentally inhale any of the potent gas. Jack took out his own breather and nose clip. "You got a watch?"

Katie nodded.

"Let me see it."

She held up her arm. Jack noted the time on it.

"Okay, in two minutes from right now, you turn on the gas. Thirty seconds after that I go up into the galley. I'll leave the sleeper sets at the top of the ladder. You come along behind me and start hooking up the escapees, then meet me at the cockpit, because I may need help."

"Um . . . all right." Katie wondered how she could possibly help in the cockpit.

"Clock's ticking." Jack ran for the tail and the ladder up into the galley.

Katie watched the seconds pass on her watch, her hand resting on the quick release valve.

* * *

Misrule frowned at the indicator light on the monitoring board. He'd noticed it flicker on for a few seconds then off. It meant a drop in internal air pressure, but it only lasted a moment—not long enough to even trigger a warning alarm. He reached out and tapped the light with a claw but it remained dark. He knew airplanes were subject to occasional gremlins in their electrical systems like any other mechanical device, but it raised his hackles nevertheless.

He switched on the automatic pilot and stood. He tapped the weapon embedded in his torso, as if he sought to comfort it, and ducked to step through the cockpit door.

Brainstorm looked over at him, a complex mixture of emotions on her face. "Etch?"

He shook his head and she dropped her face into her hands. He stepped out of First Class.

Whispered conversations between the hostages ceased as they saw Misrule. The escapees likewise stopped talking and became attentive.

"Boss? What's up?" asked Kiloton, resting from his combat injuries.

Misrule sniffed the air. Nothing seemed amiss. His eyes roved across the hostages, as if he sought an answer for a question he couldn't put into words. "How many hostages did we have when we left Deep Six?"

Nobody answered.

His voice dropped to a dangerous growl. "How . . . many . . . hostages?"

Kiloton shrugged. "I don't know, boss. I don't think nobody counted them."

"Then how do we know if we've misplaced one?"

"Seventeen," said Cassie. Doctor Mayfair had covered her burned eyes with improvised ice packs. She leaned back in a seat, a towel around her neck to catch the water that dripped from the plastic baggies as the ice melted. "There are seventeen names on the list you had me read."

"Of course there are," said Misrule. "And I see seventeen of you here. How very convenient that both counts agree."

"You think one is missing?" asked Kiloton.

Dissident turned to look right at Foster. "Oh, shit," he said, eyes widening. "Where's that chick who was sitting with you? The one who went to the bathroom to puke or something?"

Foster shrugged. "I figured she was sitting back there somewhere." He pointed in the general direction of the compartment's rear.

Misrule was on him in a flash and lifted Foster from his seat by the front of his shirt. "Who was she?" he growled. "Was it Malone? Is she still alive?"

Foster stammered as Misrule shook him like a rag doll.

A glowing point of energy appeared at the end of Misrule's other fist. He raised his hand, bathing Foster's face in the unholy light. "Speak, cur, or I'll blow your head apart."

"For God's sake, man, tell him! It's too late now!" cried Doctor Mayfair.

A guilty tear rolled down one of Foster's cheeks. "Yes," he whispered.

Misrule flung him down amid the seats. "That sneaky little bitch." He ripped a seat from the floor in anger as he passed. "I knew she wasn't dead." He raised his voice to a howl of anger that shook the plane. "I'm coming for you, Malone, you cunt! I'll rip your limbs off and drink your blood. Then I'll find that daughter of yours, then your mother, and kill them slowly. I'll slaughter hundreds—*thousands*—and all because of you, you deceitful whore!"

The plane trembled and shook. Hostages screamed in fear as it dipped suddenly. Even the escapees looked around uneasily. Misrule paused, seething with unbelievable fury. He took one more step aft, but another tremor shook the jet. Finally he spun on his heel to stalk back toward the cockpit. He pointed at Dissident and Whisper. "You two, go down below and search the cargo deck. Look for anything out of the ordinary, especially damage that we might have taken from the Italian parahumans. And if you find anyone, you bring them to me alive."

"How do we get down there?" asked Dissident.

"There should be a ladder or elevator in the galley." Misrule turned his back on everyone and returned to the cockpit to regain control of the jet.

Dissident and Whisper looked at each other, raised their assault rifles, and headed toward the tail.

* * *

Jack had just ascended the ladder when he heard people approaching. He looked around, frantic to find somewhere to hide himself until he spotted a drink cart in its niche. He yanked it out as silently as he could, and crammed himself into the niche, and then grabbed the protruding cart and pulled it in close. He hoped that whoever was approaching didn't know enough about airplane interiors to notice anything amiss.

"There it is," he heard a woman say. Grumbling ensued and weapons clattered in the narrow ladderwell as the two escapees descended to the cargo deck. Jack turned his wrist to read the faint glow of the numerals on his watch. If Katie had kept to their schedule, she had just turned on the gas.

Jack cursed to himself. The escapees would find Katie before the gas made its way back down to the cargo deck. He wanted to help her, but if he did, the timing of their plan would be ruined. He tucked the breather into his mouth, gritting his teeth against it in fury, and clamped his own nostrils shut. He inched the drink cart out of his way, held onto the gas bottle and waited for the right moment to charge.

* * *

Katie held her hands over her mouth to keep from screaming. She'd clearly heard Misrule's tirade. Somehow he knew she was still alive. Someone else must have given her up. She hoped that if it was Foster, he hadn't paid with his life. Over the pounding of her heart in her ears and the muted roar of the engines outside, Katie heard someone speak from the aft of the plane. She shrank back into the shadows and held the ultrataser out in a firm, two-handed grip to keep steady.

Dissident and Whisper approached, their assault rifles held loose and unready.

"You see anything?" Dissident sounded bored.

"No. You?"

"Nope."

They strolled up to the air conditioners and Whisper suddenly held up a hand.

Katie's blood turned icy cold as Whisper pointed at the gas bottle. "What's that?"

Dissident leaned forward. "I don't know."

"I have a bad feeling about it. I'm shutting it off."

As Whisper reached up a hand to close the valve, Katie tensed.

Whisper stopped with her hand only a few inches away and quivered like a race horse waiting for the starting bell. Her head snapped around and she gazed directly at Katie, ready to unleash psychic death.

Katie shot her in the face.

Whisper jerked like a shaken rag doll and her uncontrolled leg muscles contracted to fling her across the compartment where she lay twitching.

"Shit!" screamed Dissident, and went two-dimensional as Katie fired the other charge at him, causing it to spark harmlessly against the frame of the jet. Dissident couldn't hold his rifle in his altered form, and it fell to the floor.

It discharged as it hit, the report echoing through the empty cargo bay.

* * *

Kiloton hollered and sat down hard in the aisle, looking at the bloody hole in his leg in disbelief. "Goddammit, somebody shot me! Who the fuck shot me?"

Nightmare crouched down next to him and touched a small, ragged hole in the floor curiously. She took a deep breath to call for help, then her eyes widened and she pitched forward. Kiloton's mouth dropped open as he saw a figure running up the aisle toward him, carrying something that resembled a junior fire extinguisher. His mind reeled for a moment before the entire world spun crazily around him and he fell into oblivion.

* * *

At the sound of the shot, Misrule rushed out of the cockpit. The weapon's discharge meant something was indeed wrong, and already out of control.

As he stepped into Coach, he was nearly bowled over by a smaller man running up the aisle. The man bounced hard off Misrule and rolled backward across Kiloton and Nightmare's supine bodies. Everyone in Coach was asleep or unconscious. Misrule's eyes widened as he realized that the man held a gas canister. The cabin started to swirl around him as the gas he'd inhaled began to take effect. He forced himself to stop breathing, trusting that the oxygen in his blood and his ability to heal would be enough for him to act.

The man sprang to his feet and Misrule recognized Crackerjack from Just Cause. He knew the man was invulnerable to damage, but he still raised a hand and a burst of destructive, vivid energy blasted forth. It impacted high on Jack's chest to hurl him up and backward halfway down the cabin. The canister exploded and filled the air with more of the noxious sleep-inducing fumes.

Jack bounced right back up again, his clothes in tatters, a knife clutched in his hand. He took a single step towards Misrule, the blade raised, but then realized he'd lost his breather mask. The knife tumbled from his nerveless fingers and he toppled to the aisle floor.

Misrule smiled, but felt weak as he turned to head back to the cockpit. Black splotches filled his vision as his body cried out for oxygen. All he had to do was purge the air in the plane and he could trust to his healing abilities to clear any residual gas from his system. It wasn't far, the cockpit. Just a few steps. He took one, then two. Then he staggered and gasped.

The gas flew into his lungs and took him into its greedy darkness.

* * *

Dissident drifted to the floor like a paper cutout. He thickened to his normal three-dimensional form as consciousness fled him. The gas had taken him before Katie needed to figure out how to fight a two-dimensional foe. She took two of the sleeper sets and installed them onto Dissident and Whisper. Satisfied they were thoroughly comatose, she started to climb the ladder when a loud explosion shook the entire jet, knocking her from the ladder. She nearly lost her breather mask, only keeping her jaws clamped over it out of sheer desperation. She shook herself and then ascended the ladder once more.

The passenger section was eerily quiet. People slumped in their seats or the aisle. Katie nearly stepped on someone. With a start she realized it was Jack. His outfit was torn and burned and there was no sign of the gas canister.

"Shit," she muttered into her breather.

With Jack unconscious, nobody was flying the plane.

She ran forward, nervous as she stepped over Misrule's unconscious body in First Class, and entered the cockpit.

It was every bit as complicated as she feared. There were switches, dials, and readouts everywhere, and half of them were in Arabic. The only saving grace was a monitor that showed current flight characteristics of the jet while the words *Autopilot Engaged* flashed in red in the corner.

She dropped into the seat on the left, put the headphones on, and picked up the radio. It looked more or less like a standard CB—squeeze the button on the side and talk. She kept one hand on her breather, because she couldn't risk inhaling any cockpit air until she purged the plane. She took a deep breath, then removed the mask and activated the radio.

"Mayday . . . mayday . . ." She knew it was the appropriate thing to say, but then stopped. What was she supposed to say? "This is Officer Katie Malone from Deep Six. I'm the only person conscious on board a hijacked airliner and I don't know how to fly."

She released the button on the radio, replaced her breather mask, and waited for someone—anyone—to reply.

"Malone? Katie, is that you?"

Katie's eyes popped out of her head as she heard Garcia's voice in her ears. She nearly forgot to spit out her breather and then almost forgot to inhale from it first. She spluttered, got everything into the correct order, and spoke. "Garcia? Where are you?"

A sleek, wide-bodied jet rose into view to the starboard of the cockpit. A colorfully-painted pinup girl perched on the nose, just ahead of a large *Just Cause* logo. It waggled its wings.

"Right next to you. Where's Jack?"

"He breathed some of the gas. He's out like a light." She paused to inhale from the breather. "I need help purging the air in here so I can function. I'm going to run out of clean air soon."

"I'm giving you over to Reed, the pilot. He's going to talk you through it."

In a moment, Reed came on. He talked Katie through shutting down the automatic pilot and beginning a descent to a safer altitude. She sat white-knuckled in the pilot's chair and tried to look at everything in the cockpit at once. The altimeter crawled downward until it read 8500 feet, at which point she re-engaged the autopilot once more.

"Okay," said Reed. "This next part is going to go against every bit of conventional wisdom, but I think it's the best way to do this quickly. The escapees have firearms, don't they?"

"Yes," said Katie.

"I want you to take one and shoot a single hole through the rear-most window in the main cabin."

"I'm sorry, Reed, it sounded like you said you wanted me to shoot out a window."

"You heard me right."

"Won't that make the plane fall apart? Or suck everyone out or something?"

"Only in movies. You're flying low enough that the pressure drop isn't going to seriously inconvenience everyone and a hole that size isn't going to affect your structural integrity."

"I hope you're right . . . this breather's just about empty."

"Between the normal air-changing and the depressurization, your air should be free of the gas."

"Be right back . . . I hope." Katie took off the headset and moved aft. Everyone was still unconscious. She liberated an assault rifle from Heretic's limp hand and made her way to the tail. Finally, she stood at the last window and wondered if she had the nerve to follow through with it. She inhaled once more from the breather. It tasted sour and made spots dance in front of her eyes. It was empty.

She raised the gun, made sure it was switched to single shot, and fired it.

The bullet made a neat, starred hole in the window. The temperature dropped quickly as air flowed through the plane, making Katie's hair flap as if she were in a strong breeze. Emergency oxygen masks dropped from their berths above the seats to dangle forlornly and unused. She waited as long as she could stand it, then threw the breather away and took a tentative breath.

The air smelled sweet and clean, with a hint of sea salt. She waited to see if she, too, would drift into unconsciousness. After almost a minute, she decided it was all right, and hurried back to the cockpit.

"Katie Malone, still on the air," she said.

"Great news, Katie. It looks to us like the plane is flying pretty smooth. Can you wake anyone up to help you out?"

"These stim injector things won't wake up Jack, will they?"

"No, I'm afraid not. He requires oral medication, and it doesn't take effect very quickly."

"So I can wake up anybody except the one guy who can fly the plane. Wonderful. I'll be back in a few minutes."

Katie headed back to the cabin, slinging Jack's bag over her shoulder. She paused by Misrule and took a couple of minutes to install a sleeper set on the unconscious man. "Far as I'm concerned, you can just stay right there the rest of the trip, asshole," she said, and headed into Coach, looking for a certain head of red hair.

She found Foster slumped down in his seat next to Cassie, whose eyes were bandaged. Katie wasted no time and shot the autoinjector into Foster's arm. The vial contained a complex mixture of stimulants that would quickly counteract the effects of the anesthetic gas.

Foster started, coughed, and opened his eyes almost immediately. His pupils were dilated and he swayed in his seat.

"Good morning, Sunshine," said Katie, pleased as punch to see him once more. "The time for sleeping is now over. The time for working is now."

Foster licked his lips. "I could use a cup of water. And a Tylenol. And a mint. Jesus, it tastes like a cat shit in my mouth."

"I'll buzz for the stewardess." Katie smiled. "In the meantime, though, I wonder if you'd be a dear and fly the goddamn plane while I finish putting sleeper sets on everyone?"

"Fly the plane?" Foster's brow furrowed as he tried to wrap his mind around the concept. "But I don't know anything about flying." Nevertheless, he stood and made his way toward the cockpit.

"No problem," said Katie over her shoulder as she headed the opposite direction. "You'll fit right in with the rest of us novices."

* * *

"Everyone's out, one way or another," Katie told Foster as she flopped into the seat next to him and squeezed her eyes shut, pinching the bridge of her nose to try to manage the pain.

"Here," he said. "Tylenol." She opened her eyes and found him offering her a capsule and a can of some off-brand cola. "I found two and saved you one. Looks like you need it almost as bad as I do."

"You are an angel," she said, and meant it. She popped the capsule and cracked open the can to savor the carbonated caramel taste and let the caffeine within work its magic.

"Put those on." Katie pointed to the headphones hanging to his left. "You're officially my copilot now, and I need you in the loop."

"I'm telling you, I really don't have any idea what I'm doing." Foster fit the 'phones over his head.

"Then you're effectively doubling the experience in this cockpit," said Katie. "All right, Reed, we're both here and ready to do some flying. Talk me through it."

"First things first, Top Gun. Let's do a quick check on basic instruments. I want you to learn where they are and what to look for on each one. You remember where the altimeter is?"

"Yes," said Katie, pointing to it for Foster's benefit. "8500 feet and holding steady."

"Good. The artificial horizon is the thing that's blue on top and brown underneath. It tells you if the wings are level and whether you're climbing or diving."

"Got it. I think it says we're flat and level."

Reed continued to go over the basic instrumentation with the two of them until both Katie and Foster could identify and read their airspeed and heading. Katie's discomfort grew at the sheer number of buttons, switches, and indicators, but Reed calmed her and explained most of them weren't going to be important. He intended to act as their air traffic controller, guiding them to a landing himself so they wouldn't need to concern themselves with such esoteric concepts as VOR beacons and communication protocols.

"You just let me and Officer Garcia handle all the details. The two of you just have to land the plane, and I'll talk you through every step of the way."

"Reed?" Katie's voice sounded small and nervous, like a shy schoolgirl.

"What is it, Malone?"

"How much fuel do we need to get to where we're going?" Her voice quivered.

"Not so much, I should think. Fifteen percent of your capacity should be ample."

Katie and Foster looked at each other in horror. The fuel indicator was flashing an ominous 5%, which changed to 4% as they watched it.

"I think we're in trouble," whispered Foster.

SEVENTEEN

"You don't concentrate on risks. You concentrate on results. No risk is too great to prevent the necessary job from getting done."
—Chuck Yeager, United States Air Force pilot

July, 2007
Over the Mediterranean

"Stand by, guys," said Reed.

"What are we going to do?" whispered Katie. "We're over the goddamn ocean, for God's sake."

"I'll tell you what we're not going to do," said Foster, his voice grim and resolute. "We're not going to take the easy way out. One way or another, we're getting back home to our kids. Agreed?"

"Agreed." Katie was glad his feelings echoed hers.

"Guys, I've got bad news and worse news, but maybe some good news on top of it all," said Reed over the radio.

"Then we're worried, devastated, and hopeful all at the same time," said Foster. "What's up?"

"The bad news is that you don't have enough fuel to reach Greece. The worse news is that you don't even have enough to make landfall. The good news is that the weather is conducive to an emergency water landing."

Katie burst out in panicked laughter. "You want me to land a plane, which by the way I have never done before, on the water? Shit, I should go wake up Misrule right now. At least he can fly this thing."

"Negative," said Reed. "Not even commercial pilots are trained to ditch, so he's not going to have any better luck than you will. And you're more motivated to save everyone on board. Water landings generally have a good survival rate. Plus there is the added benefit that we're right here to provide rescue, and the *Marilyn* is less than two hours away. You're not going to get better odds than you have right now."

"Good point," said Katie. "What do we do?"

"I assume everyone else on board is still unconscious or comatose. You've got time to get everyone strapped into a seat and into a life vest. Can you awaken anyone else?"

Katie nodded, ignoring the fact that Reed couldn't see her. "Yeah, Jack brought four doses of the gas antidote. I used one on Foster. I don't suppose there's some trick to getting one inside him? He'd be awfully useful to have awake at a time like this."

"Afraid not, Katie. Use your judgment on who you want to wake up. Remember, when you hit the water you may need to get people out quickly, and you may still have a lot of unconscious or injured people."

"I understand. Give us a few minutes."

"Don't take too long."

Foster turned to Katie. "I'm thinking we should wake up Doc Mayfair and Cassie Haig. They've got cool heads and won't panic on us. Plus they're fit enough to help move people out once we're down. That leaves one more. Who do you think?"

"I agree with you," said Katie. "And I think we ought to use the last dose on Escudo."

"What?" Foster's mouth hung open in shock. "He's a convict and an escaped prisoner."

"He's a human being," said Katie. "And he's as likely to die on this plane as any of us. His powers could protect a lot of people, and he's seemed all along like he was going along with Misrule more out of fear than out of any sort of loyalty."

Foster considered it. "All right," he said. "You've been right with everything else so far."

Katie grinned. "Good of you to notice. Come on, let's get busy."

They split up. Katie headed aft to inject Cassie and Escudo, and Foster stopped in the middle of the cabin to take care of Doctor Mayfair.

Cassie awoke almost immediately and yanked the bandage from her face. She looked up at Katie with eyes filled with burst blood vessels. "Katie? What's going on? Where's Misrule?"

"He's unconscious, and we're in trouble," said Katie. "We need your help. Get yourself up and moving, and then start getting life vests on everyone and getting them buckled into their seats. We're in for a water landing."

"Water landing?" Cassie looked confused but Katie didn't have time to explain further.

"Just do it. Please, okay?" Katie hurried off to find Escudo slumped in a seat a few rows back. She wasted no time and injected him with the antidote. While waiting for him to come around, Katie looked back at Cassie, who was struggling to get a life vest over Doctor Mayfair's nurse.

Escudo stirred as he started to come out of his coma. "*Qué . . . qué está sucediendo?*"

"Rise and shine," said Katie. "Time to work, *amigo*. Help us out here and I'll see about trying to get your sentence reduced."

"Misrule? Where is he?" Escudo looked around, his chubby face frightened.

"Knocked out in First Class. You feel like being a hero instead of a villain today?"

Escudo nodded slowly, still suffering from the aftereffects of the knockout gas and the sleeper set.

"All right. We're trusting you to help us here, or we might all die. Do you understand?"

"What do you want me to do?"

"Help get everyone here ready for an emergency water landing, and then we're going to talk about your powers."

"Water landing? Powers?"

Katie hauled off and slapped him across the face. "There's no time for this!" she yelled at him. "Do you want to live or do you want to die, *cabrón*?"

"I want to live."

"Then get busy."

Foster came back to them. "Everything all right?" he asked.

"Fine. Escudo was just explaining how eager he is to earn his Good Citizenship Badge."

Foster noted the red hand print on one of the Hispanic man's cheeks and nodded. "Okay. We need to get Dissident and Whisper out of the cargo hold. Then we'd better get back up front."

Katie nodded, and they headed for the ladderwell in the galley.

* * *

"Can't this heap go any faster?" Doublecharge asked. The *Marilyn* was every bit as fast as the *Rita*, if not quite as well-apportioned inside, but without their own handy antimatter pulse drive, she had to rely on her own engines.

"I've got her runnin' at a hundred and fifteen percent," said the pilot, one Buckthorn Carter, the ex-Alaskan bush pilot who flew for Just Cause's Second Team.

"That doesn't sound safe," said Mustang Sally.

"Oh, it ain't. But any more than that and I'll melt the jet nozzles and that'd end our trip real quick."

"What's our ETA?" asked Mastiff from his seat next to Mustang Sally. He clutched her tiny hand in his massive palm.

"Call it two hours. They turned around." Buckthorn's voice dropped in volume a few decibels. "Listen, I've been talking to Reed. Things don't look so good."

"How so?" asked Doublecharge.

"It's the jet. It's . . . hell, there ain't no good way to say it. It's out of fuel. They're going to try a ditch."

"A ditch?" Desert Eagle tilted her head to one side. "I don't like the sound of that."

"It's an emergency water landing."

"I'm sure Jack is doing everything he can to bring them down safely."

"That's just it, ma'am. Crackerjack apparently got a lungful of that gas you all use. Two of the prison guards are flying the plane."

"I hope you're displaying a newly-discovered sense of humor, Buck," said Doublecharge.

"Afraid not, ma'am."

Doublecharge sighed. "Burn up whatever you have to, but get us there sooner than two hours."

"Yes, ma'am." The engines took on a higher, more ragged tone and Doublecharge felt acceleration push her back in her seat.

* * *

"Everyone locked down tight?" asked Foster as Katie stepped back into the cockpit.

"Far as I can tell." She and Doctor Mayfair had struggled to get the heavy Misrule into one of the First Class seats. She'd mentioned to the doctor he might spend the remainder of the trip brainstorming ideas for getting the bomb out of the demonic man's chest without risking whatever municipality they wound up visiting.

"All right, Reed. I guess we're all as ready as we're going to be."

"I've notified the Hellenic Coast Guard. They've already got ships and copters heading into the area. We're going to get you all out of there safely."

"I hope so," said Foster. "I've got a hot date coming up and I don't want to miss it because I'm dead." He turned to Katie and grinned. "Want to go out this weekend?"

"I don't date COs," she said, although her heart wasn't really in it.

"I'm thinking about quitting and going into gardening full-time."

"I see." Katie laughed in spite of the stress. "I guess in that case I'm free."

Foster turned back to face forward, smiling like a loon. "Talk about motivation for survival."

Reed ordered Katie to turn off the automatic pilot. At his direction, she made a few minor changes in the plane's pitch, roll, and yaw so she knew which controls did what.

"The most important thing to remember is to try to keep the nose up. If you're lucky, the jet will skip like a rock."

"And if we're not lucky?"

"It'll sink like one."

"You're doing wonders for my confidence," said Katie. "Remind me to never fly again after this."

"It'll be a long swim home from Greece unless you do."

Katie adjusted some controls. The monitor screen informed her the flaps were deployed. The plane shed velocity and altitude. She looked up to see the *Rita* overhead through the cockpit windows, shadowing their every move.

"Get your nose up," said Reed as the great blue expanse of the Mediterranean spread out beneath them.

"Do you want to do this?" said Katie through gritted teeth. "No? Then cut me some slack. It's my first day of flight school." She pulled back on the wheel and was rewarded with the jet's nose tilting above the horizon. "What's my altitude and airspeed?" she asked Foster.

"Um . . ." he looked around the control panel in front of him for a couple of seconds before he remembered which indicator showed their height. "3000 feet and dropping. Airspeed is 350 miles per hour and also dropping."

"You're going too fast and descending too quickly. Get that nose up!" shouted Reed.

"Read it off to me, Foster. I'm too busy to look."

"2500 feet . . . 325 miles per hour. No, 300 even. And down to 2000 feet now."

"How do I look, Reed?"

"Like shit, frankly. Tell everyone to assume crash positions. You and Foster better prepare to get wet. The cockpit windows might blow inward with the impact."

"That sounds lovely. Have I mentioned this is a really bad idea?"

"1500 feet. 275 miles per hour." Foster read off the numbers like a mantra.

"Don't let your speed drop below two hundred," warned Reed.

"What happens if I do?"

"Bad things."

"Got it." Katie began to check the altimeter herself. "One thousand feet. Oh shit, Foster, we're really going to do this, aren't we?"

The plane dropped lower and lower and the sparkling blue water rose up to meet them.

"Escudo, get your force field thing up and push it out as far as you can," called Foster.

"*Sì*," called the heavyset man from the main cabin.

"Get that nose up another couple of degrees, Malone," said Reed.

Katie hauled back on the wheel. "I can't see anything. How do I know when we're there?"

"Five hundred feet" Foster had a nervous tremolo in his voice.

"You're there. Hold everything just like that. Keep the nose up when you hit and keep her from rolling the best you can. I'll give you a ten-second count. Ten . . . nine . . ."

Katie wanted to close her eyes but wouldn't let herself look away. If she was going to die, she would face it head-on without a flinch. Well, she amended, maybe with a little flinch.

"Six . . . five . . . four . . ." Reed's count sped up. "Oh shit, hang on!"

* * *

The jet's tail glanced off the water and bounced back up, which tilted the craft forward. Foster and Katie found themselves looking at water as it rushed by just beneath the cockpit. Katie yanked as hard as she could on the wheel, trying to get the nose back up. With glacial slowness, the horizon dropped below their view again just as the tail hit the water again. This time it dragged along the water to carve a rooster-tail wave taller than a five-story building.

The left wing dipped too low, and caught the shimmering surface. A tremendous jolt shook the plane as its forward linear motion transformed into rotational energy. The portside engine, mounted beneath the wing, sheared away with a shriek of overstressed metal. The jetliner spun like a car on ice and pivoted around its hull, the flat surfaces of the wings making it skip across the water.

The noise of the crash was fantastic. Water roared as it rushed past and over the hull. Metal tore and support struts snapped as if the plane were being crumpled by a giant. Loose objects bounced around inside the cabin like lottery balls in a rotating barrel. Foster and Katie, at the end of the pinwheeling jet, were shaken about like test tubes in a centrifuge. Acrid smoke from melting circuits burned their eyes and nostrils.

At last, one of the wings carved into the sea like a knife and made the plane tilt low. Seawater buried the jet as it burrowed sideways and skidded to a halt. As Reed had predicted, the window to Foster's right shattered inward in a spray of safety glass and warm water that drenched the two would-be pilots. The plane wallowed like a whale breaching and threatened to slide under for good. Then, ponderously, it rolled back onto its belly and bobbed in the choppy waves its impact had created.

All lights in the cockpit had gone out. The computer screens were blank. The radio was silent. The only noise came from the sound of the sea outside and the thudding of adrenaline-charged heartbeats.

Katie felt like she'd taken about a hundred turns too many on a merry-go-round. If she'd had anything in her stomach, she'd have vomited from the severe dizziness. As it was, she could only manage a few desultory retches. "Ohhh . . ." she groaned.

Foster steadied himself on the arms of the pilot's seat. "They say any landing you can walk away from . . . *hurk*." He spat a mouthful of bile into the seawater that pooled around their calves.

"You call that a landing?" Katie fumbled with her seatbelt, which seemed to have gotten way too tight.

"Best one you ever made, I bet." said Foster. "Ow. I think I cracked a rib. Or two."

"Can you move?"

"You owe me . . . a date . . ." He winced as he got out of his own seat.

"Did I say that?" Katie staggered as the plane shifted, and then yelped as she lost her footing and fell against the side of the cockpit.

Foster was there by her side immediately, swaying with his own dizziness, but he offered her his hand. "You did. I might have a concussion, but I remember that much." He pulled her to her feet. "Let's get out of here."

Hand in hand, they staggered out of the cockpit and through First Class where Misrule was still unconscious and strapped into his seat. Katie stopped to check his vital signs. "He's still alive."

"Good thing, too. Otherwise that thing in his chest would have gone off," said Foster.

They passed into the main cabin and found that the last few rows of seats and the galley were *gone*. At some point during the impact the entire tail section of the jet had ripped away. Katie couldn't remember if anyone had been sitting that far back.

The air still shimmered around Escudo, who had extended his force field as far as he could throughout the body of the jet at impact. He looked like a fat, frightened little boy. Sweat poured off him with the effort of maintaining his field. "You can stop now." Katie used the seats to support herself as she moved up the aisle. "We've landed."

A few of the hostages within his field stirred as they shook off the effects of the knockout gas. Doctor Mayfair was already out of his seat and started to check those around him. His normally gruff demeanor was subdued. His nurse was dead. Her neck had snapped when her head crashed into the bulkhead by her seat.

Foster and Katie struggled to open a window emergency exit. They managed to loosen the hinge, aided by a hiss of compressed air that forced it all the way open. As it slid out and aside, a bright yellow raft slide tipped outward, inflating automatically.

Overhead, they heard the roar of jets as the *Rita* cruised past. A package dropped from her open bomb bay and unfolded into a second life raft. A wetsuited figure tumbled out right behind it, and then splashed toward it. Foster and Katie watched as the person climbed into the large octagonal raft and pulled aside the head covering. It was Garcia. He shouted and waved at them with a grin wider than the world. Then he pulled a harpoon spinneret from his back and fired it at the jet. The hull clanged as the barbed dart struck and embedded deep into it. Garcia reeled it in and pulled the raft alongside the base of the slide.

"Somebody call for a cab?" he shouted.

"You're late," called Foster. "My plane already landed. No tip for you."

"Go on." Katie squeezed Foster's hand. "We'll slide the unconscious people down to you."

Foster nodded and slid down the ramp into Garcia's waiting arms.

* * *

Mayfair checked over the remaining hostages and found three others besides his nurse had perished in the landing, all from broken necks. At his direction, Katie and Escudo moved the unconscious survivors one at a time to the emergency exit, and then slid them down where Foster and Garcia could place them carefully in the life raft.

The airplane shifted slightly and tilted towards the rear as it took on more water through the broken-off tail. Jack was the last of the non-escapees to go down the ramp. He was starting to awaken and mumbled something about his bag.

"I'll bring it myself," said Katie to him. Since she might never have another opportunity, she grabbed a handful of Jack's rear end and squeezed it with appreciation. He was a perennial Top Tenner on the Most Beautiful People list every year since the late 80s. It was taut and muscular and everything she'd ever imagined.

"Hey . . ." He looked sleepy and scandalized at the same time.

"Thanks for flying Deep Six Air," she said with a wink. "Mind the step." She slapped his ass and sent him down the ramp.

"Espada is dead," said Mayfair. "No surprise there, though. The others seem all right. Where's Misrule?"

"First Class," said Katie. "We'll get him last. Escudo, thank you for your help. You're done now. Get going. And behave yourself."

The heavy, perspiring Mexican nodded and dropped gratefully onto the ramp slide.

Mayfair and Katie worked quickly to move the remaining eight escapees down the ramp. None of them were difficult to move except Kiloton, who must have weighed close to three hundred pounds. The doctor wheezed after they sent him down. "I don't know how much more I've got in me. I'm not as spry as I used to be."

"What about the bodies?" asked Katie.

Mayfair shook his head. "We've got to make sure the living are rescued first before worrying about the dead. They'll keep. The Coast Guard or whoever gets here next can recover them."

Katie nodded. "Let's get Misrule and get off this plane, Doc." They moved up the aisle into First Class.

Misrule's sleeper set lay discarded in the middle of the cabin, but he was nowhere to be seen.

Katie reached for a gun that she didn't have and then cursed as she realized she was unarmed. She turned to the doctor. "Get out of here. Misrule is loose somewhere on or around the plane. Have the others move the raft away from the jet so they might have some warning if he swims toward them."

Mayfair's eyes widened. "What about you? What are you going to do?"

"My job," said Katie, her voice grim.

Misrule couldn't have gone far. He had to have headed into the cockpit. She remembered seeing a hatch there that would let him climb down into the cargo hold. If that's what he had done, he had numerous places to hide plus a way to escape the plane entirely through the ragged hole where the jet's tail had been ripped away. She couldn't let him get away, not after everything that had happened.

Then Katie remembered Jack's bag. The man was a walking arsenal. He had to have something in it that could stop someone as hardy as Misrule. She hurried back to where they'd left it. As she passed by the emergency exit, she paused and looked down at the raft. Foster brought his hands to his mouth and called to her, but his voice was drowned out by the sound of the *Rita* hovering nearby.

She raised her hands to her head, making curved devil horns from her fingers, and then pointed over her shoulder back into the plane. He shouted something urgent at Garcia, and then he turned back to her and their eyes met. A mishmash of feelings and emotions carried back and forth in that brief gaze.

Then she turned away.

Katie rifled through the bag to look for weapons, tools, anything that could help her against Misrule. She found a pistol-sized ultrataser and a spare power clip. She taped a flashlight to the ultrataser barrel, making an ungainly but useful weapon. She ignored the escapees' discarded assault rifles because she knew Misrule's skin was proof against bullets, but she tucked a flare gun into the belt of her jumpsuit at the small of her back. She wrapped a few turns of climbing rope around some seats and went to the ragged edge of the corridor.

She bent over the edge carefully and looked around for any sign of Misrule. He wasn't loitering beneath her and she couldn't see him in the water around the plane's rear. She rolled over the edge, holding tight to the rope, and swung down. She knew she'd be a great target for a moment, silhouetted against the bright sky beyond, but considered it an acceptable risk. She splashed down into several inches of water. A sharp smell assailed her nostrils and she realized a layer of fuel floated on the water. It must have leaked into the cargo hold at the impact.

"Misrule?" called Katie into the dark of the hold. "I know you're in here, Misrule." She swept the ultrataser/flashlight from side to side as she advanced cautiously into the gloom. "There's nowhere left to run. It's over. Come out and let's get out of here before the plane sinks."

As if to illustrate her point, the jet shifted. The water rose up midway up her calves. She shined the light down for a moment, watched the swirl of fuel atop the water, and shivered. She raised the light again and it illuminated Misrule's face, some twenty feet distant. A brief yelp of surprise escaped her lips and he smiled, his yellow eyes flickering in the light.

"I must commend you, Officer Malone, for a game well-played. You have proved a worthy adversary."

"Face it, Misrule, we won. We beat you. In spite of your best planning, we rescued almost all the hostages and none of you have successfully escaped. It's time to go, now come on."

"I don't think so." The tone of his voice chilled her to the bone. "I have not come this far merely to be led back like a lamb to the slaughter. I still have my ace in the hole." He tapped the canister in his chest for emphasis. "And I still have one hostage left."

Katie raised her ultrataser a little higher. "I'm not your hostage. I'm your captor, and you're coming with me right now."

"Or what? You'll shoot me with your little popgun?" Misrule took a step toward her, causing her to step back. "You don't know that it won't set off my device, do you? Your friends might be upwind and safe, or they might not be. One thing is for certain . . ." He advanced another step. "You will suffer the full effects of the toxin. It is a very unpleasant way to die."

Katie scooted back. She knew Misrule could shoot destructive energy from his hands if he chose to. But like any sadist, he was enjoying the opportunity to toy with his prey before the final strike. "You'll die too if you set it off. You won't do that. It'll ruin all your plans."

Misrule's eyes narrowed. "What do you know of my plans?"

"I know they figure with you in them."

He chuckled. "Indeed they do. However, I will not be returning to Deep Six with you, Officer Malone. You would be wise to turn about and walk away."

"So you can shoot me in the back? Not very sporting, Misrule."

"You assume that I care for rules of engagement. I do not. I will not hesitate to come after you should I feel the urge. You . . . or your loved ones. Your daughter Lindsay. Your mother. I found your personnel file an entertaining read back in the Warden's office. I'm sure you know enough about me to know I do not make idle threats."

Mommeeeeee! Katie heard Lindsay's voice as clear as if her daughter were next to her. "You . . . wouldn't . . . dare!"

Misrule's expression turned thunderous. "Do not presume to tell me what I dare!" he roared and raised his hands in preparation to blast her with his energy bolts. "Drop your weapon and I may yet let you live."

Wordlessly, Katie let the ultrataser fall from her hand. It plopped into the water at her feet. The waterproof flashlight shined eerily through the layer of fuel. An idea occurred to her. She raised her left hand and ignited flames at her fingertips. The candle-bright flames lit the cargo hold in dancing shadows.

"Interesting," remarked Misrule.

"Surrender or I'll incinerate you where you stand."

Misrule threw back his head and laughed. "If you were able, I think you already would have. I suspect you are showing me the sum total of your abilities. Your weak . . . pathetic . . . abilities."

"Can you take that chance? Give up now. You're in the middle of the sea. Where are you going to go?"

"I shall manage. I always do. I tire of your antics. You should leave now. Stay if you wish, but if you do I will kill you."

Katie steeled herself. "I'm not leaving without you. The only way you're exiting this plane is as a prisoner or a corpse."

Energy crackled around Misrule's hands. "Then go ahead, use your puny little flames. Incinerate me, Officer Malone, if you can." In spite of his bravado, he focused his attention on her hand.

"You asked for it." In the very moment he was distracted, she reached behind her, grabbed the flare gun, and shot it at him.

The round blasted into his chest. The heat of the flare burst the container in his torso and incinerated the escaping gas. Misrule staggered in surprise as his hands instinctively protected his face. The burning shell dropped, almost in slow motion, into the fuel-soaked water below.

Katie turned and ran, feeling a soft puff of heat lick at her back as the jet fuel around Misrule ignited. He roared in pain and surprise. The flames spread with unnerving speed, heading up the cargo hold toward the nose and aft toward the shattered tail and Katie. She dropped the spent flare pistol and sprinted for the circle of daylight only a few yards distant.

Impossibly, Foster was there, dangling from a cable sling and peering into the hull, an assault carbine held at the ready. He saw her racing toward him, chased by hungry flames, and dropped his weapon into the water to free up his hands. She leaped toward him, arms outstretched. As she crashed into him, her momentum swung them both back away from the plane, and she wrapped her arms around him. She realized he hung underneath the *Rita*, where Lania stared down at them, open-mouthed in surprise as flames licked out from the tail of the plane.

The *Rita*'s jet nozzles twisted and lifted Foster and Katie up and away from the burning fuel on the water. As they swung away on a dizzying bungee ride, the downed airliner exploded in a column of flame.

"We are all visitors to this time, this place. We are just passing through. Our purpose here is to observe, to learn, to grow, to love . . . and then we return home."

—Australian Aboriginal proverb

July, 2007
Athens, Greece

They couldn't find Misrule's body.

There hadn't been much fuel left in the plane to leak, but what remained had blown the fuselage apart in a spectacular fireball. Once Foster and Katie had been safely recovered into the belly of the *Rita*, Reed circled the area until fuel limits required a return to a landing field in Greece. The *Marilyn* arrived to continue the search for the missing prisoner while the *Rita* refueled. Although they could have opted to remain behind to rest—certainly they had earned such a right—Foster and Katie insisted on returning to continue the search.

In the meantime, the Hellenic Coast Guard arrived and retrieved the survivors from the life raft. When the *Rita* returned, the unconscious prisoners were on one ship under guard by Greek soldiers, supervised by Garcia and Lania, and the released hostages were recuperating and resting after their ordeal on another.

"Do you think he's dead?" asked Foster as he and Katie scanned the sea for any sign of their red-skinned escapee.

"God, I hope so," Katie shivered. But deep down, she felt that he still lived. The man was like a force of nature in his will to live, to succeed at any cost, and she didn't think her simple fire had accomplished what years of pitched battles with Just Cause couldn't. No, unless she saw a body, she would believe he was still alive, somewhere, licking his wounds in cold fury and planning his revenge.

Foster sensed her disquiet, and gently put his hand over hers on the rail. She looked up at him. His face was bruised and scratched but his eyes still sparkled with amusement as he smiled down at her. His grin was infectious and she found herself giving him back a sly smile.

"What is that?" he asked.

"Maybe I might date a CO after all."

"Is he taller than me?"

Katie punched him on the arm. "No, you dope."

"Ow, my ribs!" he yelped. She burst into giggles and leaned her head carefully—her damaged ear, though bandaged, was still very tender—against his shoulder.

Eventually they called off the search. A Canadian parahuman named Triton, whose specialty was underwater work, dove down to search the remaining wreckage of the plane. Upon his return, he reported no sign of Misrule.

The survivors spent two days in Athens under medical scrutiny, making sure none harbored any ill effects from their treatment at the hands of the escapees. American officials interviewed each one privately, but Doublecharge gave the only public press conference. She was glowing in her praise of the officers of Deep Six for their exceptional service and their willingness to go far beyond the call of duty to make sure the escapees were retrieved. The final toll was sobering. Twenty-three prisoners had been held in Deep Six. Of those, only nine survived. Half of the dead had been killed by Misrule or other escapees. Four hostages died, three in the emergency landing, and four of Deep Six's guard staff perished in the escape.

Katie felt fortunate to be alive as she sat on the rooftop balcony. The Greek government had put the hostages up in a luxurious seaside hotel. She longed to be home to see her mother and Lindsay, but her sense of duty wouldn't let her leave unless she accompanied the comatose prisoners back. The SuperMax prison in Colorado was outfitting one wing to house the Deep Six prisoners, who would be kept in their sleeper-set comas until the underground facility could come back online. They temporarily resided within a fortified military base, watched over by Garcia and Lania, a division of the Hellenic Army, and Greece's two native parahuman heroes Prometheus and Selene.

Foster ambled out from the lounge, wearing a straw hat to protect his fair complexion from the bright Greek sun. The weaving made odd dimples of light across his cheerful face. Katie smiled up at him.

"Hey, handsome. Sleep well?" she asked.

"Like a baby, except without the dirty diaper and the colic. You hungry? Want to go get breakfast?"

Katie stretched. "That sounds like a date, mister. I don't date COs."

He squatted down next to her and grinned from under his floppy hat. "Then it's a good thing we're not dating. Anyway, the phone woke me."

"Who called? The boys?" Katie's mom had taken in Foster's sons and they'd all called three times to talk to Katie and Foster. It had broken Katie's heart to tell Lindsay that she would be gone for a couple more days but that everything was just fine. Lindsay, on the other hand, told her about the new furniture, the boys and how loud they were, the latest Thomas the Tank Engine DVD Gramma had bought her, and how much she wanted a kitten.

"Nope. Better. Word's come from the powers that be," he said. "We're going home."

* * *

"Mind if I sit down?"

Cassie looked up from her thoughts to see Doublecharge standing over her. They were riding back to America on a United States Air Force transport jet, courtesy of Juice's string-pulling in Washington. The nine prisoners were strapped down to gurneys in the aft cargo bay, watched by armed soldiers. Most of Just Cause had flown back either on the *Rita* or the *Marilyn*, but Jack and Doublecharge decided to travel with the prisoners and the Deep Six staffers.

Cassie put down the magazine she'd bought along with several others for the trip. It was in Greek, which she didn't read, but the pictures were gorgeous. "No, please." She rubbed her eyes, still sore from Lumina's flash.

"Do they hurt?" asked Doublecharge.

"A little," said Cassie. "But the doctors said they're healing okay, and I can deal with the pain."

Doublecharge sat down next to her. The Air Force had transformed the front half of the cargo hold into a reasonably comfortable cabin, with first-class seating and other creature comforts. "You've faced a lot of pain in the last three days. A lot of strife and hardship, and you've handled it admirably."

"Thanks."

Doublecharge did something she did very infrequently in public; she removed her mask. Cassie had never seen her face before; she was beautiful and stately, with a grace that only came with the approach of middle age. She extended her gloved hand in greeting. "I'm Stacey, and I'm pleased to meet you."

Mystified, Cassie shook the offered hand. "Cassie."

"I've been told by my best friend that I need to be more open, more accessible to others. It's not easy for me. I'm a private person by nature."

"I see," said Cassie.

"What I want to talk about with you now is the future of Deep Six."

Cassie looked at Doublecharge. "I assume that I'll just go back to work there once it's all repaired. It is going to be repaired, right?"

"Of course. There's nowhere else to keep such dangerous felons as these. But with Silbersack gone, there's a void to be filled—Chief Warden."

"And you're looking for my recommendation? I'm just a Booking Technician. My opinion doesn't count for much."

"Mine does, and I've already thought of a suitable candidate for the position, and I wanted to discuss it with you."

"Who is it?"

"You."

"You're kidding," Cassie said when she found her voice again after the sudden shock.

"Not at all. You've exhibited exceptional poise in dealing with the unusual stresses of the breakout. You have extensive experience working with parahuman prisoners. You're one of the longest-tenured employees at Deep Six. In my mind, you are very qualified to take on the position of Chief Warden."

"I . . . I don't know what to say," said Cassie.

"Say you'll think it over. The decision is ultimately up to the Director of the Bureau of Prisons," said Stacey. "But for anything involving Deep Six, he'll listen to any recommendation made by the Parahuman Resources Agency. And the Director there happens to be my best friend."

"Nepotism at its best?"

Stacey nodded. "I'm learning it's the only way to get things accomplished at levels above the field. I'm much more of a hands-on kind of girl, which is why I get so uptight at things like reviews and budget analysis and audits."

Cassie laughed. "I get that way too." Then she sobered. "You know, Misrule 'promoted' me to this position already. At the end, he was calling me Acting Chief Warden. I think in his own twisted way he actually liked me." She shivered as she remembered the naked lust in his eyes when they'd been in the cockpit together.

Stacey leaned back in her seat. "Misrule was many things, but never a fool. He saw your potential, as do I. But I see it as something to be used for good, whereas he only saw how he could pervert it for his own purposes."

"Well . . . all right. I'll consider it. Fair enough?"

"Thank you." Stacey smiled. "You'll make us proud."

* * *

Katie hovered by the door of the Deep Six transport as it taxied to a stop outside the main hangar. The site, normally devoid of any personnel except surface guards and mechanics, swarmed with all manner of construction workers, miners, and engineers. They were working around the clock to get the prison repaired and operational once more. But Katie had eyes for none of it. Her gaze was locked on a young, black-haired head outside.

"All right, everyone. Welcome home," said Lieutenant Frankes from the cockpit.

Katie threw open the door and rushed out, with Foster half a step behind her. Her daughter, beautiful Lindsay, squealed and wriggled out of her grandmother's arms. Then Katie swept her up, laughing and swinging her around. Lindsay wrapped her arms around Katie's neck and planted a sloppy wet kiss on her lips.

"I missed you, Mommy." She laid her head on Katie's shoulder.

Tears ran unchecked down Katie's cheeks. "I missed you too, baby doll. I missed you so much."

Next to them, Foster embraced both his boys, who talked a mile a minute, each trying to overwhelm the other with the sheer power of his voice.

"I saw you on TV, Mommy. Did you catch the bad guys?" Lindsay whispered in her ear.

"Yes, sweetie, I did. They're all back in jail now."

"Good."

Gail stepped forward and embraced her daughter and grand-daughter. "I'm glad you're all right. I was so worried. So was Lindsay. She's hardly slept since this all started." Her mother's gaze turned stern. "Everything is all right now, isn't it?"

"Yes, Mom," said Katie.

"Mommy? I have something to show you," said Lindsay. "Something special."

Katie set her down and dropped to one knee so she could be at eye-level with her daughter. She put her hands on Lindsay's shoulders. "What is it, babydoll?"

Lindsay looked up at Gail, who smiled and nodded. "Can I see your magic fire fingers?"

Katie held up her hand and watched as flames sprouted from her fingertips. Lindsay gazed at them, fascinated. "What did you want to show me, sweetheart?"

Lindsay held up her hand and a bright ball of flame formed in her palm which looked like a burning softball. She flipped it up into the air. It whirled, crackled, and hissed, and then dropped into her other hand. Katie looked on in amazement as Lindsay stretched the fireball out between both hands until it was the size of a basketball, before shrinking it down to the tiniest spark and extinguishing it altogether.

"Oh, baby, that was amazing! When did you find out you could do that?"

"Yesterday. Gramma said it was because you're my mommy and you have magic fire fingers. Now I have them too!"

Doublecharge joined them. "You must be Lindsay," she said with a genuine smile. "I've heard so much about you from your mommy."

Lindsay looked up at her, wide-eyed. "Are you a princess?" she asked.

Everyone laughed at that. "No, darling, but thank you. I wish more people would make that mistake with me. May I see your 'magic fire fingers' again?"

Lindsay looked at Katie, who said "It's all right, honey."

Once more, the young girl made the flame dance around her hands.

Doublecharge clapped her hands. "Very good, Lindsay. Maybe someday you'll come and be a superhero with Just Cause."

"No," said Lindsay. "When I grow up, I'm going to be just like my mommy, because she's the best prison guard ever."

Katie smiled, and hugged her daughter to her. Tonight she'd go home with her family. Tomorrow she'd promised to go out with Foster—not for a date, because she still didn't date COs, but as a friend . . . perhaps with benefits. The day after that, she'd go back to work.

She was, after all, the best prison guard ever.

ABOUT THE AUTHOR

Ian Thomas Healy dabbles in many different genres. He's a multiple participant and winner of National Novel Writing Month. He created the popular ongoing superhero series, the *Just Cause Universe*, and is also the creator of the *Writing Better Action Through Cinematic Techniques* workshop, which helps writers to improve their action scenes.

When not writing, which is rare, he enjoys watching hockey, reading comic books (and serious books, too), and living in the great state of Colorado, which he shares with his wife, children, house-pets, and approximately five million other people.

Visit www.ianthealy.com for more information.